the silent partner

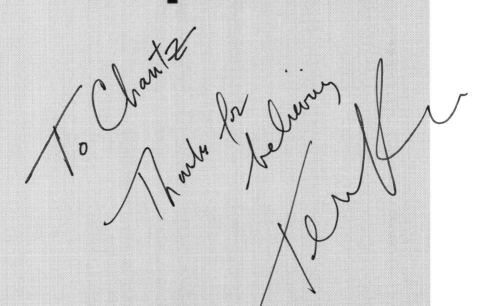

Terrence King

For more information, go to terrencejking.com.

Printed in the United States of America.

ISBN: 978-1-4669-1639-5 (sc)
ISBN: 978-1-4669-1637-1 (hc)
ISBN: 978-1-4669-1638-8 (e)

Library of Congress Control Number: 2012905125

Review Copy

Trafford rev. 05/21/2012

 www.trafford.com

North America & international
toll-free: 1 888 232 4444 (USA & Canada)
phone: 250 383 6864 ♦ fax: 812 355 4082

For Danica, Dorelie, Verena, Deanna,
Alannah, Ashley, and Katie

CHAPTER 1

She was at once bruised and lovely, with a chubby face that was dark and round and smooth and full of suspicion. The suburban neighborhood was—Homer noticed—thankfully absent of human beings, which she had come to expect to be cruel and offensive. When the sun came up later, they'd be out. Disheartened, she remained laying on the driveway, dreading the ridiculous task at hand. A stray cat hissed at her before disappearing somewhere in the shadows between parked cars, hiding from the midnight moon. If this wasn't such an awful place, she could like it here.

She craned her neck upward to the heavens. "You're not funny."

No response, of course.

Routinely stuck with the worst assignments, the last nine hundred years had been hard on her, and someone was going to pay for it. Her back was sore, and she had the celestial equivalent of a migraine.

Dead leaves rustled past her, and she teared up, her eyes quickly agitated by the night wind and its irksome debris. She cursed, determined that stalling the inevitable was pointless, and stood up. Short and nimble, her wide frame was swallowed by a grungy robe that draped her like a potato sack. She dusted herself off, her wiry braids swaying gently like velvet drapes in a sudden breeze. It was less graceful a fall than she would have preferred. Her resilient, mortal-looking form ached every time God dropped her. She hadn't figured out why she had to fall anyway. Her contempt for God—as well as humanity—had grown during her last punishment, and she was fed up with her body being thrown around like a lifeless dummy.

Nonetheless, she had to do this latest deed that God had in store for her in this supposed paradise where humans—in all their infamy—were known for killing themselves, their environment, and each other. God could try to convince her that Earth was His second-greatest kingdom all He wanted. This looked more like earthbound purgatory than Heavenly Kingdom Number Two.

But her only other choice was solitude again.

She squinted into the wind, her eyes possessing the tireless wisdom of a crestfallen owl. She beheld the tract neighborhood, and her heart sank. The flickering lamppost buzzed, illuminating everything in short flashes. All the homes, yards, driveways, even mailboxes looked the same. Homer was disappointed that God's origination of the human being had led to this homogenous arrangement of human dwellings. The suburban landscape provided no clues about where to start. So often, He expected her to understand all—without explanation—and follow orders. *He had to be vague, always making me a damn fool.* Still, this neighborhood was a slightly better location than the last place He had put her—in the desert.

She supposed she should be grateful for the opportunity for redemption. Angels—especially banished ones—usually didn't get second chances. Sometimes she cursed anyway, but it was good to keep the bigger picture in mind.

There was no way that she was going to be in confinement again while the other divine messengers enjoyed the benefits of easy tasks involving nonviolent human interaction and social leisure. They all had gossiped about her while she was nearly numbed to death in isolation. The cold lonesomeness had frightened her while she was separated from them in a dimension not even they could comprehend unless they experienced it themselves. She wasn't going to fail this time.

A young couple walked behind a dachshund that—despite its little legs and elongated body—moved faster than the two-legged humans that led it. *A new breed,* she thought. *Nothing like that existed nine hundred years ago.* She imagined God's joy in observing humans create new species. It was always about creation, and, Homer figured, Earth's preoccupation with irritating her.

A large boom filled the sky, and Homer cupped her ears in agony. Neither the young couple nor the dog blinked.

"Homer."

"Do You always have to dramatize your entrances?" she hollered up at Him, scowling, as the winds ceased. "And how did I get the name Homer anyway? Do I look like a Homer to You?"

The couple walking their dog noticed the odd hobo and picked up their pace. Awareness of the sixth dimension could clearly freak out human beings.

"No one else can make a boom like that," God said, ignoring her question. The boom subsided.

"Such ghastly entrances."

"I'm sick of people trying to be Me," God said. "Or fighting over Me."

"You're the one who gave them the ability to make war, sir."

"Welcome to your new home."

Ignorance and wickedness were bountiful, she was sure. Inspecting her surroundings, she noticed a large, discarded cardboard box nearby, folded up and tucked between trash cans overflowing with garbage and besmirched with grime. "Oh no." She glared up at Him. "Oh no! Not again."

"Now, Homer. You know how this works."

"This is outrageous! We both know all of Your other angels don't live in such abominable quarters. I've been impugned!"

"You have not been impugned, Homer," God said. He was both patient and unsurprised. "You can't be flashy, and there's important work to be done."

"Of course there is," she sighed, pulling out the cardboard box and laying it flat on the ground. She closed her eyes and remembered how God had prepped her for her assignment—albeit with limited information—and despised Him for now surprising her with such meager quarters. He was going overboard in making her inconspicuous. Preparing to surprise Him herself, she raised her hands like a magician casting a spell. The flat box magically constructed itself into a square, popping open like a knocked-over jack-in-the-box with no prize inside—the entrance to her new home.

"This is a waste of your powers, Homer. Be more judicious."

"It's not like I'm limited in the number of uses."

3

"I wish you'd find the true powers within yourself rather than relying on such flamboyant displays. Creates trouble, My friend."

Homer shook that off. "You're ridiculous . . . and so disapproving. You wonder why I'm cranky."

He didn't wonder but ignored her. "There are a couple of other things."

A small flashlight appeared in her hands. The last time Homer had been on Earth, no such thing had existed. "Interesting contraptions abound," she said, investigating her new toy. "What am I supposed to do with this?" She gazed into the flashlight's lamp, blinding herself and seeing bright circles. "Ugh."

She aimed the odd cylinder away, and light filled the darkness of her surroundings, bouncing and zigzagging around the stucco of the home nearby and the dark abyss of her cardboard box.

"Intense, focused, artificial light that eventually burns out," God said. "An interesting tool."

Quickly bored with it, she put it in one of her roomy pockets. She patted her shoulders, and a small dust cloud formed. "These detestable garments are offensive. After all of these centuries, You drop me down here to mosey around in these same clothes I wore during the Crusades? They're filthy!" She sneezed.

"Homer, I'm in a mood."

"You notice what kind of mood I'm in, sir?"

"When you're in a mood," God said, "you don't destroy things."

"That's true." She recalled once when mere irritation had caused God to tear down the Tower of Babel, defying the human race to ever again try to physically reach Him in the heavens. This created difficulty in human communication and resulted in scores of new languages, making it impossible for the world to completely unite against God again. Incidentally, the world wasn't united now.

Arranging the grubby blankets provided for her, she peered inside her new cardboard home and surveyed the limited square footage. She was depressed. "This time, I hope I'm not accosted by any of your barbaric criminals."

"Let's talk about the angel food cake you ate last night, Homer. You were supposed to be preparing for this. How did you even know about angel food cake?"

He always provided a meal of choice to His angels before they landed back on Earth. Homer had read about angel food cake while in solitude, and she knew that requesting it would bug Him. That's what He got for banishing her.

She gestured to her attire. "I'm not as stupid as I look, for starters. I broke no rules, sir. Can You provide more details on what exactly I'm supposed to do here?"

Though it was a relief being out of isolation, this human-saturated planet wasn't what she'd had in mind as an escape. She'd love to be surveying the damage from above like the League always did, from the safe observation windows of God's universe.

She crawled into the box and hit her head on the top of it, her bottom a little too wide to get into her temporary dwelling. His dirty tricks.

"It will be disastrous if Tom does not publish that book," God said. "I'm busy, and there isn't much time. We've got one chance to stop humanity from destroying itself."

"The Almighty One is doing His own intervention. Well, aren't You highfalutin!"

"Homer," God said, booming loudly.

She cupped her ears again. "You've been so sensitive the last few millennia!" She knew she was pushing His limits. In her estimation, a dose of humility was in order.

"There are problems over My green Earth. I'm here to help you."

"'My green Earth.' God's green Earth. That's funny!" she said, revolted. *The ego.*

She found little comfort in the box, backing herself into it with a tight squeeze. She lay down with her head at the opening. Fresh air. At least the blankets didn't have fleas, thank you very much. "I would think You have much bigger problems to solve than book publishing. Down here, You've still got genocide, pollution, abortion, nuclear proliferation, even global warming."

"Yes, I need to get to that."

"Recycling unread Bibles could be a start," Homer said.

He filled her universe with another boom. She covered her ears in time for it, expecting it this time.

"Tou-chy!" She'd had enough of Him.

"I'm the solution, not the problem. As a whole, they haven't accepted that it is within themselves that many of their problems lie."

Homer formed a pillow out of a dirty blanket, worn and undignified. "I could've used some clean blankets rather than these vile and horrid textiles," she muttered. A lint cloud puffed, and she coughed.

"Don't be concerned with creature comforts, Homer. We have a schedule to keep."

"Sir, I know You've got Your techniques, and they've proven to be excellent over the course of time—"

"Be careful in your boldness, Homer."

She softened, worn from God's boom abuse. "What do You care about a fictional book? There are so many Bibles already printed in so many languages, even Sanskrit, distributed all over Earth. Why do You care about this one particular soul's book when there are so many historical and political books causing severe havoc down here?"

"This book will change things for the better, that's why," God said. "I'm not concerned with previous works that have been the center of many of these problems in the first place. We have to save humankind from itself. The story in this book is powerful, and it will change things. But the book's author is lost. You, Homer, must help him."

"Ridiculous! Why don't You just give him a sign?" she asked, trying to figure out how she was going to help some misguided author publish a book. This was an odd assignment, and she didn't trust God anyway. "It's not like You haven't done it before. You know. Throw in a burning bush or a talking donkey or something."

"Humanity's free will needs to be protected and sometimes . . . nudged."

She knew all about His insistence on free will. His creations' ability to decide to believe or not believe in Him was a principle God had never ever wavered from and a gift to humanity that couldn't be refused. He wasn't known to compromise.

She wanted to do what was asked this time. Being banished from the League of Angels had been humiliating and torturous. Only Michael, the bravest of all of God's celestial beings, had stood up for her, though he detested her impatience with humanity. Right before she fell to Earth, he'd given her an earful about what the others had said about her while she'd been imprisoned. There were a couple of troublemaking angels she wanted to have a word with when she was done down here. Lollygagging all around . . . those guttersnipe angels needed to be put straight. Especially Gabriel, who always received the great assignments and was too good to talk to her.

"You are aware that You're often thought of as cruel, sir." She curled up, trying to find warmth. A flea landed on her nose. She'd been wrong about the blanket.

"Ignorance," He said. "This is an intervention. Don't underestimate the seriousness of your task, Homer. I pulled you out of confinement for good reason."

Homer swatted at the flea and missed. "Ow!"

"See this through," He said.

"You've never sent me on an assignment like this before. Usually I'm in the middle of a ridiculous war or something."

"There is a war—a war that is bigger than any of the armed battles taking place. Tom's story will perpetually affect all My loved ones and reduce the pain and hate all over My world. Once the ending and message are changed, that is."

"Oh, You didn't tell me that," Homer said, sitting up. She hit her head on the top of the box, almost knocking it over. "Now I've got to change the ending and content of erroneous prose? How the hell am I supposed to do that?"

"Homer! You know how I feel about that reference."

She was never supposed to use the word *hell*. He didn't like it, which amused her because He'd created it.

"I'm sorry, sir, but why me? I was hoping You'd pull me out of solitude and get me new digs for a few centuries, and next thing I know, we're on for another one of Your crazy adventures."

"Homer. You're perfect for this. The strength of compassion toward humanity in some cultures is seen as weakness by others, and it's compassion that you yourself greatly need."

It did feel good to be perfect for something. She had felt tremendously imperfect for a very long time. "I just do what I need to do, sir. As You ask."

This book must become accessible to the masses, He said, now in her head.

She focused so she wouldn't alarm Him with her doubts or challenging thoughts. He was especially attentive to the voice in her head. One antagonistic thought and He could reprimand her.

He must improve the ending of the book. It stinks, He thought to her, His voice echoing with the rumble of grating thunder.

Like a skunk? she joked silently, remembering the time she had been inadvertently sprayed by one that an Indonesian had kept as a pet. She had reeked for weeks.

God paused. Homer should have known that He wouldn't appreciate the joke. All of His creations were important to Him, and they all had purpose, blah blah blah.

That's enough, Homer, He said in her head.

I'm supposed to make someone want to publish it or rewrite it? Work with me here.

Now He spoke out loud. "We've got to fix this book." She didn't like it when He bounced back and forth like this. It screwed up her equilibrium, which was likely the point. Keep her guessing. "And deliver it to the person who will one day provide it to the world—though you may not interfere with anyone's intentions, good or bad. This is important, Homer. No interference with intentions. Free will cannot be compromised."

"No interference," Homer said, adjusting herself back down in her blankets. "Thanks for Your lack of interference, by the way." She was relieved they were talking aloud and that He wasn't in her head any longer. If only He'd stop communicating with her altogether and leave her alone. Things could only get worse if He brought up the past again.

"The last time I saw you in a true confrontation was with the Sadducees. I've missed it."

Ugh. This now.

She had been in deep confrontation with everyone, it seemed, during the First Crusade—long after the Sadducees—but there was no point

8

in reminding Him of what even she wanted to forget. How often He disregarded timelines, at least ones she understood.

"Now, Homer. You see that little timepiece there?"

She scanned her quarters and quickly found a large wristwatch with an illuminated faceplate. It was as big as a rat. How could she have missed it? She picked up the heavy timepiece, its silver band and glossy faceplate glistening in the brilliant moonlight. It was very twenty-first century. "This ridiculous thing? It's bigger than my head, sir."

"You see how it reads *Seven Days Left* on it? This will keep you informed of how you're doing on time. When it expires to zero, whether or not you have completed your task, you're coming back with Me."

She gasped in panic. "I've only got seven days to do this, sir?"

"You've never been slow-witted, Homer. Fail, and back to solitude you go."

Her hives broke out in overdrive. She wasn't going to be set up for failure again. "There's no way a book will be published in a week. This is preposterous!"

"I need the material in the hands of the right person, My friend. The rest will be history. Don't be so ornery. As a gift to you, Homer, the timer won't start until sunrise."

She looked up at Him, distrusting all of this. "These are regular twenty-four-hour days, right? And is this monstrosity set to Pacific standard time?"

God was silent.

"Okay, can I sleep now? Some of us have to, to function properly."

"One more thing, Homer."

"What is it?" she asked with masked patience.

"You cannot tell any mortals what you are doing. Humanity often creates fake idols when they think I'm sending down messengers. Dozens of imitators arise. Quite a species, humanity is."

"Sir, how is this different from every other time?"

"I don't want any of your excuses later."

She considered what a miracle it was that Moses had had any idea what God had been talking about those thousands of years ago. "I won't say anything," she said, dropping her head on the raggedy blanket-heap pillow and pulling another grungy blanket to her chin.

"I'm counting on you, Homer. A promotion to seraphim rides on this one."

Homer blinked, surprised that He was promising to make her part of the highest order of angels. Temptations were as plentiful for angels as they were for humans. His tasks were perpetual tests of faith in Him, and she knew it—though she didn't believe what she was hearing. She had no reason to trust Him. With depression on her left and loneliness on her right, she felt like she was being ushered by two thugs down a long corridor of unavoidable failure.

However, receiving such an honorable and splendid promotion to seraphim would show those flibbertigibbet archangels that she hadn't been overcome with devilry since her banishment. Sure, she was subject to bouts of temperamental feistiness, but she wasn't inept, and all of the heavens needed to know it. God, after all, believed in her abilities enough to send her on an assignment of this magnitude. She wasn't clear yet on how she was to accomplish her task, but she had to figure it out quickly to protect herself from spending God-knows-how-long imprisoned again—and prove wrong all of her fellow angels in that stupid League: she had not truly fallen.

Stillness surrounded her, and she breathed. He was gone.

* * *

The October moon glowed through the swaying sheer curtains, illuminating the dingy bedroom like an aqua-colored strobe light. Jamie considered it welcome company.

Being turned down by her very-acceptable-looking fiancé was unacceptable. Her pink lingerie straps were uncomfortable as hell, pissing her off, but somehow she had fallen asleep with the new, scratchy lingerie on anyway. Plus, she swore the full-sized mattress was sinking in the middle. Her petite frame felt like it was being slowly swallowed up by a black hole. The mattress was old, sure, but perhaps Tom's previous overnight guests were chunkier than he had let on. She had accepted the past as the past, and he had electively been short on details.

Now awake in the dim, blue light, Jamie sat up next to Tom, and he shifted restlessly. Something didn't feel right, and her faith in him was waning.

The night was supposed to have been different. How had she let everything get this bad? He had rejected her, and she'd let him sleep. Or try to sleep. This was more humiliating than anything she could think of, except possibly the unfortunate instance of leaving the bathroom with toilet paper sticking to her behind.

His fidgety sleeplessness made the bed cramped. He abruptly repositioned the sheets and pillows. If this continued much longer, she'd definitely struggle to get through her afternoon meetings and client dinner. This was also unacceptable.

She finally unsnapped the garters and cast them to the floor. The now-unbearable metal bra clasp felt like it was digging into her back—likely a male-devised technique to ensure the stiff, cheap fabric didn't stay on for long. The polyester lace thong had no stretch in it and wasn't comfortable. She had only agreed to wear it because—after trying it on privately—she didn't look ridiculous or fat in it.

Tom got out of bed. His slender silhouette stumbled through the moonlight as though he were drunk, passing the small windows of his cramped, two-bedroom apartment. Oak leaves rustled and crinkled outside as another soft Southern California Santa Ana draft tried to breathe warm life into the room. A six-foot-something grandfather clock cowered in the corner of the bedroom as if ashamed to be there among the cheap furniture and beaten, ratty carpeting. Ominous and foreboding, the towering clock constantly observed all the goings-on in the apartment, sometimes—Jamie felt—with judgment. Its monotonous ticktock could be heard over the room's wispy fan.

The desire for warmth had always been a great excuse to cuddle, as well as to let in the fresh air. She loved that California had more than one sunny season. Conversely, Tom hated leaving the windows open—fearing it was too risky for break-ins, though none had ever happened in this quiet San Fernando neighborhood. The fan's constant cooling usually helped him sleep. Until lately.

After shuffling a few feet toward the bathroom, he stopped and stood motionless, as if realizing he didn't need to go. It was the second night in a row that Jamie had stayed over and he was somewhere else at midnight other than in bed with her.

She adjusted her poorly-designed bra and its lame excuse for bust support, flinching as it raked her skin. If he wasn't feeling amorous, she wasn't going to torture herself. What kind of man—and it had to be a man—designed these things? Tom's intentions were good, but she needed to teach him a few things—like how to select proper lingerie for her.

Her eyes followed Tom. He—as if sensing her concern for him—came to her side of the bed, his thin, angular back facing her. This was meeting her halfway.

"What's wrong, babe?" she asked, reaching over the bed and turning the fan off. He may always sweat, but she was cold.

No answer. She felt ignored again.

Tom clicked on the only lamp in the bare room. It sat on a makeshift nightstand that was constructed of two battered milk crates camouflaged by an old bed sheet like poor-student decor.

She avoided the harsh white light at this ungodly hour. "Is it her again? Because this isn't going to work." She couldn't help herself. Somehow an ex-girlfriend had resurfaced, and she hated it. After three years together, this was too much. And with both of them pushing forty, it was ridiculous. Where was the maturity?

"Why would you even say that?"

She studied him. He looked like he was nervously hoping to avoid the inquisition in the principal's office. "Because I'm not an idiot."

"It's not her."

She moved closer. If he was lying, she would get it out of him. "Then what is it? Please stop shutting me out. What's going on?"

He dropped his head. "Oh, Tom, your brother," she realized. "I'm so sorry. I didn't even think about that." She grazed her fingers through his hair to comfort him, noticing a few new gray sprouts in Tom's dark brown hair.

"I know it's stupid."

"Don't say that." She tried to be gentle, relieved that he was bothered by someone other than his ex. "Here, come be with me."

"I can't sleep." He stood up, brushing her away.

Jamie took a breath. This was getting old. His brother's death was undeniably tragic, but 9/11 was over *ten years ago.* She was frustrated that she never broke through to him and now sighed while watching him hunch over the sink and brush his teeth, his drooping basketball shorts showing more backside than he intended. It *was* cute, though she hated to admit it when she was sore at him for keeping her up. She was bombarded by emotions that confused her.

Everything had been so much better when they got engaged a year ago. He hadn't yet considered shopping his book back then. His novel writing had merely been an outlet. *Expression.* Without professional rejection on his horizon, he had been more optimistic about his life's potential and the quality of life he could provide Jamie, despite her making considerably more money. But writing columns for *Western Mag* had gotten increasingly hellish over the last several months with layoffs of other columnists and his increased workload, and after Jamie convinced him to seek publication of his first fictional work, he became increasingly distant—from her and everyone. It was critical acclaim for his fiction writing that he now sought, and his lack of success in generating any interest in it so far made him despondent from time to time. The book unknowingly became a symbol of all he could be and all that he—currently—wasn't.

More than twelve months had passed, and they hadn't yet set a wedding date. Jamie had tried patience and all the nurturing she could muster, hoping to pull him back to her. While her efforts sometimes inspired temporary smiles, lately they often repelled their intimacy. He was increasingly self-involved, and he refused to admit that he was stalling their marriage for any reason other than to focus on polishing his manuscript and getting it out there to agents and publishers. This came to a head two weeks ago when she had pulled out of him that an ex-girlfriend had crept back into his head. An unnecessary additional obstacle to their relationship—Jamie thought—which was deteriorating quickly, and she didn't know what to do. She supported him more than anyone, but now, she found herself resenting *the book.* To her, it was the force that allowed other influences to pull him away.

Jamie's gaze drifted to the only picture on the otherwise boring eggshell walls. Its vintage, soft magenta hue made it stand out in the room that otherwise showed no artistic appreciation, making the large print awkwardly out of place. But she liked it. A young man was sitting on a motorcycle, wearing a cap, and looking longingly into the distance. He looked innocent and strangely compelling. The far-away look in his eyes reminded her of Tom. That look he got sometimes. Pondering, dreaming . . . or maybe concealing something.

She searched the enigmatic man's face for clues to where Tom's head was, hoping it would illuminate some truth about why he had let an ex from his distant past back into his consciousness. She hated that she was now insecure about her fiancé after three years of an otherwise-typical relationship in Los Angeles—a sprawling metropolis where superficial relationships ranked supreme. It was a hazardous place for delicate romance, which was often shoved aside by the weak in their quest for financial success and career validation and better, more attractive options for mates. Jamie had thought that she and Tom had beaten the odds and had a durable love. But maybe not. For the first time, she wondered why he had, of all things, this particular poster on the wall.

"You don't have to worry about getting your bad breath on me!" she yelled over the running water. She wasn't concerned about halitosis right now. Jamie would consider him a metrosexual if he wasn't such a Cro-Magnon-sexual sometimes and could actually communicate. "Come rest with me, please? I don't want to be nodding off again at work. And you can't either!"

She'd barely gotten away with being half-witted at work yesterday after a heated discussion about Tom's ex for two hours the previous night, and she didn't want to give those vicious backstabbers at her office any more ammunition. A girl needed her sleep.

Closing her eyes, she considered whether she still wanted to go through with the marriage. Every time Tom pushed her away, Jamie got scared. Her mother didn't want her to marry someone who was unsure about what he wanted, seeming more *boy* than *man*. As reluctant as Jamie was to agree with her about anything, she didn't want to marry a boy, either.

If Tom got an agent and some validation for his writing, hopefully their relationship could start moving forward again. She accepted him being temporarily distracted by rejection letters. There was no way she could handle it, though, if he had enduring feelings for this ex-girlfriend. Things had to change soon.

Jamie looked asleep by the time he got back to bed. The bright light beamed down on her while she curled up with her pillow, her blonde locks flowing. Tom loved to smell that huge mane of hair. It reminded him of honey and wheat. She looked like she belonged in a Calvin Klein ad—cute, smart, sassy, and more successful than he was, all tucked into a beautiful five-foot-four package.

How a radiant woman like Jamie had any patience with an average magazine writer like him was something he didn't understand. She loved him and supported his hopes for his ambitious novel, seven years in the making. This made her quite the optimist. For LA.

Clicking off the light, he quietly lay back down as Jamie stirred, unaware that she had freed herself from his clueless purchase. Feeling the warmth of the room and her body again, he shifted, searching for cool sheets as abstract thoughts of someone from years past returned. Jamie would be furious if she knew. He hoped he wasn't blowing it with his preoccupation with his ex, but he couldn't help himself. He had meant everything he had said to Jamie when he asked her to marry him. Now, though, he doubted everything, from his writing abilities to his desire for Jamie. Now that he was being brushed off on a global scale with rejection letters from one literary agent after another, he had become withdrawn and non-communicative. He was officially a professional failure, as he imagined Jamie saw it, no matter how much she denied it. Not until he was a successful novelist could he feel worthy enough for her, matching her professional success.

Their relationship had been on track until she had convinced him to seek actual publication of his book, not just write it. Her encouragement had inadvertently propelled his current state of discouragement. But it was the ex that catapulted him back to the memory of his youth, where he somehow found a place where insecurities disappeared—the safer place where he didn't have to worry about not being *good enough*.

He pushed back his guilt, allowing Jamie to think that it was his brother's death that haunted him tonight. He wished he could be honest with her and return to the time a few weeks ago, before his ex resurfaced. Turning his back to Jamie, he flipped the fan back on, closed his eyes, and tried to dream of a calmer place where his worries disappeared.

Jamie had almost fallen into a deep sleep when she suddenly opened her eyes, her heart hammering in her chest. The truth had crept into her subconscious and slapped her awake. She knew without a doubt that she was losing Tom.

* * *

Their last few moments inside the plummeting jet were chaotic. People frantically searched the aisles and over and around their seats, as if their human instinct to do something—anything—would in some way disrupt their impending doom. Many passengers screamed. Others held their heads down in sky-travel-recommended fashion. Some prayed; others were silent. Some held each other's hands and cried. A baby midway down the aisle screamed. Her mother desperately held her, her own wide, wet eyes searching for help that would never come. Gilbert couldn't move in his seat, and the plane tumbled violently toward the ground.

With a thunderous crash, the plane became a vacuum, everything and everyone sucked forward into nothingness.

Outside, the fury of flames engulfed the side of a towering skyscraper, and the roaring booms slammed through its exterior glass walls and concrete slabs. The cacophony of crashes and rumbles was joined by screams, yells, and crumbling girders. Terrified citizens on the ground ran away from the explosive fireball lighting up the sunny day.

Tom woke up, perspiring with the realness of the plane's impact. It had been months since he had reimagined his brother Gilbert's death, but he figured he deserved to have such a nightmare again. Deception had a price, and he knew it. Weary, he finally brought the softly lit digital clock into focus. The alarm would go off soon. Trying not to wake Jamie, he pulled himself from the damp, twisted sheets and rolled over.

An hour later, Jamie was in the shower, as usual. She had no problem jumping out of bed when the alarm went off. It was an edge she had on him, as well as a more successful career and much better social aptitude, in his opinion. Plus, she had great legs.

The shower knob squealed off. Tom eased himself up, hating Tuesdays much more than Mondays, which at least felt fresh when they started. Today, though, it was his first meeting with a literary agent that made him anxious.

Jamie was wrapped in a towel and drying her hair with another by the time Tom got to the shower. She cocked her head and scrubbed the back of her scalp, taking a brief second to spank him on the butt. He had tried to saunter by her unscathed.

Still unsettled from the night before, she tried to be enthusiastic. "Morning, babe!"

"Hey."

Jamie checked her time. Raised in Manhattan and later as a teenager in Los Angeles, she was accustomed to lines. Lines of cars. Any drive-through or coffee shop had a line. Tan lines, bust lines, and frown lines. In college, classmates had tried to get her to *do* lines. But she was mostly concerned about the lines on the 405 Freeway which, if she waited much longer, would be so congested that she may as well not leave for three hours, because either way she wouldn't arrive at the office until midmorning. Her routine was a model of efficiency: her makeup took five minutes and her hair ten. Still, she had to move it.

"Today's the day!" she hollered, starting up the hair dryer.

The steam rose above the shower door. "I know!" So much hope was riding on his meeting today.

"You have to call me right after!" Her hollow stare in the mirror made her feel pale as she tried to be authentically supportive.

"I will," he said, not feeling like yelling anymore.

How William, Tom's younger brother, didn't wake from all their racket in the mornings was a mystery. Tom wiped the cascading water from his eyes just in time to see Jamie's toweled figure through the shower door's frosted glass, and she disappeared out of the bathroom. *Enjoy this*, he thought. *You've got a long day ahead of you.*

The shower was his sanctuary. A hot shower woke him up in the morning and relaxed him so he could sleep at night, though lately, that hadn't been working so well. The hot refreshment spouting over his head was probably going to be the most pleasurable activity of his day. Normally, it was here that he contemplated his next story draft or a title that his misled editors might allow to run.

He had conceived new titles for clichéd and overused ones like "Amazing Summer Destinations"—a title that showed up each year on the cover of virtually all seven magazines that the company owned—and substituted more poignant titles like "Cheap Summer Hot Spots" and "The Nontypical Vacation," which he loved. These were modified by the boneheaded, pea-brained editors to such fashion-mag babble as "Where to Take Her" and a fresh new angle on that—titled "Where to Take Him"— which frustrated Tom greatly because it was heralded as groundbreaking by the pompous chief editor. "Don't Have Another Boring Vacation!" was changed to the crème de la crème of them all: "The Hotels, Motels, and Inns That You'll Love and She'll Love You For," which Tom felt was completely reprehensible. It was the title that didn't end.

Perhaps now he could leave the tedium of *Western Mag* behind. After six months of trying to get attention for his completed novel, he had his very first meeting with an agent in a couple of hours. He hadn't looked forward to the process of seeking representation. It was the rejection he feared, but Jamie had finally convinced him to send out query letters. Finally, someone had expressed interest in his book. He shivered with excitement under the hot water.

"Oh my God!" he hollered, jumping naked out of the shower. Shampoo lather mercilessly slid down his head and into his eyes. Water beads collected near his feet onto the vinyl floor, settling in small, effervescent pools. "The hot water's gone!"

Jamie quit primping and admired her shocked, shivering fiancé. "Did you forget to pay your gas bill again?" she asked, amused. The suds fell down his face like melting snow.

He recalled the payment he had failed to make again. "Damn it!"

She grabbed a towel and walked over to him.

"Nope," he said, wiping his eyes. "I'm not keeping this soap in my hair all day."

She calmly returned the towel, and he stepped back in the shower. If that's the way he wanted it.

"Oh, it's cold!" He shivered and frantically scrubbed his scalp, the cold water smacking down upon him like liquid hail. "This sucks!"

She smiled widely, humored by his childish outburst. At least she got her hot water. Not paying his bills, though, concerned her. Irresponsibility was *almost* cute when boys were young. For men, it usually wasn't adorable. Right now, he wasn't adorable at all.

"You sure you don't need to borrow any money, babe?" She hated herself for asking it. *Damn. You don't have to fill the silence, Jamie Owens!*

"No way!" Tom yelled, hurrying the last of his cleansing. "I'll take care of it online today." That was the last thing he wanted getting back to her meddling mother.

"Good!" She had dated all kinds of men who had the artist streak, but this one had a patent on how to make the uncomplicated complicated. She would never show him the list of all the things he needed to change—not all at once, anyway—knowing that men, like mascara, can make a mess running.

The problem was, at thirty-nine, she had never known anyone else who could help her break free from her protective mother. Tom believed Jamie was capable of doing anything she set her mind to, but he didn't push her too hard when she admitted she was afraid to leave her thankless job. She loved him for trying to understand her, and she loved him even more for accepting her, even when he didn't understand. Her first husband hadn't been half as supportive.

This didn't give her enough confidence to walk down the aisle anytime soon, though. Not with an annoying ex apparently confusing him on top of a truckload of hidden emotions that she couldn't pry out of him. She wondered how a professional writer could be so astute when it came to comparing the similarities between Kafka's *The Castle* and a feuding couple on an exploitative daytime talk show—and be able to write a full-scale essay or column on it—yet be so poor at communicating with her.

Jamie applied her mascara with the skill of an artist. "If you're stressed, we don't have to do this dinner tonight. I can just go alone. Totally fine."

"Really?" he asked. He didn't believe her.

"You've had a couple of hard nights. Though, truly, not in a good way."

He coughed a laugh, and the shower's arctic downpour ceased.

"No, I mean it. Cynthia and Jamal love you. But I get it. It makes for a long day." Still, she knew she'd think about Tom throughout the whole business dinner anyway if he wasn't there. If things went well for him at the agent meeting today, they'd need to celebrate, preferably at her place tonight, after dinner. Her bathroom was bigger, and she wouldn't have to worry about the hot water going out.

"You love doing this to me, don't you?" he asked her, pulling up his boxers while she slipped on her business skirt—smart and simple—their morning timing in sync for a moment. He couldn't believe how quickly she got ready in the mornings, and he rushed so to not be a primping male—even though he didn't primp. She dumped her purse on the bed, searching for her keys.

One hair flip, and she was done. At the front door, with her hands full of various file folders, notebooks, and her laptop, she struggled to handle it all and was grateful that Tom opened the door for her—boxers only, still dripping.

"Call me as soon as you hear something," Jamie said, "or text me if I'm in a meeting."

"Pick me up at six?"

She was delighted that he wanted to be with her too. Maybe she wasn't losing him, after all. "Nip it in the butt today!" She kissed him.

"What'd you say?" he asked, smiling. Her soft scent surrounded him.

"This is it, baby. Finally." She stared up at him, their busy worlds slowing down for an instant, a precious moment of intimacy that would get her through the day. "Everything you've worked for. Nip it in the butt!"

"You mean *bud*."

She shrugged. "Whatever."

"Actually, I think you meant, 'Break a leg.' You're hilarious," he said, endeared by her consistent destruction of clichés. This had to be the only thing he had on her.

"I am!"

Tom watched her try to manage her full arms. "Need help?"

She continued walking. "Nope, I got it!"

As she turned the corner of the house, she heard him shut the door. She was disappointed he didn't watch her walk away. It was always good when he watched her leave.

Tom sat at the small, rickety table in the kitchen. Still air-drying in his boxers, he booted up his laptop. His legs bounced impatiently, and he waited for his e-mail to kick-start. He took a breath and started to write to an old friend. He couldn't believe he was doing it, but it eased his anxiety, somehow.

* * *

Homer woke up aching; by no means had she slept on a cloud. She put her timepiece on. The monstrosity was heavy. Its glassy diamond casing sparkled, greedily absorbing the early morning light and reflecting it into magnificent little starbursts that bounced within the musty shadows of the box. She grabbed her tablet and pen—two of the few supplies she had been allowed to carry—and started writing painstakingly neat script.

Journals were normally used to document history for the greenhorn angel who inherited an expired angel's files. No angel had ever lasted more than a hundred thousand years, unless he or she was promoted to seraphim. Expired angels just disappeared. No declining health, no warning. It was common for mature angels to unexpectedly vanish, leaving no evidence of their limited existence—which she saw as mildly empowered servants on chore detail—behind. This was selfish of God but not surprising to her.

She couldn't care less about when she expired or about documenting history for history's sake. Panicked about the possibility of being banished again for centuries or longer, she wanted to prove that God had set her up to fail with this task. Her replacement would surely share her woes with the other angels—the pleasant ones she liked, as well as the aggravating ones she despised—who would then finally understand that she wasn't a disgrace. If He was going to play hardball with her, she'd make sure the story of her tragic undoing was told.

Day 1, Western Sun, Morning.
My first night in the quasi shelter was predictably abhorrent. Never before have I detested the quarters I've been provided more than I did last night. After hearing about the amenities of the so-called twenty-first century (in the Christian calendar), I was surprised by the lack of suitable accommodations. What happened to heat at the push of a

button . . . air filtration . . . or those body-contouring thingamajigs I've heard about? (This isn't pettifogging. These are legitimate gripes, for which I hold legitimate resentment, as you can see.)

I haven't yet appreciated the new sophistication of the immoral generation of humankind that I've heard so much about from the other (more) divine messengers. I must concede I've yet to have a significant run-in with a twenty-first century version of the "person." Time will tell if they improve one generation over another compared to, say, their perpetual software updates.

Last night, I heard a man and a woman in an act of copulation that I found revolting and repugnant, though I am aware—yet astounded—that the Almighty One finds this behavior beautiful in its procreativity. These sounds came from a window directly above this atrocious pasteboard that is marginal temporary storage at best. (I don't understand it as "housing" under any conditions. Desert slaves in the Stone Age were able to construct better housing out of weeds, scraps, and rocks with less-Godly resources.)

The members of this disgusting species don't appreciate their ability to test fate or own their future, and they clearly will be the reason for Earth's destruction. After the way they treated me down here last time and my resulting punishment (for which I blame them), I've realized that I don't understand the purpose of their existence.

Making matters worse, the boisterous fornication and churlish behavior of these human beings last night prevented any rest I could have had during those witching hours, leading to my uncharacteristic crankiness this morning, as well as my own pondering of angel procreation. The Almighty One hasn't shared where the new angels come from. Egad! I detest the idea of procreation of angels by this moronic human method and hope that His progressive ideas include angel "recycling" (finding a way to restore expired angels, which would surely reduce predeath anxiety for most in the League).

Uniformed as a portly hobo once again, I was sent down here with the ridiculous task of assisting some sorry soul with book publishing that somehow will assist humanity and their roguery that's integral to the flawed species. Another monumental task, challenged by limited resources, lame tools, and a ridiculously short timeline. Clearly, He intends to see me fail. For a species that can soar to great heights with abstract expression and thought, it's notably ignorant and mean. Worse, He has forbidden me any earthly comfort to assist my focus.

Dear reader, so you're aware of the magnitude of my precarious situation, a calico feline attempted to find solace within my dilapidated coverings and refused to vacate the premises of my flimsy walls. Only when I projected a squeal did this nocturnal riffraff bolt out of my grotesque shack and into a nearby neighbor's collection of trash cans (which was obviously made for easy access by scoundrels like these, with a cacophony of sound effects to summate the performance). To my further disgust, this deplorable feline had no need for further rancid retribution, for it had already urinated on the side of my meager, pitiful abode.

I'm really supposed to live in loathsome, abominable quarters by night and then, by day, blindly follow this human without explaining why I'm shadowing him on every turn? Do I confront him? From what I've been briefed, the man appears, already, somewhat lifeless when dealing with conflict. Besides, in what way can I accomplish His task without jeopardizing free will? God's objective not only lacks cohesive logic, but He has too much faith in humankind's desire to help itself. If I do indeed fail my assignment, let it be recorded that I did so with His design!

But alas, I have a job to do, however pointless an exercise it is. You, dear reader, by the time you've read this, will likely have heard of my failure. Humanity will no doubt revert to its usual wasteful hatred of itself. I will head out today on a futile quest to find this pathetic human and deliver what the Almighty One requests.

God help me.

* * *

With the sweet, honey scent of Jamie lingering in the air, Tom finished his e-mail and sent it. He knew he was doing something wrong. He dressed in loose slacks and a white T-shirt that was destroyed from hundreds of visits to the washing machine. Apparently, the only thing that was going to stop him from wearing it was the washer disposing of it—and all its shredded little pieces—down the drain. After pouring himself breakfast, he took his cereal bowl and shuffled down the narrow hallway. He glanced in his younger brother's room through the cracked-open door. William was on his stomach, his head taking cover under his pillow, one foot dangling off the end of the bed—hiding from another Tuesday, one of seven mornings he hid from. The faint, sugared scent of pot, mild and rotten, escaped from his room.

"Such a loser," Tom said. "Hurry and get cleaned up. We've got to go soon!"

William groaned and pulled his quilt over his head, wrapping himself like a cocoon. He'd clearly had another late night.

Tom hated being more of a parent than a brother. With both parents unable to raise William, and with Gilbert gone, Tom had little choice but to take on the role.

Someone pounded the metal knocker on the front door with startlingly loud clangs. Outside the meager ground-floor apartment, three skinhead punks—two male and one female—waited to see if the person they were hunting for had the courage to emerge.

Across the street, Homer searched for the residence of her subject, Tom. She noticed the colorful punks at his door. This was interesting.

Eight-Ball, a Hispanic army brat with vengeance in his eyes—both his brown eye and his green one—was the leader of the minipack and stood on the porch steps while his comrades monitored conditions a few feet behind him. His black-and-green fatigues and steel-toed black boots made him unapproachable to most, and that was the idea.

"C'mon, man!" Skinny yelled, anorexic and fidgety in his plea to avoid another confrontation gone wrong. The industrial-strength female punk could be brutal mocking him. "I think someone's coming."

Eight-Ball gave Skinny a piercing look and showed off the wide gap in his front teeth before returning with anticipation to the front door. The adrenaline in moments like this—feeding off the fear of others—made him feel like a mountain lion about to pounce on its prey.

"Relax, Skin. We got time," he said in his distinctive Hispanic accent. "Gotta make sure we're at the right place."

"Told you this was the wrong apartment," Carla said. She had more evocative tattoos than Eight-Ball and Skinny combined, plus multiple piercings in both of her ears. Her self-loathing on display for all to see, her lonesome childhood had evolved into a tough exterior. Carla would be a nightmare for any suburban mother looking for a nice girl for her preppy son.

Tom opened the door.

"Is this number 1403A?" Eight-Ball asked, looking at the number 1403B on the dull brass address plate that hung by the apartment next door.

"Yeah, why?" Tom asked. This kid was intimidating, but he had this under control. "If you're paperboys looking for your tip, I don't get the paper."

Eight-Ball moved close to Tom's face. "Holmes, we don't look like no paperboys."

"Yeah, do I look like one?" Carla asked, smacking her gum.

They were ready for a fight, and Tom winced. The kid cereal in his cereal bowl destroyed any display of toughness he may have had.

Homer sat on the curb, unnoticed. Observing these pitiful souls perpetuate humanity's demise as a species was a sadly entertaining process. If her somewhat-divine celestial being could have magically created food, she would've eaten a tub of popcorn.

"There ain't no address on your door," Eight-Ball charged. "I don't see one anywhere. Do you, *holmes*?"

"Funny story," Tom said, engaging in a foreign act of fearlessness. While the prospects of rejection for his novel were daunting—he feared this more than anything—he wasn't at all afraid of standing up for his brother. "The numbers fell down when I was pounding some nails into the wall inside. From across the hall! Shoddy construction, probably. I really do need to—"

"Quiet, cereal boy," Eight-Ball said, thrusting his index finger up under Tom's chin. "We don't wanna hear your excuses or nothin'. Just tell us where we can find your kid brother."

"Don't have one," Tom said stiffly, staring Eight-Ball down and hoping to God that William didn't choose this moment to drag himself out of bed and appear in the doorway.

"You know exactly who I'm talkin' 'bout!" Eight-Ball's tooth gap provided an easy path for the spit that expelled when he was angry, accompanied by a little whistle that only his mother thought was cute. "You scared of me?" Eight-Ball spit just inches from Tom's face.

Tom recoiled. His childhood fights—all of which he had all lost—flashed before him. The fight with the boy in fourth grade over a pomegranate seed that the kid had spit at him as a joke. The fight with the two kids in second grade who'd made fun of him because he always carried loose change in his pockets, and they'd called him "Jingle Bells, Batman Smells" one too many times. The fight in eighth grade with the two kids who'd made fun of him for wearing a Members Only jacket when he still thought they were okay to wear.

"Work him, man!" Skinny yelled, anxious about getting in another fight himself—as long as he didn't get arrested again. "You know he knows where he is!"

"Shut up, Skinny," Carla said.

"Haven't seen him," Tom said, inches from Eight-Ball's spit path. His throat was hot and dry like an oven. He had the urge to swallow, a move that would be interpreted as weak and cowardly. Focusing, he breathed regularly to appear unaffected by Eight-Ball's cartoonish intimidation. He imagined what it would be like to walk into his meeting with the literary agent, sporting a broken nose and a black eye.

Exasperated, Homer shook her head. This woefully average-looking human had humanity's fate-changing book in his hands? *Impossible.*

"I bet you have," Eight-Ball said. "And I'm gonna find William."

Skinny's anxiousness grew when he saw a woman coming up the sidewalk, twenty-five yards away. "C'mon, Eight-Ball! Someone's coming!"

"Or should I call him 'Little Willy'?" Eight-Ball asked, overwhelming Tom's senses with a concoction of salsa and morning breath. "I'm gonna jack him up, man."

Inside, William walked out of his bedroom, recognized the threatening voice on the other side of the door, and quickly disappeared back into his room, sight unseen.

"Eight!" Skinny yelled.

"Don't make me make you a part of this," Eight-Ball said. The combative leader kept his eyes fixed on Tom and walked backward down the porch stairs.

"Part of what?" Tom asked. He breathed normally again, relieved he wasn't getting slugged.

"Savin' the world, dog!" Eight-Ball yelled, with his arms wide open like he was a proud martyr on a cross or was testing the air to see if it indeed was raining or not. He pointed at Tom. "You let him know I'm gonna hang him when I find him!"

"Ugh," Homer said under her breath. *Such a waste.*

They strutted up the sidewalk, and a young black woman, William's friend Wanda, approached. She stopped as the three punks walked around her, giving Tom one last look before they disappeared. Carla glared back wickedly at Tom. She hated wimpy white boys.

Mouthing "okay" and opening her eyes wide, Wanda continued toward Tom. She was wearing a backpack. Her black hair in braids revealed her high bone structure and the silky flawlessness of her skin, rich and smooth like pure dark chocolate.

William appeared and tried to poke his head out the door. "Who the hell was that?" he asked, pretending he didn't know. He sleepily scratched his backside and his boyish blond hair fell over his eyes like a wandering wild pony.

Tom pushed William back behind the doorway, relieved that the punks didn't hear his brother's groggy inquiry and reappear with more angry taunts. Wanda's inquisitive eyes met Tom's as she reached the front door.

"Hey, Wanda," Tom said.

"Hey, Wanda," William said, poking his head out again.

Tom considered giving up and just letting the punks have at him.

"Hi, baby," Wanda said, hugging William. "What was that all about?" she asked Tom.

"Good question."

Tom confirmed that the three troublemakers weren't returning. Young or not, they were trouble. He noticed a peculiar homeless woman peering at him from the curb across the street, scratching herself in weird places and cursing. Shaking his head, he closed the door behind Wanda, considered how the unassuming neighborhood was indeed getting worse, and glared at his incorrigible brother.

"What?" William asked.

"You tell me what. Big night last night?" Tom noticed the clock. "Move your ass. We've got to leave in a few minutes!"

Right about now, William wished he had his own car. He always hitched rides from pals at work after his bartending shift at Applebee's, eventually making it home. Having blown off classes in high school, he still made more money than his older, California-State-University-educated brother. Deep down, William suspected Tom hated Applebee's.

"Every night's a big night," William said, shuffling back toward his room. If he'd known he would wake up to this, he wouldn't have come home at all last night. "Excuse me for having a life!"

"Looks to me like there's drama, and I can't believe I almost missed it," Wanda said, delighted. She loved being in on everything.

"Oh, it's still going!" Tom said, unapologetically loud. "You've got an explanation for me, pal? Who are these punks? There were three of them. One bald and angry, one skinny, and there was a girl with them too."

"I don't know what you're talking about!" William disappeared into his room.

Tom had enough. "These friends of yours are way out of line!"

"Hey," Wanda said.

"Not you."

"Don't yell at me. Don't even try to be condescending. You're not Dad!" William popped his head out of his bedroom. "You can pretend you're him, but you don't have the self-confidence. Or his talent with women." He moved to his bathroom and slammed the door.

Tom hated when William brought up their parents. Either of them. "You barely even remember him. What were you, six?"

"You know," Wanda said, smiling, "he never said those kids were his friends." She dropped her backpack, wandered into the adjoining small den, and picked up a *Writer's Digest*, the only reading material around.

"And we've got no hot water again either!" William yelled from his bathroom.

"Well, we would if you paid me your rent on time!"

Tom tried to swallow his anger. Couldn't anything be easy? He mustered some patience and spoke solemnly outside the bathroom door. "William, these guys aren't going to toilet paper our apartment, are they? I don't want to get kicked out."

"If they did, at least we'd have toilet paper!"

William opened the door and threw out an empty toilet paper roll, hitting Tom in the face. He slammed the door shut again. Wanda raised her eyebrows and flipped another page of the boring magazine, no glossy pictures to hold her interest.

"You know how much toilet paper this one goes through?" Tom asked her.

She grinned. The brothers' quibbling was welcome relief from days of studying.

William emerged and crossed the hallway to his bedroom. "I got into a little thing with his brother, okay? But I've got it handled."

"What kind of thing?" Tom asked. "I thought you didn't know these people. Whose brother?" He followed William to his unkempt room, the concoction of the fragrant scent of pot and moldy something assaulting his senses. One thing at a time.

"What's this with everybody's brothers?" interjected Wanda from the den. "Where are the sisters at?" Tom threw her a glance of disapproval. "Mmmm-hmmm," she murmured, flipping another page.

William stared at his older brother. Tom exhausted him. "I'll take care of it." He pushed Tom out of his bedroom. "Give me some privacy, please?" He shut the door and locked it.

"We leave in five minutes," Tom said through the door.

"You're old," Wanda said.

"I feel old."

"Space, you know?" Wanda said, trying to release the tension. "It does a body good."

"He has plenty of space. I don't even know where he goes between work and whenever he drags himself home," he said, following Wanda into the kitchen, small and drab with yellowed floral wallpaper screaming to be updated. Cracks in the off-white tiles on the floor showed the wear and tear over the years, as well as from earth tremors.

She reached into the decaying cabinet for a cereal bowl. "Don't tell me you always told someone who you were with or where you were going."

"Nobody cared, Wanda," he said, amused by how comfortable Wanda was in his kitchen. She got a spoon out of a drawer. He grabbed a dress shirt from the laundry closet, covering up his ripped-up T-shirt. "Big difference here. He's got someone looking after him."

She was disappointed at the selection in the minipantry. "No grits. This'll have to do," she said, pouring the most sugary cereal she could find.

"Yeah, sorry," Tom said absently, working his Windsor knot in the mirror. He must work at the only magazine that required its writers to dress like executives. It was something the CEO insisted on after a fellow entrepreneur friend of his said his writers looked like they worked at the DMV. At least he had a legitimate meeting this morning. Today, he'd wear a tie.

She watched him work on his tie and sat at the rickety kitchen table, swallowing a spoonful of cereal. "Thanks for letting me come over and study during the day, Tom. It's hard for me to do it at home with my noisy roommates."

"Wanda, quit," he said. "Anytime, and you know it."

Her face lit up. "Hey, get this. Remember that guy I told you about?"

"The white one?"

"Yeah. Blaine. He's been hinting around, but I think he may finally get the guts to ask me out."

"Go Blaine." Tom was frustrated with his rusty knot-making skills and pulled the poor knot apart and started over. "He's in a wheelchair, right?"

"Yeah."

"So sad this guy's identity to me is based on his disability and race."

"But he's not that disabled. He—"

"No!" He smiled, tightening his tie.

"Well, he'd want to, let me tell you!" she said.

"I was gonna say, if you lost your vir—"

"No!" she interrupted, laughing. She wasn't losing her virginity to anyone. "Don't say it! My roommates don't stop kidding me! I'm proud I still got it!"

"Good for you." Wanda was the only friend of William's whom he actually liked.

"It's an individual choice, Tom. Your brother convinced me I'm not broken, feeling this way. God'll let me know when it's right."

"Sure He will."

"Or She," Wanda said, pouring herself some coffee. She found the muffins by the fridge.

Tom took a second to interpret what she was talking about. "Now God's a *She*?" He looked down the hall for William.

"Whatever. Only God could've created some of these bums I get with. Last boyfriend I had, the guy had a charisma bypass, I swear. Blaine's the man, though. And loves this." She stood wide eyed, her hands showcasing her body. "You blame him?"

"Trick question." He smiled, putting on his sports jacket. "Not falling for that one." Anxiety built as he put on his jacket. He was nervous, and his gums felt numb. "Hurry up, William!"

Wanda took another bite from her muffin. "Maybe we can double-date soon?"

"Double-date? I'm a little old for that."

Wanda frowned, and William finally came down the hallway in his designer jeans and a regular T-shirt, a look he had previously described as "the hi-low." Tom inspected him disapprovingly. The casual clothes were so form-fitting that they looked like they were customized for his compact, muscular build.

"I told you we needed to dress for this," Tom said. "You're learning something today. Look at me!"

"Love the corduroy jacket," William said, approaching the refrigerator.

"Very nice," Wanda said, smiling.

Tom headed for the front door. "Let's go!"

Finding nothing he could grab, William shut the fridge door. He was starving.

Outside the apartment, Homer sat on the curb, befuddled and depressed. She eyed the mammoth timepiece on her arm and sighed, not knowing what to do or how to start. *Craaaaaap. How the hell am I going to do this?*

A brisk fall breeze suddenly knocked her over. She really hated God right now.

* * *

Westfield Shaw Advertising's red brick exterior looked like it belonged on the East Coast, but the flat roof and large reflective windows sang California. At first sight, the square building looked like a bank. In fact, it had been a bank a year before, but the struggling financial institution had been closed by the FDIC for being insolvent, leaving behind only its forsaken structural shell—including the insulated vaults, which became soundproof production studios.

From the outside, the battered office building looked weak and disillusioned—like it knew it shouldn't be standing up. Its brawny red bricks were independently strong but would crumble easily during a mild earthquake, which Jamie was sure was coming any day. This explained why she had selected places she could hide in the event of the Big One, the Small One, or the One That Destroyed Westfield Shaw Advertising. In her office, it was her desk that would save her. The sturdy table in the conference room was obvious. Under the sink in the break room wasn't.

Her relationship with Tom might be rocky, but she would be ready if an act of God shook this place up. In life, she was always prepared with a Plan B.

She rushed up the stairs that she thought could facilitate a lawsuit for the unfortunate—or fortunate, depending on the point of view—soul who fell down them. Every month after she paid her mortgage, she briefly considered free-falling down the stairs herself and paying off her house with the lawsuit proceeds.

On her way to her office, she passed the two beauty queens of the boutique ad agency, Janice and Martha, the most arrogant women Jamie had ever known. They were in Martha's office, next to hers, complaining—as usual—about the inferior office drones they abhorred. Despite their stunning looks, both women were miserable and sexually frustrated.

One recent night, Jamie had thought of them when she came across a story reported by the BBC discussing how sexual frustration had driven a mild-mannered chimpanzee in China to take up smoking and spitting. She had momentarily become concerned for the queens . . . until she remembered that, unlike her feelings for these particular coworkers, she actually loved monkeys.

"Good morning!" Jamie said, a little too warmly for Janice and Martha to consider it genuinely friendly. Her arrival forced an interruption of their malicious storytelling, which had been frothing with creative tales of woe that amounted to entertaining but unproductive schadenfreude.

They hushed their gossip to sip their daily Starbucks coffee when Jamie walked by, her hands full. They watched her struggle to unlock her office door. The top folder of the stack she held against her chest slipped to the floor, papers fanning across the carpet. Keeping her composure, Jamie pushed the door forward with her foot, kneeling down to pick everything up as her two work adversaries looked on, their uninhibited cackling within earshot. It was bad enough that she felt flanked by them, with her office in between theirs. She thought of them as the evil stepsisters, if for no other reason than her desire to be Cinderella.

Her desk was a mess, as usual. She booted up her desktop to a screensaver picture of her and Tom smiling in front of an abbey, taken in Scotland last year. The picture was her favorite, one of the few photographs suitable for anyone to see. Her smile wasn't crooked, and Tom looked especially sweet to her. A faraway time.

The conference room was on the second floor in the front corner of WSA. The room's uneven blinds hung over the large windows—open in some areas and closed in others—and looked like they were winking at each other, as if they were all in on the same joke. The colorful furniture that adorned the office had yet to make it into this room of mismatched chairs, the last unfinished room of Stephanie Shaw's decorating project. A number of the account managers were fiddling with the blinds to calm the harsh, spotty brightness. Jamie walked in with Stephanie following close behind.

"This'll be a quick one today. Mornin', everyone," Stephanie said in a slight Texan drawl. She was as sleek as a preying panther. Her eyes bobbed and weaved subtly around the room like a calculating boxer. This was how she took roll.

A number of WSA's assembled buyers, planners, and PR personnel mumbled their obligated pleasantries as Jamie and seven others took their seats at the hardy conference table. An infrequent prize was displayed proudly in the middle of it: a box of fresh muffins. Martha had wanted to impress everyone, but no one—besides Martha—touched them. Stephanie grimaced, hoping no one tried to expense them. Times were tight.

Jamie sat in the last open seat at the table, directly across from Janice and Martha, who sat in their usual seats. She tried not to stare at Janice's large, manly hands. Before meeting the aging, six-foot-two beauty, she had never thought of ex-models as intimidating.

Everyone could tell with Stephanie's curt, abrupt eye movement that she was in a huff today. Her colorful skirt suit was yellow, which made her skinny, toned legs look especially tan.

"I want y'all to know that WSA has been a successful organization the few years we've been in business," Stephanie said authoritatively at the head of the table. The large, white, dry-erase board on the wall behind her reflected sunlight from the blinds, making Jamie squint, which Stephanie interpreted as annoyance.

"But," Stephanie continued, "since we've been unable to acquire new accounts in this agency since the departure of Linden Tires and the Relax the Back franchises to those bastards at NRS, some changes are happening at this agency. The magnitude of these changes will be determined by those in this room."

The staff looked around at each other, except for Janice and Martha, who avoided eye contact with everyone. Martha took a bite of her blueberry muffin. She was a few inches shorter than her counterpart, with slightly more girth, but their perfect skin, poise, and designer fashion suggested they both felt like they were still supermodels. Both women's suits were cut perfectly for their elegant frames, and they knew they looked good. Janice just used more Botox.

"Now while this agency isn't one of them run-of-the-mill, low-cost, low-service providers, we price competitively. But we need more clients. I'm asking for your help to utilize our media contacts out there. We need to acquire some more business, or we'll have to close up shop."

Jamie tapped her pen, tried to avoid the glare, and counted her options if she were fired today.

Bobby, an assistant in PR, raised his hand and spoke—shockingly—before called upon. "So while we hunt for business for WSA, do we have to worry about our salaries being cut again?"

The whole room went silent. They waited to see how badly this would go over. The cuts had been mild several months before, but jobs weren't easy to come by in this economy. No papers shuffled, no one coughed, and no one repositioned themselves in their squeaky seats.

"Not you, Bobby." Stephanie pointed to the door. "Get out. Thank you for your service. You can pick up your last check at the end of the day."

The dumbstruck room didn't blink.

"But, I—"

"Thank you," Stephanie said.

Jamie's eyes met his as he grabbed his notepad off the table and headed for the door. He gave his former coworkers one last terrified look before closing the door behind him. It had been an uncomfortable thirty seconds for everyone.

"Now. I want y'all to know that I very much appreciate your past work and your future work. Please, people," Stephanie said, raising her volume, "I don't want this all over the market. WSA has a reputation, and we don't need it compromised because we appear desperate. Let me know if you get any good leads, okay? Plus, a full week's paid vacation for the person that brings in a good-sized account into this agency. Has to be a hundred thousand dollars a year or more. Now, I have a meeting. You can reach me by e-mail. Have a good day."

Stephanie gathered her things, signaling that the meeting was over.

"When will we know something?" Jamie asked. Everyone in the room paused, admiring her bravery.

Stephanie stopped. "What was that?"

"When will we know something?" Jamie repeated. "That we're not closing down."

"As soon as someone scores a client. Pretty simple." Jamie was fearless at times, and Stephanie liked that about her. And Jamie wasn't a threat to her business, unlike a couple of former employees Stephanie had unearthed as disloyal. "So you know," Stephanie continued, raising her voice to accentuate her point, "our creative department has been let go. I'm sorry we won't be doing a company good-bye for them due to costs, but you may do something for them on your own if you'd like. Creative will now be outsourced to freelancers."

Jamie grabbed her stuff and headed for her office, past other account reps and employees huddling in small circles, whispering about the termination they had witnessed and speculating about more changes. Not personally close to anyone at work, she wasn't drawn in to such fruitless distractions. She'd combined her work life and social life in her twenties. Now, she knew it was better to keep the two separated.

She considered how Bobby being fired publicly today threw the entire workforce into a tailspin, with a substantial reduction of productivity. She would never run a company that way.

At the thought of poor Bobby, she remembered a great job offer she had received from another ad agency three months ago and kicked herself for not having the guts to take it. It would have been a chance to be more of her own boss, but they paid commission instead of salary, and at the time, she'd thought she couldn't risk the loss of secure income. Too bad that job was long gone, or she'd go back to them.

With Tom so far away from her—emotionally anyway—a renewed focus on work would be a healthy ambition. Her clients were happy, her accounts were under control, and she'd pursue building her own client base with more zeal. Since she'd found out Tom's feelings for an ex, she hadn't been focusing on cold-calling client prospects. Working harder was a good new priority for her since she didn't have the courage to build her own business.

Janice and Martha shuffled by her office with pristine posture, as if their hallway was a runway. The beauty queens didn't mutter a thing.

She checked the time again. Tom would be in his meeting soon. She got to work and prepared her thoughts for her client dinner.

Then she noticed. Her largest client's file was missing.

CHAPTER 2

Tom paced the sidewalk, trying to dispel his overeagerness. It wasn't working. The tall, intimidating building towered above them, unashamed to loom over neighboring minimalls and sloping parking garages. Its large, mirrored windows reflected its urban surroundings, including the busy billboard advertising surrounding them. William watched Tom with amusement as vehicles whizzed by, impatient drivers too preoccupied to obey LA speed laws. Unbeknownst to them, Homer observed them from a lone park bench across the street, trying to determine the best way to approach Tom and execute her galling duty. A foolish enterprise if anyone had bothered to ask her.

"I can't believe you made us park two blocks from here," William said. He leaned against the glass wall of the building housing Maroquin and Lee Partners, oblivious to the careless smudges he was leaving or the employee he was annoying on the other side of it. "Cheap bastard. And will you quit pacing?"

"You don't have anything to be nervous about. If they don't like it, I'm the one who sucks, not you."

"Hey, I'm only here because you made me. Can we go in yet?" William asked, rolling his eyes heavenward. Tom had insisted he see how professionals work in the real world. As if Applebee's wasn't real. "We look like idiots waiting out here."

"Don't be one up there, please," Tom said. They were about to meet the only agent who had expressed any interest in his work. There was only so much rejection Tom could take before he gave up and locked his mound of paper in a drawer forever. Or destroyed it.

"I hope we finish up in time so I can still catch an Egg McMuffin."

Homer chuckled, watching the young men squabble like courting game hens. She considered going over to them, but things were moving forward. The clueless writer was already pursuing getting his book published. This may be easier than she'd thought.

"I don't expect you to understand."

"What I don't understand," William said, wanting to get this over with, "is what if they love everything but the character based on me, man!" He rubbed his palms together and overacted his idea, oddly relishing it. "They might say, 'Make this guy a little more interesting. Make him a transvestite!'"

"Seriously."

"With an incredible case of jock itch."

Homer grinned. The younger one was funny.

Tom ignored the sarcasm. "You're not William in the book. Your name's Felix in this. I thought you read the copy I gave you!"

"Felix? Like the cat? Where the hell did you come up with that?" He'd never bothered to read the book. No way could he get through five hundred pages. But he had given it to Carlos, who was supposed to get it to his stepdad, an agent. That should have gotten him out of attending this meeting. William punched Tom in the arm. "Felix, Tom? People are gonna laugh at me!"

Tom threw up his hands. "What am I talking to you about this for? You barely know how to read anyway."

"I don't read down-on-your luck stories with an ending everybody hates."

"*Calvin and Hobbes* doesn't qualify as reading."

Not bad, Homer thought. Tom was funny too.

William ignored him. "McDonald's stops serving breakfast at ten thirty."

Tom raised a brow. If William didn't work out every day, he wouldn't be hungry all the time. It was nine o'clock sharp. "Let's go."

Homer watched them disappear. How was she supposed to facilitate book publishing? Maybe she could whisper something in a publisher's ear that the ending needed to be changed. If only that didn't influence free will. She sighed. God never made it easy.

William followed his brother through the large double doors. "You know, a fat paycheck could be coming your way if you sold this."

"It's not about a paycheck."

"See," William said, running to catch up to Tom, "no wonder you're always broke. I bet you that Stephen King writes to get published—and paid—not to prove something to himself or the world. And slow down!"

"I'd have more money if you paid your rent on time," Tom said. William caught up to him at the elevator. "Suite 700. Seventh floor, you think?"

Tom hit the elevator button, and they took the slow, vertical rise to the seventh floor. He took a breath, his heart sinking fast, as if their ascent was to the top of the scariest roller coaster in the world.

He had put over a thousand hours into his manuscript. It had started as a cathartic document of his troubled childhood and evolved into a substantial piece of work that Jamie had convinced him to share. There had to be people in the world, she thought—far beyond the insulated borders of America, where child abandonment was a muted topic—who would relate to his story. But no one was interested in seeing his work. Of the dozens of query letters he had sent out, only two agents had said they'd read it. For a fee. Terse, form-letter dismissals were the norm, until Maroquin and Lee Partners invited him to meet with them today.

William wondered why Tom looked sick.

Tom's stomach sunk into his intestines. *It's only the seventh floor, for God's sake!* He closed his eyes and concentrated on not throwing up.

Dr. Seuss's first children's book had been rejected twenty-four times before he had found salvation by a publisher; over one hundred million copies of his books had sold. John Grisham's first novel, *A Time to Kill*, was declined by fifteen publishers and almost thirty agents. Tom was most inspired by Colonel Sanders, having read somewhere that his original-recipe chicken was rejected 900 times (or 1,009 times, by more lofty accounts) before it became the world-famous KFC.

Tom considered the endurance and persistence necessary to meet with that many literary agents and quickly discounted it on the belief that there couldn't be that many decent ones in the world. But at least the colonel could actually get in front of that many people. The colonel did have something, though, that Tom did not: zesty chicken, as well as guts. His work had to deliver on merit that didn't incorporate a new combination of eleven herbs and spices. Tom breathed and swallowed his vomit. The elevator opened.

Ding.

Both brothers moved through the elevator corridor into a vast, elegant reception area. A huge open space, bare and polished epoxy resin floors, and a lofty ceiling brought edgy creativity to the twelve-year-old literary agency. The receptionist, deep in the main lobby, was dwarfed by a massive curved desk. It looked like it was handcrafted to hide her so that no one would bug her.

They approached the grand reception desk, their steps echoing in the large room, its coldness intimidating. It didn't feel welcoming at all.

"Yes, hi, we're here to meet with Mr. Maroquin," Tom said. He felt his voice shake.

William smiled at the receptionist. Her classic sweater hung over her shoulders with grace. The woman clearly had style. "Hi there."

"Hi," the receptionist said, looking up from her pristine workstation.

William leaned over her desk confidently. If he was forced to roll out of bed this morning, he might as well enjoy himself a little. "You flirting with me?"

"Excuse me?" The receptionist didn't bother to conceal her annoyance. "I hope you two aren't ignorant enough to engage in sexual harassment. If you can even spell harassment."

"I know you're not flirting with *him*," William said, patting his brother on the back, almost making him throw up again. "That kind of pressure will put my brother here over the edge today."

"Ted Koppel always pronounced it hair-ass-ment," Tom said, trying to lighten the mood. Hopefully her caustic tone wasn't a sign of more bad things to come. "Mr. Maroquin, please."

"Oh, no, no, no." The receptionist shook her head. "This isn't his office."

Tom was confused. "Isn't this Maroquin and Lee Partners?"

"Yes, it is."

"Maybe we're not understanding you," Tom said, still trying not to gag. "We have an appointment with Mr. Maroquin."

"Not in this office."

"You've got to be kidding me! We're in the wrong place!" Tom stepped away from the reception desk, horrified that he'd screwed this up.

The receptionist checked her appointment calendar. "First impressions don't matter, do they?" she asked under her breath. "Tom Summers?"

Tom's blank expression was priceless.

She picked up the receiver, punched a button, and then spoke into the phone. "Your nine o'clock is here. Technically, they were here on time. Yes, ma'am." Shaky, she hung up the phone.

"Mrs. Maroquin," Tom said.

"Is there a problem, sir?" She loved asking questions she knew the answers to.

"No, thank you," Tom said, nonplussed.

The receptionist eyeballed Tom. "Have you been forced to face your own sexism, Mr. Summers, recognizing that a patriarchal society has conditioned you, a male—wow, that's hard to believe, isn't it—to stereotype gender roles so that it's become difficult to accept that a woman could own her own literary agency, let alone be the first of the two last names on the sign outside?"

William was bored with her antics. "Do you have any food here?"

"Lee?" Tom asked, ignoring his brother.

"Her husband," the receptionist said.

If Tom wasn't so nervous, he'd be embarrassed. "How'd you know we didn't want to see him?"

"Because he's a silent partner and owns a bar downtown." The two unenlightened men reminded her of why she had decided long ago she'd do whatever it took to succeed in a man's world. And a man's world it was; in no way could a sane God have intended it to be that way. "Duh."

William's eyes bulged. Even he was surprised by her abrasiveness. "Rude!"

There was an electric buzz at the desk. The receptionist fake smiled. "She's ready to see you now. Her office is through that door on the left. Oh, and don't refer to her as Mrs. Maroquin. Maroquin will do."

"Thank you," Tom said, unsure of whether or not the young woman was being helpful. He hung over the reception desk and spoke softly to the startled receptionist. "*Harassment* has one *r* and two *s*'s." He started toward Maroquin's office, his breathing steady and his stomach volcanic. He should have taken Rolaids.

Running to catch up with Tom, William stared at the receptionist who stared back at him until both brothers disappeared into Maroquin's office. "One *r* and two *s*'s . . . two asses indeed," she said, and she turned back to her computer screen.

In contrast to the spacious, echoing lobby and expensively dressed reception area, Diane Maroquin's claustrophobic office was depressing. It felt as sterile and unwelcoming as an office could, with the gloom of gray plastered everywhere. Its neutral hue was splashed on the concrete flooring and the desk and the cabinets and the shelves and the walls and in the art on the walls and even on Diane Maroquin's slicked-back bun, lacquered thick on her head. She sat rigidly at her desk—dark, polished, and solid—writing something evidently important. She lifted her head up to meet Tom and William when they walked in.

"Don't embarrass me," Tom whispered to William.

"Don't blow it."

They approached her. "Hi there," Tom said.

She didn't rise, gesturing to the seats in front of her. She didn't waste time with unnecessary, disingenuous pleasantries. The phone on the desk buzzed, and she picked it up as both men sat.

"Yes. Mmm. Really."

Tom noticed Maroquin's business cards, propped in a wooden display box. *Diane Maroquin, President.* He took one.

William studied the pictures of Maroquin displayed across the room, her static smile the same in all of them like a mannequin that simply changed outfits. Maroquin the Mannequin. *Funny.*

"Tell him we're not Simon & Schuster," she continued. "We're the rep, not the publisher. If the moron wants to negotiate like that, go to Vegas. There aren't any publishing houses, but they love cheese there. And tell him I don't hire writers with emoticons on their queries. Loser happy faces. This isn't grade school."

William looked forward to the fun starting and rolled his eyes to Tom, Maroquin seeing it.

"No, I don't want to talk to him again." She hung up the phone, annoyed by another unemployed writer/stalker.

"Hi, Mrs. Maroquin. I'm Tom Summers."

"Maroquin," she corrected.

He could kick himself for forgetting not to call her *Mrs.* so quickly. "I'm sor—"

"Save it." She looked the younger one up and down. "And this?" Maroquin asked.

"You mind if I have one of these?" Without waiting for a reply, William took a candy from the glass jar on her desk and stretched his legs out. He unwrapped the fruity sucker, the stiff wrapping crackling at an alarming decibel level in the quiet office.

Tom noticed Maroquin grimace. Apparently the noisy wrappers were meant for show only.

"Mmmmm," William said. "Mind if I have another one?" He grabbed a handful from the bowl. "Fruity."

Her attention drifted back to Tom. "He looks like the writer, and you look like the agent, in your suit there."

"It's a sports jacket."

Maroquin didn't care.

"For my day job," Tom said, smiling nervously. "William here is my little brother. He's here for support."

"Clearly," Maroquin said, forwarding a call to voice mail. "Quite inappropriate. Unless he's your manager, that is." She looked at them blankly.

Tom adjusted himself in the stiff chair, which had armrests too narrow for comfort—chairs not meant for long-term guests. Church pews were more ergonomic.

William smirked. "He made me come. I had another place to be."

Yeah, like in bed, Tom thought. Maroquin remained expressionless.

"A big-brother thing," Tom said. "I'm trying to show him more of the world—mentoring that will hopefully get him off his butt some."

"He's trying to get me to be more like him," William said.

"Now that I'm educated about your unique views on coaching younger siblings, let's move on," Maroquin sighed, perusing Tom's manuscript from a pile on her desk. She had helped and nurtured so many writers over her twenty-five-year career. None of them had ever insulted her, though, by bringing an audience. Even her best-selling writers didn't bring siblings to their meetings. "Your knowledge of industry protocol is nothing." She flipped through some pages. "So. I'd assume, then, little brother . . . Felix, is it? The uninspiring character in the manuscript."

William threw Tom an angry glance.

Tom wasn't sure he was relieved she had read at least some of his work. "Um—"

"William. I'm talking to him," she said, eyeing Tom before changing her focus.

"Okay," William said uncertainly. His stomach rumbled, and he took another candy.

"Good." She shook her head at William and transitioned quickly to Tom. So little time, so many bad writers to reject. "I understand we sent you correspondence indicating we were interested in discussing your manuscript."

"Yes, ma'am." Tom cleared his throat. He was subjected to criticism from his editors at work all the time, and yet his throat closed up when this woman asked a simple question. *Get a grip!*

"Please don't call me that. Now, I should let you know from the onset that the letter requesting a meeting was sent to you in error, as was the request for your manuscript. Once your appointment was made, it was discovered that no one here had read your material."

"Oh." Tom couldn't imagine anything worse right now.

"I had our former receptionist look this up. So strange how this happened . . . two errors . . . our request—which I did not personally make—somehow went out to you. We received it, and then—error number two—we requested a meeting with you, without having read anything. This never happens, and I almost cancelled this meeting.

"However," she sighed, "last week, my meddling husband pulled your work from one of my piles and raved about it, so I felt obligated to peruse it and meet with you today."

"It's divine intervention," William laughed.

"Not quite," Maroquin said, unamused. "This procedural oversight has since been resolved, and the employee responsible has been removed from the premises."

Tom clung to a strand of hope. "Your husband liked it?"

"He wouldn't know good literary work if it blew him," she said.

So much for hope.

"And last night, the bastard told me he's leaving me for a younger woman," she continued, her tone becoming more dismal.

Tom didn't know what to say. "I'm sorry."

"Really?" Maroquin considered how stupid she was for not getting a prenup. "But in page after page, you demonstrated why long-term relationships are destined to fail. So why don't you tell me why you wrote this story, Mr. Summers?"

"Um—"

Maroquin got up and—with her back to them—scanned over the morning city street and the adjacent gray buildings and parking garages, a foreboding dullness everywhere. A smoggy haze hung in the distance, sinking into the large buildings like the weight of the world was upon them. "So that I may be better informed about the perspective from which it was written."

"She really talks like that?" William whispered to Tom, who ignored him.

Maroquin heard William's question but continued gazing over the aggressive city she had conquered. "Defenestration," she said to herself softly.

Tom leaned in a little closer to her. "Um, did you say something?"

Her heart beat in her chest with heavy thuds. Many of the buildings she overlooked had at one time housed ambitious literary enterprises like hers. Once prosperous and successful, now closed for business. Victims of the troubled economy or themselves. She had outlived them and was professionally triumphant. It was her personal life that was destroyed. The sudden emptiness made her question everything, a new meaning for *vacancy.*

"Defenestration," she repeated louder. "Good word. Throwing someone out a window . . . can you believe there's a word for that?" Images of her pathetic husband screaming and plummeting to the ground filled her mind. Dimly, she recalled that her antidepressant bottle was empty too and had been for a month. She wouldn't have time to refill it today either. A busy schedule had its price.

Trying to carry on a conversation with her back brought to Tom's mind the image of campy soap opera staging, where the dramatizing actors and actresses don't face each other. So over the top. "Words can be powerful, can't they?"

Maroquin turned to him. "Too bad words don't necessarily good novels make."

William thought she talked like Yoda.

Maroquin turned her gaze back to the window and realized she'd had it. No more was she going to work with the writing hacks and wannabes, particularly those whose work her husband appreciated. He had twice convinced her that second-rate material was what the book-buying public wanted, not the highbrow works of the *literary elite* that she sought. He had shown her examples of trash that sold millions. *Only one hit, and we retire ten years early*, he had said.

Unfortunately, both writers he had convinced her to take on were train wrecks, their book deals a pittance (as was her commission), and their weak sales hurt her reputation and ultimately made her agency's investors balk. After accepting her husband's financial and physical shortcomings, this was how he repaid her. Her husband could ruin their marriage, but he wasn't going to destroy her business or take half of it in a divorce. Her world wasn't going to end this way.

She was drawn to a screech on the street below. A car had hit a female pedestrian, who stood in apparent shock, the car somehow wrapped around her body like a horseshoe. A small crowd stared at the woman in awe.

Homer snapped at a man trying to pull her away from the wreckage. "Get your filthy paws off me! What an abomination, this mechanical beast!"

The driver of the mangled sedan came to her. "Are you okay, ma'am?"

"Kindly step away from molesting me, sir, or I will report your cruel negligence to the proper authority."

"Mommy," a young girl said, "she stopped that car."

"Stupid, stupid," Homer muttered, walking away and hating the human species more each day. It had been a foolish idea to cross the street to be closer to Tom and William when they exited the building.

Tom selected his words carefully. Historically, he hadn't handled himself well with domineering women—his mother, for instance. He watched Maroquin stare silently out her window, lost in her thoughts. "Any constructive criticism you can make, I appreciate," Tom offered, hating his limp words after he said them. William grabbed for a few more candies.

Maroquin turned to William abruptly, as if rudely awakened. "Keep your hands out of the bowl!"

William cowered in his chair.

"You think so," Maroquin said to Tom nonchalantly, returning to her desk.

"I wrote something personal so I'd finish it," Tom said with uncertainty. He wasn't used to anyone else yelling at his brother. Then he hated what he said, the admission of an amateur. Her presence was unnerving. "My little brother here knows how I struggle to finish writing anything I start, even for my column in *Western Mag*," Tom babbled, "but I always do finish that!" This she-devil had gotten the best of him.

William entertained himself by picturing Maroquin on the toilet with cramps.

"Atrocious material in that rag," Maroquin said, discarding inconvenient industry professionalism. "Your chief editor. What a pompous fool."

Tom kept going, hoping he could avoid hitting another one of her nerves and calm his own. "You see," Tom said, trying to keep his voice from shaking, "I've always written stories, since I was a kid, but I never was able to finish any of them. Poems even. This book, though, was different. Less abstract maybe. I felt liberated."

"You felt liberated writing about doomed relationships?" she asked, surprised. Upbringing must be to blame. "Tell me, Mr. Summers. Were you a formula-fed baby?" She sat back in her chair, her hands interlocked in front of her.

What? Tom looked at her in shock. She was crazy.

"Something went wrong somewhere," she said. "Clearly."

William had never encountered someone more inappropriate than himself. "I agree with that," he said. "You, Tom?"

Tom felt attacked, unsure of the latest off chord he had struck. "I felt liberated releasing what I kept in for so long," he said, focusing directly on

Maroquin. Being rejected was one thing. If he wanted to be insulted every time he opened his mouth, he would just call his mother.

"I'm confused as to whether it's fiction or nonfiction. Clearly you are, as well." She imagined her husband reading the manuscript and contemplating abandoning her. Sexual images of him with this younger woman—whom she bet was blonde, probably fake—surged through her. "Tell me this. Have you had professional therapy?"

"What?" William coughed. "You can't ask him that." Even he didn't talk to his brother that way. Then again, their whole living bloodline could use therapy.

"Do you want to get an agent or not? I'm trying to help," Maroquin said with a fake smile, the brothers exchanging befuddled glances.

"Funny thing," Tom said, forcing a laugh. "I did. That part just didn't make it into the book."

"It's not a book yet." She looked up at the wall clock behind them. She had spent too much time with this greenhorn and his unseemly sidekick, but she wasn't done with them yet. They were going to pay for what her husband was doing to her. "So. Why didn't you include it? Could have provided more empathy for your characters."

"Because it wasn't relevant to the story. It's fiction, Mrs. Maroquin, and—"

She snapped her fingers. "Maroquin. No additional address is necessary."

"Okay," Tom said, trying to keep track of his thoughts. "I didn't want to patronize the reader with putting the guy in therapy. It would sidetrack from the point of the book . . . I mean, manuscript."

"Couldn't happen more than it did," Maroquin said.

"Excuse me?" Tom felt like he was defending himself to the Nazi proprietress. He considered just grabbing William and leaving.

"I don't know what story formula you were using, but it broke every law of good writing. What software program did you use when you wrote this, not that it would've helped?"

"I didn't use one. Did Hemingway? Tolstoy or Shakespeare?"

"Dickens?" William proudly interjected. Tom's quick glare at him was meant to discourage further unhelpful assistance.

"You, sir, are none of those." She scanned to William. "Or Dickens, especially." She rolled her eyes and lay back in her desk chair. "You are quite the *Pecksniffian* sibling, aren't you, little brother?"

Neither of them knew what that meant. William thought of the various sexual positions he could maneuver in that chair, none including Maroquin.

"That's what makes this story different," Tom said, "a new story within a new structure."

"Frankly, I found the hatred toward everyone, including God, offensive."

Tom stared at her. "The theme isn't hate or—"

"Very offensive," she interrupted. "You're not very tolerant, are you, Mr. Summers? You think people who invest in long-term relationships with other people are stupid."

"No, I'm not intolerant." He couldn't believe he had to defend his personal beliefs too. "This story has to do with certain events in my life, our lives," he said, gesturing toward William, "which inspired me to tell the story from that point of view."

"So is this fictional or autobiographical?" Maroquin asked.

"Fiction," Tom said. "I took events and people from my life, though, to help me write it. That's where inspiration comes from, isn't it?"

"I call it hate speech. Writers with talent are able to muster an imagination of some kind, create a world for the reader to explore. It doesn't have to be hurtful."

"That's not the point of the book," Tom said.

"Again. It's not a book yet."

"Story then," Tom said, finally vindicating himself. "There are chapters in it that—"

"I appreciate your passion," Maroquin said gravely, ignoring Tom's desire to engage her in debate in her own office. She wouldn't have it. "While it may appeal to the 3 percent of atheists out there, Mr. Summers, I don't see it as marketable."

"Sorry you didn't like it, but somebody will."

"And lastly, you need a better conclusion," Maroquin sighed. "The underdog story is so formulaic. Predictable. It's too safe. My advice: take some risks if you want to succeed as a writer."

Tom started to get up, William dutifully following. "Let's go, William. We'll find someone else to publish it."

"Oh, I don't think so," she said, assured. "Not trash like this. It's neither art nor literature."

"We'll see," Tom said, shrugging. "When you're wrong—"

"I won't be."

She stood behind her desk, robust and unflinching. "You can self-publish it on one of those Publishing for Dummies websites. But no self-respecting agent—or publisher—would touch this. Honestly, it's not commercially viable."

"Thanks." It was all Tom could think to say, and he and William headed for the door after William grabbed another handful of candies.

She leered at them. "If you change the ending and the nonlinear foundation and inject some life into it, give me a call. Give me something to believe in, and I'll help you find a rewriter to clean it up." She was so good at lying that she almost convinced herself she would help him.

They walked out, William feeling for his defeated brother. All a college education got you was misdirected ambition that led to more rejection in your life. High school was bad enough.

Maroquin hit a button on her phone. "April," she said loudly enough for Tom and William to hear, "get my contacts with every major literary agency. Yes, in the country. Now."

"I'm still in that other project you gave me this morning," April's voice said over the intercom. The loudspeaker's crackle reminded William of a drive-through, not helping his hunger. "Can I—"

"Do it!" she yelled, and hung up. She couldn't let smug trash like that get published. And if her pitiful husband loved it, all the more reason to make sure it didn't.

The elevator doors shut. His countless hours of writing now felt like a loss. He tried to recall the last time he had encountered a professional *anyone* who had spoken to him like Maroquin had. No way could all agents be this brutal. His work felt like a waste, and he realized he'd started down a long road of forthcoming rejection.

"Well," William said, "why don't you self-publish it?" He hoped his brother wouldn't collapse on him. He didn't want to have to carry him to the car on an empty stomach. The candies could only do so much.

"I want to get it into bookstores," Tom said.

"Use the web, dude. Screw these people!"

Ding.

Tom was obstinate. "I don't know how to market a book or get it reviewed or anything! You need an agent for that. I'm the talent."

"You're being dumb," William said, believing Tom used the term *talent* quite loosely. He'd read a couple of pages of Tom's manuscript once and was unimpressed. Too many big words. "Take overbearing control, Tom. Didn't you learn anything from Mom?"

Homer appeared from around the corner as they exited the building. She was shaken up from the car accident. God had a way of reminding her when she strayed from her assignment. His irritating booms and her fear of deafening solitary silence were an annoying combination. She could see that Tom was sulking. Anxiety flushed through her, and she wondered if she should stalk the agent or the boys. Figuring they'd probably all laugh at her, she sat on a bus bench and sulked.

"That's her!" the driver of the mangled car yelled, and a small congregation of a dozen curious onlookers started to run toward her.

"Hey, come back here!" someone yelled.

"Oh, she doesn't have insurance!" "How'd she do that to that car?" "Maybe she's a robot!" "She owes me for my damages!" "Get her!"

Despising the human race more with every interaction, she muttered to herself, "Why you're worth saving, I'll never know." She ran from them with supernatural speed, disappearing in a mere second, leaving only a slight sense of her spirit in her wake. The dozen onlookers searched around the space of her brief existence, confused.

"Where'd she go?" "Did you see that?" "I told you Hyundais didn't crash test well."

"Learn anything today?" Tom asked his brother. They moved toward his car, not noticing the commotion behind them.

"Yeah," William said, "that you're too stubborn to listen to what any of these agents have to say."

"What do you know?" As far as Tom was concerned, all William knew was how to be a slacker and spend all of his cash on pot, with all of its colorful names for it: grass, funny stuff, weed, mookah, flower tops, good giggles, joy smoke, reefer, hippie lettuce, laughing grass, herb, wacky weed, and goof butts. The terms interchanged based upon his mood more than with a difference in the quality or origin of the stuff. One time he came back from a Texas vacation with a new kind that Tom had never heard of before, Johnson Grass—a low-potency Texas marijuana—aptly named after the unfortunate and deceased Lyndon Johnson.

They didn't speak until Tom dropped William off at the apartment. Tom thought about how Maroquin had stared him down with hatred—like she saw the devil in him—and her threats of calling publishing houses. Blacklisting him, really? If his writing was that bad, no wonder he had never had a short story published. Or that Western Mag Corp, that owned *Western Mag* and a number of other publications, had given him one lousy raise in two years. And what he'd had to do for that raise made his stomach churn just thinking about it.

"I guess I'll eat the cheap junk at home," William said finally. "Thanks for nothing."

"Sorry. I've got to get to work."

"Here's two hundred bucks," William said. He unstuffed two one-hundred-dollar bills from his jeans, threw them on the passenger seat, and got out of the car. "Pay the gas bill, please? If I wanted to feel like I live in the projects, I'd move in with my friends." He slammed the door.

Tom rolled down the window, knowing damn well what the odds were of William ever living on his own. Astounding. Though Tom sometimes paid bills late, *he paid them*. "Don't slam the door to the car I use to chauffeur your ass around town!"

His brother ignored him.

Like a boxer, Tom navigated in and out of traffic. His car, a sensible, brown Toyota Corolla with over 120,000 miles of use—virtually all within a thirty-square-mile grid in its seven-year lifetime—weaved through traffic lanes until he pulled up to Western Mag Corp's sea of cars filled with the likes of BMW, Mercedes, and Lexus, many driven by nominally paid employees showcasing pseudostatus on the road.

The square, beige building's smoky-black stenciled sign was loosely attached to the boring two-story complex, looking like it had no interesting stories to tell. A satellite office for the single publication of *Western Mag,* the workplace clearly didn't try to be a Xanadu. An unadorned reception desk could be seen from outside the simple glass-door entrance. The uncreative committee behind the construction of the bland box obviously had one intention when building it: don't stand out. Numerous water stains on the stucco walls distinguished it from the otherwise identical buildings around it.

Tom parked. He wondered if Maroquin's abuse was karma for his complicity in that plagiarism incident from last year. He hoped not. After cutting the ignition, he gathered his thoughts. It was time to switch gears and be a columnist henchman.

Western Mag's writers were competitive busybodies trying to make names for themselves—in everyone's business all the time, getting the scoop, and walking the beat. In Tom's experience, all other magazine writers drowned themselves in their subjects, whether it was travel, music, dining, or dating. They invested their energy into their subjects of interest, driven to be recognized so they could get better-paying gigs somewhere else. There was no time for office shenanigans. Here, it was different.

"Morning, Tom."

Otis Bacon, the hefty security guard, pounced upon Tom getting out of the car. Sticking a half-eaten candy bar into his pocket, Otis downloaded a gaming app onto his phone and beamed at Tom.

"Hi, Otis." Tom was the only person outside of payroll who knew the security guard's name.

"You should see this great game I just downloaded! It's a cross between *Space Invaders* and *Crash Bandicoot.*"

"I don't know what that is," Tom said, smiling as Otis followed him into the building.

"Yeah, well, it's awesome!" Otis watched Tom walk up the stairs. "You ever want to play it or anything, let me know. We'll play two player!"

"You got it," Tom said, amused by Otis's exuberance.

"I've got the Wii too! You've gotta come over!"

Disappearing into the busy, uniform cubicles separated by razor-thin partitions and manufactured hallways, Tom strode toward his own personal cube. The rectangular grid of eighty cubicles filled the room neatly like they were built specifically for the large space. His cube was identified by its geometric quadrant and individualized by his framed pictures, rock music posters, and the arrangement of his personal paper mess. He logged in on his computer, trying to keep the bustle of his arrival low key. Coming in late always created a stir.

"Things must've gone well this morning, considering how late you are! Did you get a deal?" An overly cheery head popped into his cube.

"Hey, Nadia." She was the only real friend in the office he trusted enough to share anything about his book. He just wished her voice didn't carry so much. He didn't want to be mocked by other writers for his slate of rejections, by Brent in particular.

"What's up? You look peaked." Nadia frowned. "You should've gotten that flu shot. Now you're probably gonna get that plague that's infecting everyone."

"I'm not sick. You look peaked yourself."

Nadia gasped. "What?" She pinched her cheeks. "Oh em gee. I can't believe you said that to me! I need my color today. I should have gotten that shot too!" Nadia disappeared, and Tom booted his computer up. Of course, she was brushing a little color onto her face. "Do I look better now?" she asked, reappearing. A little rouge went a long way, her Persian skin creamy like milky coffee.

"You do!"

"Tom, I'm serious. I can't look sickly. I've got a lunch date and can't be pale faced!" She studied Tom for a reaction. To her, he looked like he used whitewash for sunblock. "No offense."

"Funny."

Nadia looked over him curiously as he typed away and paid his gas bill online. "How'd it go?"

"Not good," he said, closing the gas company's website and opening his e-mails. The fifty-dollar reconnect fee hurt him, but thanks to William's hundred dollar bills, he still had cash for groceries.

"That sucks. When it took you so long to get in, I had hopes."

"You're sweet. Hey, what's this e-mail from Andre that says we're moving deadline up this week?"

"Rumor is Hayes might be taking his little magazine enterprise public soon."

"Already heard that," he said. "But we're going to print faster?"

"You're snippy." She didn't respond well to irritation or impatience, especially since she got quite irritable and impatient.

"I'm not snippy." He was having trouble shaking the meeting with Maroquin, but Tom knew he needed to refocus on work now. It didn't look like he was leaving to be a full-time, self-employed writer anytime soon. "I have no idea why we're moving deadline up," he said, turning to her. "Don't get it."

"I bet there're some stories in next month's that he wants the partners to read, and you know how anxious he is. Makes me look extremely patient by comparison."

He agreed. "The silent partners."

"Brent wrote a piece on IPO success stories, and I bet the bastard can't wait for it to be out there on grocery racks and in mailboxes."

"To try to convince the partners to take this little magazine empire public." This made sense now.

"At least, I *think* Brent wrote it."

Nadia was one of the few writers who knew the whole story of how Brent—the competitive bully of the office and bloviating son of the CEO—had gotten away with plagiarism at Tom's expense. Half a year ago, Brent had bastardized an article on California's economics. Tom had carefully researched the facts, but Brent had sprinkled in so many inaccuracies, it had been an embarrassment. Unsourced, uncredited, and *stolen* paragraphs that Brent had swiped from an old *Time* magazine raised credibility flags for *Western Mag*, causing literary ripple effects nationwide. Everyone in the magazine world had heard about it. Brent's father then had put on the pressure (and dangled a small raise), and Tom agreed to publicly take the heat for the article's misstatements. Brent's writing reputation remained intact, while Tom's sense of self-worth plummeted. *Reluctant restitution* was what Tom called it when he had shared it with Nadia, disregarding the confidentiality agreement Andre had typed up. Looking back, Tom couldn't believe he had sold his literary soul.

"Unlike you *feature* writers, I've only got until tomorrow to finish my six-hundred-word column on the strife of the PTA," Nadia said, checking her cheeks again in her compact mirror. "What do you think of the title 'Cupcakes and Classrooms'?"

"Catchy," Tom said without thinking too much about it.

"Crafty?" she asked, smiling hopefully.

"Cunning."

"Alliteration is always awesome," she countered, satisfied with herself.

He returned to e-mail. "This says I have until Thursday morning to finish my piece too. He just cut my prep by a week!"

"Well, I'll let you get to it," she said. "I'm going to get myself together. Would have worn a brighter color today if I knew I looked like crap. Though the brightest top I have makes me look paunchy the way it hangs over my sides."

"I never said you looked like crap."

She strutted toward the bathroom without looking back at him. "And you're lucky you didn't."

Tom's desk phone rang, and Andre's name came up.

"Good morning." Of course, Andre wanted Tom to pop by his office. "Be right there."

* * *

She peeked at her BlackBerry. Still nothing.

"What's wrong?"

At her desk, Jamie didn't have to look up from the absence of a message from Tom to recognize that Stephanie was standing inquisitively in the doorway of her office. She was making the rounds.

"I think my phone is broken. All my e-mails aren't showing up," Jamie lied. Tom was blowing her off. He made it so hard to support him sometimes.

Jamie didn't want to appear like the weak girlfriend in front of her boss or risk filling her in on personal business. The time she had confided in Stephanie that her new Clark sandals were hurting her feet, Stephanie—quite loudly in the hallway—recommended buying Birkenstocks if she wasn't going to invest in some practical Devi Kroell clogs. Stephanie had extended the joke later at a group meeting, remarking how they were going to stomp over competitors who tried to steal their accounts—with their Birkenstocks if necessary. The chuckles in the room, accompanied by snobby looks from Janice and Martha, humiliated her. It only took once.

"Call IT. They'll take care of it."

It was hard to believe that decisive delegation like that is what catapulted Stephanie's career. "I will."

Stephanie wasn't satisfied. "You okay?"

"Oh yes," Jamie said, putting her all-consuming BlackBerry away. "My head's spinning, thinking of ideas for us."

"So tell me, who we can go after?" Stephanie asked, inviting herself in and sitting. She elegantly crossed her fake-baked legs that glistened under the fluorescent lighting like long, basted chicken thighs. "We've got to cover more of our expenses. Any ideas?"

She needed to get Tom out of her head to get through this. "What do you think of the Stone Source? I know the owner from—"

"No way," Stephanie interrupted. She inspected Jamie's office, looking for clues to how things were really going for Jamie, unable to determine anything from the uncluttered and uncharacteristically bare space. Everyone else's offices were adorned like they planned to stay awhile. "They owe money to everybody in town. Let them rip everyone else off."

Jamie relished it when she was the purveyor of new intelligence. "Purpleline is up for review with Weight Burger."

"Janice and Martha came to me on that three weeks ago, and they're already pitching it. Anything else?"

That was biting.

"I heard of this car dealership that may be coming into the market," Jamie said. "A wholesaler out of Phoenix. They don't carry an ad agency there. Maybe we could get them to carry one here."

"What—like a Cars 'R' Us or something? No, thanks. No more car dealerships."

"They're pretty consistent," Jamie asserted. "What we need here is consistent spending."

"What we need here is welcomed creativity. 'Sunday! Sunday! Sunday!' won't save WSA. This is a creative agency that I built, and only with creativity can we save it."

Jamie studied Stephanie, who had just fired their whole creative team.

"What?" Stephanie asked, alert and stiff in her seat like a patient reading an eye chart. If Jamie had any ideas, she needed to hear them, and quickly.

"If I could get a client like that to do things differently, would you consider us taking them on? Different creative."

"You're trying to sell me. You sound like one of those radio or TV ad sellers that stalk this agency."

"We need to do something," Jamie said. "Something substantial that we can get the credit for growing, instead of building the client up with our resources and watching them go across the street for the cheaper media-buying deal." She knew she struck a nerve.

"Yeah, I've had it."

Maybe Jamie was a salesperson herself. "Those buying-service agencies are vultures!"

"They're ass clowns."

"That too." Jamie's mind somehow wandered back to Tom. It was midmorning, and he still hadn't bothered to call her or text her. He was completely disregarding her, and this wasn't acceptable.

"We can't lose this agency. I've got all my savings in it. If you think you can get this dealership's creative in house, get 'em." Stephanie stood and prepared to leave the room.

"Great."

"One thing. Our expenses are as-of-now nil. So if you travel to Phoenix to see this CarMax or whatever—"

"Davey's Dealios."

"That's the name? Jamie."

"I met the owner at a party last weekend. Could be promising. He said they have a fifteen share in that market."

"Of what? Redneck pickups?" Stephanie was becoming more agitated. Her Texan roots didn't provide her a tolerance for rednecks; she'd moved to California to get away from them. "Be prudent. You're on your own for expenses."

She should have seen this coming. Stephanie never took her ideas seriously.

Martha sauntered into Jamie's office, cheery and revolting. Sweet like saccharin, she spoke directly to Stephanie, not acknowledging Jamie. "Good news! It's now down to two agencies for Weight Burger, and we're one of them. Purpleline is *out*."

Jamie wondered if her self-absorbed boss even noticed that Martha was a different person whenever Stephanie wasn't around and then quickly determined the physical impossibility of that.

"Excellent!" Stephanie looked like she was going to salivate. "Who else is up for it?"

Martha paused. "NRS."

"The hell with them! We can't lose that account to those halfwits! Do we present again?"

"They want us to." Martha noticed Jamie and quickly looked away, wishing she would disappear. "We need to present more TV creative."

"I'm proud of you, Martha. You and Janice are heroes for getting us this far."

Jamie let out a soft groan underneath her breath.

"Let's go to lunch and work through anything else we can do to take our next presentation over the top," Stephanie said, walking out. Martha followed her obediently, leaving traces of her negative aura in Jamie's office.

Jamie's eyes naturally fell to Stephanie's backside, contemplating whether she might be wearing Spanx undergarments, smoothing out any odd curves on her twig-like, undernourished body.

Grabbing her functional, lackluster purse, Jamie headed to lunch. Forlorn without the necessary attention from Tom, she was still hungry—and hoping to God that Davey's Dealios held supreme promise.

* * *

Andre Philips, chief editor extraordinaire of *Western Mag*, stood only five foot four but was bigger than life. His booming voice caught people off guard, not expecting such resonance from a small, wiry frame. Although only in his early forties, his hair was rapidly thinning, an unfortunate fact that he obsessed over. The hunger pangs from his latest carb-free diet kick made him more anxious than usual. At a mere 130 pounds, he couldn't afford to be much leaner, despite the fact that he couldn't get rid of his troublesome love handles. The only fat on his tiny frame, he considered the affectionate euphemism nothing short of a lie. No one loved them, he hated them, and his wife made fun of them.

He wouldn't eat for another dreadful hour. Being lean and mean had its costs. Standing at his desk with the phone to his ear and his head down, he waited impatiently to interrupt the boring dimwit on the other side of the receiver. He felt like a famished, restless cheetah that was letting a maimed gazelle hobble on by every time he let someone expel their common, predictable—and worse—uninteresting minutia. Surely what he had to say was much more interesting.

Popping into the impressive office, Tom halted when he saw his proud boss preoccupied on the phone. Other times that he'd walked in—even when invited—and Andre had been on the phone, he'd thrown Tom out. This time, Andre waved him in, consumed with his next thought and taking the conversation back in the more compelling direction he chose.

Andre dropped into his recliner chair and lounged back, propping up his petite frame to look grander, the way riding a horse made Napoleon look taller. His comfort in such a position suggested that he would take great pleasure with such a comparison should anyone make it.

Enormous floor-to-ceiling windows filled the refined area with majestic light, as if the dark-wood, classically furbished room offered entry into corporate nirvana. Andre had demanded upgrades to everything.

"Ah, yes, but that's the way the cookie crumbles, man!" Andre chuckled. The unfortunate participant on the receiving end was doomed. "Oh, my peeps don't roll that way," he said, with unapologetic vanity. "We got skills and don't do that smack here, pimp! We ain't *schmucks*!"

Andre had had a privileged upbringing, but he believed his *bro lingo* urbanized the aristocracy out of his embarrassingly white blood. Speaking bro lingo to the lesser social classes allowed him to fit in with the unfortunate, confused, misled commoners around him, whether they were far-left zealots or far-right Republican snobs who made less money than he did.

Tom pulled his cell phone out of his pocket and fiddled with it while he waited, wondering not for the first time why his rich boss from old money held a desk job.

Andre motioned for Tom to sit. "Look, I got someone in front of me, so I gotta bounce," he said, stretching toward the phone dock and preparing to hang up. "I'll hit you later on the scratch. Yeah. Okay, bro. Late."

Sitting, Tom considered how different Andre had been back when they were in college together. Back then, he always went by *Andy*. Tom briefly mused over when exactly Andy had become Andre.

"'Sup, pimp?" Andre asked, putting out his knuckles for a fist bump, his brotherly greeting. Tom entertained it in grateful avoidance of an actual handshake. Ever since the time he was in one of Western Mag Corp's bathroom stalls and someone didn't wash their hands, Tom had avoided shaking hands with anyone until he could figure out who the germ-ridden culprit was. That was over a year ago, and he still hadn't gotten over it. He accepted his neurosis. Andre did the fist bump just because it was cool.

"What's going on? I see deadline moved up."

"Yeah," Andre said. He was semiattentive and typed something on his keyboard. "First thing tomorrow. Sorry to do this to you, man. Ugh, my stomach is killin' me like a dagger, brah. Think I ate too much fruit."

Unfamiliar music played from Andre's iTunes playlist on his computer. Tom guessed it to be gangsta hip-hop. Andre adjusted the volume down, and Tom waited for him to reveal the purpose of this unexpected summons. Then Tom's least favorite coworker entered the office.

Brent swaggered in, his gait awkward and brutish. Charming good looks and family pedigree had gotten him far, and Brent's narcissism ran so deep that he was oblivious to his lack of talent. His boyish blond hair was too long for a respectable office job—one where his father didn't downright own the company—and Tom thought it must take the guy fifteen minutes to perfectly manicure his goatee each day.

"You wanted me in on this, Andre?"

"Come sit in, bro. Hit the door, would you?" Brent shut the door and sat next to Tom, who, for the second time this morning, had to calm his nerves in a meeting. Fearing being set up for failure, Tom had sworn to himself that he'd end it all if he had to work with Brent on a writing project again. Tom stared straight forward at Andre, waiting to compromise his professional future by pacifying the needy son of Western Mag Corp's CEO. Brent adjusted himself in his careless, masculine way.

"Hey, Andre, check this out," Brent said, leaning over Andre's desk and showing off his wrist. "Rolex number five with diamonds on the faceplate."

Tom concealed his annoyance. *Oh brother.* Now he had a different one for each day of the week.

"Let me see that," Andre said, Brent crouching up toward him. "Sweet piece! I'm buying me some bling like that when I'm done paying that vaginamony to my ex."

Brent laughed. He loved misogynist jokes. Tom wanted to punch Brent in the face. The *bromance* between Brent and Andre was nauseating. Bling is what distracted Andre from his computer, and Tom felt more like *blah* than *bling*. He craved this kind of attention from his boss but rarely received it.

"Thanks," Brent said, pleased. He sat back in his chair, confident in—yet again—having something over Tom. "This is the one Tiger *really* wears. I had to special order this one. Took months."

Tom held a straight face. Once he had heard both of them criticizing employees who had the audacity to drive base-model Mercedes Benzes. With his practical Toyota Corolla and no watch, Tom clearly didn't try to keep up with the Joneses. Hell, he didn't even like the Joneses, whom he believed died prematurely of exhaustion.

"Okay, playas," Andre said, leaning back. His thin, slicked-back dome reflected the light from the windows behind him like a glossy black helmet. "I need both your help with something *dope*."

"Name it," Brent said, his eyes fixed on Andre, aimed at him like sharpshooters.

Andre said, "Whatever is up with you two, we gotta address. You two still throwin' around the hate-o-rade? What's up?" He alternately looked at each of them.

"Nothing's up," Brent said quickly, raising his manicured eyebrows innocently.

"Yeah," Tom lied. No need for any unnecessary conflict. They already hated each other.

Andre leaned forward. "Look, pimps. Don't snow me. I respect both a ya, and I wanna see this dream machine run like it needs to. You both know about the forthcoming IPO, and I can't have internal conflict slowin' down our mojo."

An uncomfortable silence hung. Tom's anxiety swelled. He suddenly remembered he hadn't called Jamie yet. *Crap.*

"*Possible* forthcoming purchase offering," Andre said, correcting himself. "My bad. A few things need to happen first. You two need to get along, for one."

Good God. Only two hours ago, Maroquin had virtually ripped apart his dream of being a self-employed writer, and now Tom resigned himself to being stuck at Western Mag Corp working alongside Brent, this incompetent tool. "We're fine," he said finally.

"Yeah, Andre. We got this handled, totally."

Such suck-ups. Tom hated himself.

"Glad to hear it. It's good you two are volunteering success in teamwork before you're volun*told* what to do," Andre said, unconvinced. "I need you two playas to connect on somethin' for me. No cross talk. I don't wanna get in your Kool-Aid."

Often distracted by Andre's lingo, Tom concentrated so to comprehend it. An Andre dictionary to understand Andre-nacular would've been handy.

"Your sick skills combined can be a dangerous combo," Andre said. "If executed correctly. Like samurais."

"Andre," Tom said. Their last collaboration had been an abortion. "Us working together won't get you—"

Andre dismissed him. "Both of you will write the perfect piece on positive IPO success stories where the shareholders score. A couple of the partners of the firm have been burned before, and we need to illustrate—publicly—how beneficial a well-orchestrated IPO can be. Tom, drop the other project. You probably haven't started it anyway."

Tom wished he could argue that he had.

"I can write this myself," Brent said.

"Right," Andre said, ignoring Brent's fiction.

A few months before, Brent's father had made Andre write an article on IPO success stories and credit Brent, which was wrong on many levels. Brent's father considered Brent incompetent but—unfortunately for Andre—Brent was the sole Hayes heir, and Andre's job description was pretty straightforward: *do as Martin Hayes says.* Brent was to be somehow propelled into magazine publishing, with skillful people behind him to hide any misgivings of Brent's writing talent, should any exist. The well-heeled Martin Hayes was sick of his son's wasteful pursuits that had all failed. The exotic car dealership. The dating service. Even the strip club. He wanted his son to quit fooling around and, instead, continue his burgeoning empire.

The protection and buildup of the prodigal son was frustrating to Andre, but Andre knew that if the company went public and his Western Mag Corp shares on paper turned to dollars, he himself would be rich. He'd been with Martin Hayes since the beginning, almost twenty years. His seventy thousand shares would not only take care of all his debt, he might be able to retire before fifty.

The article Andre had written was *okay,* he knew, but Martin Hayes had asked him to rewrite a better one, somehow. Tens of millions were on the line for Martin Hayes, and a dynamic article had to be written if it was going to have any influence after a handful of failed talks with the partners of the firm. Andre had done some thinking, and Tom—the best writer there—would be his savior. After all, Andre was a better editor than writer. Brent was such a nepotistic spoiled brat, Andre wanted him to swallow some blood and help Tom, ultimately to expedite the powerful, high-octane column. Managed propaganda at its best.

"For this to be *dope*," Andre said, the power of his voice increasing, "it's gotta take the both of you. I expect to be substantially over the Mendoza Line on this. We need to hit the apex. We control the press clippings. I want your presentation with a blood-pumping libido!" Andre beat his chest. "It's gotta punch!"

Tom decided he would rather be forced to work with a clueless intern for two weeks, explaining the mundane inner workings of Western Mag Corp ad nauseam, than work with Brent for one day.

"No problem!" Brent insisted.

"Great!" Andre said, not blinking. "Love the enthusiasm. Now. Enough of this *mishegas*."

Brent watched Andre, trying to determine if Andre was getting testy with him.

Andre was laying down the law: Tom was going to have to work with his nemesis once again. He wondered where Andre got the guts to challenge Brent, whose father could fire him for virtually any reason. This was new. Maybe Andre had gotten a job offer at *Time* or *Vanity Fair*. Maybe he was moving away, and this was a "Screw you!" to the company.

"You two merge your mojos, and this should be a no-brainer, Brent," Andre continued. "Your liberal sensibilities with starting new businesses combined with Tom's conservative take on partnerships, and I'm pumped. We'll have a perfectly balanced story of vantage points that just needs to point to the obvious conclusion of IPO. We need the chocolate *and* the peanut butter."

Conservative? Tom had to calm his attention deficit disorder. The last time he got distracted in a "convo" with Andre, he had missed deadline because he remembered he hadn't taken the trash out the night before. Was Andre referring to him as conservative politically or conservative about partnerships like *relationships?*

With the few articles Tom had written that incorporated politics, his boss had been harsh, considering Tom's politically neutral views as intolerably—and possibly subconsciously—influenced by liberal bias. Once, Andre had torn apart the TSA for their inadequacies on 9/11 and told Tom to write that piece with a brutally critical stance because that was what *Western Mag*'s conservative readership wanted. On his own, Tom wasn't an advocate of any special interest groups, whether it was women, specific races, or the ACLU. He wasn't actively pursuing any political persuasion—particularly the redneck, Calvinist sensibility, which he thought of as people reusing plastic grocery shopping bags to somehow illustrate the sovereignty of God. But when Andre had a vision for an article, it had to be done his way.

"I want you both to figure out the research and presentation so we can get this month's issue out a week early," Andre said. "I need the partners to see that we live and breathe their mantra. I don't want 'em sweatin' like a snitch at a gangsta party. No *shvitzing* on my dime."

"You mean the guys we never see?" Tom asked, imagining the silent partners of the firm as bland personalities in white technician's coats. "I'm on board, Andre, if this is what you want us to do, but are these partners really going to be swayed one way or the other on anything if we write a positive story on IPOs? If they can be, we've got other problems. Starting with who our new board of directors should be."

"Word," Andre said agreeably. "Hotel reality, baby."

Brent gazed at Andre with an empty stare, unsure of what that meant. Andre's embroidered and aggrandized pseudourban dialect could befuddle even him sometimes.

"Sure would be great to meet them one day," Tom said, pleased with himself after having held that in for so long. It was rare that Andre outright agreed with him.

"Don't count on it," Andre said. "But I'm glad I can count on both of you to work together and timely," he said, standing up and rubbing his hands together, anxious for them to get to work. "I need this done so it's on the racks before their next meeting. Do this for me. Together we got literary jujitsu. Keepin' the negatives at bay. Okay, guys? Audio's gotta match the video."

"No problem," Brent said. He and Tom stood up, adhering to Andre's suggestive sell.

"No schlepping now! I want a solid draft by Thursday morning. You've got two days. Don't make me track you down, cuz it's not my bag!" Andre called after them. "You two cats are in charge of the kitty litter. I'll assume it's handled. Be epic!"

They both walked out of Andre's office, avoiding each other's eye contact. Making their way down the hallway, Tom spoke up first.

"So how you want to do it, Brent? Should I start, you start—"

"I don't know," Brent said, shrugging. "I can start the researching."

Tom paused, and Brent realized what Tom was thinking. Brent's poor research had gotten him into trouble before.

"Or you can," Brent said. "I know you know how to research. You tell everybody you can." His grin was taunting.

Tom pretended not to notice Brent's aggressive tactic. No point in engaging it again and giving Brent ammunition with him against his own boss. "Tell you what, Brent," Tom said, smiling faintly. "Why don't I start the research on this one and get our structural outline together?" He looked at the time on his phone. "I'll send it to you by COB."

"End of the day works for me," Brent agreed, not used to seeing Tom take control like this. But he was going to watch him. Clearly, Tom was insecure about their partnership and probably was trying to keep him at bay. *This* was not going to happen.

Tom continued, "And we can weave my notes with what you dig up. I want to see it before the final draft gets to Andre, though, okay? We've got to go through it together." He wasn't going to be bitten again by Brent's plagiarizing tactics without having a chance to rectify them.

"No problem," Brent said slowly, his imagination revving. He was in no way a chump and wasn't going to let Tom take all the glory. If this article was to be so powerful it would influence the public sale of Western Mag Corp, no one was pushing him aside. If anything, his father needed to see him own this, no matter how much he hated it. "You'll have a draft tomorrow afternoon, and we'll compare notes or discrepancies then."

"Cool," Tom said, satisfied. Progress. Maybe he was in better control of this situation—and his emotions—than he thought. He started down the hallway while Brent watched him go.

"Hey, Tom."

"Yeah." Tom turned. How many confrontations could one man face in a day? At least Brent wasn't passive-aggressive. He had the courage to be dense face to face.

"Actually, it's probably best that I do the final edit myself," Brent said. "You know, since you're distracted these days?"

"What are you talking about?" Tom asked.

Nadia came around the corner with folders in her hand. She stopped to watch the exchange between Brent the Bully and her friend.

"Oh, you know what I mean." Brent's devilish grin widened. "This silly fantasy that you can write books."

Tom froze. He had tried to keep his book writing and subsequent hunt for a publisher on the down low. "You know nothing."

Brent laughed. "What's that?" he mocked, putting his hand up to his ear. "You going deaf on me?" He approached Tom until he was just inches from him.

Nadia stood still. These boys were ridiculous. They might as well use their penises as swords.

"I think what you mean is *mute*, unless I'm inaccurate," Tom said. "But you don't concern yourself with *accuracy*, do you?"

Brent was silent, his jealous blue eyes staring Tom down in rage. His stoutness gave him confidence, and he leaned into Tom, who was the same height but half the weight. Brent's deadly coffee-and-cigarette breath irritated Tom's senses.

"I've seen you hem and haw over your *column*," Brent said. "No way do you have the aptitude to write a book, let alone publish it, Summers. You're a marginal column writer at best."

Conscious of their work surroundings, Tom didn't want to embarrass himself or get sucker punched. Brent could easily take him down. "I'm going to start the research for us," Tom said plainly, and he looked away.

"Wuss." Feeling superior, Brent finally noticed Nadia watching them, shaking her head with disapproval. "Hey, Nadia," Brent said, flashing his charismatic golden-boy smile, trying to cover up his aggressive machismo.

"Brent, what's wrong with you?" Nadia asked, not surprised Brent had nothing clever to say. She thought he looked like a Ken doll and acted like a brat.

"Nothing's wrong, sweet thing," Brent said, as Tom took a step back. "Right, Tom? We're talking about an article is all." Nadia was the only person who made him nervous.

"Tom?"

"It's fine, Nadia," Tom said, shaking it off. He couldn't look at Nadia when lying to her; she'd see right through it. "We're working it out."

"Whatever. Your alpha-male crap isn't a turn-on. Either of you."

Brent eyed Tom and spoke softly. "Don't make me look like an ass in front of her." He had no idea why, but Nadia was immune to his charms. He had looks. He had money. But Nadia remained unimpressed. Tom said nothing. Outing Brent as a hostile jackass required no assistance.

"You boys done?" Her arms were crossed.

"Tom and I are collaborating again. He's always been a bit slow on follow-through, but his ideas . . . they're okay, I guess."

Tom still wanted to punch Brent's face.

"Really." Nadia was certain that Tom had vowed to never again work with this blowhard.

Brent was keenly aware that their last writing assignment together was a mortifying experience and that it had escalated Tom's passion for his book-writing project. It was Tom's way out of Western Mag Corp. Brent had no such options. The only way to prove that he was more than a mere "daddy's boy" would be for him to take over the magazine himself. And he was impatient.

Brent jerked his meaty thumb in Tom's direction. "He learns a lot from me," he said, standing taller.

"Wow." Nadia could only shake her head.

Tom had enough. "Figure out how to use spellcheck yet?"

"Oh, ain't you chesty when a girl's around!" He smiled at Nadia, his perfect teeth gleaming. He looked like the cat that ate the canary. "But we shouldn't fight, Tom. No need to discuss this farther."

"It's *further*," Tom said. "*Farther* describes physical distance. *Further* is metaphorical or figurative distance. But then, you get *lay* and *lie* mixed up, don't you?"

Brent paused. "Don't you drive a Toyota?"

"Ugh," Nadia breathed, walking away. "Such hatred around here."

Tom backed up and started for his cube. "Great work." He held his thumb and index finger to his forehead in the shape of an *L*.

Brent fumed. "Oh, come on, sugar and spice," he called after Nadia. "I'm not all bad!"

It angered him that he could never show himself to her in a good light. As beautiful as she was, she'd be a worthy mate for him, even though she was Persian. But one day, he'd make his father accept her. One day soon.

Tom lumbered back to his desk and put his face in his hands. He hated this place. Despite their differences, Tom and Brent had one thing in common: they both wanted this partnership over with.

* * *

Homer repositioned herself on the suburban park grass and inhaled deeply, taking in the afternoon sun, convinced that she couldn't do her pointless assignment effectively without enjoying earthly comforts. She was well aware that this moment of bliss wasn't part of His way. Get the order, create a plan, work that plan, and don't plan on enjoying yourself. Thousands of years had gone by, and God was still the same.

She'd attempted to wait for Tom outside of his office, but a hefty security guard had shooed her away from the Western Mag Corp building. The paunchy butterball had garbled something about her being a vagrant and troublemaker while he munched on a Snickers bar, nougat pieces tumbling down his shirt to their dismal, abandoned future, melting into the ground.

The park, by comparison, was peaceful. She was about to snooze when three true vagrants—Eight-Ball, Carla, and Skinny—paraded up to her.

"Hey, whadda we got here?" Skinny jeered. "I didn't know losers were still allowed in the park."

Homer couldn't believe she was being talked to in such a manner by a silly, scrawny adolescent. She sat up.

"You addressing me, sonny?" Grass stuck to her all over.

"You callin' me 'sonny'?" Skinny chuckled. She looked harmless, but she'd addressed him the same way his parole officer did, and she'd have to pay for that.

Carla smiled, smacking her gum, and Eight-Ball sized up Homer.

"Skid row kick you out, bag lady?" Skinny brought his face down to her level.

Carla rolled her eyes to the back of her head. How confident Skinny became when teasing a homeless woman.

Homer stood, squinting against the sun as she tried to look at the ignorant human. Wind. Sunlight. Such frustrating elements on Earth. "How outlandish! Shouldn't you be in school or something? You know, reading, writing, and arithmetic."

"Oh, you mean 'dis, dat, and da other thing. Yeah. We're supposed to be there. Hey, ain't you supposed to have a shopping cart, some cans, blankets, and crap?"

"What's with you people?" Homer asked. "I don't need your ridiculous possessions!"

"Oh," Skinny scoffed. "*You people.* You wanna make this a *white* thing."

"Or thang," Carla said.

Homer didn't like that Skinny was in her face, blocking the warm sun on her skin. "Oh, this is because I'm *black skinned*," Homer said. "God, you're stupid. Get away from me, you ignorant delinquents. I've got work to do today and can't be distracted by the likes of *you*!"

Skinny and Carla howled while Eight-Ball looked on. Homer was proud of herself for still—after all this time—not overreacting to a confrontation. Another test, probably. Interestingly, she rarely had to stand up to *one*. Outside of God Himself, she was always in confrontations with rogues and unsavory riffraff in groups. The Romans in the First Punic War were the worst, especially with their treatment of black women. He worked in mysterious ways, indeed.

"Did you hear that, Eight-Ball?" Skinny asked, laughing. "We got ourselves a high-society homeless chick. You got work to do, do ya, lady? Got some cans to recycle?"

"I'm all about going green," Homer said.

Eight-Ball walked around her in circles, making her nervous.

"She thinks she's better than us," Carla said.

Eight-Ball and Skinny both froze in disbelief that a destitute woman could think such a thing.

Skinny grabbed Homer by her shoulder. "You think you're better than me, crack whore?" He noticed her large, shiny watch. "Ahhhh. Look at your bling! Gimme that!"

Homer had enough. God was always testing her. "Get your filthy paws off of me! I'm going to beat your ass like the Persians beat the Spartans!"

Eight-Ball was confused. "What?"

"I'm sick of you ignorant American punks!" Homer thundered. With little effort, she pushed Skinny with unbelievable strength. Eight-Ball and Carla weren't sure Homer had even touched Skinny as they watched him travel back fifteen feet before falling on his rump.

Booming thunder rolled again, only Homer's eardrums being pierced by it. She covered her ears in agony and curled down to the ground, and Eight-Ball helped up a wide-eyed Skinny, whose long legs got tangled in themselves as he tried to stand.

"Man, she's crazy," Skinny said, shaken up.

Eight-Ball led Skinny away, unaware of what was causing Homer's pain. "C'mon, man, we don't need the watch, holmes. Forget her."

Homer writhed on the ground until the overwhelming thundering stopped. His techniques didn't evolve, but they sure were effective.

71

Carla was delighted, following the other two punks down the street. "A homeless crazy woman took you down, Skinny! That chick is strong!"

"Shut up, Carla," Skinny said.

The three punks walked away, only Eight-Ball glancing back at Homer, who wrestled to her feet. This neighborhood was going downhill more than even Eight-Ball had realized.

"Seriously, can't I handle anything on my own without You barging in?" Homer yelled upward. She considered the ramifications of chasing the punks incognito and giving them nightmares of stalking poltergeists.

"You're being oversensitive, Homer," God said.

"The irony, Almighty One, is that You need my help while I don't always need Yours," she said, without concern of consequence.

"That's not technically irony."

Homer caught her breath and inspected the dead grass sticking all over her rumpled, rough clothing. "Why didn't You let me teach those punks a lesson, sir?"

"Maybe they're teaching *you* a lesson, Homer."

"I've been bamboozled!" She scrubbed her hands across her clothes as too few of the grass blades fell off her. They stuck to her like lint. She hated her duds. At best, He had provided her with Satan's fabric.

"Homer, there are no tricks here. Don't make this complicated."

"Why me?" Homer asked softly. "Don't You have better angels for these worldly tasks, helping this pathetic species? Saving the world and stuff?" Being set up to fail was overwhelming enough. She didn't want to be made fun of by the whole League of Angels on top of that. Word would get out—it always did.

"Why not you?" He asked.

Homer plopped onto the bench and plucked stray, dead grass blades off her sleeves, one by one. He had always said she was sensitive, but He was clearly the sensitive one, taking humanity's self-infliction personally. The cryptic responses and nonanswers to her questions didn't calm her at all. She didn't trust Him. Why couldn't she ever get an easy assignment like Billy Graham detail or something?

The last time He dumped her in the middle of nowhere, she had landed in the aftermath of the First Crusade in the early 1100s, and her raggedy couture ensemble had made her stand out so much that neither the English and German crusaders nor the Egyptians knew what to make of her. She roamed the deserts with no guidance, was chided in accents she deplored, and wore thin, cloth sandals that allowed her feet to burn under the scorching sun. He had lied to her too, telling her it would be an easy assignment. Then He reprimanded her for getting in the middle of a squabble in a public marketplace that left two quarreling soldiers—one Egyptian and the other German—so bewildered after her vocal, animated intrusion that they walked away, muttering vulgarities in frustration. They were looking to fight, but she had somehow—temporarily—made their holy battle objectives seem petty and not worth the effort and bloodshed. This wasn't good enough for God, and He had scolded her for intruding.

Unclear nine hundred years ago as to whether she should help the Christians or the Muslims, she had wandered through the desert, hoping silence would provide her with enlightenment. Was she wrong! Instead, she had come upon a tribe of abandoned children. She tried to guide them to safety from the bitter weather elements, but they mistook her as a criminal peasant, threw rocks at her, and insulted her with the worst profanity she had ever heard. Restraining herself from using her defensive powers against their pint-sized human forms, she had left them and continued to travel on her own, only to be assaulted and beaten by desert thieves and left for dead. Oh, how she wished that He had let her smite those horrible humans. Never in all her days—thirty thousand years of life—had she experienced being so misunderstood and unheard, not to mention being considered unattractive by little children.

She had been so furious that she had sat in a lone olive tree in the desert for twelve full days through scorching heat and thunderous rains. Dismissing Him as a showoff and braggart, she had refused to respond to Him and His brash weather elements. So what if He could make sand crawl into eighty-foot dunes with His winds and soak her with torrential rains and monsoons! Flexing His weather patterns was old hat. She had heard of the Flood of almost two hundred thousand years ago. By comparison, this was nothing, sure, but she had not been around for that. How dare He continue to punish her with His often unamazing creation called *man*!

Through it all, she sat in the tree, and she stewed on His vague instructions to prevent the mutual annihilation between Islamic leaders and the Christian crusaders. He had called her a cherub and a baby, but she didn't care. Yelling and screaming at the sky had done nothing to change His mind. He still felt that she had failed to fulfill her duties. Her ranting also failed to disturb the swarm of ugly vultures that flew overhead. The vultures—like the Almighty One—were afraid of nothing.

The vultures baited her to let them feed on her after just one day (a twenty-four-hour one). At first, she had thought the vultures' purpose was to clean, not kill. The disgusting, ugly creatures were supposed to scour carcasses, not attack living prey. Stupid idiot birds! The raggedy cloths that wrapped her appendages became increasingly torn and exposed from the scavengers' relentless assaults as they tested her to see if she was indeed still alive, the carnage continuing for eleven more days. His test was one of torture. No way would she give in to Him and His beckoning in any form, no matter how hideous, relentless, or irksome. He had been incredibly inconsiderate, and she knew she couldn't change His cruel behavior. His methods were as twisted as the trunk of the olive tree. Besides, she had seen women on Earth try to change men, and this had proven to be a futile, unproductive exercise. She could only imagine how much more of a disaster it would be to try to change God.

He had promised Homer that her task would take a week at most, but it had gone on for two full months, to His dissatisfaction. So He had brought in a "pinch angel"—whom Homer referred to unapologetically as the "Suck Up with the Stutter"—to slow down the death in His name and so that His creation could better populate Earth. If Homer couldn't accomplish the assigned task, He'd get someone else to do it—and did.

As if it wasn't humiliating enough to be superseded by Gabriel, of all angels, her blatant rebellion had angered Him to the point that finally He forcibly blew her from that lone tree in the desert dunes with His own breath, sweeping her back to the heavens and banning her from the League of Angels for nine centuries. It was there that she had faced solitude and shame, shunned by the society of heavenly beings for being particularly unheavenly, which Homer admittedly was, routinely and decisively.

Nonetheless, He refused to give up on her—unlike other exiled angels she had heard about—but not without consequence. Given what had happened with the last task, however, she didn't have faith in Him that He truly wanted her to succeed. He'd shown her how easily she could be replaced. She just wanted to get this all over with now.

"For all the free will You've given them, sir, humans are dreadfully predictable. Centuries ago, they laughed at my ridiculous clothing, and they're still mocking me today. Picking fights with me is typical. It's nothing I haven't seen before." She paused, discovering a whole new batch of dead grass on her backside. "Your tomfoolery is pushing my limits. No more booms!"

"There's much you don't see, My friend," God said. "There are much more severe problems than those three. We have to be focused on the solution now. It's West versus East, at a magnitude you do not know. We cannot fail, Homer."

A tear fell from one of Homer's eyes, out of both sadness and her growing frustration. How could He pretend she could succeed at this? She hated crying when she was mad. "How bad is it, sir? Is it Western thought that prevails? Is that why I'm here?"

He paused. "This is not about that, Homer. No culture can fight Me and win. There is good in the East and the West. I am not a Western God, My good servant. I am not an Eastern God. Sin is everywhere, not just here, and not excluding here. The origination of worldly peace will come from Thomas's book—but only if he succeeds at mass publishing it, Homer. We need to change minds and impact hearts, My friend. Billions of them."

"One book by this American is going to do the trick, sir? Hard to believe . . . not that I don't believe You!" Deep down, she knew He wasn't kidding.

"It is where it will start. The East and West will evolve from it, in their own ways. Do not underestimate the impact one book can have, Homer. You know better than that."

Wiping her brow, Homer said, "I could've changed a couple of minds a few minutes ago by wiping those punk kids' faces over the rocks down there." She pointed toward the place she had landed last night. "I would've whooped them like Achilles did Hector."

"You're not speaking like an angel, Homer."

"Have I ever?"

God sighed.

"You're right, sir," she whispered. "I know you're right."

"Make it happen, Homer. The perversion of academic and scientific freedom has created massive doubt of My existence."

"Sir? Didn't You already get a few books in circulation? You're the most published author on Earth, aren't You?"

"Oh, yes," God acknowledged. "The Bible. The Torah, or first five books. The Koran, Pearls of Great Price, the book of Thomas. Such confusion between those, looking back at them now. Everyone is believing in Me so differently. There's got to be a better way."

"Yes, why didn't You think of that? Tons of books, tons of wars. After You inspired those books, things have gotten worse. And You said it—Your influence is waning."

"Still more books published than that J. K. Rowling, though."

"Sir!" He was so competitive, even though He always won. Then she pondered. "Bringing up other authors . . . Doesn't Tom's name then become the name everyone will know when this book becomes what You say it will? How does this further Your cause for Earth? I don't understand how that stops the demise, and it's *not* easing my stress." Her hives still hadn't gone away, and now they itched with a vengeance.

"His name will be associated with Mine and facilitate humanity's need. Moses and Jesus are My children too. As are you. He is the vehicle, I am the road. You aren't expected to understand all of this, Homer."

"Americans, sir?" she pressed, glancing at the suburban neighborhood around her. The park bench advertised the construction of new condos nearby. She didn't even know what condos were. The associated picture of the silly-looking white man with an all-too-fake smile didn't help. "So many of them are blissfully ignorant of their place in the world."

"How great, Homer, that you see the irony in it. America is the country with the greatest cultural diversity. I've sought out different cultures within different geographical locations throughout humanity's history. But now, it is here . . . *here* . . . that tolerance and intolerance are colliding. It is here that the arrogance of perceived knowledge needs to be struck. At this time, it is also where Thomas and William reside, where the solution now hides. Their gifts are important, you will see."

"Oh, this is a revelation! Why both of them, sir? It's Tom that's got the book, right?" The term *struck* that He used gave her shivers. She hated when He insinuated destruction at all, and God sensed it.

"They both influence the outcome," God said. "You might have figured this out if you had started moving things along already."

"Moses, smell the roses! I get it! Humanity is on a string. Yada, yada, yada!" She got as comfy as she could back on the bench, enjoying the warm sun on her face.

God paused. "Homer, I don't know what you're doing, fooling around and wasting your time enjoying earthly spectacles. You don't have that much time."

She inspected her magnificently awkward timepiece. She hated it. "I've got six-and-a-half days." As soon as she said it, she dwelled again on the possibility of solitude again. If she didn't get moving, she would absolutely fail, just as He likely had planned.

"I don't want to sweep humanity off the Earth again, Homer. Time is ticking."

She abruptly sat up, horrified. "Sir! You didn't tell me that was what was going on here!" Though she had no love for humanity, it didn't deserve to be wiped out completely. Certain heinous individuals needed their asses kicked, sure, but this was overkill. The other angels would mock her forever too. The world ending wouldn't exactly go unnoticed. "I have less than a week to do this or the world *ends*?"

"Humanity ends."

"How dare You tell me this now!"

God thundered. Homer crouched in fear as the sky darkened and thick cumulus clouds covered the sun, sweeping through the sky like angry ghosts. The trees in the suburban park swayed angrily, and fall leaves and debris slammed into Homer like a sandstorm.

"Sir, I'm sorry, I didn't know!"

Car alarms in the neighborhood went off, windows blew out, and tires popped. A large billboard—advertising its new community starting in the low 300s—peeled off its foundation. Scaffolding on a nearby condominium construction site became unhinged and fell to its death with a deafening clang.

"Okay, sir, okay!" she yelled. A pelting wind gust slammed a canvas work towel over her face. She quickly tore it off herself. "I'm sorry! I'm on this, for real!"

He ceased. Peace returned, somehow the car alarms stopped, and the sun slowly came back out.

"I can't keep straight what You did and what You blame the humans for," she said, catching her breath and monitoring her tone. "I know how You get when You blame the whole human race. That flood thing You did. Horrible, horrible." She shook her head, lamenting the lost souls. "Will You let the species survive, sir?"

"Do you recall why I created rainbows? This was My promise to never wipe out the Earth again. But now I have to save mankind from itself. Or I'll have to do something on a grand scale again, just to preserve other life here. Do what I'm asking you to do, and I won't have to start all over again."

"How can You sleep at night?"

"I don't sleep," He said. "You know that."

"You *rest*. Whatever."

"You're still sore at Me," God said. "You can prevent this. Don't be passive."

"You're putting a lot of pressure on me here, sir! I don't know where to even start. I'm already starting to sweat."

"You don't have sweat glands, My friend."

Homer wanted to kick herself. "Humanity is counting on you, Homer. We're partners in this."

She couldn't recall a time when He had said they were partners, nor did she know how she was going to do His will without breaking His rules. Still, she knew she had to figure out how to influence without interfering. If she stopped asking questions, maybe He would shut up. She looked down at her repugnant timepiece. It was indeed ticking.

* * *

Tom sat quietly in the passenger seat, wearing distressed blue jeans and a striped polo shirt under a sports jacket, dressed perfectly for the night.

Her own white, vertically striped slacks were comfortable, and since they often earned compliments, Jamie wore them tonight. High heels helped showcase her slender yet curvy shape. Her confidence was bolstered knowing Tom often looked her up and down when she wore heels. The light pink, relaxed, cotton shirt wore well against her olive skin, and the white tank under her shirt emphasized her natural tan. She felt sexy again tonight—in her own clothes—and hoped Tom could get over his latest bout of professional rejection. She understood it, but she didn't know how to make him feel better.

"I was surprised you didn't call me right away after your meeting. I'm sorry it didn't go well," Jamie said carefully—so carefully and kind that she grated her own ears. She knew, though, that releasing her aggravation on him now could make her client dinner a disaster.

He stared out the window, not transfixed on anything in particular. They passed a gas station on Sepulveda and started up the 405 Freeway on-ramp, joining the heavy-flow direction of traffic. They passed busy commercial center signs lighting up as darkness fell.

"It's okay, babe," Jamie said. "One agent down, who knows how many more to go?" she asked, trying to be supportive. "Someone's going to love this, you know it!"

"Yep."

Tom was resentful of Andre for forcing him to work with that spoiled, crooked, rich jackass. He didn't even care about Maroquin's hateful antics right now.

"I've got to make a quick call, babe. Lame work stuff." She dialed 4-1-1. The phone rang and rang on the other side. The silence in the car felt like deadweight. "Phoenix. Arizona. Yes, Davey's Dealios, please."

While the phone rang, she watched Tom in brief one-second durations, darting back and forth between him and the slow-moving, bumper-to-bumper traffic.

"Hi, yes, is David in? Thank you. Is he in tomorrow? The next day? Oh good, I have a delivery for him in person. When's a good time to come by? No, it's a surprise delivery." She was laughing with the gatekeeper. "Okay, thank you!"

She hung up. Tom didn't flinch about her going to Phoenix.

"Is there something else?" Hopefully it wasn't that other woman again.

"Lame work stuff," Tom said. "We're trying to get the partners to agree to take the company public, and Andre wants Brent and me to work together on a propaganda piece. I hate it."

She couldn't believe she had opened the floodgates. Positivity needed to fill the car quickly if this dinner was going to be at all enjoyable.

"You can't ask for a reassignment?"

A little red pickup cut in front of her. She slammed her brakes to avoid ramming into it, instinctively stretching her arm across Tom's chest.

"Bastard! Screw yourself!" Tom yelled at the pickup.

She patted his leg, trying to soothe him, feeling ridiculous as she did it. "It's fine, babe." *Patting his leg?* It felt patronizing when people hugged her and patted her back. This couldn't be much better.

"How could he possibly think we can work well together?" Tom asked, disregarding their near collision. "I gave him some research to start, and cc'd Andre this time."

"Smart." Positive reaffirmation.

"So no one," he continued, barely hearing her, "can fraudulently put my name on a poorly written article I'm not writing! Man, that place sucks."

Jamie was listening but was distracted by the pickup, which was now riding its brakes. She wasn't going to let a fender bender ruin their night either. "So what now?"

"Maybe then we can partner up more often," he said, his sarcasm obvious. "Like Abbot and Costello or Dear Abby and her sister."

It was time to uplift the mood. "You sure Dear Abby and her sister were partners? I don't think they were." She changed lanes to move a car length a little faster.

"They weren't?"

"I don't think so. They were sisters. Are sisters, I mean. I *think* they're alive."

He nodded. "Hmmmm. Interesting."

Jamie moved on to her next concern. "Don't forget that these people are clients, Tom. Last time, it took a month for them to return my calls. Can you avoid controversial subjects this time?" She ignored the use of her blinker and moved over another lane. She was determined to get where she wanted to go.

"How was I supposed to know that he ate horse meat? Who does that?"

"This client is important to me."

Her horse-meat-loving client had brought up the subject just after Tom had finished writing about one of the last horse meat slaughterhouses in Texas being shut down. It had been legal in that state to slaughter them and sell the meat, all on taxpayers' watch. That conversation had tested Tom's debating skills, but it had also tested Jamie's diplomacy skills with the clients and—later at home—with Tom. She didn't need more ridiculous debates about the sanitary conditions of vertical toilet seats—which was illogical as hell—or HD-resolution differences between cable channels. Could they have normal conversation, please?

"Stephanie will flip her lid if they drop us because they think we're insensitive!"

"Okay, hon. I know this is your work."

"It'll be fine, babe. And fun," she assured, without patting his leg this time. "Let's have some smiles tonight. We deserve it, don't we?"

Jamie was hard to resist when her mind was set on something. "We do."

Pulling up to Melisse Restaurant's valet, a familiar voice in her head reminded her that any man in her life should be asking *her* about challenges and memorable moments of the day. Reaching out to discover the details that no one else cared about and would not ever hear about. Aching to be her confidant. Asking her who she was traveling to see in Phoenix, for God's sake! She hoped this was merely a temporary bout of *distance* and nothing more—something that hits you over the head with dismay and then, one day, poof! Gone. Much like the flu, Uggs being in, or high-rise jeans. Then she told her mother to shut up.

Two hours later, Tom and Jamie were finishing their dinner with Jamal and Cynthia. The attractive African-American couple owned a small, successful African-cultural retail chain in Los Angeles. Jamie had worked hard on this account, simply named JC Traders, which sold cultural pieces from all over the African continent. Despite being a small chain, JC Traders was a large spender in various media. Not only Jamie's largest client but also WSA's largest.

A soft, instrumental violin filled the restaurant from overhead speakers, and half-filled wine glasses and small dessert plates and forks and spoons scattered across their table. The lingering taste and smell of pinot noir surrounded them, and the waiter used his bread-crumb knife across the white tablecloth to—as far as Tom was concerned—bring attention to their sloppy manners. The last time Tom and Jamie had eaten here, it was with Jamal and Cynthia. Tom quickly figured that meant this was now *their place.*

Jamie noticed that she and Tom were the youngest adults in the large dining room. To the dismay of the older patrons, she was also the loudest. Every time she cackled, an older man two tables away gave the four of them an expression of disgust and condescension. All the while, she hoped no one would again bring up how she had first tried to order a *Neapolitan* instead of a *Cosmopolitan* before settling on the wine bottle.

"So I told him," Cynthia laughed, nudging Jamal, "to throw 'em out! We don't need their kind in our store!"

"Wow," Jamie said, her eyes glazed from the influence of the pinot noir, followed by another loud cackle. She needed to feel good, and the wine was working.

The old man a few tables away threw his fork down on his plate.

"Damn," Jamal said. "Nobody does that in my store. You got to be ignorant!"

Tom was distracted by the face of the old man, whose steamrolling eyes burned through his own, now that everyone's voice at the table exceeded a certain undefined but offensive decibel level. "So he wanted to know who exactly bought your stuff?" he asked a bit softer, hoping the old man's prickly stare would dissolve away.

"No," Jamal said, still at a high volume. "He was saying that we're hawking crap."

"We interpreted his tone to mean that only idiots would have African culture in their homes," Cynthia said. "He wasn't exactly worldly."

The waiter delivered the check, and Jamie quickly held up her credit card.

"You don't need people like that in your store," Jamie said. She loved having her conversational fiancé around clients—around period—but she realized it also stressed her out, despite her moderate buzz.

"Remember we have four stores," Jamal said, "and not all in the Valley. We can't be everywhere all the time, monitoring people's behavior."

"I can't imagine talking like that to anyone," Tom said. He quickly flashed back to the conversation with the domineering Maroquin earlier in the day, a literary virago with retribution on her mind. She had chastised him for the hatred in his book. His *manuscript*. Scolded him for his take on long-term relationships with anyone, or anything. Including God. He ignored the questions that started to gnaw at him. With all the work he had poured into those pages, no way was he undertaking a rewrite. "Except for my brother. But only him!"

Jamie laughed her loud cackle again, soon followed by her clumsily knocking over a little-filled glass of red wine onto the tablecloth. Everyone at the table stiffened back in their seats before realizing the lack of injury. She quickly erected her glass, small traces of the red wine seeping into the starched white tablecloth.

"Close one!" Cynthia said, impressed with Jamie's reflexes.

Tom gave Jamie a look of dismay for drinking so much, which she responded to with an equally offensive look that said, *Bite me.* Two glasses of wine had made her feel better—slightly—but she knew that in five minutes her buzz would be gone. By comparison, Tom's alcohol tolerance was amusingly light, a subject they joked about often because her tolerance was much higher, as was the case for most people who worked in media.

Jamie signed the bill, looking at it for the first time. Despite visions of Stephanie's rage over the dinner expense filling her imagination, Jamie ignored the temptation to cut into the waiter's tip.

"Thank you for dinner," Cynthia said, putting her hand on top of Jamie's. "I'm digging the stimulating conversation tonight!"

"So fun," Jamie said. "We love having you."

All four of them stood up, and the ladies grabbed their purses.

"This man," Jamal said, patting Tom on the back. They headed into the men's room. "Every time we do this, I don't have to worry about a boring-ass dinner!"

"That's why I bring him along," Jamie said, and she disappeared with Cynthia into the women's room.

"Oh, Jamie, I didn't tell you," Cynthia said under her breath, Jamie following her into the restroom, "but we're closing down two locations soon."

A lump arose in Jamie's throat. "Oh no."

"I'm afraid that the market for worldly art is quite depressed. As am I. So," Cynthia said, making sure her sudden tears weren't disturbing her mascara, "we'll have to cut our ad budget. In half."

"I'm so sorry."

Cynthia nodded, taking a paper towel from Jamie. "Jamal and I decided last night. We've put all of our savings into this business. Our life. We've got to protect our investment."

"It's okay," Jamie said, comforting her. "You'll bounce back. The best businesses always do."

A twinkle somehow emerged under Cynthia's tears. "So sweet." She steeled herself and put on a smile. "Let's talk soon about how we're going to go forward."

"Whatever you need," Jamie said, feeling the ground move beneath her. This would be a blow to WSA. Jamie couldn't believe this was happening. She had thought JC Traders was doing great, but WSA's biggest client was cutting their spending in half. The advertising agency was in trouble already, and this could close it down.

The men came out of the bathroom after the women, astounding both Tom and Jamal.

"How are you so quick?" Tom asked.

"Efficiency," Cynthia said, sharing a knowing nod with Jamal. Only Tom laughed before noticing that the mood of both women had sunk.

"You know, Tom," Jamal said, winging his arm around Tom, "I was kidding about the horse meat last time." He led Tom toward the exit, following the women. "Man, your face!" He howled with laughter.

All four walked out past the angry old man's table. The old woman with him concentrated on operating the comparatively large utensils in her tiny, shaking hands.

Tom shook his head at Jamal in amused defeat. "You got me!"

The old woman looked up from her food for the first time tonight. "Did you say something, Artie?" she asked.

"No, Eleanor. Eat your food."

Jamie walked in front of Tom, disappointed when she glanced back to notice he wasn't watching her walk in these slacks and heels he normally loved. She concealed her disappointment, and they approached the valet, not saying a word.

In the car on the way home, Jamie and Tom were quiet at first. The dinner and wine had taken a lot out of both of them. Jamie's feet hurt, so she drove barefoot. She cursed Leonardo Da Vinci, or whoever was responsible for creating high heels.

"You sure you're okay to drive?" Tom asked, checking his phone for the time. It was after nine o'clock. No wonder he was exhausted.

She forced a smile. "I know I have precious cargo," she said. "Can't let anything happen to you. I'm sober and alert."

Tom kissed her hand. They whizzed southbound on the 405 Freeway without talking for several minutes, Jamie driving calmly and steadily in the fast lane—or the barbecue lane, as a cop ex-boyfriend of hers had called it once. The hot place to catch speedy drivers.

"How bad was the bill?" Tom asked finally.

"Bad enough to make me dread going into work tomorrow. And Cynthia told me in the bathroom that their spending is going to cut in half! Oh my God, Tom! This is not good, not good."

"Oh, that's what happened."

"Stephanie's going to kill me."

"I wasn't bad, was I?" Tom asked.

"Tom, don't make this about you."

"Sorry."

She sighed. "I might be out of a job soon," she said, resigned to the fact.

"What?"

Then she realized. "Oh, I didn't tell you the latest. The shop's in trouble, Tom. JC Traders killing their spending like this is going to put Stephanie on the brink of homicide."

"Oh."

She beat the steering wheel. "I'm so stupid for not taking that job offer a few months ago. I'm such a *wimp*!"

"It wasn't the right time for you, that's all. Keep knocking their socks off there, and another opportunity will pop up."

She was mad at herself. "I get on you again and again about sending your work out to be critiqued the hell out of, and I didn't have the courage—"

"It's not the same thing. You've got a mortgage. Don't beat yourself up for being more responsible. Besides, it's your own business you've said you wanted anyway. And one day, you will, I have no doubt."

She felt love for him again. Maybe the night could be better than she had hoped. "Thanks for coming tonight. Means a lot to me that you did."

"You'd do it for me," he said, rubbing his eyes with his palm. He needed more sleep than she did, his violent dreams and those about *her* disturbing what would otherwise be refreshing REM. He thought back to Maroquin. *That witch.* "Can we not talk about our stupid jobs anymore?"

"My job's not stupid." She was surprised how quickly his tone had changed. "Well, only I can say it is. One minute you're supportive, the next you're not."

His freeway exit was coming up soon. "I think I'm just going to be alone tonight. I've got to get some sleep." He felt like a wuss for saying it.

"Okay," Jamie said, disappointed that he was distancing himself from her when she could very much use being close to him. She put her hand over his, desperately trying to reach him, hoping her touch was all he needed to change his mind. Seeing the freeway exit, she moved to the slower lanes.

"Don't be mad."

"I'm not mad," Jamie said, keeping her eyes on the road. She let his hand go, realizing she *was* mad. Such a letdown after looking forward to tonight's possibilities all day. Tom's emotional pendulum drained her energy. She pulled onto the off-ramp.

He was silent again, watching nothing along Sepulveda. Jamie made the last turn into his residential apartment complex. She parked, and they sat there.

The stillness of them sitting in the car together could easily trigger waterworks, but she wasn't going to let herself cry. It didn't matter that he was tired; she was too. He was further and further away, and she was losing him.

"What do I have to do for you not to be distant all the time?" she asked, abruptly turning to him with glassy eyes. "Is it her? Are you still pining for your ex?"

"Why do you ask me that?"

"Answer the question." She looked at him dead-on.

He paused. It had been a day of confrontations. Telling the truth was supposed to be the right thing, and one lie always led to others. He'd read that somewhere once. "Sometimes," he said finally.

"I knew it! Tom, we're supposed to be getting married!"

"Jamie, I've got a few questions in the back of my head, that's all. I'm not being a jackass about it."

"Yes, you are," Jamie said, sniffling. At least she wasn't bawling. "You're somewhere else, and I want you here. With me." She hit him on the arm with frustration, unable to stop herself from tearing up. She couldn't help but wonder why her boyfriend picks were always so poor. "If you're thinking about her when you're with me, something's not right! Right?"

"I guess so."

"You know what, Tom? I know this ex-love of yours went and married somebody else—"

"Do you have to call her my ex-love?" He realized he wasn't helping his cause, but he'd sure feel better if she stopped calling Teri that. It made him feel worse.

"I could call her your current love, I guess. Love of your life, maybe. Ever since you started getting rejections for your book, our relationship has been falling apart."

"I have no idea where my thoughts of her came from."

"You're searching. You're unhappy. And you're reaching to some unrealistic past relationship to feel better about it. This isn't rocket surgery, Tom."

"You mean brain surgery?" he asked meekly.

"Yeah, parsing my grammar right now . . . that's productive," she said. "You should keep doing that."

"You asked me a question, and I just answered honestly, Jamie. I'm not trying to hurt you. Or us."

"Well, maybe you're too honest."

"You want me to lie?" Any direction he went, there was collateral damage.

"Are you stupid?" Jamie asked him blankly. "Honestly. I can't live like this, don't you understand that? Tom, could you be with me if I was thinking of someone else? And it's worse than that, because this woman has ahold of your heart after *three* years of us being together, and I can't touch it. I think the most awful, painful things."

"It's not like I'm sleeping with her. I'm not cheating, and I wouldn't."

"Emotionally, you are."

He searched, wondering if that was true. "I'm trying to be a man here, okay? Some of this stuff I'm trying to figure out how to handle. Your parents were better—"

"My parents have nothing to do with your lame emotional unavailability! Can we be together when I lie next to you every night and I try and I try . . . your terrorist dreams and all . . . you want to blame this on my upbringing? Tom! Geez! This is so pathetic! How old are you? We can't even have sex anymore with it feeling okay."

Tom looked down, which he'd been doing a lot lately. She was right about everything—though he didn't understand what she meant about the sex, but now wasn't the time to ask her about it. He reached out to hug her, but she pushed him away. He tried to reassure her. "We'll work it out."

"You've said that before, Tom. And sex is supposed to be the reset button, remember? It used to be that way for us."

"We'll work it out," he repeated, doubt suddenly sweeping through him.

"I can't do this," she said, wishing she could pull farther away, but she had the limitation of the driver's door. "You need to figure out what you want. Get in the pot or off it."

"You mean shit or get off the pot?"

"Keep it up."

"I'm kidding."

"I can't compete with a dream of your book, your past relationships, or whatever combination of the two," she said, ignoring him.

"I'm working off my gut right now."

"Well, right now I hate your guts."

Tom forced a smile to try to ease them both of their discomfort, but Jamie didn't smile back. He shivered. "It's something I have to work through." Flashbacks of his previously failed relationships rushed through him. No originality with this rerun.

"You know how many times you've said that?" Jamie asked. "You're searching . . . God knows for what. If there's something you're looking for in life, Tom, you have to go get it. *You've* got to happen to life and quit waiting for it to happen to you. I'm here for you, but that's not good enough, is it?"

"I just have to succeed with my book, Jamie. And everything will be fine."

"Really, Tom? You need that kind of validation to be communicative with me? And why you're reaching to an ex to make you feel better about agent rejections astounds me. I *hate* being ignored. You didn't even ask me anything about my trip to Phoenix."

"What trip to Phoenix?"

That was it. Hoping to rouse him from his ridiculous relationship slumber, she pulled off her ring and reached to give it to him.

Tom sighed, staring at it in her hand. "Will you put your ring back on, please?" She didn't blink. "You're kidding me, right?"

"Do I look like it?" Her eyes were dry now. *Please wake up, you idiot!*

"You're mad," Tom said, refusing to take it. "Thinking about an ex doesn't mean I don't love you."

She placed it on his knee. "Take it. I don't want it anymore."

"I can't believe this."

He wasn't fighting for her. Her head filled with flashes of their beginning, and she wondered if this was it. Was she really sitting in a car on a Tuesday night, dumping her fiancé? He wasn't supposed to allow this to happen. Men were supposed to fight for the woman they love, weren't they?

Tom shook his head reluctantly. He didn't believe she was breaking up with him. This day had gone from awful to horrible. He gazed out the window, until he finally noticed the homeless woman sitting there on the steps of his building, looking squarely at both of them in the car.

CHAPTER 3

Luigi loved pizza. And pasta—baked ziti in particular—and calzones, and, on occasion, lasagna, though it caused bloating so unpleasant that it could bring about household seismic shifts. When it came to Italian food, Luigi didn't care what was on it or in it or if it was hot or tepid, fresh or frozen. His mama had raised him on it all, literally. When he and his brother were teenagers, she had opened a pizza shop after their father died. Now as an adult, his main trouble in his life was losing the gut that his belts desperately tried to restrain, the leather slowly rupturing under the stress. On heavy pasta days—when his sluggish, steady gait was a bit slower—he felt like he ballooned in his trousers. He was pretty sure that if someone pushed him over, he'd pop when he hit the ground. To the dismay of his wife, his resulting grouchiness was accompanied by excessive and unapologetic gas.

His belching was out of hand now too, his pleas for forgiveness competing with her complaints. He needed to clear the gassy obstructions in the passageways of his bowels and esophagus. Blockages could lead to involuntary convulsions and, likely, an irregular heartbeat, and maybe even death.

But Teri didn't buy it.

The door slammed behind her, and she walked in with the mail. Luigi stood at the kitchen counter, eating again. Though they had both had a decent meal a couple of hours ago in first class, Luigi felt that dinner should be a substantial caloric achievement. A six-ounce chicken breast? Vegetables? *One* roll? A little bread may suffice at lunch, but for dinner, that just didn't do it. It being ten o'clock at night wasn't going to stop him from completing his meal.

Up the street from the trolley station in San Francisco, the Steffanci home was perched at the top of the hill, looking down with grandeur at the other affluent residences around it. Somehow, gravity didn't work here on Shadow Hill Lane; the houses didn't roll down on top of each other. Inside, their spacious home was an interior designer's oasis, with textured paint throughout and adobe-like Euro plaster accentuating its Spanish influence. Light hardwood floors and warm colors provided a homey and inviting space for their friends, should they ever invite them over. At night, neighbors walking along the inclined sidewalk could often see the married couple feuding through the enormous windows—like a large television screen showcasing a muted sitcom.

"A lot?" Luigi asked in his distinctive, husky voice. He stuffed his fork into his mouth, strings of cheese lasagna collecting on the tips of his wiry mustache. His cheeks were pink and flushed. Eating was exercise, and a bead of sweat rolled from his balding forehead down his brow. He was studying the sports page, irate that the Red Sox just lost a key pitcher, confirmed for retirement. With the world in turmoil, Luigi's mood soured.

Teri struggled to carry the heavy load of magazines, shoppers, bills, and junk mail. "It was stuffed in the mailbox so tight I could hardly get it out."

Luigi pulled his *Sports Illustrated* from the pile. "It's ripped, Teri."

"Next time you make me go with you back home to New Jersey, we should hold the mail while we're gone. That God-awful place. Where the drinking water isn't fit for drinking. And I've never seen so many Dunkin' Doughnuts in my life."

On the trip back home, she had pondered how she'd ended up with him. It dumbfounded her now—how she had let her material desires strip her of her one unyielding need: to love a man she could admire.

The allure of a man with wealth had been powerful. The money had been too intoxicating to refuse; the pleasure she got from displaying it was a high. A gorgeous home in a desirable neighborhood, so many levels above her parents' humble cracker box. The designer clothes. Her two-carat ring. The Porsche Boxster.

But it wasn't enough. Regret had been building for three years, their entire marriage. On the way home from the airport, Teri had had the fleeting thought of grabbing the steering wheel from him and crashing them into the freeway divider. At seventy miles per hour, her empty existence would end. She didn't want to die, just get away from all of this.

Her head had sunk when they drove up the hill to their home. What had once been her upper-crust escape from simple and average was now the House of Misery.

It hadn't always been this way. Luigi's once-attractive self-assuredness had given way to insecurity. She missed the way she used to laugh with him. It was like losing a favorite blanket, not knowing where it was or how to replace it. He didn't make her feel good about herself anymore. He didn't make her proud of him. Their mundane routines bored her, and sometimes she'd watch him, wondering who he was.

She had thought about leaving him, of course. After all, this was California, the *I'll-take-half-of-everything* state. Her parents would have her ass if she left him. They had attended both of her weddings—and they'd taken out a hefty loan to pay for the first one. They didn't understand how anyone could *divorce* anyway. Her parents had reluctantly forgotten about her first youthful indiscretion—a short-lived union with a carefree surfer, whom her parents never referred to by name; rather, they called him "the surfer" with overt disdain—blaming an American culture in decline. No way would they take her in. She had no siblings to fall back on, and all of her friends had their own families. Kids, bake sales, and baseball games.

If she left him, she'd be alone. She was scared of staying with him and terrified of being without him. She had tried being on her own in her early twenties and almost became addicted to antidepressants just to make it through every empty day. Since then, she'd bounced from relationship to relationship. And then she married Luigi.

He went through the pile of mail, aggravated. "If you stopped buying so much crap, we wouldn't get all these stupid catalogs." A blob of sauce splattered onto the travertine floor. Luigi ignored it.

She eyeballed the meat sauce that decorated his ribbed, white tank top. It confounded her that men—this man—loved these wifebeaters, the name clearly explaining them as something women hated. The kinky hair that peeked from the back of his head in the shape of a horseshoe was bristly and choppy again, a result of his Flowbee hair-cutting system that he insisted on using, refusing to let any *broad* cut his hair. Walking into a traditional barber shop made him feel old too, so despite being well off, he insisted on using the vacuum hair chopper himself.

"Or we could get a bigger mailbox!" She opened a bottle of water, threw the cap at him, and booted up her laptop on the kitchen counter.

Ignoring the bottle cap, Luigi said, "Bigger is always better with you," realizing what he said a moment too late. Her breasts were augmented, which he knew she loved and her parents despised. It didn't keep with her family's cultural sensibilities.

"When is smaller ever good?" she asked. There was one appropriate answer. "Smaller gut. That's good."

"My gut will get smaller when your ass gets smaller," he said. "You gonna start with me again, hon? Ain't a good idea."

"My ass is fine. You're just an ass." She grabbed her laptop charger, plugged it in the wall, and then checked her e-mails.

Luigi eyed her up and down. Her black, form-fitting yoga pants wore her well. Her ass *was* getting smaller, and he had yet to make any gloat-worthy progress on his protruding potbelly. At five foot ten, she was the tallest Chinese woman in America, in Luigi's opinion, and her statuesque and athletic physique caught the eyes of all straight men. And she had the most beautiful hair he'd ever seen.

Her long, black hair was so amazingly soft that it made him think of his own as curly horsehair. Luigi loved it so much that he'd become repulsed by other women's hair, which he determined to be saturated with products. When she let him caress her hair, now and then, he'd run his fingers through Teri's silky locks, appreciating her un-white-American-ness.

Luigi slurped another mouthful of the lasagna and read the paper, dribbling meat sauce down his chin. Teri ignored him and came upon Tom's e-mail. Her heart stopped.

"That better not be another tax bill there," he said, clearing his throat and staring at one of the envelopes in the pile. "I prepaid those sum bitches."

"Uh-huh."

He looked at Teri's toned butt again as she stood over her laptop and then considered his beer. *What the hell.* He liked drinking more at bars anyway. There, he wasn't judged. He put the beer down and moved to the walk-in cabinet, looking for a bottle of water instead. Teri wasn't the only person who could look better.

After opening the cabinet door, Luigi looked confused.

"There are some in the fridge," Teri said, not taking her eyes off her computer.

"Teri, you know I hate drinking the water cold."

She quickly moved to the freezer and pulled out a frozen bottle of water and placed it on the counter for him. "I don't know how you drink it warm."

"How do you drink it iced?"

"You can burn more calories when your body absorbs the cold," she said, returning quickly to her e-mail. "Would be good for you."

He ignored the bottle but had to comment on her running back to her computer. "If it's your mother complaining about the money, I sent her a double payment this month too. So there better be no bitchin' outta her either. Everybody wants a piece."

"Shut up, Luigi. The world's not after you." Teri took a breath. "Tom wrote me. He wants to see me."

"Jesus," he said. Tom was one of the few subjects that warranted Luigi putting his fork down. "The one with the hair?" In Teri and Tom's homecoming picture from high school, Tom had an Elvis-inspired coif, which Luigi had always lacked.

Teri read for unwritten clues or subtext that revealed Tom's affection for her. "I bet he's cut his hair since then," she said.

"I bet," Luigi said, thinking of his hair implant debacle last year. After spending a few grand on grafts of hair that were transplanted from the back of his head to his thinning top, he had stared at them in horror in the bathroom of the transplant facility. Then he had pulled the plugs out one by one, leaving the expensive mess all over the sink to make a blatant statement to the doctors, who needed to know their geometric planting sucked. Cornrows were what they were, he didn't care what the hair surgeons and prep videos said. "Doesn't that guy quit? This ex-boyfriend is pissing me off, Teri."

"Are we doing this again?" She was exhausted from the thought of another fight over Tom.

"Obviously we have to, honeybunch."

She didn't like *honeybunch*, which he used when he was sore at her. "He was my first real love."

"You were a late bloomer," he blurted back.

She started to leave the room.

"Wait, baby." The last time she was furious with him it had cost him a week's vacation with her family and two months of celibacy. Horrible. "You're married to the man you love now," he said.

She turned to him.

"And he knows you're married to me, not him," Luigi said. "He screwed up. You left him, remember?" He looked at her hopefully, waiting for her to appreciate the man in front of her versus the boy of her past.

She raised her eyebrows. "Which is why you shouldn't be threatened by him." If she weren't so rattled right now by Tom's letter, she might have been endeared by Luigi trying to prevent another trip to her mother's and an extended dry spell.

"You're freakin' kiddin' me, right?" Luigi asked, approaching her. "Look at you. Look at me!"

She noticed the fresh pasta stains on his wifebeater. It was like a child's painting, the red paint splattered on cardboard paper and proudly displayed on the family refrigerator. Except Luigi was neither proud nor ashamed, merely oblivious to his ridiculous appearance.

"I don't wanna lose you to that guy, honeybunch," he said, trying to sound sensitive.

"Don't worry, Luigi. I'm all yours," she said, poking his bulging stomach with her finger. She tried to walk away, but he grabbed her arm.

"Do you still think of him that way?"

"What way?" she asked, shaking him off.

"Like a juvenile first love, Teri! We all have it when we're young."

She stared him down. Her feelings for Tom went back twenty-five years, and they were *not* juvenile. The nerve.

"Answer the question!" Every time this came up, she avoided answering questions head-on.

"It's a stupid question."

Despite his hefty physique, even when Luigi was mad she wasn't afraid of him. He could yell, but if he kept it up, they both knew he'd suffer for it. They would be spending Thanksgiving *and* Christmas with her family this year.

"I don't think so." He was indignant.

"Don't you trust me?" she asked, crossing her arms.

"Um," Luigi said, pretending to grab straws in the air, "maybe you married me, but I think you're still stuck on some guy with a perverse love of Elvis!"

Teri told herself to remain calm. Luigi sometimes let his temper flare. That would mean his blood pressure would surge again too, which would be a bad thing. They would be in the ER all night.

"He's got a girlfriend, I'll have you know," she said as reassuringly as she could.

Luigi wiped sweat off his forehead with one of his hairy arms while Teri noticed how intensely the familiar, rancid odor was seeping from Luigi's pores, permeating the air around him. Teri considered turning on the air conditioning full blast, despite it being forty-two degrees outside, at least until she bought one of those Ionic Breezes that she had seen on TV. She needed to remember to do that. They were supposed to be really good at neutralizing odors.

"Yep," he said, "and she's probably as irritated as I am."

Tom was the good-looking guy that Luigi always thought of as her *type.* The kind of guy he thought of when he saw other abundantly haired, fit guys with chiseled features and lazy, brown bangs. The pneumonia-resistant guy who showed off his abs at Baker Beach despite it being so chilly, windy, and foggy that swimming was out of the question unless you brought your wet suit. The hairless guy who strolled naked through the gym's locker room with a towel hanging over his shoulder, as if to say, "That's right. They love to be free."

"What's with you and your ex-boyfriend communicatin' behind my back anyway? I ain't one of them punks you can deceive. Don't forget. I come from the streets. No one gets one over on Luigi Angelo Steffanci. No one!"

Teri would have considered leaving the room again, but she was distracted by his unusual reference to himself in third person. His full name at that. "We're just friends, Luigi. And you can't take my friends away from me."

She successfully left the room this time, Luigi missing his chance at grabbing her arm again. Stomping past the thermostat, she noticed that it was only sixty-eight degrees in their home. How could the beast be sweating?

She turned around, about to yell something else back at him, when Luigi surprised her by being right behind her.

"Yes, I can," he said softly, inches from her face.

Teri wasn't intimidated by his sinister physical presence or the cheese dangling from his mustache, the stains on his shirt, his breath—courtesy of Mrs. Stouffer—or the anxious bead falling from his brow. She was furious and focused. Teri looked at her husband, easily twice her weight, without blinking. "What'd you say?"

"I said, 'Yes, I can.' You're my wife. You're my lucky wife who doesn't have to worry about her husband running off with other women. I don't have any female friends that are ex-girlfriends or 'lost loves'—whatever the hell you call him—that you need to worry about."

"You barely have any friends at all. Besides those schmoes at the bar."

He only went to the bar when she wasn't around, and he hadn't been there for weeks. Always bustin' his balls since she lost the weight and felt good about herself again.

"Funny, Teri. But you don't have to worry about me being like what's-his-face in *Fatal Attraction*."

"And you don't have to worry about me being like *what's-her-name* and taking you back, because if you did screw someone, I'd be gone!"

"Sure," Luigi said, hoping he sounded like he didn't believe she was capable of leaving him. Her sass had increased since they married.

"Outta here!" she hollered. Luigi snickered, backing off. She stood up to him brazenly. "If you think I'd stick around, try me."

"And leave all this?" he asked, forcing a laugh. He knew she loved not having to work and enjoyed the security he provided her. He didn't even demand she cook for him, which she'd refuse if he tried. But of course, he didn't have faith in an Asian cooking Italian food anyway. "Fuhgetaboutit!

Who'd you run to, your parents? They'll disown you if you're a disgraceful wife."

She knew that was true, so she dodged the question. "I'd run to nobody. And don't get me started about your judging folks. That whole Italian *It's about the family, we need to talk about everything that no one else talks about.* Give me a break."

"Don't tell me you'd run to that brochure-writing loser who can barely feed himself. You know how hard I work to give you all this?" he asked, gesturing at the room with his arms like a car salesman proudly presenting the vast selection of models on the floor. His prosperous furniture store provided them a life of luxuries. Luigi Angelo Steffanci and his wife could afford to live in one of the premier neighborhoods in San Francisco, a long way from his childhood home in Guttenberg, New Jersey.

Luigi was satisfied that he'd made his point. He belched and considered turning back to the kitchen to rescue his lonely lasagna, still in the tinfoil.

"I told you I wouldn't run to anybody," she said, ignoring his uncontrolled bodily functions. "And he doesn't write brochures anymore. You don't have to insult him. He's only talked about you with respect."

"I bet he has," Luigi said, barely hearing her. He resented her right now. "Don't tell me you're flying down there to see him."

"I am."

"I can't believe this!"

She was wide eyed, feigning innocence she wasn't sure she had. The light creases around her eyes disappeared. "Luigi, I love you. But my friend needs me, and I promise I won't do anything wrong."

"That's cuz you're not going!" he yelled, burping painful gas. He couldn't believe she thought he'd be okay with this. Particularly when he'd be the one footing the bill for this ridiculous rendezvous.

Without a word, she marched into the bedroom and slammed the door.

He returned to the kitchen, took a bite of his lasagna, and spit it out. *Broads.* Suddenly, he couldn't stand the taste of his lukewarm pasta. He wanted to wash it down with something but ignored the bottled water that had barely started to thaw. It stared at him like it was mocking his weight.

He snubbed it and grabbed a can out of the fridge instead. *Let's see how many calories I can burn with a cold beer.*

* * *

This morning, Jamie lay in bed thinking. *Tom . . . are we really broken up? What the hell is wrong with you?* She dreaded the idea of telling Stephanie of JC Traders' cutbacks . . . the two evil women at work, Martha and Janice . . . Stephanie and her domineering ways . . . Davey's Dealios . . . she needed to book her flight to Phoenix. If this client prospect worked out, it could be bigger than JC Traders, maybe. WSA represented no car dealers, and their ad spending could be substantial. If the background information she'd acquired was correct, Davey's Dealios could more than make up for JC Traders' cuts. She needed to prepare for her surprise meeting with the owner. This could be huge.

Then she remembered a dream she'd had. Drowning. She was drowning while holding her BlackBerry safely over her head, untouched by the still, cold water. An achievement she remembered acutely. She figured she didn't have to Google "drowning dreams while holding a BlackBerry" to see what it meant. She was truly addicted to her CrackBerry and insecure without it. Being in constant communication with those she cared about, Tom particularly, gave her comfort. The technological wonder was more than an accessory. It was a *partner*—unlike Tom, one that she could depend upon.

Eventually she'd have to get up. It was almost 6:00 a.m. She'd had a restless night after the breakup—if it indeed was one—and she had a lot of work to do today. One moment they're breaking up and she's giving Tom back her ring, the next—after refusing to take it—he's staring out the window at a homeless woman and clamming up even more. It stupefied her how Tom's newfound passion for getting his book published could be the epicenter of their relationship's problems, breaking their world together into pieces. He should be using her for support, not distant, despondent, and emotionally involved with an ex. It wasn't perfection she was seeking—just perfect *for her.* She wasn't a wallflower, and she wasn't going to let herself fall into a depression over a guy either. Tom wasn't just a guy, but he sure could act like one sometimes. No calls or texts from him last night. She'd checked a couple of times through the night.

Her cell phone rang. Jamie picked it up, still connected to its tangled power cord. She shifted in her bed and looked at the caller ID. It was too early for this.

"Hi, Mom." She held a hand over her face. The early morning sun peeked through the clouds, light winds breezing through her window in small gusts.

"Jamie, are you still in bed? You sick? What's wrong with you? Need me to come by? I'm not too far from you."

"Mom, it's barely 6:00 a.m., that's what's wrong."

"Oh, darling," her mother gushed, ignoring her daughter's sleepiness. "I had such a great time with him last night. I told you he'd treat me nicely."

"Mom!" Jamie sat up in her bed. She couldn't remember a time when her mother had doted on a man, or as her mother said, "a gentleman caller." "I can't believe you!"

"I told you that I knew what I was doing, didn't I? I don't know if I ever told you his name, but his name is Pete. He's nice and sweet and good and rich too."

Jamie was relieved, considering her mother's prior roster of vagabond boyfriends. She sat up with her legs crossed on the bed, smiling and listening to her mother's rapid overflow of details.

Always optimistic when on the prowl, her mother often met her temporary younger male companions when she went alone to high-end, ocean-front food establishments. She picked spots where older people hung out so she'd look younger by comparison.

"We went to a nice dinner at this cute little place near the water," her mother continued, unaware of her loud, grating, early morning volume. Jamie figured mothers were like that, completely oblivious when they were annoying. "Lordy, what's the name of it? I can't remember, but anyway, you'd love it. He reminds me of your father, God bless him. Almost as handsome too. We finished off a whole box of wine last night."

Her mother had bought boxed wine for years. Nothing was going to change that. The little corner grocery store with its splashy displays always had it in stock. Great Oaky Flavor and Berry and Grape Delight signs, often written in crayon, created a hard-to-resist temptation. Jamie got up and opened the drapes wider, wishing for more light to flood the room. Abundant, natural light would hopefully somehow make post-breakup day easier. "How many dates now?"

"With this gentleman caller, two real dates, if you call those dates. The first one with all those people from church, and last night ended early because we drank too much."

"A whole box of wine, Mom? How are you even driving right now?" She put her mother on speaker phone and examined herself in the mirror. A new zit on her cheek. *Great.*

"Something's wrong, Jamie. I can tell," her mother said.

"Nothing, Mother." Talking about Tom with her was worse than a trip to the gynecologist.

"Don't lie to me."

"Mom," Jamie moaned.

"You've got twenty minutes to clean up. I'm making breakfast." She hung up.

Jamie looked at her disconnected phone in shock and quickly ran the shower to prepare for her mother's inquisition. She wouldn't be close to ready by then.

Eighteen minutes later, her mother let herself in downstairs, carrying two bags of groceries. The door slammed behind her.

Upstairs, Jamie towel-dried her hair and contemplated her boundary issues. Scrambling to get some clothes on, she remembered that her mother hadn't given back the key after she'd borrowed it last time. She struggled to be as resourceful as her mother, even if just at her job.

"You still like your eggs poached, right, honey?" her mother yelled up the stairwell.

"Yes, that's fine!" She never ever liked her eggs poached. Sometimes it was like her mother didn't even know her. "Nothing fancy, Mom! I have to leave soon!"

"Flapjacks? Five minutes!"

"Love it!" Jamie yelled back down the stairs.

Jamie quickly put herself together. Stress was getting to her. She couldn't figure out what to wear, and her hair wasn't cooperating. The engagement ring stared at her on her dresser, calling to her like those aliens called to Richard Dreyfuss in *Close Encounters of the Something-or-Other*. She put it on. She wasn't up for the gossip queens at work speculating about her love life today. *Breathe.*

Her mother accomplished a lot in the kitchen. Jamie admired her for finding the skillet. She hadn't been able to find it for months.

"You still like salsa with your eggs?"

"Sure," Jamie said. Salsa with poached eggs. No sense in disrupting her flow. "You went shopping too? How fast do you shop?" She walked over to help her.

"Have a seat. I've got everything done here."

Admiring the results of efficient multitasking, Jamie sat down at the counter to a fruit plate and orange juice, and her mother delivered eggs and flapjacks. The butter and hot syrup were waiting for her.

"Mom. This is better than any room service I've ever had." Carb-loading wasn't going to solve her problems, but the flapjacks looked really good. No carb left behind.

"So you've forgotten all my other meals! Great. Now," she said, sitting eagerly next to Jamie, "tell me."

Jamie tried camouflaging her stress. "You're crazy. I'm fine!"

Her mother wasn't going to bother with a stealth mission. "Don't lie to me," she said, generously pouring hot syrup over her pancakes.

Jamie enviously watched her mother inhale the carbs that never affected her. If Jamie ate three pancakes herself, she'd be bloated for two days.

"And you know how I feel about throwing that word *crazy* around, for God's sake," her mother said.

Her father had called her mother crazy when she left him, not believing she could make it on her own as a single mother. Never tell her she's crazy.

"Let's move on this. I'm getting my hair done in a couple of hours."

Images of her mother at the salon styling her way-out-of-date bouffant hairdo stole Jamie's attention. Her hair was striking, standing atop her head like a proud, dark beehive. The coiffure travesty stood so tall over her head that men often eyed her mother's hair rather than her breasts, which were often on grand display in a dramatic, form-fitting, cleavage-baring outfit. Once, as a lost child, Jamie had found her mother in a crowded mall by looking for her old-fashioned hair-nest.

"Jamie!"

"Yeah, Mom," she said, awaking from her daze and buttering her pancake. She'd have *one*.

"Tell me the truth," her mother said, sucking pancake off her fork. "I don't have a lot of time today either."

It was motherly waterboarding. As soon as Jamie spoke, she knew she was giving her mother ammunition against her. "Tom and I—"

"Oh, that one," her mother said. "He's never going to be what you need him to be. You're too old to be waiting for him to become a man."

Her mother could be so brusque. "Well, we kind of broke up again last night, so—"

"It's about time," her mother said, relieved. "Good Lord, that boy's got to get it together, Jamie. Though I heard you say you *kinda* broke up."

"He's not a boy. Most of the time."

"So now you're on his side. You always take the other person's side."

Jamie hated when her mother got like this. "Mom."

"I'm just a dumb mother that's out of her mind!" her mother exclaimed, thrusting her passive-aggressiveness into overdrive.

"You know I don't think that," Jamie said calmly, having seen her mother's manipulative tactics so many times before. "Tom's got to figure out if we're supposed to be together. I used to think so, but I've been wrong before."

"He doesn't treat you right. I left your father for the same reasons. Even though you were only ten years old, I'd rather be alone than be talked to like I'm ignorant. I could've been a lawyer if I wanted!"

"Mom, Tom never mistreated me. And before you say anything else about Dad again, don't. Just don't."

Her mother put her fork down on her empty plate. She was a speed-eater. It couldn't be good for her, but Jamie knew how far she'd get by saying anything.

"No need to warn me. I know the boundaries of a mother."

Apparently not. Jamie kept her disagreement to herself.

Her mother placed her hand over Jamie's. "I also know you love poached eggs." She stood up with her plate and rinsed it in the kitchen sink. "You need to date other men, Jamie."

Here we go. She should have seen this coming. "Dating helps me how?"

Her mother scrubbed the skillet. She'd have Jamie's attention only for a few more moments before Jamie realized she had left her BlackBerry in the other room. "You need to find a man that is set up better, child. Would be especially good if he had money, truth."

Being referred to as *child* meant more condescension was coming. "I make my own money."

"People running all around this earth," her mother said, not hearing her, "don't know half the reasons why they do the things they do. You have to find the strength within yourself to make the right decisions, even the ones that bring you pain. You have to find power within yourself, Jamie. Your fate, young lady, is much bigger than you. You just need to be willing to take the risks so fate takes its desired course."

"Mother," Jamie said. "Not another debate on challenging fate and what the future holds." She noticed that her BlackBerry wasn't nearby.

Her mother pounced on her quickly, sitting back down and holding Jamie's hand, her own hands wet and soapy. Jamie raised her eyebrows at her mother's urgent need for her attention.

"There's something about your father."

The last time her mother had shared secrets about her father, she'd been treated to the unnecessary details of his mole cluster. "I don't have time for this now."

Her mother stared steadfastly at her. "I've wanted to tell you this, but—"

"What?" It was easy to get impatient with her mother's long setups.

"I was with another man while I was still with your father."

Jamie didn't blink, but her rounded shoulders said, *Okay. I give up.* "You're dropping this bomb on me right before I go to work," she said, waiting woefully for her mother to continue. A shiver brought goose bumps all over her legs.

"I settled for less than I should have," her mother said, "and then I had an affair that I hid from everyone."

Jamie was silent.

"Anyways, I loved your dad. I still visit his grave on our anniversary every year. Seven years now. I've also gone a few of his birthdays.

"In the middle of our marriage, I experienced something with someone that brought me out of the funk of life, where everything was predictable. No, I never said a thing to your father about him. Would've killed him before the tobacco companies got to him. I ended the affair about a year before I left your father. This other man wasn't what I needed either, necessarily. I was missing something in the marriage, and of course, I didn't know that at the beginning. Don't let this happen to you, child. I don't want you to go through what I went through. If you think this young man isn't going to work out long term, don't move forward with him. Some days I didn't even know who I was anymore. Didn't know if I was happy or sad. And I don't want you sad."

Jamie had to stop her mother's nonstop spluttering or she would continue past midnight on this monologue. "Mom, don't worry about me."

Her parents' relationship had been worse than she ever knew. She should be fearing long-term commitment more than Tom was. She didn't really want details, but she couldn't stop herself from asking questions. "How long?" Jamie groaned, unsure if she was angry or upset.

"Was I with him? Almost two years. Best and worst of my life."

"Geez Louise, Mom."

Her mother's eyes scanned the ceiling. "Memorial Day 1977. Lordy, so long ago. He was a neighbor. Came to one of our block parties. Remember those?"

"Dad didn't know?"

"After so many years, I could *hear* him not pay attention. He violently ignored me. Sometimes I looked at him and thought he might think something, but nope, I don't think he ever gave it a thought. If it was the other way around, I would've made him pay for a long time, I tell you that!"

"What were you doing, getting together while I was at Girl Scout meetings?"

Her mother smirked in embarrassment. This kid was going to make her smoke again. "Remember when I would go to church by myself on Sunday mornings?"

"Wow," Jamie said. Suddenly things made sense to her.

"You never saw a Bible around the house, did you?" her mother asked. She squinted mischievously.

"My God, Mom."

"The heart makes you do unimaginable things. You've been unhappy with that boy for so long now that you don't remember what it's like when your heart's beating like a drum."

She remembered, all right. "And those church retreats?"

"Getaways to his second home in Colorado. We'd go hiking and fishing. God, I miss the outdoors there."

"You've always hated the outdoors," Jamie said, unable to imagine her mother settling down enough on a boat to fish. "You never did stuff like that with me."

"I'm very outdoorsy. I love the outdoors."

"Outdoor malls, maybe," Jamie said dryly.

"He had this incredible log cabin in the mountains with this smoke chimney that I used to love to cuddle up to with him," her mother said, reminiscing about her secrets, ignoring her daughter who was cringing at these details. "It was made of cedar. Cedar! And it always smelled like cinnamon. To this day, I smell a Cinnabon and—"

"Why, now, are you telling me all this?" Jamie's mind searched for anything she could remember that would have hinted that her mother was in love with another man and came up with nothing.

"Because you need to know, child," her mother said, "how important it is that you're with the right person and learn from my mistakes. I had to make a move with my life or be miserable. There are people that you can love, but being with the right one is the art of your life. Or you end up having affairs like I did. And you'll learn the hard way that passion isn't the same thing as true love."

Jamie put her head in her hands. "It's really something that I haven't committed myself to an institution yet."

"Oh, Lordy, what am I saying?" her mother said, shaking her head. "I'm calling *that* art, but I was able to experience different kinds of loves and have you, and that's art too. I know now that marriage is like a loaf of bread. When it goes stale, you've got to sprinkle water on it, plop it in the microwave, and moisten it up some. There are things I could have done differently, looking back now."

"Poor Dad!" Jamie said, defending her father, which she'd never done before.

"I know, I know," her mother said, sinking in defeat.

There was no way her father hadn't known what was going on. He had always picked up on the unspoken communications between her and her mother. He might have seemed oblivious, but he'd been far from that. How awful it must have been for him to know that he wasn't enough for her mother.

Jamie felt a wave of nausea. Tom was now doing what her mother had done. He was fixated on Teri because he was looking for whatever it was that Jamie wasn't providing him. Certainly Jamie hadn't plopped their relationship in the microwave.

Sitting silently, Jamie pushed aside thoughts of Tom and considered everything her mother had just revealed. She wasn't all that upset about her mother's adulterous escapade. After all, her mother's affair took place decades ago. She wasn't about to go wallowing in her childhood pain again. The constant fighting at home before the divorce, moving from place to place after it. Eating Top Ramen when there was little money for food or anything else. She had blocked out that part of her life. She had more immediate concerns now—like her job. And Tom.

She thought about him obsessing over his ex. If they were really broken up, nothing was stopping him now. Maybe he'd already set up a rendezvous with his lost love. She felt sick.

As if she sensed Jamie's thoughts, her mother straightened up, switched gears, and focused on her next target. "Jamie, I'm worried about you. I'm not a fan of this Tom boy. Or Tom man, if that's what you want me to call him. Such a weird one. I've never really liked writers anyway. Always observing the world, making judgments on people and things. All questionable, if you ask me. Writers write about the world. That doesn't mean they know the world they live in."

"If we're not together, you have nothing to worry about, okay?" She noticed the kitchen clock. She had to go. Throw up.

Her mother noticed the ring on Jamie's finger. "You kept the ring. Good for you."

"It's not like that." Her stomach was churning.

"You hate me now, don't you?"

"Of course not," Jamie said with obligation to her mother's manipulation but meaning it. "It's a lot to hit me with this morning." She quickly got up and ran to the bathroom and slammed the door.

Her mother followed her and spoke to her through the bathroom door, continuing as if she'd expected such a reaction from her daughter. "I know it's not my cooking." She picked at a stray cuticle. "Clarity is better than blissful ignorance. I should have told you this long ago, Jamie. Sorry I didn't."

Jamie knew her mother was pouting. "It's okay, Mom," she said. If she wasn't kneeling over the toilet, she would've felt like their roles were reversed. "It's water near the bridge." She hurled.

"What I need to do," her mother realized, "is get a better look at Pete's buttocks."

Jamie hurled again.

"I only felt them briefly last night," her mother continued. "I needed more light for a good study anyways."

Her mother was a recent casual student of *rumpology*, the study of the lines, crevices, and folds of a person's buttocks. Or, as Jamie thought of it, palm reading of the ass. Jamie wasn't up to hearing the differences in character again between someone with an apple-shaped rump versus a pear-shaped one. Her mother had guessed that her daughter's naturally muscular bubble butt—which she hadn't seen bare since Jamie was seven years old—suggested that she was charismatic, confident, dynamic, and creative. Not a conversation she wanted to prolong any morning, but especially not when she was late.

"Okay, now I really gotta go," Jamie said, after opening the bathroom door. She was exhausted already, and the day had barely begun.

* * *

The office was empty. Only a superachiever would be in the cubicle farm at Western Mag Corp before 7:00 a.m. Here, writers and editors worked late, not early. The interior lights were off, except for one desk light. Down one row, there was some activity.

Tom was on the phone, trying not to think of Jamie and the fact that their relationship was no longer flying in a holding pattern. He was unsure where they were going to land—or if they had already crashed.

"I'm sorry, Mr. Summers," the male voice said without much inflection on the other side of the receiver. "We're not in the market for unsolicited submissions at this time. Thank you, though. Good luck to you." The line went dead.

He noticed the clock. The office would soon be humming with semidiligent work dogs and fresh-faced underdogs competing for attention, and the limited minutes available on his thrifty cell phone plan necessitated use of the company phone. He didn't want gossipmongers or Brent the Plagiarist meddling in his business. He'd have to quit his calls soon.

Rejection by one literary agency after another could have exhausted him, but the return e-mail from Teri late last night somehow brought light to his day. She had agreed to come visit him, making no jabs at him for his financial limitations in visiting her.

He dialed again. "Hi, my name is Tom Summers. I sent you my book about two months ago. I'm looking for representation—"

"One moment," the receiver said.

He waited impatiently. As the cube farm started to wake from its twelve-hour slumber, he'd have to quit his early morning calls to the East Coast soon, or he would surely face a reprimand from Andre for using the office for personal matters.

"Tom Summers?" the new voice on the receiver asked.

"Yes," Tom coughed. "Hi."

"Keith Levy here. We received your submission. It's not what we're looking for right now. If you ever have any other material to send us, though, we'd be happy to look at it. I'm a personal fan of your column in *Western Mag*. This just doesn't fit our needs right now."

How frustrating. The book was considerably better than his columns, which were quickly whipped up and then chopped up by the editors. He'd done so many revisions to his book, where his passion bled on the pages. Someone being a fan of his columns and rejecting his manuscript was ridiculous. "Do you have any suggestions on anyone who would be interested? I think my manuscript's got undiscovered potential," he said, uncomfortable with talking up his own material. He never was a good salesman.

"I wish I could tell you," Levy said. "To be honest, I'm surprised that you don't have representation already. You've got talent. No juice here on the West Coast? I don't know how this would play on the East Coast, thinking about it. Sometimes it seems like there are competing philosophies between East and West. Different preferences. Culturally. And not good for you, agencies are getting more selective these days."

"I'm shopping it around," Tom said. He tried to smile, having read somewhere that smiling while on the phone could ease conversational tension. For Tom, it wasn't working.

"I read your work personally," Levy said with what Tom hoped was respect. "Quite good. Though your ending . . . personal taste . . . I was surprised you killed the lead protagonist."

No one—including Jamie—could get past his unhappy ending. Did it have to end up all tidy and happy like *A Christmas Carol*?

"You might want to take this to one of those writers' conferences. Here or even one of those international ones," Levy said. He spoke with the resonance of a public speaker who loved what he did for a living. "Take it to England. Germany! They're always looking for new talent, and they pay close attention to new American writers. Hoping they get their hands on the good stuff here in America before we even do." He rustled through some papers on his desk. "There's one here in LA tomorrow."

Those conferences were expensive. Much more than Tom could afford. "Well, I'll go tomorrow," Tom said.

"Ahh." Levy was pleased. "Take it there. Take five-page samples and copies of the first chapter in case anyone asks for your work. But don't, under any circumstances, provide the last chapter. Tell them it's coming. Keep 'em hanging while you rewrite it."

"Hmm." Who said he *would* rewrite it?

"Tell you what," Levy said, "I'm in my LA office on Friday. Swing by around eleven o'clock if you can. I've got a couple of ideas for you. You're on the right track."

"Oh, that's great!" This was different. Someone saw he needed help and was intervening. "I'll be there, sure."

"Really, think about the ending. You know how to write."

"Thanks," Tom said, "I appreciate any insight. I'll see you Friday." They hung up.

He hated the idea of changing his ending, finding a rewrite of the whole last chapter particularly daunting. *Do I believe in the ending or am I just lazy?* For the first time, Tom wanted to throw away everything he'd written and forget he even started it.

Elsewhere in the boxy quarters of Western Mag Corp walked Brent Hayes. The superachieving gene in his DNA that had always eluded him—frustrating his father—had finally appeared. His phone to his ear, he strolled to his cube, impatient to leave it and all it represented behind, ready to move into an office befitting his rank and power. This would all be his one day.

Inconveniently for both Brent and Tom, Brent's desk shared a cube wall with Tom, who was silent on the other side of the cube wall, reading another rejection e-mail.

"Listen to me," Brent said into the phone. He moved the computer mouse, and Tom's notes for their IPO article glowed on his computer screen. Glancing down his vacant, quiet cubicle row, Brent continued his phone conversation, believing he was alone. He had been on his cell for so long, it was hot. His superhydrated skin was making the faceplate—a boon and haven for Brent bacteria—sticky. He quickly wiped the grime off onto his shirt and looked up and down the row again before he sat at his desk. In the clear. "I need you to listen to me, damn it! No more of this dainty, prissy, I'm-scared-to-do-the-job-I-was-hired-to-do crap. I want this done before all of the partners of the firm vote. You got me?"

Tom perked up at his desk.

"I need him taken *out.*"

Who? Brent the Great Jackass was conspiring, devising an evil scheme of some sort. Tom found himself eager, even aroused, by the prospect of Brent wreaking havoc in the world of Western Mag Corp.

"I'm telling you," Brent threatened, "I don't have time for lofty promises and missed opportunities. Finish Andre off. I don't want him holding me back anymore."

Andre? Tom tried not to breathe. With no phones ringing or other sounds in the cube farm, if he moved even the tiniest bit, he knew his swivel desk chair would make a squeak that could be heard as far away as Maine.

"We've got a dwindling time window here. Get it done." Brent killed the call.

Tom's mind raced, but he suppressed his urge to investigate what was going on between Brent and Andre. It couldn't be *murder* that Brent was talking about. Those two were buddy-buddy, not adversaries. Anyway, keeping himself off Brent's target list was a noble ambition.

It was absolutely quiet up and down the cube farm, until a text message popped up on Tom's phone, accompanied by the phone's tri-tone signal of its arrival. From Jamie, it read: *I miss my best friend.*

Brent's eyes widened madly when he heard the chime. He hadn't been alone after all. He bolted to his feet.

Tom panicked, knowing Brent would swing around to his cube any moment. He quickly clicked off his small desk lamp and turned off his computer monitor. He swiftly scampered down the aisle and jumped into a dark cubicle.

The foreboding figure appeared in the aisle.

Brent peered into Tom's cubicle, the source of the text message chime. It was dark and still. The phone sat by Tom's computer. Brent saw it and was relieved. *No big deal. The stupid douche bag left his phone at the office. What a moron.*

He picked up the phone, scanning Tom's messages, fixated on the one from Jamie. *Ah, trouble in paradise.*

Suddenly, one of the overhead lights turned on. The bustling of someone entering the room immediately changed the dark and desolate mood of the office. Nadia appeared down the cube aisle, her head cocked, propping her cell phone to her ear with her shoulder, holding her coffee.

Tom's endorphins pumped. Brent couldn't know he'd been overheard, nor did Tom want to be caught lurking in someone else's cube. Which was worse?

"Yeah," Nadia said into the phone, "I'm not sure what to do next. I don't know how to tell him. I know it's weird." Her eyes met Brent's. She quickly realized that Brent had Tom's phone. "What the hell are you doing?"

Brent was frozen. "I—"

"Give me that." She grabbed the phone from him and fake smiled at Brent, who stood there foolishly. "Yeah, that one's an idiot," she said into her phone, making her way to her cube. "He's more of an idiot than Ozone and Turbo from *Breakin'.*" Brent could smile, compliment her, or even provide her gifts. Nothing was going to happen between them—ever.

Brent retreated to his cube, infuriated by the way Nadia disrespected him. That would change when he ran Western Mag Corp. This kingdom would one day be his.

Nadia turned to her desk, and Tom darted for his cube and quietly turned his monitor back on, proud of himself for not being caught. His heart was pounding so fast that his chest was heaving. He clicked his lamp light back on, relieved to hear other employees entering the office.

Back at his own cube, Brent determined that he indeed hated *the world.* The one woman he sought was repelled by everything he did. He got no respect at his workplace. His father discounted him as lazy and unable to create a successful career trajectory on his own. The incompetent hit man Brent employed had failed to dispose of the other inept moron that aggravated his bowels: Andre. Who had been the one who had convinced his father of the benefits of finally going public? Who had the ear of the silent partners of the firm? Who had to be stopped from turning Western Mag Corp public?

The cost to implement the IPO was $3.5 million, thanks to a regulatory act passed by Congress in the wake of the dot-com boom and bust back in the early '90s. That money was supposed to be *his*, not the government's. It was a lot of cash pulled from his forthcoming inheritance, considering his father had refused to give him share in Western Mag Corp at all. Brent had wasted too much on his own failed ventures, which his father had determined to be materialistic vanity projects focused more on attention from the ladies and his pals than on running a successful business—which is why Brent was to learn the ropes of Western Mag Corp. Become a real businessman.

But turning the magazine public would strip away Brent's ability to take control once his father was gone, and it would substantially reduce his family fortune. He had no faith that the stock would ever have legs. A fledgling magazine empire could no way thrive while depending on poor management and bad writers like Tom. Brent's millions could be better invested than into this worthless stock . . . and it'd all be junk, he was sure. He wasn't going to allow his family's estate to be swallowed up by the government or scheming shareholders like Andre while the company sunk. He couldn't depend on himself becoming rich this way. It was bad enough Brent had to wait for his father to croak to be truly rich, if he would be hugely rewarded in his father's will at all at this point. He had to do something drastic.

Brent massaged his pulsating temples. He despised Tom and being forced to work with him on the pro-IPO article, but Tom was just a workhorse. Andre had the whip, and he had to go.

"You forget something?"

Tom looked over his shoulder to see Nadia holding out his phone.

"I didn't see you come in," Nadia said. "You left this. Jackass was reading it."

His eyebrows furrowed, and he took his phone back.

"Don't pretend you don't know who I'm talking about," Nadia said. "There's only one jackass around here."

On the other side of the cubicle partition, Brent steamed. This place was due for a shake-up.

* * *

Jamie struggled to open her office door. It swung open and—as usual—a folder dropped onto the floor and papers fell out. Her purse slid off of her shoulder and was caught by her arm. She bent down to pick it all up, and her BlackBerry and lip gloss clunked on the floor. Her morning was not improving.

With the thoughts of her mother fornicating with another man on getaway weekends refusing to fade, she unlocked her keyboard and pulled up her computer screen, preparing herself for the photo screensaver of her and Tom. The Internet couldn't come up fast enough.

Her anxiety over telling Stephanie about JC Traders was making her tremble. She could only postpone it so long, imagining Stephanie's various emotions making great effort to overpower the paralyzing effects of her Botox.

Martha, in all of her unpleasant beauty and glory, popped her head in Jamie's office. "Jamie."

Jamie cringed, startled. Martha's voice ranked only behind chalkboard scratching and cats mating. "Hi," Jamie said, faking cheeriness.

"We're repitching Weight Burger tomorrow. We're going to lock it down. You might as well hold off your trip to Phoenix. There's no point, really."

"I hope you guys rock! Screw NRS! Take 'em out!" Jamie shouted, hoping she sounded genuine. While she didn't want either half of the yenta sisters to upstage her, she wanted the agency to succeed. She told herself it felt good to take the high road.

Martha stared at Jamie, unsure of what to say. No matter how hard she tried to get under Jamie's skin, she was frustrated that she could never predict Jamie's reaction. "Don't make yourself look stupid," she said finally. "You don't need it, Stephanie doesn't need it, and neither does WSA. It's unnecessary. Why don't you do something useful around here? There's a lot of filing work I need done."

Jamie had a smile on her face that Martha, to her credit, knew was acting. "You know what, Martha? I bet if we scored two huge accounts for this agency, we'd save a whole bunch of jobs, don't you?"

Martha looked bored.

"By the way," Jamie said, searching her desk, "have you seen my file on JC Traders? I can't find it anywhere."

"Nope," Martha grunted, and she walked out.

Jamie threw her hair back in frustration and booked her last-minute flight to Phoenix, a red-eye tonight. She had high hopes for a Davey's Dealios score.

Her BlackBerry rang. She didn't recognize the number but answered it. Could be a new business lead.

"Hi Jamie! It's Wanda."

Immediate recognition. "Hey." She had met William's friend a number of times and liked her but didn't know her well. Sometimes Jamie and Tom had woken up on the weekends to see Wanda studying at Tom's compact kitchen table, waiting for William to eventually ease himself out of bed. "How are you?"

"Great! Got a weird favor to ask."

"Oh," Jamie discounted, "no weirdness here. What's up?"

"I'd ask Tom, but I thought he might automatically say no, so I thought I'd ask you first, to see what you thought about you guys doing a double date with me and this guy I'm into. I dig him, but I don't really know him well, and I want a good, comfortable first date. You never know, there're a lot of weirdos out there."

"Oh, I know," Jamie said. Tom aside, her dating history was a kaleidoscope of weirdos. A particular one that stood out—back in college—had severely reprimanded her with a dazzling sequence of profane insults for being ten minutes late. She hadn't stuck around for more, and she never let her mother set her up on a blind date again.

"I'd ask William or one of my girlfriends, but everyone's busy tomorrow night. So I'm hoping you can talk Tom into it and that you both can come along so it's a legit double date."

"And you thought we wouldn't have plans for tomorrow night."

Wanda stuttered. "Um, I—"

"I'm kidding, Wanda, don't worry about it. There's a problem, though. Tom and I broke up last night."

"Oh no."

"As weird as your first date with the guy might be, it'd be weirder for us to go."

Wanda became uncomfortable. "No doubt! Oh my gosh, you guys were getting married, weren't you?" Wanda couldn't believe she had asked Jamie that. "Are you okay?"

"I will be." Stephanie walked briskly by her office, Martha trailing her. "Look, I've got to go. I've got to handle something here at work."

"I'm sorry. Look, if you want," Wanda said quickly, "Blaine has a friend. I don't know him, but if you could use a night out . . . we could all get together."

Jamie laughed, trying to hurry off the phone. "I don't think so, Wanda. It's too soon, you understand."

"Sure. Think about it? Dinner's on me. I'd pick you up."

"We'll talk soon, okay?" Jamie asked, trying to hang up. As much as she feared Stephanie's reaction, she wanted to get this over with.

Awkwardness wouldn't stop Wanda. "Let me know if you change your mind?"

"Bye, Wanda."

They hung up, and Jamie hurried down the hall to find Stephanie. She was gone. Jamie raced down the stairs to catch her before she got in her car, only to come upon Martha and Janice huddling at the front exit. Stephanie was driving off in her white BMW.

Martha was scolding Janice, her quivering finger pointed at her. "I told you!"

"It's all handled!" Janice shouted back in a loud whisper. "Now quit telling me what to do!"

The two beauty queens hushed upon Jamie's hurried arrival. They had been whispering tall, mischievous tales of meanness, Jamie was sure of it. If they thought that she was giving up on saving the agency, they were wrong. It would be clear to Stephanie who was indeed valuable to WSA.

"Oh, man," Jamie said. "When is she coming back?"

Martha and Janice were uncomfortably quiet, Jamie noticed, before Martha finally said, "We don't know."

Janice nodded. "We don't know."

Returning to the stairwell, Jamie heard a slap, unsure of who slapped whom.

"Ow!" From the stairwell, it sounded like Janice.

"Listen to me!" Jamie could hear Martha say.

"Why'd you hit me?"

Jamie continued to ascend the stairs and snickered. The troublesome women were their own enemies.

By the time Jamie returned to her office, she'd decided to call Stephanie. It'd be equally dreadful if Stephanie heard of JC Traders' cutbacks from Cynthia or Jamal. Hiding facts from the boss would be unforgivable.

She called Stephanie's cell to no answer. Jamie hung up, choosing not to leave her name, number, and a detailed message. Normally, Stephanie would call back her missed calls.

But the day went by, and Stephanie never called her back.

"You have your part of the article done, Brent? I want to get out of here."

Brent turned in his cube and hid his computer screen from Tom, who hovered over him. It was six o'clock, it'd been dark over an hour, and Brent had barely started the article Tom was waiting for.

"No, Tom. I've been busy."

"Busy?"

What a joke. Everyone in the office knew Brent didn't do much at Western Mag Corp. He asked for help doing almost anything. Tom believed Brent spent his energy contemplating his next opportunity to feign incompetence, keeping his attention and efforts on getting out of doing things he didn't want to do. By perpetuating his sadly believable charade, Brent could avoid mundane and unimaginative tasks that interns had mastered. It was much easier for others to do the lowly, nonskilled tasks than for them to explain to exhaustion how he did them wrong over and over again.

No one subscribed, it appeared, to the philosophy of teaching to fish. Everyone—the writers, editors, junior staffers, and assistants; the mail sorters; and the interns alike—preferred to do all of the fishing and let the CEO's son take his ineptitude to another department rather than face retribution from above. It was widely joked that Brent Hayes could not find his ass with both hands.

Brent knew it, and he had vowed to remember that. Soon enough, he'd own this place, and then he could fire whomever he didn't like. Anyone who thought he was incompetent didn't deserve to work there under his watch. In the meantime, he had spent most of the day working on his imaginative restructuring of the organization.

Tom checked his phone. After her text this morning, he had called Jamie twice, and she hadn't called him back. It wasn't like her not to answer his calls. He realized he was freaking out. "I can't stay here all night and wait for you to finish it, Brent. I told you I needed to see it before deadline. You're not sending it to Andre without me reviewing it."

Brent studied Tom coolly. *I'm not, am I?* "Get out of here. I'll e-mail it to you later. Check it from home."

"Brent."

"Don't worry about it." Brent waved him off. "I don't want to keep you from whatever social life you pretend you have."

Tom shook his head and left, and Brent returned to his plans. Western Mag Corp was to have a revolution.

Tom pulled up to the curb of Jamie's home. An old couple who lived in a small, quaint box of a house across the street sat on their porch drinking lemonade in unison like they had been doing it for so many years that no coaching was necessary for their consumption to be in absolute harmony. The old man was busy fixing strings on an antique guitar, his shaky hands desperately holding on to their desire to fix things. Nursing a glass next to him, the woman rocked in her swing chair back and forth, thinking back to a time when she cared about her hair, her clothes, and the guitar strumming of her handy-dandy husband of fifty-two years.

"Look, Ed," she said, the first words she had said in a long time. "He's still courting that young lady."

Her husband didn't look up from his seat and continued his work on the guitar.

"What a cute couple," she continued, satisfied with her assumption. "Remember when we were that age, going after what we wanted?"

The old man grunted and continued his work.

The woman noticed Homer creeping around the cars on the street like a cat, stalking the familiar man approaching Jamie's front door. "We need to call Neighborhood Watch."

This got the old man's attention. He finally looked up and squinted over his spectacles. No way was he going to let his neighborhood be overrun by criminals. He disappeared into the house to make the call.

Across the street, Homer felt like she was being smothered. "Leave me alone!" she whispered to Him. "You're micromanaging me!"

"You've got to get things moving along, Homer," God said. "I don't have all the time in the world."

"Great way of putting it." She saw Tom press the doorbell, and she crouched behind a sedan. An inquisitive rat moseyed by on the bumper. "Rats!" She scowled at the rodent. It scampered away.

"Another missed opportunity, My friend. You let him walk right by you into his apartment last night. Tonight, you follow him and do nothing. The clock is ticking."

"I'm aware!" she whispered back at Him. She was so angry her nostrils heaved like fish gills. "I know what I'm doing!"

"What are you afraid of?"

"Besides Your aggravating booms? Nothing."

"You're afraid of failing, aren't you, Homer? You said you could do this."

"I'm afraid of nothing." The rat returned, scooting along the car bumper. It lifted its head and flared its nostrils at Homer, imitating her. Startled, she fell back on her rump against another car. "Umpf!" The car's alarm went off.

The rat taunted her, standing on its hind legs.

"I swear I hate all Your creations," she said to Him, glaring back at the rodent. The sedan was its turf, clearly. She hissed at it. It hissed back.

At Jamie's front door, Tom looked back to the car alarm, the whirring and honking switching to a loud, deep blare like a foghorn summoning lost ships in the night.

Homer bumped against the car again, and its ear-piercing alarm stopped abruptly. "Good God." As far as she was concerned, each of humanity's inventions was more maddening than the next.

Now that calm had returned, Tom turned back to Jamie's front door, waiting and hoping for her to answer.

The old man popped his head out the screen door of the house across the street. "What's all this racket? It's after seven o'clock at night, for God's sake."

"Heh? Just get the cops here!" the old woman exclaimed. He never did anything quickly enough.

"I'm on hold," he said, returning inside.

Jamie opened the door, surprised to see Tom standing there, looking relieved and hopeful. For a moment, she thought of how he must have looked as a young boy. She used to picture him a lot that way, imagining his innocence when he opened his first Christmas presents or hit his first baseball. These things made her feel like she knew him better.

"Hi."

"Hi, Tom," she said.

"You didn't answer my calls."

"You could have just texted me back."

He smiled apologetically. "Busy?"

"Can you tell? Sloughing my feet before I catch my flight." They both looked down at her feet, covered with foot scrub. Answering the phone earlier surely would have been easier than coming to the door. "Pretty gross, huh?"

"Just don't ask me to suck your toes right now, okay?"

Homer rolled her eyes, observing Tom and Jamie. "Ugh," she said under her breath. The rat snickered at her. Homer ignored it.

"Taking the red-eye, huh?"

"My mom's here," Jamie said. The last thing she needed was her mom to lecture her—or Tom.

Tom considered for a moment why she had answered the door in such a messy state while her mother could have done it. "She doesn't have to know I'm here, does she?"

Jamie knew this was trouble but opened the door and allowed him inside. Homer felt her eyes bulge as she watched Tom disappear into the house. Once again she was stuck outside, waiting.

"I know," Homer said.

"I don't understand you."

"And everyone's got You figured out," Homer quipped.

From the entryway inside, Tom could see Jamie's mother working at a desk in the living room, her back to them. He quietly followed Jamie up the stairs to her bedroom. She was putting extreme and comical effort into walking on her heels, as if less slough would make it onto the floor.

"So when did you start this with your feet?" he asked softly.

"Since I was a teenager."

"Who was it?" her mother called from the living room. She was entering bill payments online. The Internet having access to her bank account still scared her. She continued to double—and triple-check her work and verify that her money was still there.

"Just Tom! Dropping off something!"

"You better quit it with that man, Jamie!" her mother yelled. "He's nothing but trouble, that one!"

Jamie stopped. "He's coming upstairs, Mother. He's *here*." She grinned uncertainly at Tom.

"You know how I feel about him, Jamie!"

"Such a nice woman," Tom said, shrugging off his embarrassment.

"You know how you and your mother don't have a relationship at all? Consider yourself lucky sometimes," Jamie said, continuing up the stairs.

"Don't close your bedroom door!" her mother yelled from her chair. "No hanky-panky with me in the house!"

They walked into her bedroom, and Jamie shut the door loudly enough for her mother to hear. She escorted Tom into her master bathroom and sat on a bath towel on the floor by the tub.

"So you ready to talk?" She was a bit tired to get into another fruitless debate with him, but she would if it brought them closer again.

"I have talked, haven't I?" He noticed the skin shavings, or something, on the towel with her. He tried not to look at it.

"You spoke, but you didn't talk." He wasn't giving her the direct answers she wanted.

"Jamie, did you close your door?" her mother yelled from downstairs.

"It's my house, Mother!" Jamie yelled back abruptly, jarring Tom.

"How did you beat your mom to the door, crazy girl?" he asked, hoping changing the subject would make him more comfortable.

"I was going to get myself some hot tea, which now I don't have because I brought you up here instead."

"Sorry. Want me to get it for you? I will."

"I'm not telling you that so you'd apologize," she said, calming her combative tone. "It's okay. Though it's sweet for you to offer to face my mother if I asked you to go get it. I chose to bring you in here. And I didn't mean to miss your calls earlier, babe." The term of endearment snuck off her tongue. "Work's just a bear right now." She looked up at him, concerned. "So what do you want to talk about?"

He sat down on the side of the tub next to her, watching her expertly wipe her feet of scrub. "I'm thinking this book thing is a mistake. I have no idea where I got the idea I could do it. Everyone hates the ending. I mean everyone."

A part of her agreed with him that the book was a mistake, but she should have known that he wasn't here to talk about their relationship. "I know you're against changing the ending," she said, trying not to be angry with him. Who did he think he was, showing up at her door and acting like everything was fine? *They were broken up.* "But maybe you could change it a little." She chose her words carefully. "Make it commercially viable for the powers that be, you know?"

"And make it 'pop culture-esque'?" he snorted. "That wasn't the idea when I started."

He looked lost to her. Helpless. "I'm just saying," she said, compassion creeping into her tone. "It's an option. Or you can do the self-publishing thing."

"No one would ever read it if I did that," he said. Like she even knew what she was talking about. "It would be printed and bound, but that's it. I can't afford to promote it, and I want my art to be read."

No one knew what he was going through, and he felt alone through it all. Jamie understood the best, but even she didn't fully get it.

"So you came here," Jamie said. She couldn't help but be humored by Tom's use of the word *art*, remembering how her mother had used it earlier in the day. She refrained from telling him that being misunderstood didn't necessarily make him an artist.

"What do you want me to say?"

She sighed. He was clueless. "The truth. We both know you don't have a problem with that." She got up and stood in the tub to rinse her feet and watched him stare at the remains on the towel, much like a young boy would look at roadkill that's been ignored for days. "No point in hiding this from you now, is there?" she asked over the noise of the faucet.

"Your *feet* are cute."

"Aren't they?" she asked, showing them off under the warm water.

"It's this *stuff.*"

"It's not as effortless as I've made you believe."

"I never knew you scrubbed your feet like that."

"Sloughed. Sloughed my feet." She turned off the faucet. "If you're an aspiring Steinbeck, you better get your vernacular right."

"Hey."

She knew saying Steinbeck that way was abrasive but couldn't help herself. It was hard to hide the hurt. "I'm trying to help you out with the correct terminology so you don't have to write *Western Mag* columns for the rest of your life. Not with your talent, Tom."

She took her feet out of the tub and threw another towel down on the floor and stepped down onto it. Tom knelt before her and wiped her feet dry. He looked up at her beaming down at him. Under other circumstances, Jamie thought this would melt any woman.

"If you write *scrub* and not *slough*," she said, trying not to be pedantic, "you may have inaccuracies in your masterpiece."

"Thank God I didn't." He stopped himself from pointing out that she couldn't even get clichés right.

"Yup," she said, looking down at him and remembering what a great couple she used to think they were. She was getting drawn into him but resisted it, and she screamed at him inside. *Where is your your moxie, or whatever you call it? You're down on your knees, but why aren't you pleading to be with me? You need to figure yourself out!*

He finished drying her off and stood up. "You're being facetious, aren't you? I sense contempt, resentment, or something."

No kidding. Tom's aloofness was infuriating her. She wanted closure, but she didn't want to fight. "It's nothing," she lied, realizing that sarcasm, such as her use of *masterpiece*, kept worming its way into her sentences. "You know I think you're an awesome writer. I want you to achieve whatever it is you need to achieve." Though she hated the ending to his book too, she wanted him to reach his dream. It was this ex-girlfriend that she had the big problem with. *And quit pushing me away!*

"No, I mean it," he said, confronting her. "You're resenting me."

She faced him. "Yes." She was satisfied that she had the guts to say it. "But I want you to face these demons you've got, with you needing to be a literary commercial success to love me or whatever it is you're dealing with. These nightmares about your dead brother too. You've gone through a lot in your life. I'm pissed about this thing you've still got for Teri, though. But there's nothing I can do about it."

Her resignation hit him hard, and he didn't know how to respond. Jamie sat on the tub and put on her socks. Tom remained silent. Then she walked away.

"Jamie," Tom said, following her into her bedroom.

She was over crying. "Sucks being the one causing you to run away rather than the one you run to. That's why we need to be over. At least for now."

"We're just going to meet. Talk. Just talking!"

"What? You're meeting her? Oh my God!"

"We're not going to have sex or anything."

Jamie thought saying that was just stupid. "I'm not stopping you, am I?" she asked him squarely. "So you've been communicating with her! You're a piece of work."

"Getting you upset wasn't my objective," Tom said. His words had an unintended clinical tone.

"And being unhappy was mine." Her sarcasm came out freely. "I don't even want to know how long you've been talking to her."

Tom pulled her to him.

"Don't," she said, pulling away. Hugging him made her feel dizzy with need for him. "I can't do this. While we're like this."

"Okay."

"It's not fair for you to expect me to put my life on hold while you deal with this midlife crisis crap. You're almost forty years old, for Christ's sake."

"It's not midlife."

"It is if you die at seventy or eighty! My dad died at seventy. I want a family one day, Tom. You know, kids. A husband to come home to. I'm not getting any younger."

"You want kids?"

"You never asked." She looked at him blankly. She wished he had asked.

"You used to say that having a kid was like the ultimate bowel movement."

She needed to scream. "Three years ago I said that, Tom!" She collected herself, not wanting her mother to barge in. "Some of us change. Apparently you don't."

"How was I supposed to know? You should've told me this!"

"What do you want from me, Tom? Did you think that you could come here, I'd make you feel better about your life, and you would leave and go along your merry way? You're going to see your ex while we fall apart. You wanted this."

Sitting on her bed, Tom realized that this might be the closest he ever got to sleeping in it again. He put his face in his hands. He didn't understand everything himself; how could he expect Jamie to? He wasn't sure what he wanted or what he expected.

Jamie had had enough of this. What would it take to get a reaction out of him? "Life is short, Tom. So . . . I'm going to be going out myself," she said with more courage than she thought she possessed. But once the words were out of her mouth, she realized she wasn't taunting him. If Tom wasn't going to do something profound to keep her, something dramatic to win her . . . something *intelligent*, she was ready to move on. "On a date."

Tom's mouth fell open in shock.

Jamie's mother opened the bedroom door and appeared in the doorway, showcasing the disciplinary attention that was the hallmark of good parenting. "The bedroom door has to be open while I'm in the house."

"Mother, get out of my room!" Jamie pleaded. She slammed the door. "I'm not fifteen!"

Tom tried to get hold of himself. "You're dating already?"

She crossed her arms. "Are you telling me I can't?"

"No, no," Tom stuttered. "Of course not. I hope you take off your engagement ring there before your date."

"Oh, this," she said, admiring the modest carat reflecting her bedroom's yellow light. "I can't part with this *quite yet*."

"I'm not moving on. You're moving on!"

"It's a group of us, no big deal," she shrugged, watching his expressions carefully. "I'm going out with Wanda. She feels weird going out alone with that Blaine guy. I promised her I'd go hang out with them and one of his friends. It's no crazy hookup."

"William's Wanda?"

"Yeah," she said, humored. "What other Wanda do you know?"

"One of my brother's best friends is taking my girlfriend out on a *date*?" He couldn't believe this.

"Ex-girlfriend," Jamie said, scrunching her nose.

Her BlackBerry vibrated on the bathroom counter.

"This all sucks," he said, louder than necessary.

"Again, just being honest."

"Look. I'm gonna go. I just wanted someone to talk to. And you're always that person. Things going on at work—"

"Oh, that stuff with the quiet partners?"

"The silent partners," he said dryly. "Changes are coming. Speculation is wild through the office. Another distraction from my writing, the book . . . us."

She breathed. She was losing him. Had already lost him. "If I knew you truly wanted to be with me, Tom," she said, "then I'd be here for you. Through anything, until the end. If only you'd be there for me."

"I would," he said automatically. He didn't know how else to respond, a feeling that was becoming routine.

"I know that's the way you say it will be."

He headed for the bedroom door, allowing Jamie to open it for him. Jamie's mother fell into the room, her ear having been on the door.

"Mom," Jamie sighed.

"Hi, Miss Owens."

"Sorry," her mother said. "I'm not going to allow hanky-panky—"

Jamie was furious. "Out!"

Her mother disappeared.

"Tom," Jamie said, hugging him, "go after what makes you happy. I wish I was that person is all."

"I—"

She put her finger to his lips. "Do what you need to do. Sure, I hate you right now. But I'll be okay. Down the road, we can be friends . . . but not right now."

He tried to speak but couldn't. She walked him down the stairs and to the door, a long silence following them, both feeling worse as they descended. Jamie glared at her mother, who stood in the hallway observing them. After Jamie opened the door for him, Tom walked through it, stopped, and turned to her. She waved awkwardly, and he turned back. She watched him walk away, wondering why he tortured himself so much. Why he tortured *her* so much. The loss of him started to overwhelm her, and she welled up, imagining him with this other woman. She pulled back, not wanting to succumb to the release there and then, and shut the door.

"Would you like some tea, dear?" Jamie's mother asked.

"No, Mother! This is hard enough without you hovering."

"It's all for the best, though, child."

"Ugh." She ran up the stairs, and her mother watched her go.

A police car pulled up, its front wheels braking abruptly onto Jamie's driveway. Blue and red lights whirred like a disco ball. Homer's eyes popped open wide, and she darted, disappearing in a flash. The two policemen got out of their vehicle and looked around, confused. They thought they had seen someone.

"The car prowler was *right there*," the old man said, appearing by their side. "I saw it with my two darn eyes."

"Where'd he go?" the first policeman asked.

"I swear he went that way," the other one said.

"I think he went *that* way."

"You sure it was a *he*?"

"Bah! What do you know?" The old man walked back to his porch. "You boys are slower than my mother, and she can't even walk."

The second policeman said, "We'll search around."

"Looks like you've got this 'protect and serve' thing down," the old man muttered, and he walked up his porch steps.

The first policeman watched Tom closely, approaching the street. "Did you see what direction the suspect went, sir?"

Tom shook his head. "Nope."

"Are you blind?" the old man yelled at Tom. "The prowler was right in front of you!" The old woman watched her longtime husband's spit collect in the corner of his mouth. She couldn't remember the last time she'd seen him so worked up.

"Apparently, very," Tom said, surprised by the old man's outburst.

The policemen shrugged at each other and got back in their car, windows down. Tom sauntered to his car, puzzled by the goings-on.

"Have a good night," the first policeman said to Tom, who waved back nonchalantly and got into his car.

"To you too, sir!" the other policeman called to the old man.

"We'll keep our eyes out, sir!" the second one said.

"Bah!"

The policemen drove away, and the old woman watched her husband go back into the house.

"There's no hope for this world," the old man said.

Jamie picked up her BlackBerry and texted Wanda. *We're on. Make sure Blaine's friend is cute at least.*

She collapsed onto her bed, next to her packed travel bag. Her mother had told her once that she would have to kiss a lot of frogs before she found her prince. Perhaps that was true. Was she not good enough or pretty enough to deserve love? She quickly convinced herself she surely was pretty enough.

He had needed her—for what exactly, she wasn't sure—and she had sent him away. She couldn't believe she had done that. The thought that she might never see him again surged through her. She felt guilty for being unable to help Tom through his trials, but she stopped herself. *He* wasn't sure exactly what he was working through. You can lead a horse to water, but you shouldn't have to drown it. She couldn't help but now see Tom as weak, and she had never felt that way before tonight. If only Tom would allow himself to love her before he became commercially successful. Perhaps her more successful career had been more threatening to him than she had thought. If she had been pursuing her own dream of owning her own business instead of taking the secure income at Westfield Shaw, she'd surely be living more modestly. She looked around her master bedroom. It was almost as big as Tom's whole apartment. Her closet was full of more work clothes than she had ever imagined having. Her own voice, telling Tom she hated him, played in her head. She held her pillow and bawled as quietly as she could, wishing Tom's engagement ring pulled him back to her.

From one of the front windows, Jamie's mother watched Tom sitting in his car. "Goodbye, Tom," she said.

The warm rusty hue of the lamplight flickered dimly upon the street, gnats dancing under the soft buzz. In his car, Tom sat still, mystified by his own idiocy. He knew hearts could change, but his love for Jamie had not. Jamie was letting go of him, and he hated that he was allowing it.

All breakups needed purpose, so he believed. Other people—that is, the desire for other people—were often a catalyst that could jettison a relationship to oblivion. When they had first started dating, they had promised they'd be honest if someone else ever got between them. Jamie was emphatic about it, specifically threatening him Lorena-Bobbitt-style if he ever strayed.

He had catapulted Jamie out to single-hood and had practically forced her to go out with someone else, all on his own, without a clear motivation. *Brilliant.* There was no *It's not you, it's me.* No *I need some time to figure things out.* And, thankfully, no *I think it's time we see other people*, which Tom believed really meant, *I don't have the guts to break up with you, but I want to screw other people.* She had allowed him to break up with her without full closure and explanation. Then he realized that she had broken up with *him*.

A car's passing headlights swept across his face, reminding him that he was still in front of Jamie's house. With the revelation that he'd taken Jamie for granted, he felt alone for the first time. Her love was disappearing down the drain while he watched it vanish. He had become insecure about his lack of success and couldn't be close to her no matter how he tried. He needed to see Teri in person so he could move on with Jamie. If only Jamie could understand that.

He studied his hands, for what he could see in the dark of the car. So much he had accomplished with them. They had written celebrated columns that demanded magazine-cover teases, though many of them— once edited by *Western Mag* trolls—were some of the most ordinary, dull, and uninspired stories he had ever read. Hands that had opened—and closed—doors to his life. Doors that invited some and shut out others. He thought of the small whispers of scars that remained just a few inches up his forearms, unnoticeable to anyone else. Tom always tried to forget them. Forget how good they felt being cut. Cathartic emotional releases that he'd never told anyone about. Anyone.

Some lazy mornings, when early western sun filtered through the windows of his apartment, he looked up at the ceiling . . . his walls . . . and then his bare skin. He inspected the small traces of the incisions between the soft, even hairs on his arms that reflected the morning light. Cuts he had made with an old hunting knife.

His broken skin had healed well. The sharp, burning sting that had accompanied the peeled breaking of his skin somehow had made him feel better then. Grateful that he had learned to cope with the lonesomeness of that period of his life—when he and his older brother Gilbert were raising

William on their own—Tom still resented his parents for abandoning their three sons. Disposable like garbage.

How inadequate Tom had felt back then. He had struggled with focus while studying in high school, trying to raise a little brother while not yet a man himself, floundering in all of his relationships. He and Gilbert had been so distracted with school and work that the three brothers had spent little time together. There was little time or energy provided to William's maturation or even Tom's and Gilbert's outside friendships. To this day, Tom didn't have any friends—except for his work pal, Nadia—and he'd convinced himself this was his parents' fault. The solitude he still often felt around circles of people was odd, he knew, and something he didn't want to make worse by shutting himself down. He didn't want to again go down the lonesome road of self-infliction. He feared it and narrowly succeeded sweeping the rapture of the pain to the back of his head, not wanting to give in to its calling.

Through college and into his midthirties, he had sometimes come close to seeking out the physical pain that would release any inner despair. But not since he met Jamie. She had, in a way, saved him.

Taking life head-on required taking risks, which Tom had been adverse to before her. He hadn't felt confident enough in himself to try anything new and had lived in the same apartment for over twenty years now. Even when Gilbert had died, Tom had refused to move to a new apartment, took Gilbert's old bedroom, and William—eventually—got rid of the bunk bed. Tom had feared that memories he'd had of Gilbert in the place would fade, which, of course, they did. But then, he didn't want to lose the great deal on the rent.

Tom also had taken little initiative beyond creative columns at Western Mag Corp, his only job since graduating high school. With Jamie, he had realized a bigger dream, an aspiration to do something bigger than himself. Finishing his novel became that, and harming himself no longer provided him an escape from his loneliness. His work—the writing that Western Mag Corp didn't own—did. Jamie believed in him and all that he wanted to be, and he opened his life to more possibilities. Because of her, the pain continued to become a more distant desire. Out of feeling, out of mind. He had begun to feel like what he imagined normal people felt like: somewhat ambitious. Ironically, once she had convinced him to pitch the book for publication, he wasn't able to move forward with *her*. His feelings of inadequacy had snuck back tenfold.

There in the car, he hated that getting the rejection letters had escalated yearning of his youthful past with Teri, overshadowing Jamie's goodness. Jamie was good for him, and he knew it—but he couldn't help his forlorn thoughts of Teri. Why did he feel the need to see an ex that had broken up with him, her explaining at the time that he wouldn't be successful enough for her? He was sure he still wasn't. Somehow, his desire to prove himself as worthy to Teri hadn't escaped him. *What did he need to prove?* He wasn't able to move forward in any aspect, and he considered dropping this meeting with Teri altogether.

Opening his car door, he stalled. He stood there, imagining himself standing confidently at Jamie's door—until her mother opened it and denounced him for this or that. His heart was pumping without coherent words to explain why he would be standing before her and why she would even accept him back. Jamie wasn't a person he wished to shut out. She filled a void he didn't understand, and unless he walked back in quickly, it would be too late with her. Jamie's porch light went out, and his hopefulness sank.

Suddenly, William dashed past him, narrowly missing Tom's open car door. "Damn!" William shouted.

Wide eyed with surprise, Tom gaped at William running down the street with the punk kids from the other morning mere seconds behind him. William turned the corner, and Tom wondered how far he had been running. Their own apartment was back in the Valley, a considerable drive from here.

"I'm gonna kill you, punk!" Eight-Ball yelled, Carla and Skinny following behind him.

Skinny noticed Tom as he ran past him. "Hey, Ball, that's his brother, man!"

"I don't care! Move your ass!"

Tom quickly pondered his next action, unsure if he could run after these three hoodlums in his work clothes or if he should use his Corolla's speed instead, unsure of its aging zero-to-sixty performance. He glanced at Jamie's house, dark and oblivious to the commotion outside. Figuring it would be faster to run after them, he took a quick breath and ran.

What felt like ten minutes of running by various buildings and parked and moving cars was in truth only a matter of seconds. Tom came upon the three punks cornering William at the end of a new building complex, where the skeleton of a developing housing project was under way, its empty scaffolds and trestles haunting them from above. Bright security lights over the building starkly shined down upon them all on the dusty street below. A stiff breeze swept through the framework of the building, stirring sheets of clear plastic that hung over the bridges and planks, swaying and slapping with the wind.

Reaching the dead end, William turned around and saw the three punks coming at him. He stood tall as Eight-Ball, Skinny, and Carla slowed their approach, all breathing heavily. Skinny's hands held his knees, and he tried not to vomit.

"Boy, you're gonna pay for makin' us all run like that," Skinny said, pretty sure that hoodlums like themselves were supposed to be in good shape. He knew it was embarrassing.

Carla laughed, catching her own breath and smacking her gum.

Beads of sweat collected on Eight-Ball's forehead like condensation on a cold glass. He wanted to terrorize William. "You little bitch."

Seconds later, Tom appeared, his slapping shoes on the asphalt a startling announcement of his arrival.

William was relieved to see his brother, an unfamiliar sensation. "Tom, please don't scrap with these guys! You're a black belt!" he invented. "And a black belt's hands are lethal weapons, remember? You'll go to jail if you hurt any of 'em!" He eyed Tom hopefully.

Eight-Ball sized up his possibly formidable foe, but he wasn't concerned with martial-arts nonsense, considering Tom, too, was heaving and could barely stand vertical. Aware of their desolate surroundings, Tom tried to collect his wits. Intimidation with weapons wasn't a factor since there were no spare two-by-fours conveniently available.

"This ain't your business, holmes," Eight-Ball muttered to Tom, watching William intensely. He hated chasing anyone around town. Wasn't his style.

"Why are you all chasing him?" Tom asked. He couldn't believe he was going to rumble with these ridiculous troublemakers. He was too old for this.

"Somebody wants to be a hero," Skinny said, delighted.

"Bring on the show," Carla said, blowing a bubble and popping it. She spanked Eight-Ball on the butt. She hoped it would be Eight-Ball taking both of the brothers, not wanting to endure Skinny's inevitable shame if he got brave.

Eight-Ball shifted as Tom moved closer to William in the standoff. It was easier to watch both brothers if they stood near each other anyway.

The menacing, shaved-head gang member was staring William down like a cheetah on the hunt. "I'm gonna kill him," Eight-Ball said to Tom. "I'll jack you up too, if you want."

"Stay away from my brother," Tom said.

"Kill me?" William mocked Eight-Ball. "You don't have what it takes, man. My brother's going to *kick your ass!*"

Tom shook his head at his brother. "You're not helping." He couldn't believe that William wasn't scared of this thug. His own heart rate was through the roof, and he was having visions of their dead bodies being found by work crews in the morning.

Eight-Ball approached them and threatened William. "Keep your hands off my brother, you little runt. I'm not gonna tell you this again! You ain't turnin' him into a cupcake, punkass!"

"Ooohhhhhh." Skinny circled around them. He was carrying a short wood plank he'd found. Tom kept an eye on him, wishing he'd found the plank first.

Carla smiled and smacked, looking on. One brother was lame, and the other looked preppy. Eight-Ball could easily take them both.

"What are you doing over here?" Tom asked William from the corner of his mouth. "And what the hell did you do?"

"My buddy lives nearby. And don't worry, nothing illegal."

"How illegal could it be when street thugs are pissed?" Tom cracked.

"His brother and I are close. Eduardo here, that is, *Eight-Ball*, is bugged by it. This is inconvenient for me too, you know. I'm missing my Applebee's shift."

"Damn it, will you take this seriously?" Tom said. "We're going to get assaulted by kids while you're being an ass!" He'd never thought of how he was meant to die, but here in a cul-de-sac at the hands of a trio of adolescent thugs wasn't an option he would've ever come up with.

Eight-Ball steamed. "I'm gonna hang your little wee-wee so it never works again, *pinche wey*."

Carla chuckled.

William was fearless. "You're not touching my anything, so you better get that fantasy out of your head. My brother and I will take you all out!"

"Brave boy!" Skinny hit his palm rhythmically with the plank, waiting for Eight-Ball's go-ahead, ready for redemption by beating these guys to a pulp. He would take the older, reluctant brother. Carla laughed.

Tom tried to be calm and looked at his brother, feeling parental, as usual. "You're going to make it worse with these guys."

"And girl," Carla interjected.

Tom appealed to Eight-Ball. "Can't we talk this through?"

"Yeah, *vato*?" Eight-Ball suddenly punched William's face and knocked him to the ground. "I'm gonna kick his nuts so hard he won't need 'em anymore!" He stood over William, impatient for his sorry prey to get up.

"Hey." Tom put his palms up like a traffic cop. "We can figure this out, right?"

William struggled to his feet, and Skinny approached Tom with the wood plank. Tom flinched at him, and Skinny quickly retreated a couple of feet. Eight-Ball smiled devilishly, enjoying the ruckus, much like a Rottweiler might enjoy watching an injured cat writhe after the first maiming bite.

"I'm standing up for myself, Tom," William said, massaging his chin. He'd never been punched in the face before by anyone other than Tom, and that was when they were kids. What a wallop. "Which is what you've always taught me to do."

"I'm not through with you," Eight-Ball said.

"I didn't teach you to get us into street fights," Tom said, ignoring Eight-Ball's menacing grimace, which froze in stunned amazement that the brothers were ignoring him. "That was grade school, Will. We're not kids anymore!"

"Well, you keep treating me like one," William said, eyeballing Tom. Eight-Ball was perplexed, watching the brothers bicker back and forth.

"I don't treat you like a kid," Tom said. "Do I?" He considered how often he talked down to William, but he certainly deserved it.

"I know you don't mean to, Tom," William said solemnly. Then his attitude kicked in again. "It's not like you had a great role model for a father. You can't help being so damned judgmental."

Eight-Ball was seething. "Enough of this *Dr. Phil* show!"

Tom held his hand up to Eight-Ball again. "Wait a sec. Your name's Eight-Ball, right?" Tom asked. "Can I just get to the bottom of something here?"

"I'm not waiting for this psychotherapy session to end, man! This nasty-assed brother of yours keeps molesting my brother, and it's gotta stop!"

"Yeah, it's gotta stop!" Skinny howled.

Tom looked at William, shocked. "You're not—"

"Yes, I'm gay!" William yelled, unleashing embarrassment and relief. "There! Got what you wanted to know? I'm gay, Tom! Such a shocker." Eight-Ball watched the brothers, gritting his teeth, frustrated by his own hesitation. He wanted to knock this kid into oblivion, but he only fought prey that would fight back. It wasn't worthwhile any other way.

Tom stopped. He couldn't believe this. "What?"

"It's not molesting like you're thinking," William said. "His brother's older than I am. Still younger than you, though."

"You're gay? And this is how I find out?"

"Boy, you're slow," Carla muttered under her breath.

"Do you have to make this about you?" William demanded. "I knew you'd be disappointed. I didn't need that additional baggage to carry around or to hear your crap about it."

"Ball, you're right about him," said Carla. "The dude is jacked up."

"Is gonna be jacked up!" Skinny yelled, looking to Eight-Ball for approval, worrying about trying to hit Tom with the plank by himself.

Eight-Ball wiped a bead of sweat from his brow and approached William for the kill.

"Wait!" Tom yelled at Eight-Ball as loudly as he could, stalling the thug's trounce. "Will." Tom spoke directly to William. "Is that why you're into hot yoga?"

Eight-Ball was more perplexed than ever.

"It's called Bikram," William said. "And the answer's no. Tons of straight people do it."

Eight-Ball threw his hands down in frustration. He couldn't fight this way. Like all sharks, he loved wounded, flailing prey. This target wasn't defending himself or even running away.

"Whatcha waitin' for? This sucks," Carla said.

"Shut up," Eight-Ball said to her. He wasn't sure if he should pummel both of them quickly or just go home.

Carla stared at Eight-Ball in astonishment. No one talked to her that way.

Tom couldn't believe he'd never figured it all out. He quickly replayed various situations in his head—like the time he questioned William about the collection of Nair products in his bathroom, which William had defended using by saying they were a time saver so he wouldn't have to shave his face every day.

And when he caught William watching a DVD called *Princes and Princesses* that William insisted he had thought was an instructional video on romantic courting, complete with fantastic picnic locations and exciting wardrobe ideas.

And how he never put it together after discovering that William was a fan of Margaret Cho.

Straight-faced as he could muster, Tom was as direct as he could be. "If anything, I would've been more patient with your constant replaying of all those George Michael and ABBA songs."

"Hey!" Eight-Ball yelled. "Shut the hell up!" This was humiliating.

"You shut up," Carla finally quipped to Eight-Ball, who glared back at her in surprise. "Yeah, that's right. I said it."

"Leave me alone, *chica*," Eight-Ball said. "I got a handle on this little punk."

"I ain't little," William said, too proudly in Tom's estimation. "Trust me, your brother would know."

"That's it!" Eight-Ball jumped toward William again. Skinny was immediately behind him, ready to throw wild swings with his plank, when suddenly, a loud female voice boomed.

"*Stop!*" the voice said with such power that several windows of the incomplete building exploded. For a couple of blocks around, dogs barked and inquisitive neighbors came out of their homes to watch the commotion, only to see nothing.

In the cul-de-sac, everyone froze. Homer approached them authoritatively. She stood in front of Tom and William and pushed away Eight-Ball and Skinny, more with her presence than her arms. "You boys get back now."

Tom and William both waited in silence. The street punks backed off, their bodies trying to keep up with their legs. Eight-Ball, Skinny, and Carla felt like they were in a trance for a moment but quickly woke themselves out of it, Skinny last.

"Not you again," Skinny sighed.

"Hey, wuss!" Eight-Ball knew he should have kicked the hell out of William on the ground while he had the chance. "Why you gotta hide behind the ol' lady?"

"Old, yes. Wiser, still," Homer mused.

Skinny jumped up and down. "Cuz they're both scared little pansies!"

"Who you calling pansy?" Tom said, not believing he asked after he said it. He was no hero.

Eight-Ball raised his eyebrows. "What'd you say, punk?" The guts of these two. So far, they'd gotten off easy. "I'll knock your teeth so far down your throat you'll be cryin' for Mommy like your little sister here!"

"Go for it! *Right now!*" Tom yelled at the top of his lungs, his throat going hoarse.

William wondered what the hell Tom was doing.

"Come on, Eight-Ball!" Tom popped off, stepping in front of Homer. He knew that he was losing it, but he allowed himself to let it all go. His frustrations were being released, right here, right now. "You talk all bad, but I bet you ain't nothin'! Your cue-ball, Mr.-Clean head and your loser sidekicks in diapers. Let's see what you got! And what's the girl gonna do? She Barb Wire or somethin'?"

"Without the implants!" William hollered, thrilled to see his brother lose his mind.

Carla inspected her chest.

Homer stood firmly in front of Eight-Ball and waved her arm across the sky. Eight-Ball ignored her and tried to jump at William, but his body wouldn't let him—like he was stuck in quicksand. Homer admired her work.

"Who's Barb Wire?" Carla asked.

Waiting for Eight-Ball to rush him, Tom thought he had intimidated the punk, who was motionless in front of him. He got bold. "Eight-Ball! Let's get this over with!"

Homer was bemused by Tom's belief that his dopey taunts had worked.

Eight-Ball struggled. "I'm stuck! I can't move my legs!"

"She's a witch," Skinny pointed. "Witchcraft!"

Tom couldn't believe Eight-Ball would be faking this. He held his fists up. "C'mon!"

"I can tolerate you boys calling me old," Homer said, not letting the reference to her age go, "but I'm not a witch, young man. Curse you!" She wasn't going to be mistreated by humans again. Closing her eyes, she opened them to see Skinny's striped shorts swiftly fall down his knees. Colorful devils and ghosts painted his underwear. Then they dropped to his ankles.

Skinny freaked and covered up, dropping his wooden plank. "Oh my God!"

Carla laughed.

William didn't blink. "Oh my *God*."

"What I've got is *experience*," Homer yawned. "Yeah, you should be threatened by that. Both pious followers of God and pagans alike throughout all of history have been."

"What?" Eight-Ball asked, befuddled and angry. His discomfort grew by the second with his inability to move. He struggled, but nothing.

"Someone's scared," Tom said, putting his fists down. "Hope I didn't make you pee your pants."

"Shoo," Homer said, waving her hands away at the punks. By now, she was a bit annoyed that Tom thought himself the hero of this scuffle, though she did wish she had thought of releasing the ruffian leader's urinary tract. That would have been amusing. "Shoo! Go home and play."

Eight-Ball regained control over his legs and started backing away, stiff and disoriented. He pointed at Homer and the brothers. "We're not finished! We're not done with you, man!" Skinny and Carla followed his lead, Skinny holding his pants up.

"I'm not a man," Homer said, "thank you very much."

"This sucks!" Skinny was upset at another confrontation ending without victory. Carla shook her head, asking herself why she was hanging out with the two weakest intimidators on the planet.

"Watch yourself!" Eight-Ball hollered at the brothers, now twenty yards away. "Both of you are on my list."

"Maybe you're on *my* list!" Tom yelled back. He and William watched in disbelief as the thugs retreated.

Homer turned to Tom. "Shut up, Thomas. Calm down, and quit acting like a numbskull." Her patience with human beings was exhausted, and *this one* was already driving her crazy with his ill-mannered outbursts. She shook her head, muttering, "Contemptible humans abound. Maybe God should just kill them all. Worthless."

Hearing her, Tom couldn't believe what she was saying. *Apparently she doesn't count herself among those who should be struck down.* He finally realized that she was the same homeless woman he had seen on the steps of his apartment. *Why is this crazy woman following me?* An odd coincidence, perhaps. He could hear Jamie in his head too, saying *Don't always make it about you.*

Skinny yelled back to them. "They don't call him Eight-Ball for nothin'!"

"Shut up," Eight-Ball said.

The brothers watched Carla punch Eight-Ball in the arm; then the three punks disappeared around the corner.

Being upstaged by the punks—and that's what they were—was no good, Homer decided. She'd had enough of this sneaking around too, following Tom around town while God nagged her. This whole assignment was asinine, really. Could God have plunked her down into any more of a dysfunctional situation? This senseless man clearly had relationship woes, a sibling rivalry of sorts, some kind of work problems, and—from what she could gather from his mood—comical disdain for mischievous punks, which was the one attribute she related to. But she was not going to give up. She spoke to him like a teacher would to a rambunctious student. "Thomas."

He turned to Homer to see her appealing to him with her hands open, a sign of peace, so he guessed. He wondered why she'd even gotten involved. "It was unnecessary to get in the middle of our scuffle."

"I'm blown away by her Jedi mind tricks," William added.

"You're such a pain." Tom sat down on the curb. His dress shoes weren't made for running. A blister or two was beginning to form, he was sure of it.

"Thomas," she said again.

He was somehow certain that this woman was about to blame him for this absurd skirmish with *kids*. He'd had a bad day already, and a homeless stalker wasn't going to talk down to him too. "I didn't do anything wrong!"

Homer sat down next to Tom. "You must calm down, my boy."

"I am calm!"

She was amused. "Are you now?"

Tom took off one of his socks.

"Being mad is totally unproductive," William said. He kicked a rock on the street. "Fun to watch, though."

After inspecting both of his blisters, Tom carefully put his sock back on. "I'm on edge. Who wouldn't be, considering the ridiculous circumstances?" He scowled at his brother. "You make everything complicated. Everything! Always a problem!"

"You need to get over yourself," William said. "My problems have nothing to do with you."

"They do now!"

Homer raised her voice. She'd wasted enough time. "Boys."

"I want you to know, miss," Tom said, "I really appreciate you helping my brother here not get his ass kicked."

"And helping *my* brother not get *his* ass kicked," William said, ungrateful.

"Whatever."

"They wouldn't have taken me down," William offered.

"That's great, Will. Now *shut up*! I'm sick of your crap!" Tom yelled. Homer was amazed at how loud this one particular mortal could get. "The lying, the laziness! Sick of it, man! Such a pain in my ass! Everything's a freakin' battle!"

He winced while putting his shoe back on. What a night. After getting officially dumped by Jamie and chasing a minigang around town, the last thing he could deal with was his brother pretending he could kick *anyone's* ass. Then there were the blisters.

"Most battles are won by facing the aggressor's confrontation," Homer said soberly, looking to the distance.

Tom was unsure how to respond.

"And lost probably," William sighed.

"No, William," Homer said. "Most losses are a result of individual weakness. Giving up on the possibility of triumph."

"You're joking, right?" William asked.

"I don't kid."

"Well," Tom said, standing up and testing the pressure on his blisters, "I appreciate the philosophy lesson, Aristotle."

His sarcasm jolted Homer. He couldn't talk to her like that. *The humanity! How dare he.*

Tom bounced off his sore foot. "But confronting punks at night in a cul-de-sac is what we were doing. In case you were lost in the land of theory, I was standing up for myself and my newly out-of-the-closet brother! No weakness here. I didn't want to have to scrape him off one of these two-by-fours in the morning because I didn't do anything to help."

"Hoodlums." William took in the developing building around them, squinting at the bright security lights.

Homer narrowed her eyes at Tom, yet another human being she had little faith in. "You're misunderstanding me. A confrontation must be faced from the beginning. It's unfortunate that the bigger battle isn't finished," she said, more to herself than the brothers.

"What are you saying, woman?" Tom was frustrated. "We should have fought these idiots before I met them? What's wrong with you?"

"We don't even know who you are," William said.

"Sometimes we see the error of our ways through other people's actions," Homer said. "And we forge a path of our own to correct what we can while here on Earth. Before this stupid species ruins it to spite themselves."

"What are you talking about?" Tom asked. He paused, trying not to allow this homeless woman to get him any more riled up.

"Can I go now?" William asked. He had no place to be but wanted to be anywhere else.

"I can't believe you're asking me for permission for anything," Tom quipped.

"Thomas. William. You boys have plenty to discuss." She eyed Tom up and down. He was to publish something that was going to save humanity? *Impossible.* Nonetheless, if this was her task, she had to move things along. Time was wasting away while the brothers quibbled. "I can see by how you're dressed that you've got a lot of work to do. Probably got some project you need to get done or something."

"I'll say," Tom said, nodding at William. "Let's go." Exhaustion weighed hard on him. "You okay?" he asked Homer. "Need a ride or anything?" He hoped she'd say no.

"Nah, I got these splendid walking shoes." She was wearing old, torn-up moccasins that looked like they'd been worn for twenty years.

"You sure?"

"I'll be seeing you soon, Thomas."

The brothers walked up the street, leaving her standing alone in the desolate cul-de-sac, the security lights shining down upon her like God's interrogation from above. She hated that He watched her every move, adequate or not. As if He needed lights at all.

Tom turned back to Homer, realizing something. "Hey, how'd you know our names?"

She shrugged and knocked her head. "Using my noggin."

William smiled, and Tom shook his head. They continued up the block silently, both thinking through the action-packed events of the night.

Everything was different now, William believed. He hadn't felt it necessary to declare his sexuality to anyone, including and particularly his brother. But maybe this had been the best way for Tom to find out. At least now, the truth was out.

Tom was tired. The last couple of days had been full of battles. Life had a way of parlaying drama on top of drama. Today, a drama sandwich. He walked with a limp, careful of the pressure on his sensitive foot, not wanting to pop a blister. "I can't believe you," he said finally as they approached his car. The outdoor lights of Jamie's house were still dark. Closed for business. The cop car drove by them slowly, the cops inspecting them but continuing along.

William was amused. "Oh, now the cops are here."

Unable to care less, Tom opened his car's door. "You've been going on dates with girls!"

"I also watch football and collect *Star Wars* figures," William said.

"Get in the car."

"I couldn't turn myself straight," William said, opening the passenger door.

"No wonder you wanted to see *Mamma Mia*."

"I know You're listening," Homer said softly, the boys too far away now to hear her or see her. She didn't need them watching her talking to herself.

"Oh, come on, Homer," God said. "I didn't even understand what you meant with that 'forging a path of our own to correct what we can while here on Earth' stuff."

"What am I supposed to do? Put Yourself in my shoes—these sucky, tired-ass shoes, and You can talk."

"You're upset about something."

"How am I supposed to even do this? Get a book published? Sir, the boy's got demons!" She sat on the curb. "Why do Your absurd creations make so much trouble? Your people down here are loud and nasty. Their perversions grate my whole being. Honestly, I'm confused by the objectives of their creation in the first place. I question Your entire worldview."

God was incensed. "You're not supposed to interfere with free will, Homer. You got in the middle of that squabble, in a physical conflict."

Homer gasped. She hadn't predicted He'd be so sore with her. "But—"

"Free will," God repeated.

A loud boom filled her head, and she covered her ears, feeling her eardrums ring. "Okay!" she bellowed. "You're not making this easy on me! I've got to do *this*, but I can't do *that*. I don't know where to start!"

"My orders were clear, Homer. Do you not understand that without choice, there would be no humanity? This is why free will is so important to preserve."

She thought of how He had abandoned her during the First Crusade and how she would have loved for Him to intrude back then, saving her from the humiliation of two beatings by thieves, among other atrocities. Her watch read: *Five-and-a-half Days Left*. She was depressed. The prospect of finishing off her existence in solitude was sinking in as a real possibility. These humans were idiots. "Tomorrow," she said. "I'll make something happen tomorrow."

"I hope so, Homer. You need to quit abusing your unearthly powers, Homer. It's important that you succeed in your task, but I expect you to use your head. As it is, I'm getting impatient."

Dramatic pronouncements weren't going to deter her. "Heavens, no!"

* * *

Squeezing into her cardboard hut, Homer pondered a solution to her predicament. She needed better preparation if she was to succeed. She lay down on her stomach with her writing tablet in front of her and gazed out of her box, briefly distracted by her disgust with the lazy architecture of the tract homes that surrounded her, recounting various periods of building design that had offended her in the past. The Mayans' crude mud-and-thatch construction. The Egyptians' pretentious, over-the-top pyramids. But nothing had been more unimaginative or spiritless than these adobe-plastered, uniform dwellings.

The full moon's light fell upon the pages of her writing tablet, and she reflected upon what was—in her mind—a purposeless day. After almost a full hour of biting the top of her pen and then her nails, she started to compose.

Day 2, Western Night, Evening.
This is going to be even more difficult than I had thought. Two days into this is all it has taken for me to become frustrated by the challenging deficiencies of the ineffectual criminals, oxygen-hogging nonessentials, and Thomas, the—sadly—pitiful luminary here on Earth.
A couple of weak links in particular—who've shaved their heads in apparent rebellion to the species' status quo—were of the oddest sort. Two encounters with these mortals and their temperamental female sidekick illustrated that the dissatisfaction and frustration of the younger generation with older authority, which date back to Cain and Abel, still live today. (Unlike those two descendants of Eve and Adam, however,

I hope there are no murders or future sacrifices coming from these riffraff. Unfortunately, these young people aren't likely to evolve for the better.) I could have been forced to wield more of my spine-chilling abilities, encasing their fragile mortal forms in prolonged punishment and thrusting their minds into phantasmagorias of horror, sending their ignorant gray matter into orbit with wild dreams that God would save them! This would have undoubtedly led to another ludicrous reprimand from Him.

Her venting on the page was cathartic but discouraging. "This is woeful dribble," she said aloud to herself, knowing she should be focused on the task at hand. The grand intrusion of intrusions disrupted her concentration.

"Dribble it is, Homer," God said.

"May I have some privacy, please!" Homer screamed, trying not to lose her train of thought. Her wordy paragraphs were her business, and she didn't care for His opinions about them. "I'm busy working on a particularly succinct passage."

A dog barked up the street.

"Why is it My presence disturbs you, My friend?"

She dropped her head to her tablet. There was nothing to gain by sugarcoating it. "Do You have any other guidance to offer me, sir, or are You trying to get my hives to act up again? It's inconceivable, now that I think of it, that You would provide me a human vessel that is continually susceptible to such uncomfortable blight."

"I'm here to help."

"You are not! You clearly want to divert my attention away from solving the unfortunate conundrum that is the ominous future of humankind by barging in on me!" She banged her head with her tablet; she was so frustrated. "Leave me alone!"

He was silent. Or He was gone, she figured. *That's all it took?*

After taking a breath, she shut Him out of her mind and returned to her journal.

My disdain for humankind has escalated, as predicted. Their modes of transportation are crude wrecking machines that—despite their grating, unrefined noises—were no match for your humble correspondent. Upon impact, these swift machines are like clay. (I would destroy all of them myself during this mission, if it weren't for my downright fear of perpetual desolation for the rest of my existence. God forbid, as literally as I write it.)

Chronic fatigue is setting in after just two days on this non-Godforsaken planet. More wretched sores are developing under these worn garments that aren't suited for the least discriminating humans, and my itching will undoubtedly get worse. I must be allergic! But it is what He has in store for humanity that scares me. Despite humans' utilization of off-putting street jargon and the inclinations of some to partake in violent altercations, the death of humankind is an awful extreme for penance. Though the Almighty One chose not to put me in the middle of murderous warfare (should I say, I'm grateful), I observe bloodshed of another magnitude taking place. Humanity is dying within itself.

Free will, I discovered through admonishment, is not negotiable. I don't understand the strict adherence to rules indoctrinated by the Rule Maker, but I predict it will be a frustrating process to work within such ludicrous parameters to acquire His "desired result," which very well may be a ruse. Upon simple reflection, it is He who gave them the power to destroy themselves in the first place.

As I rest tonight in anticipation of the dawn, the Almighty Omniscient (and Omnipresent One) will be watching as He enjoys the drama within His proscenium. Why He sent me down here is now clear: He felt I, of all angels, was most competent in matters like failing. God will destroy the Earth. It is inevitable, but He will satisfy Himself with the falsehood that He tried to prevent it and that I was the perfect candidate for this doomed assignment. He believes I'm the perfect angel to fail? Damn Him!

Even though she couldn't hear Him, Homer was certain that God was watching her, reading her journal, in effect. She was, admittedly, a bit fearful of His reaction to her cursing Him, but she *wanted* Him to see her rage.

She imagined different tactics to save the humans. There were particular details of her plan she couldn't write down because she had no plan. If God had a plan for her to fail, she wasn't going to go down easy.

* * *

The cool San Francisco rain pattered relentlessly on the windowpanes while Teri packed her bag in awkward silence. It was late. Luigi sat in bed propped up against the headboard, pretending to read a review on his laptop about the differences between luxury coupes. He was unable to determine which two-door was less embarrassing to drive than the other. No matter how fast they were, they still weren't trucks. Back in Jersey, that was all he had driven. But he had a new West Coast life—three years now. Though he hadn't graduated to four-door sedans yet, he had—as Teri had put it—"grown up."

What he changed to be with her . . . to be accepted by her . . . now made his stomach churn more than normal. He strained to contain his unpleasant bloating, sure that any release of his valve would result in an unpleasant reek and her disdain for its source. He had spent plenty of time on the toilet earlier, to no avail. He was constipated. The trapped air was extremely uncomfortable, but he didn't want to miss any details of his wife's packing, while he pretended to be oblivious. Meanwhile, the pressure built within the walls of his stomach, and he felt it heave, feeling for a moment that—with a little helium—he could indeed float over the bed.

His heart beat loudly against his chest. Teri was leaving him—for a day—to see the ex who had never escaped her consciousness. He imagined them kissing, Teri's head rolling back in ecstasy. Compounding the aggravation of his constipation, his stomach growled from hunger pangs brought on by a—surely—misdirected, guilt-driven diet. Again, for her.

He felt confined air trying to escape and hoped that a slow release of it would be camouflaged—the sound at least—by the timely thunder outside. He gambled and lost.

"Ewwwwwwwwwwwwwww." Teri disappeared into her magnificent walk-in closet, which used to be theirs. She had taken over the whole thing.

Luigi hated himself.

"I swear," she said. Self-conscious packing with him in the room, Teri took advantage of her time out of Luigi's line of sight. She preferred to conceal what she was bringing. Tom, without question, would think she looked good. This aroused her as she tucked her favorite revealing pieces into her carry-on, which was open on her closet floor.

"The Infiniti is cheaper," Luigi said, knowing he'd never buy it, especially since his buddies would bust on him and never let it go. Still, he was attempting to initiate any conversation possible with his wife, who was disinterested in all things Luigi. It had gotten worse the last few months. The last year.

"That's nice," Teri said. Unable to decide which bra to bring, she threw three into her suitcase, despite the fact that she was only traveling for a day.

"Yeah," Luigi said. "It's very nice."

She pondered over one of her closet drawers. "Yeah, it is. Fuhgetaboutit!"

He hated it when she made fun of his Jersey roots. "I ain't *fuhgettin'* about which sports car I'm gonna get."

Teri found some sexy boy shorts and threw them into the suitcase. They had a large red heart on the back of them. "Go ahead. Looks like we aren't having a baby. No need for a practical car."

They had tried to find a solution to Luigi's low sperm count over the past year. Or, as Luigi put it, he wanted her to stop bitching. They had gone to a fertility clinic so his seed could be better situated so as to best fertilize her eggs. Having sat in the waiting room for hour upon fruitless hour, on various days over many months, Luigi had resigned himself to reading *Redbook* magazine. Apparently, there was little need in the waiting room for men's reading material. He was stuck breezing through articles on weight loss—which he was already nagged about—"What Men Really Think of Women," and worse, a recipe for wheat lasagna. All for nothing. Teri wasn't pregnant, and Luigi was still hooked on good ol' white pasta, with as little nutritional value as possible.

"That's right, doll." He immediately regretted saying it. *SportsCenter* started in seven minutes. This could take a while.

"Doll? You know I hate it when you call me that." Teri contemplated bringing her boots. They looked good with jeans, but she didn't want to try too hard.

"Yeah, toots. I do." He adjusted himself on the bed. "Does he know you're even coming?"

The jealous Italian was exhausting her. She reappeared, leaning against the wall and crossing her arms. He had to be longing for her, seeing her in her skimpy underwear. She relished it. "It's just one day."

"You're packing for a lot more than one day! A lot can happen in *one day*." He couldn't believe she was trying to tease him, standing there in panties and nothing else. It was almost working.

"You can sure as hell eat a lot in one day."

Luigi was astounded. He was crash dieting, which meant barely eating and taking diet pills that made him queasy. He was miserable pretending those pills actually suppressed hunger like they were supposed to. Though Teri was stuck with his thinning crown, maybe he could drop a few pant sizes if he missed some meals. He didn't want to have to start exercising, for God's sake. Teri hadn't even noticed his day-old thinner physique, though he was bloated. He released again.

"I've got to get out of here, Luigi," she said, deciding on heels, which would lift her butt just right. She went back to the closet and put them by her suitcase for the morning. "A little space would be good for both of us. Show you what it's like when I'm not around."

"Teri, if you wanna play a disappearing act, why don't you just go to a coffee klatch or something? Stay local. Like you're seeing this Tom guy for the benefit of our marriage. Right."

"I'm gone for one day. Then I'll be back, and we can return to our old, boring routine."

"Do what you'll do. I don't care."

"Oh, I'll do what I'll do, all right." To think she could have finished school and made something of her life. Things would've been so different. She was proud of herself for taking this step to see Tom. For once, she had found the courage to move outside her comfort zone. Risk was something she had always avoided, and she knew it would be dangerous seeing Tom again. He had asked to see her likely for the same reason she wanted to see him. They'd never let go of each other, all of this time.

She reappeared in the bedroom and watched Luigi pull some lint from between his toes and throw it to her side of the bed. "You're an idiot," she said.

"That all ya got, buttacup?"

Luigi was making it easier for her to make the trip without guilt. "You seen my brown belt?" she asked.

"Yeah, try the hall closet. Maybe you'll accidentally lock yourself in there."

He realized he had spoken without thinking. Teri walked out with her long stride, and Luigi watched the legs and butt that he swore were, indeed, getting smaller. He swallowed in nervousness while he waited.

She reappeared holding three porno mags. "What's this?" she asked, already knowing the answer.

"What's what?"

"Luigi, I can't believe you." She was exasperated. "You've been masturbating in the closet?"

"Um, I—" he stuttered, searching for something coherent. He had been in a hurry a couple of weeks before when Teri had come home from the store, and he had hidden the magazines under shoes. He'd meant to stash them somewhere less obvious.

"Damn, my purses are in there!" She wanted to get away like people did in the Southwest Airline commercials.

He belched, providing gaseous relief and surprising himself, considering he had not eaten much at all that day. She threw his porn magazines on the floor and glared at him in disdain before stomping into the closet.

"Don't push me, Luigi. Or I won't come back at all."

Luigi sighed, scrolling his mouse on the laptop and pretending it was necessary. Why hadn't he just used Internet porn?

She yelled at him from the closet. "And will you stop making that noise?"

"I was just breathing!" He needed to change something, or this was going to get worse. "Touchy."

"That's right!" She picked through her drawer. There was a pair of particular sexy panties she'd wear for Tom tomorrow. "I'm going to the kitchen," she said, reappearing now in her sleep sweats. "Want anything?"

If she was trying to reach out to him halfway, it wasn't working. "Water, please," he said.

"Quit pouting," she said, leaving the room.

"I'm not pouting. I'm pissed off." He knew he was pouting, but he didn't care. "No ice!"

* * *

Tom tried to find free parking around Staples Center in Los Angeles. It was the first day of the three-day conference, and cars quickly maneuvered into three-point parking spaces with nervous energy. This morning, Tom's focus was on getting representation and proving Maroquin wrong while trying to forget the happenings of the previous night. It was emotionally draining.

He sat at a light. A crowd of important-looking people carried attaché cases, notebooks, and banners toward the convention center, a huge network arena. One young guy was so sharply dressed, wearing an expensive designer suit, that the dapper lad must have been an agent. Tom decided that no self-respecting writer would dress that well.

The men and women looked more like executives than writers, making him question whether there'd be more agents and publishers than writers at this conference or if he was even in the right place. Though he briefly considered this a plus—there being less competition looking for agency or publishing representation—he was intimidated, and he hadn't even parked yet.

Driving around the congested blocks searching for a spot made him ponder the grief-to-dollar ratio of paying for parking in the arena's lot—patronizing the criminals running what surely had to be a felonious operation versus walking several blocks on his blistered foot to the conference. Reluctantly, he drove toward the main lot to pay the twenty-dollar ransom.

Tom waited impatiently at an intersection for all the bright-eyed and aspiring professionals, young and old, walking at speeds in a spectrum that varied from *Why am I here?* to *I'm so damn late.* He searched their faces to try to determine the level of fear, anxiety, and—in the case of one particular fellow in Dockers—vacancy.

After parking, he traveled with a flock on the crosswalk toward the formidable building and a lonesome table with a posted sign that read Vendor Services. A bored young woman behind it kept herself awake by reading a celebrity gossip magazine he didn't recognize. "Hi. How can I get inside?" he asked. "I tried to order tickets online but couldn't."

The young woman's tired eyes looked like they were going to roll into the back of her head. It was clear she found the latest stories of the paparazzi's favorite glam gals and hunks more interesting than the anonymous herds swarming into the building . . . and now this clueless loser. "We're almost sold out. It's late to register. How many of you are there?"

"Just me," he said. A pack of serious, well-dressed people briskly passed him, the women dressed in sharp skirts and slacks and the men in sports jackets, a number of them in dark-rimmed glasses. Nervous, Tom couldn't stop himself from speaking. "Been busy working, forgot about this thing."

"There's a lot involved, but I'll see what I can do," the woman behind the table said. She smiled gratuitously, punching the keyboard of her laptop.

"I want to see if someone will read my stuff." He did a double take on the sign at the table again. "Oh, I'm not a vendor," he said quickly. "Just general admission."

"We're sold out of entry tickets, sir. There're no more available."

He pulled out his business card and spoke to her like he was about to ask a favor that he didn't want anyone else to hear, like someone trying to score a table at a busy restaurant. "I'm a *Western Mag* columnist. Can I get in as a representative of one of our greatest local magazines?" It pained him to speak so well of the company that ran its operation so poorly. He hoped it didn't show.

The woman inspected his card. The intoxication of celebrity smut had been postponed because of this buffoon. "Tom Summers. Columnist."

"Yep," he smiled. "Building my platform."

"Wait, Tom Summers?" She looked at her clipboard.

"That's me," he said. "You ever read any of my stuff? If you read last month's article, 'The Truth About America's Processed Food Supply,' that's me." He wasn't used to being recognized.

"I'm sorry, sir. I can't admit you into the convention center under any circumstance." She got on her walkie-talkie. "Security. You're needed at the main entrance."

Tom was shocked. "What do you mean you can't admit me?" His mind raced. "I didn't even register! How can I be unadmittable?" He knew it wasn't a word but didn't care.

"Your name is on a list, Mr. Summers," the woman said, now wide eyed and alert. "A list that you don't want to be on. A newly generated list that few people know about. A list that, unfortunately, forbids you from entering the conference."

"What?" He wanted to jump over the table.

"You will now be escorted off the property."

Two sorry excuses for security guards came up from behind him.

"Wait a second!" Tom yelled as one of the security guards grabbed his arm. "There's no such thing!"

She was visibly threatened by him now. "You need to step back. You should be ashamed, sir."

"Sir," the heftier one huffed, and Tom glared at the woman in awe.

"I do what my clipboard says," the woman said.

"Your clipboard's broken!" Tom hollered.

"You need to leave with us now, sir," the heftier security guard said, struggling to hold on to Tom's billowing arm.

Tom briefly considered the training that went into the delivery and brevity of that statement. "This is Orwellian, don't you think?" He broke free from the security guard's grip and swiftly approached the table again, confused and humiliated. He tried, ineffectually, not to appear threatening or angry. "Or it's purely a bald-faced lie! Can you tell me how I got on this supposed list?"

"Sir," the woman behind the table said before asking for more security forces on her walkie-talkie.

"Sir," the heftier security guard said, self-conscious of his bare dome, "I believe you meant *bold*-faced lie." He smiled patronizingly and grabbed Tom's arm again, the lesser guard watching on, clearly the apprentice.

"No, I meant *bald*-faced lie, you ignorant mongoloid!" Tom swung his arm, stepped backward, and broke free from the guard's grip with strength that existed only from adrenaline. "It originated centuries ago to describe men so good at lying they didn't need to wear facial hair as a mask." He couldn't believe he had bothered to explain that. Jamie had always hated him correcting her, and now he was giving etymology lessons to meatballs in uniform. How low he had sunk.

Deciding to step up and show off his new authority, the apprentice guard grabbed for Tom, his clumsy grasp resulting in him losing his balance. The guard fell toward the vendor table, hitting his head against the top. "Owwwwwwww."

The bigger guard advanced toward Tom, shifting his weight from one hip to another, sauntering on elephantine legs. His grin showed a mouth stuffed with too many teeth. "Not good, mister."

Inspecting the guard's overstretched belts and puffed-out regalia, Tom backed up from him and said, "I didn't mean to disturb you from breakfast. But who would be able to blacklist me from this event? And why?" He had a fleeting thought of Maroquin but discounted it. *No way.* He moved backward at an accelerated pace to avoid the brutish figure drawing toward him. Tom turned to the vendor woman—who was visibly unnerved—and pleaded, "If you have a boss I can talk to, I'm sure I can clear all of this up. I'm a professional writer, for God's sake!"

"That's enough," the hefty security guard said, lumbering at him with steady confidence. He salivated at the opportunity to take this unruly troublemaker down himself.

Two more security guards suddenly arrived, and Tom decided to retreat. "Okay, okay," he said. "No need to call in for backup. Seriously, I'm not worth a siege by a gaggle of rent-a-cops."

The apprentice was shaken up but wobbled to his feet. The other guards smiled at one another—victorious in the expulsion of trouble—except for the big one, who was disappointed that the need to physically remove the terrorist with bodily force had been averted.

It was undeniable that he encountered resistance at every angle in everything, so Tom was forced to consider the possibility that he was his own biggest enemy. He was making his own choices, but they were clearly bad ones.

Rounding the corner outside the conference arena, he ran into Homer holding two hot dogs from a stand nearby. Globs of catsup, mustard, relish, and onions were stacked on both of them, remnants of each on her chin after just one bite.

"God, you're everywhere," Tom said.

"Funny how it is, Thomas," Homer deadpanned. She found the fusion of condiment flavors and odd meat invigorating.

Tom stopped. "I never learned your name."

"God Damn is fine," she said absently, using her sleeve to wipe the catsup running down her chin. "Call me that." She licked mustard and onions off one of her fingers and dropped a hot dog onto the pavement. *Ugh.* Reluctantly, she let the tubular meat roll down the pavement so to put her attention on Tom before he was gone again.

A rumble started to increase in volume, Tom and passersby never hearing it.

She laughed nervously. "Just kidding." The rumbling subsided. "Homer. Call me Homer." Although she knew better than to kid about taking God's name in vain, she wasn't sure if those Ten Commandments—pesky to so many humans—applied to angels. She never had asked God about that. Safeguarding her lone hot dog, Homer outstretched her freshly licked hand to Tom.

"Nice to meet you," he winced, deciding not to shake her hand. "Everywhere."

She shrugged and took another sloppy bite.

"So you know where I am all the time," he said. "Are you following me? Searching through my garbage too?" He wasn't sure what to do about this stalker.

"Ah, interesting story. Though I just stole these hot dogs from an unsuspecting vendor, so if you see some vengeful security guards seeking payment, let me know. Want to sit down with me? I'll give you half. It's so hard for me to eat these things standing up. Amazing what you do with food these days," she said, gesturing toward a bus bench a few yards away.

He started to follow her and realized, "I can't." He read the time on his phone. "I was hoping to get in front of some agents or publishers today, but since they won't let me in the building, I'd better get to the office."

She sat on the bench. "So you're a writer," she said, playing it up as a revelation. This was her chance to try to get through to him. "I've always wanted to write."

"Yeah?" Tom asked, uninterested.

She eyed him carefully. Bored mortals had the worst attention spans. "Enough about me. Any criticisms on your work yet?" She took a huge bite of her hot dog, her round cheeks ballooning with moisture-resistant bread.

"Not any worthwhile ones," he said, unsure how to read her. This wasn't your average homeless woman, though he didn't know any other homeless women to compare her against.

"Maybe you should change something in it. Anything you can improve on? Do what you need to do to get your work read. Don't waste any time!"

Was he in *The Twilight Zone*? "I've got to go." He wasn't changing anything, especially at this weird woman's prodding. "Enjoy your lunch."

"My prayers are for you," she called to him. He walked away and didn't look back. "Damn it, Homer," she mumbled to herself. "This is the one we're counting on to save the world?"

Tom headed for his car, considering how to get his work read by the right people. That batty homeless woman was right. He needed to get everyone's attention somehow, despite what obstacles came at him and from wherever they came.

An older couple came upon Homer and looked down at her on the bench. "Are you waiting for the bus?" the old man asked. "This bench isn't for vagrants."

Homer was disgusted. Another irritating mortal was assaulting her, ignorant that she was trying to save their existence. The whole species' arrogance was grating. "There's room on the other side of the bench, mister."

"I don't need God's power up above to move you."

"Yeah? What's the opposite of *above me*?" Homer asked, itching herself.

"Below me?" the man replied, and Homer nodded.

The old woman replayed her husband's reply in her head and gasped.

Homer heard a thunderous roll so perilously loud that it knocked her off the bench onto her rump, and the rest of her hot dog rolled down the sidewalk into the gutter. "Egad."

Inside the convention center, Maroquin was engaged in a conversation with a colleague, able to hold her saccharine smile while he went on in a snobby, nauseated fashion about his latest roster of new clients. Her assistant whispered something into her ear, only briefly pausing Maroquin's active listening to the other agent. Not missing a beat, Maroquin smiled with satisfaction. Mission accomplished.

As Tom approached his car, his heart almost stopped. He had forgotten about the draft he was supposed to get from Brent. With everything going on, he had never even checked his e-mail. He pounded his fist on the roof of the Corolla. Time had gotten away from him, and the world was crashing down.

CHAPTER 4

The parking attendant refused to give Tom back any of his money, despite a mere twenty-minute parking stint. The firm rules of this monopolistic enterprise left no room for compromise. Tom had to abide by a lot of rules that he now understood were envisioned, developed, and enforced purely to incense him and pile on to his day. He was sure of it.

How could I have forgotten to check Brent's notes?

He questioned the whole point of writing. Not writing the book or magazine columns but *writing*. The modest pay he received from Western Mag Corp. The stress of working there. He felt somewhat respected but mostly ignored by Andre, his superior—a term he used loosely. The many years he had worked there were supposed to have provided him a platform of some kind to help him get a book published. He'd learned how to write and even how to appeal to the lowest common denominator—or, as Nadia had put it, "the common unread American public." It was inconceivable that he'd be unable to get agency representation, much less be blackballed by an agent who abhorred his employer. It all wasn't worth it. Publishing this manuscript was his escape route. His exit strategy out of Western Mag Corp. His Plan B. After the thousand hours he had poured into it, he realized he had never really considered the obstacles he'd face in getting it published. To think he'd been afraid to send out query letters. *Ha!* Little had he known that far more rejection than mere form letters awaited him. Plan B might as well have been Plan Z. William's and Jamie's voices were in his head again, telling him to self-publish. Being in the Local Authors section at a single Barnes & Noble up the street wasn't what he had in mind. This wasn't success to him. He wanted to be in bookstores everywhere and *be read*. The thought of compromising the work's integrity by altering the ending to appease commercial sensibilities gave him hemorrhoids. If he only knew how to prevent those embarrassing symptoms of stress. Preparation and Preparation H were two very different things, and he needed both.

On the outside, Western Mag Corp was as dull as ever. The early morning sun had given way to cumulus cloud formations, making the drab building look more depressing—like the gray sky sucked out any positive energy it may have once had.

On the second floor, Nadia was standing at her cubicle, stretching to see the parking lot. She thought she had seen Tom's car arrive. "Let me call you back." She hung up her phone and ran to the window. She had to get to him before Andre's imposing authority knocked him on his ass. Taking quick notice to make sure no one was watching, she ran down the stairs, impressing herself for not scuffing her heels.

Tom wearily made toward the entrance. He had dropped the ball with Brent and placed the blame on himself if there were consequences for it.

"Hey, Otis," Tom said, approaching the security guard beyond the glass door.

Otis nodded approvingly from a chair too small for him. He chewed on his fingernails, and his phone fell from his belt to the floor, its Velcro backing having perished. His efforts to quit dropping or losing his phone had failed. "Oh no. My mom's going to kill me!"

Nadia hurriedly appeared in the lobby. "Tom, quick!"

"Hi, Nadia," Otis said, flirting, his rosy cheeks more flushed than usual.

Nadia noticed Otis's name tag for the first time.

Tom stopped. "What's wrong?"

"Andre's on the rampage!" She tried to calm herself down. "He was looking for you earlier, and no one knew where you were."

"Is Brent here?" Tom asked, trying to get around her. She blocked his progress and was clearly frustrated with him.

"He didn't ask everyone in the office where Brent was," Nadia said, "just where you were."

This was more serious than he had thought. "This isn't good."

"Thank you!" Finally, he was listening to her.

"So, is Brent here?" Tom asked again. If Andre's fury had to do with their article, Brent wasn't going to get away with hanging Tom out to dry.

"Um, no," Nadia said.

"This sucks. Who knows what I'm walking into?"

"Um, yeah!"

Nadia thought that the situation sucking was quite evident. Now that she had heroically prevented him from being blindsided, she allowed him to step by her. She said nothing as he passed. He didn't look good, but she knew his resilience would see him through. And, like every time he was under pressure or couldn't get his column up to par and on deadline, he refused her assistance. And she continued to hide that she loved him all the way. If he ever dumped Jamie, she'd jump on him like saffron on rice.

Weathered for the second morning in a row, he found it within him to hurry up the stairs. He needed to find out if Brent had set him up for failure again.

Midmorning on the second floor at Western Mag Corp was quiet and reeked of artificial people who hated their jobs but faked loving them, as if a positive attitude could assist elevation through the ranks. These writers and editors struggled to be energetic and make it through their mornings—aided by the ready supply of generic coffee in the break room that was so bad that few drank it. Only the lowly junior staffers and overeager interns drank the stale grounds, not knowing any better. Its flat aroma floated through the cube farm.

Nadia was sly and separated from Tom by taking an alternate route to her cubicle. Her heart beat faster as she made her way around the large maze of rows, arriving back at her cube undetected. Having this crush on Tom was risky. If Andre caught her warning him of troubles ahead, she'd get reprimanded. Or worse, demoted to advice-column support for months. The thought of providing love advice to the anonymous masses made her puke. (Andre referred to such rebellious shenanigans on his floor as "*meshugge* mutiny" or "*shlamazel* anarchy.")

Tom wasn't so sly. He literally bumped into Andre and his exotic cup of coffee that he had made for himself—and himself only.

"Dude!" Andre bellowed. His distinctive voice boomed through the partitioned cubes, catching the attention of the whole floor. Tom thought that Andre sounded like James Earl Jones on crack.

"Hey, Andre," Tom said eagerly, as if his lightheartedness would diffuse Andre's aggravation over the narrowly missed coffee collision. Only a few dark droplets had fallen to the floor.

"Gotta watch it, holmes," Andre said. "I'm filled to the rim—"

"Sorry about that," Tom said. He felt a little bad.

"But not with Brim," Andre said, observing Tom move down his cubicle row. Tom felt Andre's eyes pierce him from behind.

"Tom," Andre said, slicking his thinning hair back with his free hand. "Pop by my office. Let's pony up." He left, not bothering to wait for Tom to respond.

Tom's stomach dropped. There was no escape. He breathed deeply and slowly followed Andre. Nadia watched him in pity. Getting called in on one of Andre's bad days was never good.

"So talk to me, playa," Andre said as Tom followed him into his office. Andre plopped into his chair at his desk and swiveled it with his thumbs crossed in his lap, a position that Tom considered to be a power posture. Subordinates don't sit in their chairs like that.

"About what?" Tom asked, sitting in front of him.

"Not about your choice of Folgers over Sanka. I need a better kick to wake me up." He refilled his own cup, noticeably not offering Tom any.

"It just says *coffee* on the bags in the break room, Andre," Tom said, unsure if any quality of coffee could wake up this place. He was uncomfortable with Andre's casualness. It was unlike him. "Did you get our article?"

"That's why I scored," Andre said, ignoring Tom and pointing to his personal coffeemaker, "my own exotic Godiva gourmet coffee brewin' in here, homeslice. You won't catch me drinkin' that piss water. I find that the crème brûlée in particular soothes my yawning palate while I'm achin' in the a.m. A cock has got to wake, dig what I'm sayin'?"

Tom resigned himself to play along. "Decaf in the afternoons?"

Andre looked at him like he was crazy. Clearly he didn't believe in decaf at all. "I need supercharge in the p.m., bro, not supersnore," Andre said, proudly showing off a designer bag of grounds. "And what's even better is that this crème brûlée doesn't take longer to make than regular coffeehouse, yo."

Tom was bewildered. "Get it?" Andre joked, raising his eyebrows. "You know, man, how it always takes longer for restaurants to make crème brûlée dessert over regular pies and stuff?"

Tom had no response.

"Yeah, well, that's another *Oprah*," Andre dismissed. Often misunderstood by the inept around him, he believed he was a victim of smart person's disease.

"Hmm." Tom didn't care for any of Andre's esteemed coffee anyway. He just wanted to know what was really brewing in here.

"What we gotta talk about is the IPO story," Andre said, his tone turning cold. "The partners meet soon, and I don't have what I told you two I needed. What up wit dat?"

"We started it and—"

"And where is it?" Andre interrupted.

"You ask Brent yet?" Though he'd never seen Andre lose his quasi-professional composure, Tom had a sense that it could go at any time.

"I'm askin' the questions." Andre stared steadfastly at Tom, who looked a bit too comfortable. The confining chairs across from his desk were supposed to facilitate uncomfortable experiences from his office guests. "Where the hell's my story?" Andre hollered, darting up from his chair, startling Tom and the two secretaries outside the office who quickly pretended they were busy with other tasks.

"I don't know!" Tom surprised himself by yelling back from his chair. "We've started it, but I haven't seen the last work Brent's done on it. We meant to have it to you first thing this morning."

"The video's not matchin' the audio," Andre warned, his hands out and his head cocked like the dog on the RCA logo, a gesture he often gave when pleading and threatening his audience at the same time. "Don't hate. Celebrate. Participate."

"Where's Brent?" Tom asked, hating the cramped chair more than ever. "I'll take the fall, Andre, for balls I drop, but I passed this one." It stung as he said it, feeling like he was crucifying himself with every word he said.

"Sucks to say this, bro." Andre sat back down. "I'm gonna commission another writer for this story," he said calmly. "There's gotta be a better place for you if you can't pull out your pimp hand when I need you to." He needed what he needed. If the IPO went through, his personal payout would pay off all of his debt. Tom and Brent didn't understand what was on the line.

"*What?*" Tom exclaimed. It was too easy for Andre to look him in the eyes. "You think that's the right thing to do? With my notes in Brent's hands?"

"Look, you're a great writer," Andre said, "but you were unable to deliver. Don't fret on it too much. Even supermodels have herpes."

What?

Tom recalled the phone conversation he had overheard the day before. Maybe it was a good time to divulge that he had eavesdropped on something. Something sinister and deadly. He contemplated how to bring it up to Andre. It was risky to suggest treacherous motives that he couldn't confirm. He'd be thrown out of Andre's office. Or fired. He considered that he could've misheard Brent but discounted the possibility on account of his own lucidity—which he considered to be abundant—both as a writer and as a person, though clearly not as a fiancé. Brent was engaging in something dangerous, he was sure.

Tom said, "Andre—"

Then Brent walked in. "It's done." The stupid look of marginal accomplishment on Brent's face made Tom feel sick.

"It's about time," Andre said, trying to dilute the impact of the authority behind the statement. Under no circumstances was firing the owner's son an option.

"Sent it to your e-mail," Brent said.

"Coolio," Andre said, tapping at his computer.

With Andre in constant fear of retribution by Brent—or worse, his father—Tom figured Brent had nothing to worry about missing deadline.

"Your backup, Summers," Brent said, condescending. "I used some of it."

The notes he had given Brent were relevant and should have made the story. As if Brent ever knew what he was talking or writing about. "There you go," Tom said, the only thing he could think to say that wouldn't be construed as combative.

Andre was reading the article intently on his computer screen. "This works," he said with relief. The partners would buy this write-up. "How much of this is you and how much is Tom, holmes?"

Tom shifted in his chair. Brent hated the petite chairs too, which made him feel smooshed like when sitting in the middle seat on an airplane. Only it was his own stocky girth that made the seat uncomfortable, not portly passengers as neighbors. He remained standing.

"Truthfully, I wrote it," Brent said. "Tom was the background. Kind of like the twin suns in *Star Wars.* An interesting component but not substantial."

"Great analogy, *brah,*" Andre said, fist bumping him. Tom grimaced. "This is a problem, though."

Brent smiled. Hopefully now Andre would pull the trigger. He wanted Tom out of the firm.

"Brent, you know I did more than that," Tom said, looking up at him. "I wrote the whole opening for you, with the points for the body. Set you up for the closing summary."

"Oh, don't be such a wuss, Summers," Brent chuckled. "It is what it is." He hoped sabotaging Tom wouldn't hurt his chance of getting in Nadia's pants.

Andre raised his eyebrows. "Seriously? Tom did nothing?"

"I can't lie," Brent said casually. It was easy for him to lie.

"Yes, you can!"

"Pimps," Andre said, dismissing them. "You guys produced. I'll edit tonight. It'll be on the stands just in time. See. Indeed, happy cows come from California." He gave both of them his signature fist bump, and they both automatically obliged him, Brent stunned that Tom still worked there. "It looks like it's exactly what we need to help this friggin' thing go through," Andre said proudly, "and I appreciate you two homeys playin' nice in the sandbox and kickin' it up a couple of notches to version 2.0 for us. This is business, not friends-ness, but I'm stoked to see you two utilizing each others' mojo."

"I told you, Andre. I wrote it," Brent said, furious.

Andre gestured to Tom. "Nah, I know how this cat rolls."

Brent was disgusted. "What?"

Tom raised his eyebrows. He hadn't expected Andre to stand up to the CEO's son—at all.

"No matter. This is important, not just to me," Andre bellowed, ignoring Brent's glare, "but to the partners of the firm, and I'll make sure both of you *mensches* get recognized for your quick turnaround. All the prime filet of our competitors doesn't match our porterhouse. Good job, fellas. I think we've now reached critical mass. You two boys are the gift that keeps on giving. Like the clap."

"Thanks, Andre," Tom said. He hadn't gotten a compliment half this magnitude—nor nearly as ridiculous—all year.

Brent's rage was building. Nothing was going according to plan.

"So, I've got to get this other project done," Tom said, trying to get out of Andre's office. Now was his chance. Strong praise didn't prevent Andre's space from feeling like the principal's office. "'Christmas Shopping Tips for Champions: Shopping Overseas with the Weakening US Dollar.'"

Andre laughed with approval. "Well that's better than last year's 'Christmas Regifting: How to Get Around Being Labeled an Indian Giver,'" Andre said. "We got a bunch of complaints on that one."

"That wasn't me." Tom smirked before walking out.

"I did that one, Andre," Brent said. "You told me you loved it and that you didn't care that it wasn't PC."

"That was you, huh, brother?"

"Yeah," Brent said, making sure Tom had left, "and you found it so hilarious when Tom pointed out that the title *alluded* to the problem of being labeled an Indian giver more than actually being one."

"Oh yeah, I remember," Andre said. Alone with Brent, he knew the hammer was coming down.

"Andre, Andre," Brent said, slowly moving to Andre's side of the desk.

"Yes," Andre said with uncertainty, his pupils enlarged. Sitting back in his chair didn't make him feel grand or powerful like usual.

Brent hovered over him. "Don't look at me like that. You know what you were supposed to do. And you embarrassed me."

So what that he was the sole heir of the Hayes fortune. Andre tried not to be intimidated by this *kid*. "What's on your mind, Brent?"

Brent tapped a finger on Andre's desk. He was relishing this position, standing on Andre's side of it. "You were supposed to fire him."

Andre said nothing.

"We've gone over this. My father doesn't know how dense you are, but I do. And this article is mine. Hell, you know this whole company will be one day."

"I know you wish I would fire him," Andre said, shaking his head, "but I won't do it. He's the best writer here. And it seems to me, homeslice, that you both worked on it."

The best writer here? Brent was losing his patience. "I just told you he didn't! And will you quit it with the *homeslice*? His name won't be on this." His eyes pierced Andre. "Period."

"You don't want—"

"I said," Brent interrupted, his voice soft and restrained, "his name won't be on this at all. No *with reporting by, additional reporting by.*"

Andre was shocked that he was being talked to like this. "Lemme get this straight, holmes—you want me to completely pull his name off?"

The nicknames grated Brent's eardrums like scratching a chalkboard. "His name won't be on this article. I've got ideas for another article for him. It's about time I got credit for what I do at this rag," Brent snorted back. "Your boy Tom's not hogging all the credit on this." He needed to earn his stripes in his father's eyes, and this imbecile was in the way. "Holmes."

"What you're asking me to do breaks one of the most important journalistic rules in our business," Andre said, uncomfortable with Brent breathing over him. "Forget the ethics, Brent. Word gets out in the journalism community that we steal credit from writers, we'll only be able to get hacks to work here. You want to destroy your father's business that he's built from the ground up? You're like the termite of the family tree."

Without question, Martin Hayes would fire him if this came to light, and Andre's compromised journalistic integrity would forever follow him wherever he went. He quickly considered the prospect of telling Martin of his insubordinate son's mutiny, but he'd likely be fired then anyway. *Blood is thicker than water*, he imagined Martin Hayes thinking.

"Don't make me laugh," Brent said. He was infuriated that Andre hadn't been whacked yet. He'd paid that imbecile weeks ago, and the job still wasn't done. "My father's business. Ethics. While you're requesting a positioning piece on IPOs for your own financial interest? Well, *this* isn't a request," Brent said calmly. "I know how important your *Western Mag* income is to your family."

Andre gulped for the first time in his adult memory. Brent was right. His wife would have his ass.

"You wouldn't know this about me, bro," Andre said, searching for a response, "but it's not about what you make, it's about what you have. Why you mad doggin' me like this? You've been one of my boys!" Deep down, he hated the privileged snot.

Brent shook his head and sat on Andre's desk. "*Bro*, I've checked out your financials."

"Ha!" Andre roared. "Right!"

"Oh, you don't believe me." Brent was amused.

"Whatever, cool cat," Andre threw out. "You know how many times fools think they know my details? My *wife* doesn't even know where all the bodies are buried."

Brent almost pitied the poor little deluded man sitting in his chair. "Your two checking accounts—only one of which your wife knows about—have been low on funds for almost two years. Why is that? My dad not paying you enough?"

Andre tried to stare through him.

"This cool cat got your tongue?" Brent asked. He felt the devil within him.

"Anybody who's got what I've got has an extra account on the side. Whatever."

Brent sighed. "Andre, you should consider paying off that hot tub a little more than the minimum payment each month. You're getting nailed on the interest."

Andre's blood pressure was rising.

"Your municipal bond fund," Brent continued. "You know, a responsible investor would pay off your hot tub and credit cards before stockpiling cash in a 3 percent savings account. But at least you don't have to pay taxes on it, right? I wonder what your wife would do if she knew you didn't trust her and were hiding money while putting your family into debt."

Andre stood up, huffing in Brent's face.

"Don't touch me," Brent warned. He put his hands up defensively, backing up and circling to the other side of the desk. "Your windows there—anyone can see. Don't make me tell my *dad*."

Andre glanced at the large windows and door that faced the journalistic floor. No one was peeking or hanging around at the moment. He walked steadily toward Brent, who was easily three times his size. "You think I give a rat's ass if you tell your poppa?" Brent fell back into a chair, his burly girth providing him a tight squeeze. "Come on, you little shit. Threaten me again."

A smirk slowly crossed Brent's face. He held enormous calm as Andre placed each of his own hands on the armrests and spoke down to him angrily.

"I said, threaten me again, silver spoon."

"You really want me to?" Brent asked with a sarcastic woefulness—like he was bored. He didn't blink, mere inches from Andre's red face.

"Excuse me, Andre."

At the door of his office stood his receptionist, who looked quizzically at Andre standing over Brent. She wore clothes that suggested she was ashamed of her bosom that was unnaturally larger than it should be, given her petite frame. "I've got Mr. Hayes on the phone."

"Thank you, Grace."

"Would you like me to grab your lunch today again?"

"No. Thank you, Grace," Andre said again, more forcefully. She scuttled out.

"I'm gonna have to tell Martin about this, Brent," Andre breathed, trying to gain his composure. "He won't be pleased."

"You're not a stupid man."

"You pampered little shit. I know Martin ain't gonna put up with your spoiled ass breakin' into my personal info. Ain't cool, man."

"*I'm* spoiled? He'd hate it more if he knew about the checks you received from Stewart . . . um," he searched, "Mantlebee . . . oh, and there was another one . . . Hansen! Yes, that's the name."

Andre stopped. A freight train had hit him.

"Hansen." Brent grinned devilishly, comfortable again. "Partner bribes, Andre? You think *anyone* would accept that kind of behavior in this country nowadays?"

"You're crazy, man," Andre said, trying not to reveal any clues on his face while he collected himself. He backed up to his desk.

"Oh am I?" Brent asked, showcasing his position of strength in a new, slow, confident stride. His regained upper hand. "Crazy enough to review your financial statements to look for obvious weaknesses. I've got to know who I'm dealing with here, *holmes.* Let's see. Do you really think that the SEC would tolerate this? Let's say my dad, or Martin—that's what we both call him—was just a little pissed at you for narcing on his son. I'm sure SEC would put you away for a long time . . . once and *if* we went public, that is. You've got a lot of stock options at stake, Andre, and those thousands of shares could make a pretty pension. But bribes to the board? And now, publishing stories in this rag to rally the partners of the firm? You really think that's right?"

Andre's shoulders sunk, and he fell into his desk chair.

"He can fire you, Andre. He won't disown me," Brent said. He stood over Andre, his eyes drilling at him. "My mother's dead, so that leaves me and Martin and the company. And with his blood pressure, I don't expect him around for long. I don't care what journalistic code you think you live by, and I don't know how you could possibly think that I believe you have publishing integrity, filtering your right-wing propaganda into my old man's magazine anyway. He's too stupid to see it, but I don't miss it, you ghetto-talkin' white boy!"

Andre wanted to smack him but knew he was now under Brent's cruel thumb.

"I know I don't have to threaten you," Brent said. "You're too sensitive for that. You could lose your *cool.* And that, we both know, that would be heinously uncool."

"Homey don't play that way," Andre said. This sucked.

"That's right," Brent said. Patronization was dripping off him. "I know you won't. Now. I want my name on this article and that literary pain in my ass, Tom, off of it." He wanted his father to be proud of him before he keeled over.

Brent turned to leave Andre's office and then stopped. "Oh, and I want Tom fired. By tomorrow—or else. Don't make your pissant life worse than it is."

All Andre could do was watch Brent leave. He couldn't believe what Brent was forcing him to do.

"Everything cool?" Nadia asked, poking her head in Tom's cubicle after he dropped into his chair.

"So cool," Tom said, collecting himself. Shockingly, Andre hadn't taken Brent's side on the article. At least he had somewhat of an ally in Andre, the comparisons of Tom to an STD aside.

Brent came by a couple of minutes later, flashing a flirting twinkle at Nadia. She turned her back to him in disgust. He walked away, wondering what it would take for that hot little bitch to respond to him instead of always being so attentive to that loser. Both Tom and Andre were definitely in the way.

* * *

Her disdain for car lots was so intense that, a couple of years ago, Jamie had bought her new Acura over the phone. It was delivered to her apartment without her stepping foot on the dreaded lot. The thought of predictable bogus sales pitches of extended warranties and rust proofing nauseated her. She had picked out all of her options online and waited patiently three weeks for delivery. Since then, she forever swore to anyone who'd listen that she never again would step foot onto sleazy car lots, until now.

Davey's Dealios was the oldest car dealership in Phoenix, and it strived to do only one thing: sell cars. And from the look of the place, it didn't do that very well. The drab business was little more than a local landmark, its vertical sign reading Quality Used Cars. At night, when the dated sign was lit, its bulbs read Qu It S Car. The grungy building's outdoor paint was peeling, and the lot's loose gravel and potholes guaranteed bumpy rides, warning off high-end shoppers and good credit scores.

Immediately upon arrival, she considered turning around. Online, she had seen it as a clean, sparkling, bright car dealership, not the sad, debilitated building that had obviously been Photoshopped. She had been duped into flying out here on her own dime. *Who am I to think she could be Wonder Woman and save WSA?* Janice and Martha would ridicule her behind her back if they found out about this, and Stephanie would be proven right. Jamie's shoulders slumped as she turned the steering wheel into a parking space.

This was bad. Stephanie would surely consider who was generating accounts and who wasn't when she did her predictable forthcoming layoffs—if the agency stayed open. Jamie hated herself again for not having had the courage to start her own business.

She checked herself in her rearview mirror. Her hair wasn't too flat at least, as it often got when she flew. She had been up, in her mind, since the crackle of dawn.

Suddenly, a hand knocked on the driver's side window. Jamie jumped in her seat. She could have peed her pants. A mustached man appeared, beaming. She breathed in calmly and rolled her window down.

"Hi," the friendly mustached man said, his voice thick with a Middle Eastern accent. "Can I help you today?"

"God, you scared me there!" Jamie laughed nervously, holding her hand to her chest.

"Looking to trade this in?" the mustached man asked hopefully, ignoring the Enterprise Rent-A-Car license plate frame. His suggestive sell wasn't subtle.

She smiled. "Um, no, I'm here to meet with David. Or Davey."

"You want to look around? All our cars are certified by Davey's world-famous guarantee."

She collected her stuff and opened her car door. "That famous, huh?" It sounded like a small-town lemonade stand.

"World famous," he repeated, appreciating her playfulness.

"Tell you what, Samuel," she said, reading his name tag as she got out of her car, "show me where Davey's office is, and I guarantee I won't let you waste your time trying to sell me a car today."

Samuel laughed. "Thank you so much, miss. But these cars sell themselves. You can't waste my time."

Jamie patted his shoulder, and they walked toward the building's entrance. "Thank you, Samuel. You're sweet."

"I don't want to be sweet, miss. I wanna sell some cars! I've only sold five today so far."

Only five today? Jamie thought that sounded like a lot of cars to sell—and before lunch. The guy must sell them in droves over a week. Looking at the poor condition of the car lot, she concluded there was no way this could be true.

"Great weather today out here, huh?" Samuel asked.

Unsure of his sales accuracy, she still loved his accent. It made her think of great Middle Eastern cooking, though she was unable to pinpoint the specific food exactly. "It's very sunny here."

"I love the sun. You can't buy this weather at the store," he announced, holding the door open for her.

"I never thought of it that way," she said, catching her breath. She couldn't believe what she saw, entering the lobby of Davey's Dealios. The yellow-stained walls bore the evidence of decades of Davey's employees ignoring surgeon generals' warnings and the lack of ventilation within the small, boxy reception area. The glass door slammed shut behind them, startling her.

"I'll get him for you." Samuel disappeared into the service area, no more than twenty feet from the front door.

"Thanks, Sam." Jamie surveyed the room. It smelled of burned coffee and newspapers. A lonesome, orange, torn-up couch sat in the corner, with cigarette burns on the well-used, butt-depressed cushions. Used Styrofoam coffee cups overstuffed the small trash can nearby, spilling onto the skid-marked tile floor. Dusty, crooked blinds tried desperately to open the claustrophobic room to the world outside as loud drills and tool clangs could be heard from the garage nearby. Jamie was horrified.

Inconveniently, she suddenly needed to pee. The unisex bathroom she saw wouldn't work. Experience had taught her that twenty or thirty years of standing and urinating didn't mean that men could hit a target, even if it was the broad side of a barn. The last thing she wanted to do was squat—which she would do if there were no bowl liners, which she guessed there were *not*—and have her suit pants at her ankles, absorbing random people's urine off the ground. She'd hold it in.

The spectacled young woman behind the information/service desk was highlighting a history textbook she was reading. Jamie wondered how the woman could concentrate with all the clanging noise around her.

"Hey, Lois, a guy from Saturn is here," a husky voice said, entering from the garage. The tattooed and goateed forty-something mechanic smoked his cigarette, it floating on his lips by its tip, defying gravity. He looked like he had never washed his fatigue shorts or his grimy T-shirt, greased like he'd been working three days straight.

Lois eyeballed him through her reading glasses, bored with his interruption. "Where's he from?" Lois asked.

"Saturn."

"You're saying the guy's from Saturn."

"Yeah, Saturn," he said, noticing Jamie standing by the front door. He wiped his hands on a blue work towel and salivated over her in her pants suit.

Jamie looked around uncomfortably. She ran through all of the reasons she had come out to Phoenix for this account, from proving the evil stepsisters wrong to being heroic at the agency. At the party, Davey had told her about his vision for LA car dealerships. Meeting the owner of a company in such a setting was supposed to provide her an *in*. Everyone knew that. Another lick of the grease monkey's chops and in a few brief seconds, she considered quietly leaving again.

"You're saying the guy's from another planet. I don't know who to send him to."

"He may be from another planet," the mechanic said, wiping his brow, "but he's from Saturn, *the auto manufacturer*. He's got info for us on parts we need. Dumb ass."

"Didn't Saturn go out of business?" Lois asked. "Who's the dumb ass now?"

Jamie couldn't contain her smile. The mechanic eyed her up and down one more time and left, leaving her feeling violated. She had read once how women could determine the likelihood of mate-hood after a mere thirty-second encounter. Today, three seconds was enough.

Samuel came back into the reception room with Davey, a handsome man who looked out of place in the low-rate pit. Wearing jeans and a polo shirt, he was casually professional and clearly ran the place.

"She was just here," Samuel said.

"Oh no," Davey said. "We didn't scare another one off, did we?"

While Davey was rebuilding his father's automotive empire, he was hoping for the right media allies to help catapult his sales numbers to new heights so he could expand from Phoenix into Los Angeles by next spring. Despite the heavier tax burden and costs of doing business in California—

payroll and the lease of the property, specifically—Los Angeles was the ultimate automobile market. Everyone needed a car in sprawling Southern California.

Since selling two other dealerships earlier in the year and moving unsold inventory to this old, signature location, Davey Junior was increasingly embarrassed by the deterioration of the property, but Senior had refused to put money into it, believing his customers thought that upgrades to the property would be construed as frivolous luxuries, with additional fees then added to the car prices. And he was right. The property's no-frills presentation was no gimmick. They maintained huge car sales with tremendous customer loyalty and word of mouth. Because they actually owned the property versus leasing it, it was by far the cheapest to operate, and their profits were through the roof, helping to finance their future expansion.

He was disgusted by the place. How they had a fifteen share of all used cars in the market was beyond him. Davey Junior was ready to get LA going, and it couldn't happen fast enough. He couldn't wait to get out of this hellhole, and he wasn't surprised that yet another potential media partner couldn't wait either.

Samuel opened the front door and peered outside. Jamie was gone.

* * *

LAX was called "the Zoo" for good reason. There were so many cars, planes, and people that it was hard to get in and out of the airport. The traffic was congested, and the taxi drivers drove like animals. In many parts of California, people planned their lives around traffic, unlike in New York where they planned around weather or Washington DC where they planned around political demonstrations. The traffic was constant and chaotic. Like the workers at an actual zoo, the LAX workers wore vests and used whistles to control the animals and keep things in check.

Teri was in line for a taxi. Her direct flight from San Francisco had been smooth, and she was anxious to see Tom. The line crawled steadily along, and she thought of different things she could say to him. Funny memories she had. How much she had studied his pictures on Facebook for traces of the boy she once knew. How things could have been different had she not broken up with him.

Her feet were already killing her. Though not that accustomed to wearing heels, she looked sexy in them, just as long as she remembered to be graceful. Walking like an ape would kill any sex appeal. Normally, she didn't show off her firm, shapely calves. There was no one to show them off to. Her hair was down, and––after deciding against the jeans––a solid beige dress completed her look. She liked how good she looked dressed up, which she had not done since church last Christmas. Without a job, a fashionable wardrobe of self-consciousness wasn't necessary, and Luigi certainly never took her out anymore.

She was curious why Tom wanted to see her. Obsessively curious. If they saw each other and there were sparks, her whole world could change drastically. Deep down, she was pretty sure she still loved Luigi, but the unknown was exciting. Exactly how exciting, she'd see—which was why she had packed lingerie in her bag . . . just in case.

She approached the front of the line and noticed a familiar blonde woman approaching a shuttle for car pickup. The woman was petite and beautiful in a girl-next-door kind of way, reminding Teri of the kind of women she had always known Tom to be attracted to. Or *feared* he was attracted to, as if she had a right to feel threatened in any way.

Teri moved forward. An attendant pointed the couple in front of her toward the next taxi, and she realized that the woman had to be Jamie. Teri couldn't take her eyes off her. The woman dropped a folder she was holding, and as she bent to pick it up, her purse fell off her arm. The woman scrambled to pick up the items falling out of it. Teri gaped at her, not blinking as she waited to get a better look at the woman's facial features. The attendant motioned for Teri to move to the next available taxi, but she was so engrossed in the woman she didn't notice.

"Ma'am."

The woman got up and searched around, making sure she had picked everything up that had fallen on the asphalt.

"Your taxi, ma'am."

Teri ignored him. When the woman's side profile changed to face her direction, Teri recognized her from Tom's Facebook pictures. *That's Jamie, all right.*

Finally, the taxi driver grabbed Teri's suitcase and threw it in the trunk with more force than necessary. She got into the car, her heart pounding, and continued to watch Jamie until she disappeared into the shuttle. Somehow, seeing Jamie in person had made her more nervous about all of this.

So nervous, she hadn't noticed Luigi in line a few people behind her. He did all he could not to be detected, anxious to get a taxi quickly himself and follow her. Popping his gum, he watched her from behind his sunglasses, sticking out like someone trying not to stick out.

* * *

On the plane ride back to LA, Jamie had decided she'd had no right to think it was up to her to save WSA from closing. She could have better invested her time into another client project, preferably one that was better thought out. Nothing was going right. Cynthia and Jamal's shrinking business didn't make her shine professionally, and she hadn't yet shared that news with Stephanie before pursuing Davey's Dealios. Stephanie wasn't known for taking bad news well.

She missed Tom terribly. Though it had been less than a day since they had broken up, he was already the memory she wished she could forget. It hurt too much.

Back at WSA, she walked in to dispirited and morose faces. Gloom hovered over everyone. Something terrible had happened. "What's going on?" she asked a group of coworkers congregating in the hallway.

"Check your e-mail," one of them said.

Jamie realized she hadn't checked her BlackBerry since arriving back in LA. How depressed could she be if she wasn't checking her BlackBerry?

Her office was unlocked. *What the hell?* She turned on the light. Everything looked normal but her computer. Someone had been going through her e-mails. Immediate concerns of a breach in privacy—and the companion argument of privacy rights in the work environment— weakened when she saw the title of an unopened e-mail at the top of her e-mail list. It had come from Stephanie and was titled "Immediate Changes." With a title like that, those changes couldn't be good. She took a breath and read:

Everyone,

It saddens me to say that today I must announce that WSA has been hit by the loss of not one, but two large accounts that bring cause for immediate changes to this ad agency. Today, we received notice that JC Traders, our largest account, has left us to be represented by NRS, one of our notorious competitors. Secondly, we were up for the acquisition of Weight Burger but have lost that opportunity also to NRS, despite the valiant efforts of Martha and Janice, who put together an over-the-top proposal that, despite its dramatic brilliance, did not suit the taste of the client.

That being said, I'm announcing the layoffs of the entire buying department. All four positions will be replaced by freelancers. You've seen me fire poor performers before, but I hate laying off people for this reason. I'm sorry, y'all.

There's some good news, though. I'm promoting both Martha Lakewood and Janice Knight to senior account managers, to oversee our new Account Acquisition Team. Their unwavering support for this agency and their wherewithal to fight for our accounts' best interests has earned these talented ladies the opportunity to help build this agency into the kind of powerhouse I've envisioned since I opened it. All support staff will report to them on all new account prospects, and they will report all progress to me directly.

Now. Let's go get some new accounts!

Stephanie

Jamie's heart sank. Jamal and Cynthia had gone to NRS? Did they hate her? Everything had seemed fine at dinner until Cynthia's tearful pronouncement. Leaving the agency was the same as firing her. Another misjudgment. She couldn't believe she had to learn this way—in a work e-mail—that her account had left WSA. No calls or anything. When a client cuts its ad spending, it was merely a smaller commitment to advertising. On the other hand, completely changing media buying and creative services was a powerful statement that what the current ad agency was doing wasn't working. Another ad agency had weaseled its way into stealing JC Traders from WSA. This other shop had covertly been pitching the business, and no one at WSA must have known about it. As the account executive, Jamie should have known about it. Stephanie had to be livid.

Jamie imagined the beauty queens reading this e-mail over and over again with glee, satisfied that she now reported to them. How was it that they could lose a pitch for a prospective client and still get promoted?

She reviewed her schedule in Outlook and noticed her blind date was only hours away. *Why did I allow Wanda to talk me into this tonight? Why did I allow myself to talk me into it?*

* * *

Tom arrived at the agent's office at 11:00 sharp, as requested. A meeting with a second agent in the same week. The first one had been a disaster, and he hoped this one would go better. It couldn't be much worse.

He waited patiently in the carpeted waiting room. It wasn't grand or artsy like Maroquin's. A boutique literary agency, the compact lobby was outfitted like an old folks' home with its upholstered couch and television. The thick flokati shag rug under the coffee table in the middle of the room had to be a haven for dust mites, Tom was sure. The small room's stale air made him think of sweaters in a closet.

"Mr. Summers." Tom stood up from his chair. "Hi, Keith Levy." They shook hands, and Keith Levy inspected Tom oddly.

"Hi."

"Have a seat."

"No need to go into your office?" Tom asked.

"No, out here's fine," Levy said, his assistant eyeing them from behind a desk. "We need to talk." Levy was a heavyset older man, bouncy in his walking rhythm in high-waisted pants that Tom thought could be tweed, though he'd only ever seen sports jackets made of such a material. His mustache was twisted at the ends with the exuberance of Santa Claus.

Tom got right to it. "So what do you think? Do I have promise?" he asked, looking for some sign of hope.

"You do," Levy said. "In fact, with a few changes, I'd consider representing you. Unfortunately, some information that's come to light makes this impossible."

Tom let out a breath. "What kind of information? I already know you hate the ending."

"Well," Levy sighed, "I wouldn't say I *hated* it. I appreciate many structural forms of storytelling. I'm just interested in what's *marketable*. Problem is, I don't represent plagiarizing authors. Barbara, do I have any messages?"

His assistant shook her head.

"What?" Tom asked.

"Plagiarists aren't authors at all. Little opinion of mine. Developed it over the years."

Tom was too blown away to appreciate Keith Levy's animation. Under different circumstances, Tom may have actually liked the guy.

"See," Levy continued, "an e-mail from one of my contacts in town said that you aren't the original writer of this work. She's not a fan of it like I am, but after talking to her this morning, she insists that it was stolen from one of her other clients."

The confined space of the office helped Tom feel like the world was closing in on him. Claustrophobic, trapped in a box. "Maroquin. Maroquin told you this."

Levy smiled. "I'm glad you're aware of your predicament, Mr. Summers. And now, mine."

"She's full of it, sir."

Levy looked at him questionably. "I understand there's a lot of pressure to succeed in this town, Mr. Summers. There's a lot of competition, I know, in this business, but this isn't the type of behavior that endears you to agents. We're not *lawyers*."

"So that's why I was blackballed from that writer's conference you recommended I go to."

"Oh, you went!" Levy said, satisfaction beaming. "I'm glad you listened to me." He turned to his bored receptionist. "You see, some people do listen to me!"

"I can't believe Maroquin's blackballing me."

"I've never met a real plagiarist. Thanks for coming in!" He was overly jovial.

The work that Tom had put into his manuscript was being challenged all over town, possibly all over the country. Maroquin wasn't kidding when she'd told him it wasn't getting published. Tom wondered how someone could hate his work so much.

Levy stood up. "Well, my work's done here!" He rubbed his palms, ready and cheery for happier tasks. "So. I can't represent you." He put out his hand for Tom to shake. "Good luck!"

As insensitive as Tom thought Levy's happy-go-lucky presentation was, he couldn't think of a better way that Levy could have rejected him. Tom stood and shook his hand, severely deflated.

"If I can prove it's my work—"

"Then let's talk. Until then, good day!"

* * *

Maroquin sat at her desk, contemplating the next insult for her soon-to-be ex-husband, Lee. She wondered what it was about men and younger women. It was an epidemic in American society. She considered using a specific sharp kitchen utensil to sever his most treasured and what she thought had been his least used body part, but she decided the consequences of such heinousness—despite the fact that it would be righteously deserved—weren't worth it. Losing her business wasn't an option, and going to prison frightened her. She sighed, deleting another soliciting e-mail that she'd barely read. Life itself was a stress test, and she wasn't happy. It was with no humor that she determined that chopping off his penis would surely be such a bloody mess that it would it destroy her eight-hundred-thread-count Egyptian sheets. And he wasn't going to take those from her, also.

A handsome, sophisticated-looking man and his younger female companion abruptly welcomed themselves into her office. He was at least twenty years older than she, his plentiful, gray hair falling loosely over his forehead—the envy of every thin-haired man in his fifties. His good looks were striking, with rich, piercing brown eyes that could make even her forget her idiot husband. dark, textured suits provided them trim silhouettes and flattering contours that gave them an eye-catching presence.

"Good afternoon, Maroquin," GQ said. His voice was rich and deep like a tuba.

She looked up from her computer screen, surprised that anyone had the gall to waltz into her office unannounced.

"We sent your assistant home," the woman said. Soft, pale skin contrasted her long, dark hair that hung over her shoulders, light and easy. She was what Maroquin considered *too* attractive. And, in her midtwenties—too *young*.

The couple adjusted their suit jackets and arranged themselves in the sofa chairs.

Maroquin was miffed. "It's almost six o'clock, and I asked her to stay late."

The young woman didn't care. "Hmm."

GQ shrugged. "That explains why she took off like a bat out of hell."

"I'm running a business here," Maroquin said. "It would have been nice for you to have let me know you were coming. Can I get you anything? Coffee? Iced tea?"

"No, thank you," they said in unison.

"Glad to see you offer refreshments," the young woman said, to the approval of her husband.

"Don't worry, I'm running the business responsibly—and profitably. You're getting a fruitful return, aren't you? I'm sure I'm one of your best investments, with the business doing what it's doing."

"That's what we're here to talk to you about," GQ said.

The young woman gazed around her office, imagining herself in Maroquin's chair. If only her husband believed in her enough to run the business herself.

"Is everything okay? I've made my payments on time. On both loans."

"Yes, Maroquin," GQ said. "The loans have been on track. But we've missed some great opportunities, don't you think?"

She was languishing internally, but her business was a tight ship. Never before had they called her out for questionable business practices. "I'm sure you're aware of the economic challenges of the day, so I'm not going to provide remedial training."

"Appreciate that," the young woman said.

GQ crossed his legs and rested his palms comfortably on his lap. "We're down 20 percent this year."

Maroquin laughed. "You're lucky we're not down 30 percent."

"Is that a fact?" the young woman asked. She was truculent, but Maroquin was unaffected by the trophy wife's contentious attitude and felt no need to stand. She was still in control, in her office.

"Brick-and-mortar bookstores are closing," Maroquin said. She spoke with the exhaustion of someone having told the story many times before. "Walmart and Target are trying to outdo Amazon on seeing who can be the first to strip away all profits on books. The chains are doing smaller runs, trying to keep less inventory, even on best-selling authors with great track records. You know this. You're surprised profits are down? If I have this right, you forbade me to risk time or money on new writers. We've missed no opportunities with our current client roster. Tell me what to do differently."

She had continued to search for new talent anyway—despite the challenges of actually finding it—looking for the next great book. If she found something or someone promising, she felt she could somehow convince these hacks to allow her to sign a new writer.

True literary fans in publication and talent representation savored the next new find that they discovered before anyone else—great work with tremendous marketability. These discoveries happened infrequently, but book lovers who got into editing and publishing thirsted for the next great book, fiction or nonfiction. The people behind the money often couldn't care less. Maroquin thought this couple invested in her agency a couple of years ago because of the prestige involved with book publication. And they couldn't afford to fund movies.

"Just always looking for better," the older one said. "Not just different."

Maroquin nodded. "I agree with that."

"I don't buy it," the young woman said. "Digital book sales are up."

"True," Maroquin said. She continued to be articulate and polished. "Which is why being down 20 percent this year is miraculous, considering how much worse last year was. We're still heavy in the black, and we'll be up again next year. Likely."

"Against poor comps," the young woman said.

"Rachelle and I don't want our investment to be a bad one is all," GQ said.

"Does the sign outside say Husband, Fourth Wife, and Maroquin? It doesn't." The young woman rolled her eyes in frustration, and her husband stared through Maroquin. "You're the money, yes. But I'm the brains of this operation and number one in this town for a reason."

Maroquin hated that she was having this conversation. She would have gone to a regular bank for the loans if her husband's bar hadn't already been maxed out in equity to cover the 35 percent of Maroquin and Lee Partners that the GQ loan sharks didn't own. If things had gone as planned, if she wouldn't have had a couple of other professional misfires, she would have bought them out already. She wasn't used to being in an inferior position.

"I don't appreciate you two barging in on my shop," she said, grasping for authority, "in such an accusatory fashion with a problem, and—predictably—no solution."

"Correction," Rachelle said. "As a reminder, you own a minority stake."

"You can't fire me out of my own business. You're the money, folks. While I appreciate your input and understand your frustrations with the numbers, the industry, the economy, for God's sake—"

"Save it," GQ said, holding up his hand. "The papers we signed indicated that misconduct of any kind that hurt this business made the proprietor of the funds—that's me—owner of the business. Which, of course, then I'd have Rachelle here run."

Rachelle cocked her head at Maroquin, amused. Maybe she'd run this publishing business after all.

Maroquin's head almost exploded. "Misconduct? There has been no misconduct, and you know it."

"We're watching," Rachelle said.

"In need of a hobby?" Maroquin asked.

Rachelle smirked back at her.

Maroquin knew they had always paid attention to the numbers—but not to the degree of challenging her on how the business was run. If only her husband had put his law school education to good use and passed the bar instead of buying a bar, these clowns wouldn't be sitting in front of her right now. That's what she got for thinking she didn't need an attorney to look over the papers.

Ding.

This rise to the seventh floor hadn't been as nerve-racking a ride as last time. Tom stepped out of the elevator and marched as calmly as he could through the grand lobby of Maroquin and Lee Partners, observed an empty reception desk, and poked his head into Maroquin's office.

He knocked on the doorframe. "Maroquin?"

* * *

The van was difficult to drive. Its stick was long and awkward to shift and made grinding noises every time she shifted down gears. Embarrassed by the accompanying rattle of the loosely attached muffler, Wanda shrugged toward Blaine in the passenger seat. "Sorry."

"No worries," Blaine said, nervously watching her handle the huge gearshift. He imagined Wanda steering a barge in a lake. "Why'd you get a van, anyway? Eats up the gas."

"It's not good for the environment, but I could afford it. Plus, it's kind of fun." Their seats bounced due to the absence of shocks.

"Sure it is!"

Her date's wheelchair fit in the van wonderfully. It rolled and jiggled against the floor of the van every few seconds. Wanda struggled to maneuver the aging behemoth off the highway.

"Show respect to the van," Wanda said, Blaine laughing and holding on to a handle.

She navigated up a curvy hill. Dusk had fallen. She shifted up to third gear with all her might and pushed her body forward. The engine roared.

"Flatline it!" Blaine yelled.

"I'm trying to!" Wanda laughed. "Don't be tellin' a black woman she can't drive now!"

Grrrrrrrrrrrrrrrrrrrrrrrrrr. Her shift into third gear wasn't smooth, but she was satisfied with her accomplishment.

"Turn here!" Blaine called out. She immediately made a right turn into more residential suburbia. "Okay, okay, slow down. It's just a couple of houses up."

A suave twenty-something stood at the curb texting on his cell phone and holding a flower bouquet in cellophane and a case of beer.

"There he is," Blaine said. "Looking studly as usual."

Wanda pulled over and got her first look at Blaine's friend, Don, dressed in designer jeans and a white, long-sleeved shirt. Starched to the hilt. His chiseled looks were striking, but she immediately knew the type—self-absorbed and a bit younger than she expected. The van stalled, and she started it again. *Grooowwwwwlllllll.*

Don opened the van's sliding door and said, "You're late." He climbed in the back, slammed the door shut, and sat down on top of the case of beer he'd brought for the night. "I should've waited inside."

"Why? Missing *America's Next Top Model* or something?" Blaine cracked.

Don winced. "It's too windy, tool."

Wanda had never noticed the wind, and she disliked Don immediately. Looking out, she saw leaves in the trees barely moving and then noticed Don primping his hair. The guy had a complex over a few wispy hairs out of place.

"Hi, I'm Wanda. Sorry we ran a bit late."

Grrrrrrrrrrrrrrrrrrrr. Upshift.

"We didn't anticipate the traffic in *the Valley,*" Blaine said.

"No prob," Don said, ignoring their sarcasm and Wanda's rough gear shifting.

"You're the one who insisted we pick you up, man," Blaine said, sharing a glance with Wanda. "You could've met us there."

Don finished primping his hair. He knew it well enough to do it without a mirror. "I don't know this chick yet. I'm not waiting in a restaurant by myself."

"So high maintenance," Blaine said. "The world doesn't revolve around you, Don."

* * *

Eyeballing Tom from her desk, Maroquin wasn't sure if she was more frustrated that everyone in the world seemed to be barging into her office—after hours—or more relieved that someone, anyone, was interrupting the most asinine conversation she'd ever had. Outside of her bedroom, of course. "Yes," she sighed.

"I'm Tom Summers. I met with you two days ago?"

GQ and Rachelle stretched their necks, turning toward the source of the interruption.

"Of course I know who you are," Maroquin said. "I don't have Alzheimer's. Can't you see I'm in a meeting?"

Tom acknowledged the couple. "I'm sorry to interrupt—"

"No," Rachelle said. "It's fine."

Maroquin's eyebrows furrowed. She wished the trophy wife would die of convulsions.

"Yes," GQ said, turning back toward Maroquin. "We're business partners of Maroquin's. You can say whatever it is you have to say."

Rachelle smirked at Maroquin again. She loved it when her husband put Maroquin in her place.

Business partners? Maroquin couldn't believe this. They had never had any say. A philandering husband on one hand threatened to take half of all she had, and these sharks were bullying her about her agency. The last thing she needed was a troublemaking writer somehow escalating her life's downward spiral.

She put her hands up, as if to hinder them going forward. "Folks—"

"It's fine," GQ said. He was stern.

Tom entered her office warily. This was more awkward than he had imagined. He had intended to privately confront her on the charges of plagiarism that she was spreading. If his points were to be taken seriously, now was the time, he guessed.

"I had a meeting with an agent today," Tom started.

"Surprising," Maroquin said. Summers was proving to be a nuisance.

"Surprising that he met with an agent?" Rachelle asked.

"Yes," Maroquin said.

"Anyway," Tom continued, "someone has been spreading rumors that my manuscript is plagiarized."

"Well, you shouldn't be ripping off other writers then," Maroquin snapped. "How's this a problem that has incited you to interrupt my meeting—" She was pained to finish her sentence, "with my partners?"

"I'm not doing it, Maroquin. That's just it. I understand you're the source of the lies."

He had the couple's attention.

Maroquin was expressionless and direct. "That's preposterous."

"What I don't understand is how I can be accused of plagiarism when I wrote an original novel inspired by my own life? I've been a victim of plagiarism in the past. It's a serious charge you're making, Maroquin. And getting me banned from the writers' convention? This isn't limited to ethics. There are legal consequences."

Rachelle arched her eyebrows and observed her husband's wooden poker face. This was getting better.

"So you've been involved with plagiarism before, have you, Mr. Summers?"

"I just said—"

"I recall that you were indeed reprimanded in your own company, for that rag *Western Mag*, for exactly that. Am I correct?"

Tom hadn't seen this coming.

"It's my job to know all," she said, pleased with herself. Having read up on Summers's writing history after he had left her office two days ago had been a constructive exercise. LA was a competitive environment, and so was the publishing industry. She was on top for a reason.

Tom frowned. "That was a misunderstanding."

"I'm sure it was. Are you surprised that plagiarism is following you?"

"That wasn't me. There was an agreement made internally—"

"You're focusing on the wrong thing, Mr. Summers," Maroquin interrupted. "Have you considered the possibility that the problem is with you and your work, not with the entire publishing industry?"

"The whole industry isn't my problem."

"Sounds to me like it is. I've given you some free advice already. Here's some more. Cope with your inner demons before you barge in my office and accuse me of unethical or illegal activities."

Tom was speechless. Like with Jamie, he understood that he wasn't good at facing opposing points of view head-on. With Brent at work. With work. With William. He realized he was most comfortable when writing, safe behind the shroud of editing and well-constructed prose. Sticking his neck felt like he was killing himself.

"Well?" Maroquin asked, staring Tom down.

"I—"

Her tone became more caustic. "Spit it out, Summers."

He couldn't think of anything else to say. "I'm sorry to disturb you." He left.

"Wow," Rachelle said. The couple glared at Maroquin.

Uneasy, Maroquin took a breath. "What?"

"Does it suck?" GQ asked, Rachelle delighted by her husband's inquisitive directness.

"No, it doesn't suck. But you two instructed me not to sign any new writers, your sole request of me the last couple of years. And I agreed, though this is *my business*. The ending was deplorable, and he refuses to change it. Otherwise, it's quite good." She paused. "But if I can't have it, no one else can either."

"Good play," GQ said, and Rachelle's face soured.

* * *

A half hour later, Wanda's van pulled up to Jamie's home. The old couple across the street was sitting on their porch watching the television the old man had proudly situated onto a bench, delivering crisp cable reception. His enjoyment of *Jeopardy* coincided with being out of the house, figuring when he died he would be in a box 24-7, so he should be outdoors while he could. They both noticed Jamie come out of her house and walk toward the van.

"Boy, that is one busy girl over there," the old woman said.

"*Angels and Demons*," the old man said to the television.

"What is *The Da Vinci Code*," the *Jeopardy* contestant said correctly, only to be cursed to by the old man. She was unaware of a particular viewer's infuriation with her being more well read.

Jamie wore jeans and a white blouse, simple and comfortable. Wanda waved at her enthusiastically from the driver's seat, and Blaine's passenger window was down.

"Hey there, Jamie, I'm Blaine," he said, his arm folded over the window. The lines that cut his face suggested that he was a bit older than a college freshman.

"Hi." She noticed the wind. "Think I'll need a jacket?"

"No, we'll be safely indoors," Wanda said.

The van door slid open, and Don stepped out, ridiculously suave.

Oh great, Jamie though to herself. It was too late to back out now.

"Ooh, look at you!" Don beamed. "Aren't you a little red Corvette? I'm Don. You ready for the most exciting night of your life?" He provided her the cellophane-wrapped bouquet. Dead flower petals fell to the ground. She pretended she didn't see the $13.99 price tag on the wrapper.

"Oh, brother," Wanda said. The van stalled again.

"Pleased to meet you," Jamie said, politely extending her hand out to take the flowers. She hopped in the van, disappointing Don, who wanted a hug.

"All righty then," Don said, jumping in after her.

Jamie glared at Wanda. "Nice guy." She already regretted coming out tonight. It felt weird to be out without Tom. Her first blind date since college.

"Great flowers, huh?" Don asked lamely.

"Very nice," Jamie said with obligation. She laid the limping flowers on the seat next to her. "Are you a florist?"

Don pulled out some marijuana and started to roll it in a wrapper. "Nope, I'm a waiter. Got a light?"

"My gosh!" Wanda exclaimed. She checked through the front window, afraid of anyone catching them engaging in such illegal activity. "What are you doing?"

"Dude, right now?" Blaine asked. He should have known that taking Don out would be a bad idea. The last time they went out together, they almost got arrested when, in stop-and-go traffic on the formidable 405 Freeway during Friday night rush hour, Don had dribbled his basketball on the pavement to prove he had *skills*.

"Don't make me come back there," Wanda said, fixated on him in the rearview mirror. "You get that crap out of the van, or I swear to God I'll hit you upside the head!"

"I know what I'm doing," Don said, shrugging. "I'm a pro, don't worry. I take this seriously. I don't recreationally do recreational drugs."

"I mean it!" Wanda yelled. "Don't push me, mister man. You get rid of it now. I'm not going to put up with that."

"It's only weed," Don said. "What's your problem?"

Wanda turned her head around him. "You want to live?"

"Okay, okay," Don laughed, quickly throwing it out the window.

"Don't do that!" Wanda yelled. "You want some kid to find it?"

"You said get rid of it," Don said. "I'm glad I didn't bring any H." He gave a mischievous grin to Jamie. "I can take orders from women when the mood's right."

Jamie glared at Wanda again through the rearview mirror, and they made their way to dinner. She wondered how she was going to make it through this night. *Every relationship is designed to fail until you find the right one*, she reminded herself. Her mother had taught her that. Every relationship of Jamie's had always started with the question, *Once I get in, how do I get out?* Tom had been the sole exception. Followed by, *Girl, this one is gonna hurt. You sure it's worth it?* For a time, Tom had been.

* * *

Bright lights from the inside of Peppertree's Diner spilled out of the large windows onto the shrubs, hibiscus plants, and well-manicured grass outside, illuminating the walkway. The throwback restaurant's low windows allowed anyone standing outside to see into the treasured world of the envied seated guests. This was fairly common and expected on the busy weekends at Peppertree's due to their "world-famous" braised ham.

But tonight, the '60s-themed joint was dead. Friday nights didn't bring in the crowds until after midnight, when teenagers were jonesing for eats where they likely wouldn't get kicked out for their offensive auditory levels.

Tom sat at a small table in the corner working on his laptop. Anticipating seeing Teri made him more nervous than he had been walking in to Maroquin's office. Either time. He knew it had been a mistake to allow Jamie to break up with him, but he had to see this through—so he could move on and quit dreaming about her. For all he knew, his violent dreams of Gilbert could have been brought on by his tumultuous emotions for Teri. He still questioned why he had allowed that breakup to happen, over two decades ago.

He somewhat reduced his anxiety now by taking advantage of the time waiting for her, looking up every literary agency he could find—from California to New York—making sure he didn't miss any that he planned to send submissions. Thanks to Maroquin's evil tactics, he had to do something differently. She had humiliated him—again—and he was searching for a way to trump her. If he could get the personal drama of Jamie and Teri out of his head, maybe then he could better focus on getting professional representation. *One thing at a time.* He shook his head. *Impossible.*

A cab pulled up outside. Teri got out and handed the driver fifty-five dollars. The driver handed her his card. The last ten minutes in the cab, she couldn't stop watching the meter, cursing herself. She could have rented a car for a full day for that.

She walked into the diner while Luigi's cab pulled up half a block away. Luigi got out, and the driver gave him the toll.

"You're freakin' kiddin' me," Luigi complained. "We went ten miles!"

"The rates are posted on the side of the car."

"This is downright rippin' off."

"Do you have the toll?"

Luigi searched for his money clip, noticing his wife walking into the restaurant. He hated spending money over Teri's punk ex-boyfriend. Worse returns than the worst weeks in the stock market. "It's a real racket you guys got goin' on down here. Just call it a day and join one of them inner-city gangs you guys are famous for. Or just rob some ol' ladies, instead!"

"I like this job," the driver said, bored.

Luigi handed the driver the money and slammed the door. "You're all criminals!" he called through the open passenger window. "Criminals, ya hear me?"

"God help you."

"If I believed in God, I'm sure He would."

The driver peeled off, flipping off Luigi nonchalantly.

"Oh, that's just great! Friggin' *great!*" he hollered after the driver. He couldn't remember the last time he had been flipped off by a cab driver back in Jersey *or* New York. These Southern California drivers were rude and gutsy. He was surprised that his masculine girth didn't intimidate these brazen cabbies. LA wasn't as full of pansies as he'd thought. He approached the diner up the block.

Four years ago, Luigi had met Teri, and soon after that, he was married and living on the Left Coast. Time passed quickly after they had met. After a brief four-month courtship, he agreed to move west because of her family there, opening another furniture store just to be with her. This is what he told everyone, but he moved because he didn't trust her. After all, both of his previous girlfriends had cheated on him. For those few short months before they got married, Luigi showered her with lavish gifts that opened her eyes wide with surprise but distracted her from the jealousy and insecurities he harbored. She swooned after each unexpected gift. After the Goldendoodle was a hit, he learned the way to her heart, and it allowed him to hide his fear.

Now, after all that, he was officially a stalker of his own wife.

Luigi stood on the street holding nothing more than his crisp and unused vinyl gym bag, staring into the window of the diner. He wished he was enjoying the Jersey Shore right now instead of being down here in *Smell A*, the best term he'd conjured up for Los Angeles. He would hang with the boys and whistle at the girls who would shrug them off as rude tourists or *bennies*. Instead, he was here watching people eat, which would surely make him hungry again.

He got closer to the revealing windows, watching Teri walk toward a man sitting at a table. Tom looked much younger than Luigi, despite them being about the same age. His hair no longer looked Elvis-ish but like an older version of the kid from *The Jungle Book* or just someone he would hate. Tom's *GQ*-ish looks infuriated him. Teri had a soft spot for the clean-cut white-guy model type, though sometimes she was into the second-rate *GQ*-like guys in magazines like *Men's Journal*. Luigi pondered how easy it would be to knock Tom out if he touched his wife.

From the bushes outside, Homer tried to position herself comfortably while getting a good look at what Tom was doing inside the diner. She sat among leaves, branches, and—to her disgust—hungry rodents.

"Get off of me, you dirty things!" she whispered loudly, using the light from her flashlight to scare them off. "God's yucky creatures, yes, you are."

Continually adjusting her location for the best possible vantage point, she tried to stay out of view. She didn't know what Tom was doing inside the diner or who the Asian woman was. All Homer knew was she had only days to do His will.

"Hi, Tom," Teri said, approaching him at his table. She would have noticed him a block away.

He looked up from his laptop to see Teri standing just a few feet from him. "Teri." He grinned widely and stood to hug her. "You look great. Almost the same!"

"You too." She smiled nervously.

Outside, Luigi flinched, wondering if the hug warranted an ass kicking. From the bushes, Homer noticed Luigi watching the goings-on inside the restaurant, quickly figuring out that he was involved with the woman.

"Uh-oh," she said softly to herself. She couldn't get in the middle of an altercation between mortals again. God had made His point clear.

"Weird, huh?" Teri asked rhetorically.

"I had to see you. We're crazy, aren't we? Doing this?" Tom folded his laptop away.

"Luigi was totally against me coming to see you."

"Why did you? I was surprised you wanted to meet up. I just wanted to talk to you."

She had lied to Luigi. She had wanted to see Tom, and now stared at him and breathed him in. "I wanted to see you too." Lying to Luigi had been easy for her.

Tom didn't blink. "All of my relationships have suffered because of us. Some just took longer to disintegrate."

"Mine too."

"When you leave . . . tomorrow, right?" Tom asked.

"First thing. I'm here for one night."

"Everything'll go back," he said. "You'll have your mansion, your vacations—"

"My husband," she said, thinking of her packed lingerie-in-waiting.

"Your husband."

Outside, any measure of wind had stopped. Luigi started to sweat in the still, tepid air, wondering what was going on inside.

"It's not quite a mansion," Teri said, trying to inject energy into a story she had told a hundred times. "It's nice, don't get me wrong. I'm grateful for where and how we live. The street's a little hilly for my taste."

"Whole city's hilly, isn't it?"

"Pictures are on Facebook."

He nodded. "Missed that."

"That's weird too," she said, pointing at him. "I wrote way more detailed messages to you than you to me. You're the writer."

"I just thought," he said, searching, "you'd hit Delete after you read them."

"After I found you on Facebook? Why would I search you, find you, and delete your messages?"

"Because in your first message to me you said you couldn't keep stuff like that with Luigi going through everything of yours."

"And I mean *everything*. My e-mail is more private. I told you he's a bit possessive."

The waitress came by looking for an order. She was disappointed that they ordered nothing.

"After your first note, I had to see you."

"Though I haven't forgotten," Teri continued, "about those *other* love letters."

Tom knew she'd bring this up again. "She wrote them to me, I didn't write them to her."

Teri laughed. "I can't believe we let that stupid cheerleader's letters break us up."

Tom held his hands up. "Not my fault."

"It was high school."

"Over twenty years ago."

"And she was blonde." She still compared herself to that bombshell. Her *Chinese-ness* was definitely not blonde American apple pie.

"Nothing ever happened with that."

"I hated her." She couldn't hold back a smile.

"I know. Sorry. So," he said, trying to change the subject, "how are you and Luigi doing?"

"He's an idiot." All she wanted right now was Tom to *want her.* Tomorrow she could go back to the life she endured day after day.

Homer watched the large, sweaty man intently observing Tom and the woman through the window. Trying to be incognito, he moved a little closer to the window, mesmerized by the two of them in the diner. Homer didn't know if she should start praying or get the perspiring man some water.

"Are you happy?"

"Sometimes," she said after a brief pause, "I catch myself grabbing at an opportunity when one affords itself, do you know what I mean?" Teri waited, watching Tom's reaction closely.

"I took the opportunity to see you, though Jamie wasn't happy about it."

She wasn't grasping what he was saying. "Go on."

"We actually broke up. I don't know if I'm miserable, happy, or lonely. There's something missing, and I haven't been able to figure it out."

"Something missing with Jamie?" Teri asked. Hope was meeting opportunity.

"I don't know."

Teri was in disbelief. "You're doing the same thing to her that you did to me. A couple of love letters from a former flame, and you're confused. You sure you're not screwing up a good thing?"

"I have a way of doing that. Your messages . . . your e-mails. Financially now, too, I'm a mess."

"I thought that you were in the big time now. Don't you write for a magazine?" She didn't need him for his money anyway. She wanted something else from him.

"It's never been about the money for me," he said, frowning. "Ever. How it was important to you when we were in high school is beyond me."

"No judgment!" She put her hands up, surrendering. "You needed time to grow up into success, that's all."

"I write a column for *Western Mag.* It's not success to the degree of your husband's, I'm sure," he said. "But it's not like I'm still writing travel brochures for that casino."

"Tom," she said, trying to calm him down, "your head in the clouds attracted me at one time, but priorities change, people change. Luigi's a little older, but he's got his shit together."

"You found *the one,* I guess." It came out more sarcastic than he meant.

She breathed. "What you are is *that one.* Always have been."

He paused, distracted by an eerie feeling of being watched. He looked around the restaurant and then at the windows. Someone moved in the bushes outside, but maybe he was mistaken.

Teri remembered their heated make-out sessions so many years before. She was unable to forget them. "More like *that one I can't get over.* I don't know if there really is *the one.* If that were true, I wouldn't be with Luigi."

After she and Tom had split and she went to college, she dated so many *boys* that she had desperately hoped would be *the one* she would marry. They all had insisted they were men who were looking for their *one* also, despite their inability to move out of their parents' houses, support themselves, or grow chest hair. Later, with Luigi—after her first husband—she got more hair than she asked for, except for on his head.

"I have one request. A single . . . lonesome . . . request." She hoped she wouldn't have to say it, and his eyes eventually met hers.

He couldn't believe what Teri was suggesting. "Are you thinking—"

"You've always read me," she said, relieved he was not a typical stupid man.

Tom quickly pondered intimacy with Teri, which he had fantasized about since high school. They'd fooled around, but they were never fully intimate. He was sure he wouldn't have even known what to do back then anyway. "Always? That's overstating it a bit, isn't it? Considering we haven't seen each other in two decades?"

She ignored him. "I need to. I think we both need to. So we can get on with our lives finally, don't you think?" Her eyes were open wide with innocence.

Now having moved a bit closer to the windows of the diner, Luigi was able to clearly see both of their facial expressions. Luigi wished he could read lips. Maybe a full-on confrontation filled with berating, profane name-calling and a straight punch to the face was in order, or a sucker punch followed by berating, profane name-calling and more punches. If he knew what they were talking about, he was sure he'd make the best decision.

An angry white cat discovered Homer in its territory and turned its nose away, detesting what it determined to be Homer's dirty, foreign stench.

"Oh, you think I smell, do you?" Homer asked the cat softly. "At least I don't have to dig and cover my own ammonia tracks." She shined her flashlight at the feline, who snubbed her and moved on, as if she'd spoken some kind of weird cat code.

"You're speechless," Teri said in awe. "I can't believe it. I don't think I've ever known you to be mum."

They both were silent.

"The thing is," Tom started, "our respect for each other would change so much that—"

"No, it wouldn't. I could never lose respect for you or for what you've always aspired to be."

"I know that," he dismissed. "Aspired to be," he mumbled under his breath. Clearly, she didn't see the man he already was. Jamie flashed back in his mind. She had pushed him but appreciated him, possibly despite his fears of rejection in the literary world. He imagined Jamie's joy in hearing about how he had confronted Maroquin earlier.

"Come on, Tom!" she insisted. "I've dreamed about it for so long. Sometimes I lay in bed with my husband, our backs to each other as usual, and I imagine what it'd be like."

"It's questionably legal to even hug you."

"You know how long it's been since Luigi's held me?"

There, Luigi thought to himself, grateful that he thought her lips had said his name.

"There's another person involved," Tom said firmly.

"Oh, Luigi?"

Luigi smiled and moved a bit closer to the window now.

"Oh, don't worry about him," Teri said assuredly. "I'm the queen of the house."

"I mean," Tom said, "two people. Jamie. She trusts me."

"Luigi doesn't trust me. So what. Besides, I thought you broke up."

"We did," he said.

She looked back at him questioningly.

"I needed to see you to get over you," he said. "I know it's weird, but I just figured it out. You've been—or the idea of you has been—an obstacle in all of my relationships. An overromanticization I've allowed to destroy good things in my heart and in my life."

She looked at him straight-faced. Even her selfish husband didn't speak to her that way.

"I've destroyed things in your heart and life," she repeated. "My God."

"I'm not trying to be mean."

"Are you saying you aren't still in love with me?" Teri asked directly. She had always figured that he had felt as deeply for her.

Tom looked across the table at a woman he didn't know. She wasn't the immaculate, unrealistic image anymore that he had carried through college and a half-dozen short-lived relationships. If he could get over his consuming—and silly—adulthood extension of high-school infatuation, he could now look Jamie honestly in the eyes when he told her he loved her. And only her. "I haven't been in love with you since high school, Teri. Even then, I was more in love with the idea of you than the person. I was young and stupid."

"I was in love with you, Tom. I wasn't stupid. Or maybe I was!"

"I'm not saying you're stupid. We were immature. I'm sorry if you feel coming to see me was a waste of time."

She stared at him. "So that's it?" She couldn't believe she'd been suckered to fly down here to be rejected by someone she broke up with two decades ago.

He sighed. This woman who had haunted his dreams for so long. To whom he had compared all subsequent girlfriends and potential loves.

"Is this because I'm Chinese, Tom? I saw how pretty Jamie is, and she's white. Of course."

"Of course not. I just had to close this chapter that I've carried around with me for what seems like my whole life. Since I was old enough to be into girls anyway."

"I've just always wondered," she said, "what'd it be like."

He was expressionless. "We're both going to always wonder."

Teri's hopes were dashed. Things had been troubled at home with Luigi a long time because of Tom and, she now realized, her own obsession with the past.

"So none of this has been real," she said, exasperated. "All a bunch of fake crap."

Guilt swept through him like a gust. "We embellished our own feelings, Teri, don't you think? Won't letting go help you in your marriage?"

Teri thought Tom was an idiot, an even bigger one than her husband. "You're such a wuss. And no, it doesn't help me," she said, getting up. "You're lucky that I don't have Luigi come down here and kick your ass for playing with my emotions all this time."

"I haven't been playing with you, Teri," he said, watching her get ready to leave. "I've been trying to get over you. You reemerged two weeks ago! I figured you are—or I thought you were—unattainable."

"Fine," she said angrily, looming over him. "Figure away. What you missed out on tonight!"

A patron eating at the diner's counter turned to watch the commotion.

"Don't ever call me again, okay?" Teri asked, not really asking. "Don't e-mail me, send me letters, or even think of me. And I'm *unfriending* you. God, that's what this was about? Seeing me was about getting over us? I guess you're the one hitting the Delete button."

Tom was silent, and she turned on her heel and walked toward the exit, rolling her small suitcase behind her. She was so different now from his romanticized puff dreams and empty yearning. Finally, he let her go.

Luigi saw that Teri was getting ready to walk outside. He quickly jumped back into the bushes to hide and fell on top of Homer.

"Excuse you, mister!" Homer hollered, startled by the odd, profusely perspiring man.

"What the—" Luigi stammered.

"Don't 'what the' me, you half-wit!" Homer shouted. "I was minding my own business!"

Luigi curled down in the bushes, knowing Teri would be coming out of the glass double doors any moment. "Shhhhhh!" He pulled Homer down with him.

"Ow!" Homer whispered loudly. She crouched down with him, trying to avoid being pricked by the thorny shrubs.

Teri came out of the restaurant on her cell phone, holding the card the cab driver had given her. "Yes," she said into her phone, "Peppertree's Diner. Thanks." She hung up and strutted briskly down the walkway, her heels clicking with angry determination on the pavement.

"You smell somethin'?" Luigi asked softly, his adrenaline screeching from its high gear. He made a sour face, still holding Homer's arm.

"I'm telling you right now, you imbecile," Homer whispered angrily, "I don't smell. You don't want to push me either. I know you're hiding from that woman there. I believe you're the one with the foul stench. You people and your offensive bodily functions."

"Us people?" Luigi was confused, unaware of what that meant. No way would she be disparaging *Italians*. He sniffed. "Is that urine?"

"I will yell for her, mister. I mean what I say."

"Okay, okay," Luigi pleaded. "Just stay down with me. Who you hidin' from?"

"Who are *you* hiding from?" she countered.

Teri turned around quickly when she reached the street and saw Tom through the window, still at the restaurant table. He looked lonely under the overhead lamps, their light fanning out over the dark bushes outside the windows. She hated and pitied him, grateful that she was saying goodbye to him. For the first time in a long time, she looked forward to getting back home, which suddenly felt so far away.

Across the way from Restaurant Row, Wanda drove the old van through the parking lot into Sam's Doughnuts. Rihanna was singing on the radio about being a crying man's umbrella.

"I need a little sugar kick," Wanda said. "Or else it will be a long night."

"Man, forget dinner. Let's go to a party!" Don hollered up to the front of the van, holding his beer.

Blaine turned to the backseat of the van. "Looks like you've got your own party back there."

Wanda yelled at the rearview mirror. "I told you to stop drinking, Don! Not while I'm driving!"

"You can't tell me what to do," Don said. He had devoured several beers already.

Jamie was bored and gazed wishfully out the side window. She should have stayed home and rented a movie.

"Anybody want anything?" Wanda asked with a sigh. She pulled up to the drive-through speaker of the doughnut shop. She missed her hometown beignets, the chewy dough being a more savory experience. Doughnuts would have to do.

"I want some action tonight!" Don yelled from the backseat of the van.

"Puh-leeze," Jamie said, wanting to slap him.

Blaine laughed, and Wanda ordered her doughnut.

"C'mon, sweetheart," Don chided Jamie, moving closer to her. "Have another beer with me."

"I don't drink beer," she said, pushing him away.

Wanda pulled forward, and Don fell on his ass. "Ow!" He hit the floor hard, and Jamie couldn't contain her laugh.

"I thought you said she had a great personality, Wanda," Don said, struggling to talk without slurring. "Chick's probably got bush growing hip bone to hip bone."

Blaine raised his eyebrows. "Dude. Really?"

Wanda mouthed *I'm sorry* to Jamie in the rearview mirror and pulled up to the front of the drive-through. She paid for her chocolate éclair—completely with change—and received her little white bag. All the while, Jamie grimaced, not believing the endurance test she had before her with this jackass. She considered making up a reason to leave—like her mother needed her, or a fabricated emergency, or a faked illness. *How bad would it be to just end this thing now?* Jamie wondered what Tom would think of her right now and then wondered what he could be doing. If he was meeting with that ex he obsessed over.

"You guys, I'm going to just pull over," Wanda warned. "I want the open containers out of here!" A ticket or arrest with drinking passengers, or at least one actively drinking passenger, would jettison any possibility of a good night.

"I'm going to be sick," Don said, picking himself back up into his seat.

"Maybe you should pull over anyway," Blaine said. He wished he'd intervened with Don opening beer number one.

"You're not hurling in this van!" Wanda leaned up and yelled to her rearview mirror. "I'm not cleaning your nasty-ass mess up!"

"Ohhhhhhh," Don moaned.

Wanda pulled the van into the parking spot. She killed the ignition and the radio and pulled her chocolate éclair out of the little bag in her lap. At the edge of Restaurant Row, it was desolate and quiet. Nothing else was around.

"I'm so having a bite of that," Blaine said.

Wanda slapped Blaine's reaching hand, and Jamie slid open the side door of the van and jumped out. She needed to get out of there. Moments later, Wanda came out, the rest of the doughnut in her mouth, pulling out Blaine's wheelchair and helping him get out of the van and into it.

"Hey, I don't need any help here!" she sarcastically called to Jamie, who was looking out over the empty parking lot.

The lot was lit by bright lampposts positioned all through Restaurant Row like a grid, equidistant from each other, so far apart that huge patches of darkness seeped between their small circles of direct, white light. It fell directly and brightly onto the pavement in defined circles, making Jamie think of interrogation lights in dark rooms like in the movies and on cop shows on television, except these attracted hundreds of gnats and other flying bugs. Thankfully, they were in a dark patch.

"I'm sorry," Jamie said. She ran back to the van to help get Blaine into the chair.

"I know he's an asshole," Blaine said, looking up to Jamie.

"Then why'd you want to set them up, Blaine?" Wanda asked. "I said one of your nice friends. He's a jackass."

"It's okay," Jamie said, leaning up against the van's passenger door. "I don't want be a sacrificial lamb for the night, though. Any way you guys can drop me off?"

"Really?" Wanda asked, watching Blaine push himself off toward one of the light patches on the asphalt. She pleaded softly. "I'm sorry, Jamie. This wasn't what I had in mind for us tonight, but I really like him. Can we see how the rest of the night goes first?"

She and Jamie watched Blaine push himself under one of the lampposts, gazing up at the fluttering bugs circling in maddening chaos.

"Wow, guys, look at this!" Blaine said. "Heavenly creatures above!"

"Ewww, I don't think so," Jamie said. "I'm close enough."

Wanda was gushing. "Look at him. He's sooo cute! Okay, not the bug thing. But in general."

This wasn't Jamie's idea of a date. Come to think of it, she couldn't think of the last time she was in a *van,* which, before Wanda, she had associated only with child molesters and the bug man—which, right now, was fitting.

"Got any condoms in here?" Don called from inside the van, going through Jamie's purse. He had already pulled out a small makeup bag and her precious BlackBerry.

Jamie peered into the van. "Hey!" She jumped through the open side door and confronted him. "What do you think you're doing?" She pulled her birth control pill case out of his hands. "Give me that!"

Don quickly shut the van door behind her, locking Jamie in and everybody else out. Right there, Wanda reached over and tried to open the door from the outside.

"Bastard!" Wanda shouted. She rushed to the front passenger door. Don was there inside the van in front of the cab. He locked the other door, eyeing her menacingly through the glass.

"Why are you pushing Wanda's buttons, Don?" Jamie asked from the backseat, unaware of Don's increasingly hostile behavior as she recovered her items back in her purse. "You know she won't have it."

Outside in the front of the van, Wanda watched Don lock the front passenger door before she could get around to it and frowned when she saw her keys dangling in the ignition. She couldn't believe she'd left her cell sitting on the front seat. "Ugh."

Blaine quickly pushed himself back to the van. "What's going on?"

Inside, Jamie put her last personal item back in her purse, she hoped. "She will kick your drunk ass."

Don turned to Jamie. "Another couple around can really ruin the mood," he said, slowly stumbling toward her, his stomach queasy.

She didn't look up at him, checking her purse for anything missing. "We're not a couple, Don."

He quickly moved to her and kissed her neck.

"Gross," she said, shaking him away. "As if. And you better not get sick all over me, either!" She reached for the door, and Don blocked her.

Blaine pounded on the side door. "Don, open the door!" He turned his wheelchair around and searched helplessly, seeing no one else in the vast parking lot. A lonesome pickup that sat outside the doughnut shop seemed like it was a mile away. He slammed his wheelchair against the side door. "Dude! Open the door, man!"

Wanda pounded on the door with him and then the window, wishing her fists could break the glass.

"You said you were ready for the time of your life," Don said, jumping on top of Jamie. Anger and determination flushed his face a feverish red.

"No, I didn't!" She struggled, but he was too strong. In a quick second, her top was ripped open, and he was between her breasts. She screamed and kicked but couldn't force him away. "No!" Jamie cried. "Get off me!"

All Wanda could do was punch the door. "Oh God!"

"Leave her alone, Don!" Blaine shouted, clobbering the door harder and harder.

"Don, stop!" Wanda yelled through the walls of the van. She peered through the backseat window and tried pleading with him. "Please stop! Unlock the doors, and we'll forget this!"

Blaine kept pounding on the van with his fists. "I'm going to kill you, man!" He craned his neck, trying to see through the window. Frustrated, he climbed out of his wheelchair and tried to scale up the side of the van to see Don in the back passenger window but fell to the ground. His wheelchair toppled over.

"Please, Don!" Wanda cried. "Somebody help us!"

From across five empty restaurant parking lots down, Teri stood at the curb waiting for her taxi, trying to determine the source of the commotion she was hearing.

Luigi and Homer stayed hidden in the bushes, his fat belly laying over one of her legs. She cursed to herself, hoping God wouldn't hear her; His disruptions didn't help. In fact, every time He barged in on her, her equilibrium was disrupted, and the task became more daunting. Now, she swore her leg was asleep.

"Who's yellin'?" Luigi whispered to Homer. "You know?"

"What do I look like to you, Nostradamus?" she whispered back angrily. Her angelic senses had to be allergic to the rancid garlic that permeated through Luigi's pores. When he whispered, his breath offended her unlike anything she ever encountered before, including anything she had experienced in the Middle Ages.

"Somebody needs help," he said, stating the obvious.

"Well, why don't you go do something about it before you kill the circulation of my mortal body here?"

Luigi looked at her oddly.

Homer warned in her stern whisper. "I've seen more evil by man than you ever will."

Luigi let out some unapologetic gas.

"Oh, you're kidding me!" Homer whispered with revolt. "What do you eat?"

"I think I had too much fruit at lunch."

"Consider a different diet," she said, holding her nose. "And you'll have a different stench, if you do indeed have a problem with objectionable odors."

"You people."

"*You people*?"

"Women," he whispered back, peering up over the prickly hedge. Teri was still oblivious to their presence, checking her watch. "You women. Don't flip out, sweet Jesus."

"Watch yourself, mister. Time is ticking while you're engaging in reckless debauchery and indecency with, I presume, your betrothed."

He shook his head. "What's that mean? Time is ticking. You got a bomb or somethin'?"

"Oh, I don't have a bomb," Homer said, trying to kick Luigi off her leg. Refraining from using her God-given strengths—if to merely avoid another one of His intrusions—had its uncomfortable price. But it was still worth it. "And get off me, you animal! *You people* do a great job wrecking this place all by yourselves." Her timepiece indicated time *was* ticking, but she was held back by God's rules, and she still didn't know what she could do to successfully complete her task without violating free will. She was getting resigned to the fact that there was nothing she could do. Humanity was doomed.

Teri considered that though she'd be alone tonight, she wouldn't have to endure *SportsCenter*. Whatever was going on a couple of hundred yards away wasn't her problem. If there was one thing that Luigi had taught her, it was not to get involved in other people's beefs. She'd been reckless enough today already.

Don was on top of Jamie, who sobbed helplessly and bucked, trying to get him off her. He turned his head to Wanda through the van's window and unzipped his jeans, sneering devilishly. Wanda bounced helplessly in place outside the vehicle and cried.

Peering out of the bushes, Luigi saw Teri looking out across the empty parking lot, waiting impatiently for her taxi. He heard a call for help. A memory of celebrated heroism flashed before him. He remembered the time a drunk guy in a bar catcalled Teri when they were dating, back when she still would go to bars with him. After Luigi had stood up to the guy, he and Teri had passionate lovemaking for weeks. He thought of how differently Teri looked at him now, with his diluted charm and larger potbelly. He yearned to feel good about himself again.

"I've got to do somethin'," Luigi whispered to himself. He got up. The risk of being caught following Teri was worth the possible reward. He hoped she wouldn't immediately divorce him without hearing his story of why he was here—that he'd likely make up—after he emerged from the bushes and shrubs.

Homer was relieved that Luigi's large stomach was no longer on her leg. "Thank the Lord." Her mortal knees felt weak.

"Somebody help us!" Wanda screamed to the deserted parking lot. "Please!"

Jumping out of the bushes, Luigi startled Teri and rushed past her.

"Luigi?" Teri asked. She couldn't believe what she was seeing. Her husband—all two hundred and fifty pounds of him—was sprinting.

Homer stood up and contemplated following him into the parking lot but stopped. "Oh no," she said to herself. "Free will again. Damn!" Her knees buckled. "Oh!" she blurted, falling back into the bushes.

Teri's attention scanned to the bushes just as Homer fell out of sight. She was bewildered by the location from where Luigi emerged.

"Luigi, get back here!" she called after him angrily.

"No!" Jamie cried as Don struggled to take off her jeans. Tom's face flashed in her mind, and she kicked with all her might, also elbowing Don in the face.

"Ow!" Don yelled. He hoped she didn't break his nose. "Think you're tough, huh? And too good for me?" He slapped her.

Suddenly the window next to them smashed. Don saw Luigi holding the wheelchair. He slammed it through the window again, the glass shattering inside the van.

"What the—" Don said.

"Yes!" Wanda cheered.

"Man, you're crazy!" Don yelled. He got off of Jamie, who continued to kick at him.

Luigi's hairy arm reached through the broken window and found the door latch. He slid the door open and dragged Don out. "Get out here, punk ass."

"You lunatic!" Don yelled. "Don't rip the shirt!"

Luigi pulled him out of the van by his ripped shirt collar and threw him to the ground.

"Can I cut off his dick, please?" Wanda asked.

"You asshole!" Blaine yelled, laying on the pavement not far from Don, who wept when he noticed his shirt was torn. Blaine turned his attention to his toppled wheelchair on the ground. His expensive self-propelled vehicle was severely bent and damaged, looking like scrapped metal junk.

Wanda picked up the chair onto its wheels. It still worked. Surprised by its smooth operation, she helped Blaine back into it.

"How about we all kick the hell out of him?" Blaine asked, rolling his wrecked wheelchair toward Don.

Looking up at all them meekly from the ground, Don realized he couldn't defend himself against all of them, especially the hairy ape. He finally got sick, vomiting his excess alcohol into a small pool under him.

Wanda winced.

"I can't believe you!" Jamie yelled, emerging from the van. She covered her ripped blouse with her arms so to not expose herself. She ran to Don and kicked him until Luigi pulled her back. "How dare you do that to me!" she screamed, tears streaming.

"Let her kick him!" Blaine yelled at Luigi.

"Who do you think you are?" Jamie yelled to Don, who almost dropped his face into his vomit.

"You've got balls, you little weasel," Luigi said, looming over him.

Blaine rammed his chair into Don. "I see no balls at all!"

"Ow!" Don writhed and pushed his leg off the blunt edge of one of the wheelchair legs. "I'm sorry!"

"That's not good enough!" Jamie kicked him once more.

"Owww!" Don was sure he'd puke again.

Knowing things could get more out of hand, Luigi pulled Jamie back again and motioned for Blaine to cool it. As it was, he wanted to disappear before Teri emerged in this mess. "Miss, you've gotta stop," he said.

Jamie ripped away from him and sat on the ledge of the open door of the van. Wanda consoled her.

"Thanks for letting me borrow your chair," Luigi said.

"No problem," Blaine said, rolling forward to Jamie and Wanda. "I'm so sorry, you guys, for inviting him along."

Wanda caressed Jamie's arms tenderly, soothing her. "What were you thinking?"

"I've only known him for a few months," Blaine said. "I hadn't seen this side of him."

"I'm sorry too, man," Don said to no one in particular, sitting up. "I'm not really a drinker at all and—"

"You're weak!" Luigi yelled straight into his ear.

"I know, I—"

"Weak!" Luigi yelled again.

"We should call the police," Wanda said.

"They'll be here in a few," a female voice said.

Teri's taxi had pulled up. She got out of the car. "Wait here," she said to the driver.

"Honeybunch," Luigi said hopefully to his wife.

"Luigi! What the hell are you doing here?" She rushed to him. "You followed me?"

"What?" He acted as if nothing could possibly be odd about him being here, now.

Jamie moved in front of Luigi. She had quickly turned weary. "Luigi?"

Teri stopped, curious what this woman with the ripped blouse was saying to her husband.

"Thank you, Luigi," Jamie said. "Thank you for saving me from this man."

"This asshole!" Blaine yelled.

"I mean it," Jamie continued. "Thank you for doing what you did. You're an angel."

Teri was puzzled. "You just saved her?"

"Who's this woman?" Wanda asked, coming up to them from the van.

"This *woman* is this jackass's *wife!*" Teri said. "And who are you to question who I am?" She turned to Luigi. "You idiot, why are you here?"

"I don't want to get into it with this one," Wanda said, walking away with her hands up in annoyance. She didn't want to be incited to getting into her own fistfight.

"You can call him an idiot, miss," Jamie said to Teri, her adrenaline fading, "and he may even *let* you call him that. But I'm grateful to him for saving me from this would-be *rapist!*" she yelled, eyeing Don on the ground, who threw up again.

"Get in the cab, Luigi," Teri said. "We're going home."

He stood motionless for a moment, not wanting to get into the car and be verbally abused the whole way home. There was the prospect of drinking heavily—a much more favorable option—or eating pasta, which he had missed the last couple of days due to some half-assed diet he didn't take seriously. "I'll catch my own cab, Teri," Luigi said finally. "I'll meet you at home."

Teri was shocked. Her husband was willfully embarrassing her in front of these people. "Luigi Steffanci. This is not a request. Now get in the frigging car with me right now!"

Everyone was silent.

Wanda shrugged. Teri was the kind of woman that Wanda hated: bitchy, demanding, and privileged. She could tell.

"I said I'll meet you at home," Luigi said stubbornly. He raised his head proudly, feeling better about himself than he had in a long time—though passionate lovemaking with his wife wasn't on the menu anytime soon. Clearly.

Teri's harshness softened. How was it that others were admiring him like she used to? She remembered how she used to feel about him. How could these strangers so easily see the man in him that she had struggled to see in him lately? She suddenly yearned to be close to him. "You're not going to come home with me?" she asked softly.

"I can't believe he's going home with you at all," Wanda said. She wasn't falling for Teri's act of victimization.

Jamie threw Wanda a look.

"What?" Wanda asked, opening her hands innocently. Maybe she would kick this bitch's ass anyway. "So he's hairy! He's more man than I've seen in a long time! Except for you, honey." She tousled Blaine's hair, and he smiled.

"I am hairy," Luigi admitted.

"You okay, honey?" Wanda asked Jamie, providing her a sweatshirt from inside the van.

"Thanks," Jamie said, putting the sweatshirt on. "I will be." She read the lettering on it and cocked her head at Wanda. *We'll get along fine as soon as you realize I'm God.*

"It was a gift," Wanda said.

A few yards away, Homer watched the goings-on, her aching leg returning to normal. *An impotent angel.* This was a story she would take back with her to the heavens. At least the young woman hadn't been raped . . . she'd merely been assaulted. Homer looked up angrily at the sky and walked briskly away into the darkness.

Don got to his feet, and Wanda got in his face.

"Sit the hell back down," she warned, "or I will hang your little dick by a rope, you understand?"

Don reluctantly complied.

"Hey, man," Luigi called to the taxi driver. "Can you order me another taxi? I'm not goin' with her."

"Yup," the taxi driver said, carefully eyeing his meter.

Teri sulked. Her husband was distant, and she didn't like it. After getting into her cab, she directed the driver to her hotel and wondered if she was ashamed or not for how Tom had rejected her. She had flown down here with unrealistic, overromanticized expectations and put her already-rocky marriage at unnecessary risk. She realized Luigi had watched her virtually *plead* for Tom to sleep with her. Now her husband rejected her too, and she considered how she had rejected him so many times before. But he had always stood by her, even when she didn't deserve it.

She couldn't believe that Luigi had cared enough to follow her. It brought her back to his Italian machismo, which had greatly attracted her to him in the beginning, as did at one time—interestingly—his thick body hair. She decided she needed to save their relationship from ruin. She tried to figure out how to find something in herself to do it. A cop car pulled up, and Teri's cab pulled away.

Jamie's impulse was to call Tom. He would've wanted to be there to save her from this awful incident. At least she *hoped* he would have. She noticed a missed call from him, no voice mail. So that's the way he was going to continue, reaching for her but not truly talking to her. No way was she going to tell him what happened and let him try to rekindle their relationship on the basis of *guilt*. She could hear him now, explaining that none of this would've happened had they stayed together. While true, she didn't need anyone to save her—anymore after Luigi, anyway. Her BlackBerry rang. It was Tom. Not wanting to deal with him, she forwarded it to voice mail. She wanted this night over and couldn't wait to take a hot bath when she got home and get that idiot Don's scent off her. In the morning, she'd make sure he was featured colorfully on dontdatehimgirl. com.

* * *

It had been impossible for him to get any more work done at the restaurant. Sorting through the lists of literary agencies and publishing houses became more daunting. He wanted to give up. He couldn't focus at all, fighting his reflection on Teri's abrupt departure. He couldn't help contemplating how to repair his damaged relationship with his fiancée. So he kept calling Jamie. If she was going to ignore his calls, maybe he'd ignore hers. He could have seized the opportunity to sleep with Teri, especially since he had been fantasizing about it for twenty years, culminating in a two-week daydreaming affair. Who was he kidding?

When he got home, he turned his phone off and plopped onto his bed, wanting to disappear from the world, feeling the weight of everything.

He was a jackass for meeting with Teri, even though nothing happened. He had hurt Jamie, a foreseeable consequence he could've prevented had he thought it through. And he hurt Teri too, which made him even more stupid. His job sucked. He raised his brother and—somehow—didn't know he was gay. He was being persecuted by Maroquin, and he was a fool to think he could publish a novel. Staring at the popcorn ceiling, his eyes eventually fell upon a copy of his manuscript laying on his makeshift nightstand. He hated his work. All of it. He got up and let the anger fuel through him as he ripped it apart into little pieces.

* * *

A cab pulled up to the front of the bar. Luigi looked out his passenger window up at the burning neon sign that read Lee's Downtown Bar. With no windows, it looked seedy, but the last thing he wanted was to be lonely in a hotel room. Even when he and Teri were distant from each other, he felt an odd security sleeping next to her every night. He wanted a drink right now. Badly.

"This the only bar around here?"

"The closest one was what you told me," the driver said. "Want me to find another one?"

"Hmmm." Maybe getting a little buzz in a dive bar was just what he needed.

"The meter's running," the driver said, indifferent.

"I'll pay the damage." He dug cash out of his pocket, closely measuring it against the meter.

"Have a good time!" the driver said, counting his cash quickly until he came to the one-dollar tip.

"It's all I got!" Luigi said, slamming the door. Everybody wanted to rip him off. Small victories mattered a *hell of a lot.*

Two flamboyant gay men walked out of the bar and headed down the sidewalk of the dark street. It was quiet here, and the small joint seemed out of place, segregated away from the nearest commercial center two blocks away. The cab took off, and Luigi chuckled, realizing it was a gay bar. *Now who's got the last laugh?* He was too emotionally exhausted to care.

Luigi moseyed into the dark tavern to see twirling disco lights complemented by a cheesy, generic hip-hop beat oozing from the aged sound system, setting a unique throwback ambiance to the '80s. A small stage with a karaoke setup was in the corner, and raucous laughter and conversation filled the suffocating, dingy joint.

"Fantastic!" "He's the greatest guy." "I love Gloria Gaynor." "Such sensitivity in her voice." "Want to go to Vegas?" "Do you have underwear that's small in the waist but big in the basket?"

The dozen or so male patrons in the bar all turned to notice the newcomer that walked in. Luigi quickly realized this was not only a gay bar but a *male* gay bar. He thought there would be some cute lesbians at least, but there were none to be found. *Of course not.*

"Amazing." "Please play something from *Hairspray*." "Where have all the cowboys gone?" "I miss Aunt Ethel."

He wasn't homophobic, but Luigi didn't know a lot of gay people, although San Francisco had a substantial and growing population. He didn't hang out with them. His friends weren't gay—or refused to own up to it—his employees weren't, and no one in his family was—except for his cousin on his mother's side, whom no one knew was gay until she was in her late twenties. The cutest female in his bloodline was a lesbian, his first reason for deciding that God didn't exist in the first place, or that if He did exist, He had an awful sense of humor.

He felt self-conscious that all eyes were on him. Ambling up to the bar, he was greeted by a bartender wearing a name tag. Luigi had never seen a bartender wear a name tag in a dive bar before.

Two gay men made room for Luigi as he walked up, one of them eyeing him up and down, not normally seeing a short, 250-pound pudge in the bar. The other slapped his gawking partner on the arm.

"JD and Coke," Luigi said to Lee, the bartender. "Please."

A patron nodded, impressed with Luigi's choice of drink. Luigi gave him a *how-you-doin'* pursed-lip nod right back. He remembered his self-consciousness about often being the fattest guy at the beach and felt similarly now. The guy looking over the karaoke machine got creative and played a generic techno tune.

"This is lame." "Since when did cords come back in style?" "Just no *American Idol*, please." "Have you considered veneers?"

The bartender slid the drink to Luigi.

"William!" someone in the bar yelled.

Like everyone else, Luigi turned to the front of the bar to see the young man beaming at the front door.

"Hey, Carlos!" William said. He was greeted by a young man in black jeans and white T-shirt, showing off a kanji-symbol tattoo on his bicep.

Luigi took a swig of his drink and watched several guys crowd around William, taking turns shaking hands and hugging him. He was very popular. Everyone was unbelievably joyful, making Luigi wonder how exactly anyone could really be that happy. He felt like a sourpuss, putting his drink down.

"Um, excuse me, Lee. Can I just have some water? By itself."

The man who had been impressed with his drink choice frowned.

"You okay, my man?" Lee asked, picking up the drink. "Something wrong with this one?" He sniffed it.

"Doesn't feel good to drink right now."

"God doesn't care if you have a drink, my man," Lee said.

"I don't believe in God," Luigi said, "so that's not the problem. Just tryin' to cut down a little."

"You came to a great place for that," Lee said, disappointed in the atheist.

Luigi couldn't stop admiring the happiness of the guys who were doting over William. He wished he and Teri could be that way again, knowing he had bottled himself up over the last couple of years.

Luigi thought back to their first summer trip to Las Vegas when his knees had hurt from walking up and down the bridges overlooking the Strip, connecting many of the premiere hotels. He had set out to do two things on that trip. One was to place a big—and what proved to be worthless—bet on the Yankees winning the World Series. The other was locking down exclusivity with this beautiful Chinese woman. When Luigi had decided to propose, getting down on one knee itself wasn't the problem. He had not thought out how much his knee would burn on the hard, hot cement of the sidewalk outside of the Bellagio Hotel at three in the afternoon, when it couldn't have been hotter. The air was 118 degrees that day. The sidewalk must have been 130 degrees plus. He had winced when he put his knee down as the powerful fountain water streams at the front of the hotel danced gracefully to Elvis Presley's "Viva Las Vegas" blaring through the speakers. The submerged water cannons blasted and puffed the dozens of water streams into the air as they zigged and zagged, rising and falling with grace to the tackiest Elvis tune that Teri had ever heard—second only to "Kissin' Cousins"—in the cheesiest town she knew that ever existed, with its faux everything. (Only in Las Vegas could you find a fake castle, sphinx, and even a skyscraper skyline.) She had caught her breath when he pulled out the ring box and kneeled down. Luigi had bungled his prepared speech, but she had been endeared by him. He had pulled off one of his flip-flops and put it under his knee so it wouldn't burn on the sidewalk. Despite her parents' pleas to marry a Chinese man, she had accepted, though he recognized she probably regretted it later.

Guzzling the tepid water, he realized he had been happier when he had faced his stupid insecurities that Teri wouldn't want to be with him. Confronting the possibilities and peril of rejection had brought him happiness like that of these young men at the door of the bar. He missed Teri and suddenly wished he had gotten in her cab.

"Can I get some ice in this?"

"You said you wanted water by itself," Lee said.

He shrugged. "I didn't know I wanted it."

The doors of Lee's Downtown Bar opened, and William and his friend Carlos—proudly strutting—walked out onto the desolate sidewalk, illuminated by the pink and green glow of Lee's neon sign.

"I loved it until the last ten pages," Carlos said. "There's some pretty messed-up stuff. Compelling, though. Finished it in three days."

"Wow," William said, surprised. He couldn't get past page one.

Carlos shrugged. "You said it was important I read it."

"You think you could pass it on to your dad? Tom needs an agent, and he's working on changing the ending right now," William lied.

"I hope so. How great you remembered my dad's an agent. At least I know you listen to me. That's good he knows that he needs to fix the ending."

"Yep," William said, trying to avoid eye contact. He had always been a terrible liar, except to Tom, for some reason. Tom's defiance to revision would be his undoing in getting it published, William swore.

They walked by a bum, asleep against one of the walls of the empty storefronts.

"What'd you think of it?" Carlos asked, checking texts on his cell phone.

"Loved it," William said with lame conviction. He had taken the lazy route of forming his optimist opinion with Tom's rants and defenses to agents like Maroquin. "It's a personal story for him. He doesn't want sell out to commercialism or whatever. I don't understand where he gets the passion for it, actually. My bro's got passion, with some left over to give me crap all the time."

"Interesting," Carlos said. They continued to walk.

"You're the only person I know who can help, with your dad." William was sure that Tom would forgive him for giving away his personal copy for such a cause.

"It's my brother's dad," Carlos said. "Didn't I tell you that Eduardo is my half brother?" He changed his mind that William listened to him. "And I don't see his dad. I've got to give the book to Eduardo. He'll get it to his father. Though that may be a problem, since he now hates you *and* Tom."

"Oh," William said, disappointed. *Eduardo.* He had only known him by his street name, *Eight-Ball.* And Eight-Ball had made it clear he wasn't a fan of Carlos and him being sexually involved, and he would never help him or his brother.

"I mean," Carlos faltered, "how was I supposed to know he would hunt you guys down? I can't blame your brother for standing up for you, though. He's not as big of a wuss as you said."

"Surprised me too."

"My brother has anger management issues."

"Man, this sucks," William said, kicking the sidewalk. "Maybe you can just change the name of the author or something. Just to get in his hands."

They continued their moderate pace down the sidewalk that was becoming more desolate as they got farther from Lee's. "Don't worry, he'll give it to him," Carlos said with confidence. "I'll make sure of it."

"Thanks," William said with uncertainty.

"Hey," Carlos said, forcing eye contact, "it'll be okay. He's just protective."

William forced a smile.

"Will, I told you I would," Carlos said convincingly. "It's very interesting. He'll absolutely give it to his dad if I ask him to. Promise."

"Thanks, man."

"No worries! Being there for each other. It's what it's all about, right?" He threw his arm around William's neck.

"Totally."

"You silly, silly boy," Carlos said, playfully rubbing William's scalp with his knuckle.

Finally, William felt like he had something good to share with Tom. He'd always been treated like the baby of the family, always needing his older brother's help with everything. Now he could contribute something substantial.

"So weird the two of you have separate dads," William said.

"Wish we had different moms instead," Carlos joked. "My mother's got hang-ups with wire hangers and shit like Joan Crawford. Drives me crazy."

William's laughter was cut off when a Mercedes screeched by them.

"Faggots!" one of the punks in the Mercedes yelled, throwing a half-filled water bottle at them. It sprayed William and swept across the sidewalk and hit a dark storefront.

"I hate this town, man!" William shouted, giving the departing sedan the finger. It hit its brakes.

"Oh my God," Carlos said under his breath.

"Great," William said. The car sat still, its red brake lights illuminating the street blood red. He didn't want trouble, remembering something his brother had said about guys with inadequacy complexes carrying guns in their cars. It was too dangerous these days to flip somebody off when road rage was an American-created commonality that was more frequently implemented by frustrated suburban, white-collar yuppies than by ignorant rednecks with gun racks.

The Mercedes backed up slowly on the quiet, dark street until the two hatemongers in the car were able to have clear and direct eye contact with William and Carlos.

"What?" Carlos yelled.

Both doors of the sedan opened, and two angry, preppy guys sprang out with baseball bats and ran toward William and Carlos, leaving the car running on the street. The passenger wore long camouflaged shorts and a backward cap, holding his bat like a club. The driver held his bat in both palms.

"Got something to say?" the passenger shouted, hoping someone, anyone, would answer his question with a yes.

"What'd you say to me, you little bitch?" the driver yelled.

"Back inside!" William yelled to Carlos, and they bolted back toward Lee's bar. The empty street with no open establishments didn't provide any other cover.

Both hatemongers ran after them, gaining ground on William and Carlos, who had the door of the bar in their sights.

Only a few yards from the door to the bar, the thug with the hat grabbed hold of Carlos's shirt and pulled him backward to the ground.

"Hey, pretty boy," the capped hatemonger said, holding him to the ground with his foot, breathing a bit heavier than anyone should after running just thirty yards. "Ain't so quick!"

Carlos was scared.

William ran to the front of the bar and grabbed the door handle only to be pushed up against the heavy, wooden door. The hoodlum threw his bat and tried to pry William's hands off the door. There was no way he was going to let him back in that hellhole for sinners.

"Leave us alone!" William yelled. His fingers were pried off the door handle. He was surprised to see Carlos down, being kicked and beaten with the bat. Carlos managed to kick the capped thug in the groin from the ground. The sleeping homeless man nearby turned over, ignoring the ruckus.

"Ow, you little mother—" the capped thug yelled at Carlos, who futilely tried to kick the thug's legs away from him.

"Put this in your mouth!" the thug yelled. He slugged Carlos in the head one more time with the bat. William watched him writhe, blood spattering the concrete.

"Carlos!" William yelled helplessly, thrown to the ground himself. Before he could get up, he was kicked and punched back down. Soon, he blacked out.

On the other side of the door, the bar was in an uproar. Customers laughed raucously and applauded as one of them walked gracefully up to the small karaoke stage ready to perform. Luigi figured the entertainment was just starting. He took a swig of his ice water, and it tasted good.

All the while, no one heard a thing that was going on just on the other side of the bar's front door.

* * *

Homer's watch struck midnight and read *Three-and-a-half Days Left*. She rested on the pavement on Restaurant Row, the cares of the world not her concern. If God was going to hold her back with His free will nonsense, there was nothing she could do. She would sit by and watch ridiculous altercations and observe the expanding suffering. In just days, she feared humanity would be damned. But then, who was she to think she could change it anyway?

She sat up abruptly, visions of William's and Carlos's beating manifesting within her. She could feel both of the young men's suffering. She scrunched her eyes tightly and tried to see and feel it all, while moths and bugs fought each other for the perfect light above her. Her eyes opened in horror.

Things were getting worse down here. Human beings were their own worst enemy.

"Hey!" Homer yelled angrily to the sky. Nothing. "*Hey!*" she shouted again.

"Do you need to talk about it?" God asked finally.

She stood up. "Sir, it's a mess down here! William is badly hurt." She shut her eyes and felt the truth. "His friend . . . is worse."

"I see."

"You've prevented me from doing anything! And excuse me for saying, but a different assignment helping some of the people down here not kill each other could use Your attention more than this stupid book."

"It's not stupid, Homer."

"I feel like a stalker, sir. I'm dealing with thugs, I'm hiding in bushes. And did You see this heinous human being with the offensive odor? And then he saves Tom's girlfriend, who's not his girlfriend? I can't tell what's up and what's down in this place. He almost crippled me too!" She felt a pang through her innards.

"Homer, you could be instrumental in affecting the lives of human beings for centuries—"

"The suffering that's going on!" Homer cried, interrupting Him. "What's happening to these two young men? This isn't right!"

"I did not ask your opinion."

"Flapdoodle!"

"Homer."

She got hold of herself. Maybe she could get through to Him. "May I be frank, sir?" If angels could throw up, that's what she'd be doing right now.

"Whoever you want to be, Homer. You've always got plenty to say."

"You're selfish, sir! While ignoring so many of the other problems on Earth, You're focusing on a book that's supposed to restore faith and belief in *You*!"

He sighed. "That's why I'm God and you're an angel, Homer. This has nothing to do with Me. I can't concern Myself with how My decisions are interpreted. There are other angels handling a multitude of tasks right now. You, My faithful servant, are handling the most important one, globally speaking. Decisions had to be made. As you know, I've had to make difficult ones for many millennia."

She figured if He knew all and created all, it was probably easy to get bored. It was enough to almost feel sorry for the old guy. She stepped out of the light and into a patch of darkness, away from the flying insects that were starting to really annoy her. "Destroying human life with boils, gnats, and flies like you did those thousands of years ago . . . how is that any different from what You're doing now? Do You enjoy bringing pain among people? They shouldn't be treated as subjects, sir. I'm not so sure You respect the species at all."

The ten plagues in Egypt were still a sore point with her, and using thunder and hail to convince the pharaoh to let the Israelites go was still devastation. Mass death was mass death, any way you sliced it.

"It's very different."

"Frogs, locusts, death of the firstborn?"

"I do what's necessary."

"What's left?" Homer asked. "Livestock disease, darkness, rivers of blood?"

"Don't mock Me, Homer. What happened in Egypt was necessary. Ultimately, it was the best thing. I still have not used asteroids or allowed man to destroy himself. I'm hoping it won't come to that."

He couldn't be serious, and He was making her nervous. What kind of destruction of human civilization did He have in mind exactly? "You've used volcanos, sir." The eruption of Mount Vesuvius in Pompeii had killed thousands, as did Krakatoa in the sixth century, and again from Mount Tambora in Indonesia in the 1800s. Quite possibly, volcanos were His favorite human annihilation tool.

"I don't want mass extinction, Homer. I'm avoiding more global cataclysms at the hands of nature. Right now, I'm trying to prevent mankind from destroying itself. You don't understand, and this is why you fail."

With all of His resources available, He had talked directly to human beings before, sent prophets and saints, shown chosen people signs, and even used torrid, precipitous weather to get things done. She was flying blind, which was ironic since angels could not fly, despite human mythology. Why was He fussing around with a lowly, disgraced angel like herself, offering her redemption? He wasn't testing her abilities or patience. He was playing with her.

"I'm sick of You!" she yelled, her pain for William and Carlos welling up through her.

"My intentions are often misunderstood, even by My most faithful messengers."

"Skullduggery! You are cruel, toying with me and Your creation of humanity, who You only *claim* to be precious! Truthfully, You're a puzzlewit."

God was silent.

"I'm telling You," she said, turning her back to Him, "that I'm done! You're no help at all. We're through!" She started to walk away.

"Where are you going?"

"I'm doing this my way. I don't need You and Your unhelpful platitudes!" She walked away mumbling expletives no angelic being should ever utter.

"Homer!" He rumbled. "You only have three-and-a-half days left on your timepiece."

"I can read!" she called to Him, strolling deeper into the darkness, and avoiding any circles of light.

CHAPTER 5

That night, Jamie's nightmares had her reeling. In one, her teeth were crumbling and falling out, dissolving like Pop Rocks and tasting like vanilla. In another, she was endlessly falling and lost the jelly shoes she was wearing, which was odd because—among other reasons—she didn't own any. In the worst one——the one that caused her to wake up in a cold sweat with her hair stuck to her face——she was back home living with her mother.

It was after 6:00 am. In denial that she had to get up, she dropped her head back onto her pillow. Tom hadn't responded to her text message last night. She hadn't been able to help herself. She'd asked him to call her.

The rape attempt ran through her head again. Being out on a date wasn't what she should've been doing. She should have been *with Tom*, not trying to escape the pain and rejection he'd given her. Classic. She had read about how rape victims often blamed themselves, and she had thought it was ridiculous. But now she was doing it herself.

Imagining her mother's grating tone, she decided not to tell her mother about it at all. The last thing she needed was judgment or unrestrained meddling.

Eventually getting out of bed, she replayed the emotional and scary events again and again. She was grateful she hadn't dreamed of being raped or stalked. One night after watching *Night of the Living Dead* with Tom—which he somehow had convinced her was a movie classic—she had had nightmares of being chased by a scary, stiff-legged, no-faced assailant for a week.

Suppressing nightmare-induced yawns at her desk, she avoided seeing Stephanie, dreading the conversation about JC Traders. It was a pointless attempt; she'd have to face her eventually. She sat at her computer reading, filing, and deleting e-mails. One in particular that her mother forwarded her detailed predictions of the fates of a number of celebrities—including Miley Cyrus, Sylvester Stallone, and Paris Hilton (whom Jamie couldn't believe were linked together in any possible way)—with superclose stills of their buttocks being examined by rumpology experts across the globe. Their folds, dimples, and muscularity were examined in surprising detail. Jamie kept this e-mail in a file she called Laughs. She decided to print the keeper, still unsure if the The Asses of the Stars was serious or truly a parody of the science of studying people's future by what's left behind.

At the community printer, she accidentally picked up a Word document listing contact names, phone numbers, and spending histories of all of Westfield Shaw's accounts over the last few years. The shuffling of Martha and her open-toed sandals approaching from down the hall rattled her. Jamie quickly realized she was reading something she wasn't supposed to and swapped it in the printer's tray with her printed e-mail, just as Martha snatched the private document from her.

"Give me that," Martha said, scowling.

The moment Jamie saw Martha's snarl, she swore there was already something green in Martha's teeth—and before lunch. She'd hold that piece of information to herself, not feeling bad about it one bit. "Sorry about that," Jamie said.

Martha gave her a dirty look and trudged away. Jamie observed her slow, flat-footed huff, realizing with incredulity that at one time Martha had not only been walking the runway but had been the fastest sperm to reach the egg.

"Hey, uh, Martha."

Martha turned in supreme impatience, reminding Jamie of how an annoyed teenager acted with his or her parents.

"Yes, Jamie," Martha breathed. She and Janice had a schedule to keep; she didn't have it in her to deal with clumsy, jovial Jamie.

"I saw you had a list of all our clients' histories there. You cataloging everything for us?" she asked as innocently as she could. It was all suspicious.

"Something like that," Martha said curtly, irked by the irritating snoop's probing.

"Can I see it when you're done?" Jamie asked, concealing her suspicion of what Martha was up to. "I'd love to use it to review the highest revenue categories."

Martha glared at her.

"You know," Jamie continued, aware she was irritating the bullying shrew, "to make sure I'm spending my time going after the best client prospects."

Martha took a deep breath, her augmented chest heaving in her bright-orange top. "Sure," Martha said with dread. Jamie had to be on to her and Janice.

"Thanks," Jamie said. The heavy air around her made her gums shiver. She pretended to read the rumpology e-mail she'd printed, and she started down the opposite direction of the hallway, knowing Martha was up to no good.

Martha hated that woman. She watched Jamie turn the corner down her own hallway and then rushed back toward her own office, her sandals clapping against her soles.

Getting back to her desk, Jamie pondered calling Jamal and Cynthia. Their defection to NRS puzzled her. She was sure Stephanie had probably contacted them already to find out why they'd left, but no one had given her a heads-up about it. A lot of hours, energy, and personal sacrifice had gone into her servicing of that account. Finding out about it in a company-wide e-mail that was also congratulating the promotion of the evil stepsisters was embarrassing.

Stephanie's name popped up on Jamie's desk phone.

"Hi, Stephanie." She tried unsuccessfully to not sound anxious.

"Busy?"

"No," Jamie said and then changed her mind. "I mean, I'm always busy, you know? Going to get us some new accounts!" she added enthusiastically into the phone, punching her hand in the air with gusto. "I've got some calls to a few friends of mine at a couple of other shops, trying to get some info on some accounts under review somewhere maybe we can snatch."

The lie escaped her lips before she could stop it, and she hated herself for not looking into that before. It made total sense. She'd have to do that.

Her overacting was a bit much, but she needed to be busy—productively busy—when the prospect of being fired hovered over her like a black cloud. This black cloud happened to wear colorful suits and spray tan.

"Want to come by?" Stephanie asked, ignoring Jamie's zeal.

This couldn't be good. The hammer was coming down because of JC Traders. Too bad Davey's Dealios didn't work out. Researching a prospective client more thoroughly before booking a flight would be a good idea next time. Their website alone clearly wasn't enough.

"Know what, I'll come down there," Stephanie said. "I've been at my stupid desk for two hours already. See you in a minute."

Jamie's head filled with job options. She wondered if she should consult or something. Many businesses were unhappy with the results from their marketing these days. What was she thinking? She didn't want any of this. She wanted to run her own business, but the whole prospect scared the hell out of her. Convincing Tom to take risks was different, she was sure.

Stephanie quickly swung in and closed the door behind her. She stood there in her bright yellow suit, which she had just worn a couple of days ago. Pending doom had walked into her office rather than a ray of sunshine.

"A lot of changes around here," Jamie said, trying to conceal any nervousness.

"JC Traders," Stephanie said, plopping down across from Jamie. "What the hell?"

"Right? Though not my fault! Cynthia told me two nights ago, and I—"

"I know," Stephanie said, keeping her cool. "It's an epidemic. Companies, big and small, pulling back. This economy has got to turn."

"Yeah," Jamie said, watching Stephanie carefully.

"It was odd I heard it from *Martha*."

"Yes, I—"

Stephanie interrupted her again. "But I appreciate your efforts in flying to Phoenix on your own dime. So I forgive you. Martha also tells me that didn't work out."

"Nope," Jamie said. She didn't know where to go with the conversation. No one at Westfield Shaw knew she had walked out of the dealership before she had even met with the owner.

"I know," Stephanie said. "It's all a mess. All the energy I've put into this." She looked up at the ceiling thoughtfully. "Everything happens for a reason, though, right?"

Jamie nodded.

"God has a way." Stephanie breathed in and sighed, pausing before staring directly at Jamie. "So tell me. You and Martha and Janice. Y'all gonna be able to work together? I sense—I've always sensed—that the three of you aren't doing sleepovers."

"Um, no." Jamie imagined the three of them during a sleepover, picturing them in a place humankind wouldn't catch them all being together, like in a secluded log cabin somewhere. Janice was ordering her to scrub the floor a bit harder while Martha laughed with her mouth full of kaiser roll.

"I don't want to lose any of you," Stephanie said. "As long as I can afford it, and I hope to for a while."

"That's good news," Jamie said, dreading deep down that she'd be stuck in this job. "And no, we don't do pajama parties, but seriously, could you imagine us in pillow fights?" It hung in the air for a bit, until Jamie was relieved to see a soft grin emerge.

"Would be a mighty Kodak moment," Stephanie said. She folded one of her tan, skinny legs over the other, showing off her Prada shoes. The woman wasn't shy about her fashion, though only Stephanie knew that her shoes of pride were two seasons old.

"I'll bring the camera!"

"I'm serious, Jamie." Stephanie's smile disappeared, which made Jamie think it was quite possible that Stephanie was bipolar—something she'd read in a psychology book once about quick changes in emotion.

"Oh, we're fine," Jamie lied. "We're all like quarreling sisters, really."

Stephanie's tan forehead crinkled. This was new information to her, particularly since she was privy to Martha's and Janice's many complaints regarding Jamie's loud, cackling laugh, the most extreme irritant. Little did she know, it was Jamie who felt trapped between their offices.

"I know they can gang up on you," Stephanie said, surprising Jamie, who wondered why then she didn't do anything about it.

"Well, I wouldn't say *gang* up on me," Jamie said. She wanted Stephanie to see her as the bigger person, though she didn't have the statuesque model height of the other two. "It's more like . . . I sing a different tune, you know? Dance to a different beat."

"I would say," Stephanie said, "you do a lot more than sing differently. You dress, walk, and laugh to a different tune. It's like you're a Shetland pony, and both of them are Clydesdales."

"Okay," Jamie surrendered, "though I'm probably more of the Clydesdale."

Stephanie ignored her and continued. "I've talked to them, and they agree you're invaluable here." She stood up, signaling the end of their discussion was near. "Janice, particularly. And as long as you can get along with those two invaluable talents, we're good."

Calling those two trolls *talents* made Jamie's insides hurt. *Invaluable*? They'd try to get her fired if they had the chance.

"Absolutely," Jamie said. She questioned her adequacy as an actress, while her job depended on it.

"Good to hear," Stephanie said, remembering something else to tell her, though more delicately. "I'm proud of your ambition to do what it takes to win, Jamie. Something I would've done myself years ago."

Jamie faked a smile, and Stephanie walked out.

Martha was hysterical, her head down on her desk. "That little bitch is on to us," she whispered, her voice shaking into the phone. "We've got do something fast!"

Two offices away, Janice was calm, staring at a copy of the report that Martha had e-mailed her. "You shouldn't be printing stuff like this anyway."

"I'm the one with the plan, remember? You're supposed to follow my lead."

Janice took a breath. "I've got worthwhile contributions, Martha!"

"Keep your voice down!" Martha whispered.

In the office between them, Jamie was oblivious to their infighting.

"I'm just saying," Janice said, correcting her volume. Sometimes she hated her partner's bossiness. "I've got unused skills. I'm sick of being on the bottom rungs."

"You're either with me or against me."

"Who are you, George Bush?"

"Shut up, Janice. I think Jamie's getting suspicious of us. We've got to neutralize her."

"What?"

"I don't mean *kill* her," Martha snapped. "She's a great distraction here at Westfield Shaw while we're finishing up what we're doing, but now we need to get her blown out. She's going to find something."

"Would you make up your mind, Martha? One minute, keep her here. The next, get her fired. And you promised me we wouldn't get caught. We're supposed to retire one day with our vineyards, remember?"

"We're not going to get caught. Stephanie's too stupid—too busy riding horses and doing tanning salons and all. We'll need the printouts when our e-mails are shut down. It's not my fault she's too cheap to give us all printers in our offices! How was I supposed to know that Little Miss Muffet was going to be right there at the printer?"

"Little Miss Muffet?" Janice asked, humored. Martha could be so high strung. "Where'd you come up with that one?"

"Shut up," Martha yell-whispered into the phone. "I hate nursery rhymes, and I hate her." This was all her own idea anyway. Janice was along for the ride and would reap the benefits once NRS brought them into the company as co-owners with quarterly profit sharing at the agency, hopefully shutting Westfield Shaw down. Their new leadership roles here gave them access to all client billings and history, valuable information to help them steal the clients. She was the one who'd brought Janice into the deal. Janice *owed her.*

"Don't freak out," Janice said. "She won't be here much longer."

"Why didn't we just get her out of here when we had the chance? Damn."

"We've gone over this, Martha," Janice quipped. "She's a distraction. You want Stephanie in your shit? Or in *her* shit? You're going to screw everything up."

"You're right," Martha said, exhausted. She cradled the phone against her head and closed her eyes. They had promised NRS they'd have all the information they needed two days ago.

Stephanie poked her head in Janice's office. Janice looked up at her, holding the phone to her ear.

"Jamie'll be fine," Stephanie said.

"Great! She's awesome," Janice said, the joy from her face disappearing as quickly as Stephanie did.

"We've got to get this done quickly," Martha said into the phone. "Move it!"

"We're keeping her here like we planned. It'll be fine," Janice said calmly, swearing to herself that she needed new friends.

Martha growled and hung up.

* * *

Tom struggled this morning, depressed over the sight of his manuscript in little pieces in the corner of his room like pieces of white shrapnel. Perhaps his manuscript had a similar fate in agents' offices across the country. Of course, he had saved his work on his weathered laptop. Maybe throwing out his computer was the next step to recovering from his idiotic neurosis over his book. Jamie. His job.

On the way out the door for work, he realized William had never made it home last night. Tom considered calling him, if only to scold him again and educate him on the traits of a time-wasting juvenile versus that of a time-wasting professional. Possibly, there was a difference.

At work, Tom's first task was fielding more denials of his queries, and he wondered how many were influenced by Maroquin's evil lies. Even if the she-devil didn't exist, *Western Mag* columns seemed to repel any opportunity to get his book considered by literary agents and publishers on their own. It was as if *Western Mag* was a joke to the industry. He needed to get out of here.

He rushed on a new column he was toying with for the next edition, titled "Manscaping America: It's Unnatural." Andre hadn't yet approved the *manscaping* concept of male grooming, but Tom looked forward to his reaction. He'd come up with the idea after showering at the gym one day and seeing—despite his conscious effort to look away—men without any pubic hair. The world was running amuck, and the Apocalypse was nigh.

Nadia popped her head in his cube. "Hey, baby," she said with more cheer than he could handle. "My date was awesome last night; thanks for asking me."

"Sorry," Tom said, tapping away.

"You always ask me about my dates," Nadia said, sitting on his desk where he couldn't ignore her. "Don't tell me you're letting this place throw you off track."

"Not this place." Sarcasm oozed out of him.

She should have known. "Screw Brent. He's rich but stupid. Now, this boy last night," Nadia said, applying lip balm. "Though he's not really a boy, but all men are boys, aren't they?" she laughed. "Anyway, he's handsome and loaded, though that doesn't matter to me," she tried convincing herself. "I don't need a man taking care of my bills like Amanda Jones in accounting. That ho."

"Okay," Tom chuckled. His computer beeped, signaling an e-mail arrival. He multitasked and read the latest agency rejection letter. "Handsome and loaded. What else?"

She was disappointed Tom wasn't jealous at all. "Well, he doesn't have a job," she conceded, adding quickly, "but he's written a few things."

This was more uninteresting than the now-common rejection letter, which he deleted. He was more annoyed than he wanted to be, hating his manuscript in its entirely, hating that Jamie had ignored his calls when out on a *date*, and William was God knows where. Rejection letters kept coming, and his manscaping column now made him sick. It sucked too. The world could blow up, he didn't care. He turned to her. "Like what?"

"I mean, not like books or mags."

"Well, what then?"

"I don't want you to look down on him—"

"Nadia," Tom interrupted. "Just tell me."

"Travel brochures."

"Oh, I've written those," he dismissed. "That isn't the worst thing in the world." He had written for them while in high school, sure, but it was legitimate writing or, at the very least, concise documenting, with industry buzzwords like *enjoy, recreation,* and his all-time clichéd favorite, *getaway,* an industry staple for travel brochures. As if the intended readers of the travel brochure didn't yet know that they were going away somewhere.

"I know," Nadia said, unsuccessful in convincing herself. She frowned. "He also said I shouldn't swallow any more corporate mandate suppositories."

"Ha!"

"Yup," Nadia said. "Doesn't think I should follow this corporate IPO stuff. He thinks it represents all that's wrong with society. His rich family—yes, *rich*—believes financial growth trumps the health of the business or the employees or *the customers*. Hell, the health of Earth itself. Corporations are superficial and shallow."

Tom didn't care about any of this. He tried to be patient so to avoid the consequences of upsetting her. If he pushed her, she could ignore him for weeks, and he needed an ally at the office besides Andre. She wasn't one to quickly forgive you for your sins. "Not that I disagree with him, Nadia, but Western Mag Corp is barely a corporation. We're this little building. That's it."

"True dat, but we're gonna be," she said. "We're probably going public soon, and that's pretty much the big time."

Suddenly, the new copy of *Western Mag* plopped into his hands. A young intern was scurrying down the cubicle rows throwing copies on everyone's desks.

Nadia saw Tom's disagreeable look. "That's what you get for calling them *the help*," she said, grinning widely. "Ever hear of the intern mafia?"

"No."

"Word gets around," she said, getting back to work. "I think they have a network on Facebook or something."

Tom flipped through the magazine looking for his article, "The Success of the Merger." He never knew what graphics would accompany his article, if any. Sometimes another writer on the floor would contribute a different angle on the same subject matter, juxtaposed within the pages of his article. He had anxiety every time the new edition came out, not knowing if his column would be a premier, highlighted feature, a supplemental feature for another writer's main headline, or merely filler, where he felt his text was just *the crap between the ads.*

There it was. It was highlighted, all right.

Initial Purchase Offerings—Bad for Everyone
by Tom Summers

He scanned the article. The words weren't his. The accurate research was presented inaccurately. The parts he had provided to Brent with initial question marks—inviting Brent's opinion—were transcribed into the article erroneously. Brent had contributed to the article, all right. He had written a blasphemously inaccurate story about successful IPOs and left the inaccuracies and poor journalism all over Tom's face. Wrong sources and timelines were layered throughout. The facts about the merger of Time Warner and AOL were completely wrong. Clearly, the writer couldn't accurately define *stock split*, either.

Tom shook his head, again seeing his name on the article. His credibility was shot. Wonder of how this could have happened turned quickly to anger. He was being pushed around by that narcissistic and nepotistic bully with the passive condoning of Andre. The article got a full-page photo, and upon closer inspection, the story made the cover. He'd never before gotten the cover for a story he had actually written.

He flipped the page to see another article written by Brent.

Successful IPOs: Where Everyone Wins
Everything You've Read Before is Wrong
by Brent Hayes

The story contradicted Tom's *fake* article on every point. It blatantly discredited Tom's story as fiction, challenged his ability as a journalist, and compromised his journalistic honesty and integrity—with Brent's research discrediting the article in Tom's name. *How were there two articles?*

This was war.

His cell phone rang with an unknown number. Tom ignored it and left it at his desk. Marching toward Andre's office, there was a foreign strength in his brisk stride. He normally didn't challenge the little man's Napoleon complex, but this fake column couldn't be ignored. He didn't care about the consequences. He'd had enough.

"Andre," Tom exhaled, storming into Andre's office.

"I don't want you to be pissed," Andre said, uncharacteristically popping out of his chair defensively. He turned down the volume of the music blaring from his computer. X was singing something about Los Angeles.

"You're screwing me." He found no comfort in the fact that Andre expected his outrage. Tom had read once that the most stressed-out lab rats knew the shock was coming.

"I needed to get people's attention and light up the positive position of the other article. A lot of rumors out there, gotta play defense with offense. I didn't screw you," Andre said, wishing he could come up with a more plausible explanation.

"Yeah," Tom said defiantly. "You did."

"It's a mistake for you to—"

"We both know it wasn't a mistake, Andre!" Tom yelled. "I did the work on the propagandist article like you told me to, and you allowed that jackass to screw me! Your operation here is crap!"

"Now, that's not necessary, Tom," Andre said, shifting gears back to authoritative supervisor. Otherwise, it would get around that he could be pushed around. "You don't want to call it crap."

"It's barely even your operation!"

"Tom," Andre warned, putting his hand up. "Stop."

Two assistants outside Andre's office poked their heads in to check out the commotion, quickly disappearing when they saw Tom striding up to Andre, pointing his finger in his face.

"I don't care about your little rules here anymore, Andre. I don't care about your poor systems or your inability to be a responsible editor with the spirit of journalism and all that we went to school for."

"Get your finger out of my face," Andre said. "Uncle Sam's the only cat that points at me, and that's cuz he knows he's only pinching pennies from me." He eyed the ceiling, uncomfortable with being justifiably attacked. Tom was considerably taller than he was, which, deep down, Andre disliked. Someone physically larger attacking him made him jittery.

"You cower to Brent and his poppa," Tom continued, ignoring him. "Now, you have to fix it because I'm not going to stand for journalistic fraud."

Andre kept his composure. He knew the whole office would be chattering about this insubordination within the hour. "Is that even a term?" he asked, humored. "There was no journalistic fraud."

"Hell there wasn't!" Tom yelled back at him, his confidence building. "You need to run a correction! I demand it."

"Nobody demands from me," Andre chuckled, concealing his nervousness the best he could. "I'm the chief editor. You, Tom. You're just the workhorse."

"That's too bad," Tom said.

"Yes, it is," Andre said, collecting himself. He needed to fire Tom, or his own livelihood was at stake. "And you no longer work here at Western Mag Corp."

Tom stared at him. A correction in the following month's issue would have sufficed.

"Unfortunately," Andre continued, "it's come to light that you've been using company resources—our e-mail *and* long-distance phone calls—for personal use, pursuing other writing pursuits. I'll give you a moment to ponder the consequences of theft, playa."

"You've got no proof," Tom said. He visibly had the wind knocked out of him.

"On the phone calls? Those are documented." He'd never cared about Tom utilizing the firm's resources before, but he had nothing else on him. Nothing. "Anyway, it's your word against mine, pimp. And my word is golden around here."

Tom was stumped, unable to refute the charges. His mind raced. "Calls for my novel isn't for another employer."

Andre nodded and stood up. "I'll make sure Dolores gets your stuff to you. See yourself out with no trouble, and I won't call security."

Andre's assistant quickly walked by the office. She had to collect Tom's stuff immediately, or she'd risk the same unemployed fate, though she wondered who Andre would sic to collect her stuff in such a case.

"What you're doing here has to be illegal," Tom said with unfamiliar confidence. He had nothing to lose now, his financial situation barely solvent anyway. "Phone calls to the East Coast aren't theft. It would've been corrected behavior on my part if someone *told me* it was frowned upon. Which no one did. And e-mail costs you nothing. That's not theft. I don't recall anything in the Western Mag Corp handbook that prohibits it. Show me how this has affected my performance."

Andre shrugged, and Tom swiped the papers, folders, and magazines off Andre's desk.

"I wish you could call HR," Andre said, sarcasm falling off his tongue, "but as you know, we laid HR off. Damned downsizing. More frustrating than itchy pubes, right?"

Tom was furious. "You can't do this!"

"California employment law won't side with a former employee terminated for stealing company resources. Take it to the highest power you want. Dolores, call security!" Andre snickered. "Be glad I'm not calling the police. Imagine sitting in a jail cell. Bubba hasn't got a cuddling hand."

"This is wrong, Andre."

"Wrong? Try *right*. I've got an early printing with two perfectly timed featured pieces on IPOs. One *tries* to discredit what we're doing, throws all the knives at the board. The second column—and this is important—burns the argument against IPOs like this one into flames. Get the issues on the table, and then burn, baby, burn. Everything falls into place here like *Tetris*. Can you believe I hear applause in my head? Dolores!"

Tom swallowed his own vomit. "You put my name on something I didn't write."

"Yes, Andre," Dolores said, fidgeting one step inside his office.

"Got his stuff?" Andre asked. She nodded, and he noticed the time. "Oh, and get me a sandwich. Turkey on wheat, no mayo." She scurried out.

Tom was humiliated, and he stared Andre down. "The facts will come back to haunt you."

"Oh, you'll get your correction. But the partners will have all voted their approval by then," Andre said. "And you won't work here anyway."

Otis, the security guard, approached quietly from behind Tom.

"You knew you were going to fire me from the beginning, didn't you? I don't hate you. I feel sorry for you."

"Aww, don't cry for me, Argentina!" Andre said with fake remorse. "Don't make me out to be a monster, Tom. I'm paying you two months' severance. Which, in this business climate, ain't half bad. Oh, and your unused vacation. You can come back at the end of the day, and accounting should have your last check for you."

Tom noticed Otis behind him. "So that's the way it is."

"Got my A plan and B plan. You were the C plan. It all starts with a seed," Andre said, knocking his knuckle on his own crown as he nodded to Otis, who took Tom's arm weakly. Tom was the only guy who worked here that Otis liked. "It ends with a wilted leaf, bro. And you, my man, are wilted."

"Let go of me!" Tom yelled, ripping his arm away from Otis's lame grip, the second time in mere hours that he was in a beef with security. "I'll leave, but my way."

"Swallow and smile, Tom," Andre said, beaming.

Tom shook his head in disbelief. There was no point in fighting anymore.

"I'm sorry, Tom," Otis said, scratching an itch on his butt.

"What do we pay you for?" Andre hollered. "Whatever your name is, escort this cat outta here!"

"It's okay, Otis. I'll let myself out," Tom said. He walked out.

"And no reference either!" Andre yelled after him.

"Hear that? My name's Otis, sir." He followed Tom out the office.

Andre plopped back in his chair and sulked. The Oscar performance of a lifetime. He couldn't believe what he'd done, but he had to protect all he knew. His career, his savings. His marriage. God, he wished Tom hadn't pushed him. He hated spewing his rage at Tom when it should have been targeted at Brent. It had erupted with no warning, pent-up frustration toward Brent that hit its nadir. Leaning back in his chair, Andre hated himself for not having the strength to stand up for what he believed in.

Compared to how he had entered Andre's office, Tom left the building quietly. Otis watched him leave. Tom's stuff had rudely been thrown into a tattered cardboard box that desperately held itself together with masking tape.

Brent strutted by him in the stairwell, pretending surprise by the sight of Tom carrying the box. "Oh, you're out? What happened?"

"I guess I was that much of a threat to you, Brent," Tom said. A side of the box gave way, and miscellaneous items fell out and rolled down the stairs, including a framed picture of Jamie and him that finally cracked in half when it hit the bottom of the stairs.

"Threat to me?" Brent stopped. He watched Tom kneel down to pick up the broken glass. With his hands in his pockets, his comfortable Tom Ford suit felt especially good. Wearing the best clothes in the building always made him feel rich, inside and out. With Tom out of the office and Nadia not being so close to him at work every day, Brent felt wealthy beyond his hopes.

"Why would I be threatened by you, Summers? Because you're better than me at finding other people's research? Please. In everyone's mind, whether it's Nadia or that little girlfriend of yours, my ownership of this magazine's now looming, and I'm more of a man than you'll ever be—while you rent that crappy little apartment with your lofty dreams. What's this unpublished *War and Peace* you've been working on for years? Pretending you're Yeats. Like I have anything to be jealous about." Brent convinced himself this was true.

"Tolstoy wrote that," Tom said, trying to hold the box together. "You're pathetic." He exited the building, and Brent followed him.

A crowd of writers from the second floor gathered at the windows of Western Mag Corp and watched the exchange—Nadia among them— unable to make out what Tom and Brent were saying. Outside, Brent immediately became conscientious when he saw the figures standing at the windows upstairs.

"Let me help you with that," Brent said and grabbed a side of the box as it gave way, Tom begrudgingly grateful.

They both held the box together, approaching the car. Tom pulled his keys out of his pocket, and they muscled the box into his trunk. It completely broke apart, spilling its contents inside.

"I'm going to miss you, man," Brent said with no conviction.

Tom slammed the trunk. "I'm sure you'll get over it."

"Wow, Summers. Getting a bit of a ball sack?" He laughed, knowing Tom's recent bout of manhood was futile now. He was out.

Tom looked to the windows and noticed Nadia waving at him.

"You're out of here. And," Brent continued, "I get to see Nadia every day."

"She's great," Tom said, making his way to the driver's side of the car. He hated all of this. "And the magazine needs her."

"Speaking of *need*," Brent said, "I need you to not come back here again. Nadia doesn't know that she's moving on to a much brighter opportunity for her career than hanging around with a talentless lug like your ass."

Tom stared at him. Oh, she'd have a fit if she knew that Brent was acting like he owned her. It would surely cost him, and Tom wasn't going to warn him.

"Get this, Summers. Talk to her, I mean at all, and I'll fire her. I'll blacklist her from writing anywhere."

"You're hilarious," Tom said, opening his car door. "Your fake power's going to your head."

Brent slammed it shut and leered at Tom against the door and then remembered that everyone was still watching them from the second floor. He politely opened the car door again for Tom with showmanship. "You think I'm funny, Summers? If you contact her, or even just return contact, I swear you'll regret it, and she'll pay for it."

Nadia would in no way tolerate that. She needed constant attention, and if he didn't talk to her, she'd resent him and, worse, stalk him through text messages and e-mails until he did.

"Don't you have enough to worry about right now—like the partners finding out that you're writing fake articles?"

Brent's anger was simmering. He figured he could prevent Western Mag Corp from going public—with Andre's listless leadership *out*—and it could be run correctly under his watch. Andre would be gone, and his propaganda would be discredited. Brent would soon claim that the pro-IPO article wasn't his but Andre's. The fool would be dead *and* disgraced. He felt like a considerably better-dressed Judas.

If Tom was threatening to out him in any way, it had to be mitigated.

"It's dangerous talk coming out of your trap right now," Brent said.

Tom scoffed. "Dangerous? Tell my brother I'm dangerous, and he'll laugh at you." He slid into his front seat and tried to close the door, but Brent got in the way and smiled for the audience.

"How about I just laugh at you, dumb ass? Figure this. I find out that you say anything that facilitates this IPO or you get in touch with Nadia, and I'll destroy your future as a writer, okay? The whole pathetic thing. You don't wanna mess with me, Summers."

Looking up to Western Mag Corp's second floor, Tom saw Nadia through the window putting her fingers to the side of her head, gesturing that she would call him. "I'm doing a great job not getting published on my own, Brent," Tom said, starting the ignition. "I don't need your help."

Brent backed up, and Tom shut the door, reversed, and drove off. Turning onto the highway, Tom noticed a message and accessed his voice mail. Then he drove madly.

Tom rushed into the hospital room, antiseptic compounds and the fear of the worst overwhelming his senses. A woman sat bedside next to William, holding his hand with her back facing the door. Tom quickly realized it was their mother. She rose to Tom's steps alerting her to his presence. His stride was still distinguishable to her after over twenty years of no contact.

"What happened to him?" Tom asked her. He approached William on the opposite side of the bed.

With his head half-bandaged and a cast on his left arm, William moved, wincing in pain.

"He was beaten up," their mother said. She sat back down, avoiding eye contact with her older son. She had hoped for a better greeting.

"Dude." William smiled.

"Hey, big man," Tom said. He delicately ran his hand over William's other arm, not looking at their mother.

"This sucks," William groaned. His body ached all over, and the painkillers made him lethargic.

"Looks like it," Tom said, inspecting him up and down. Bruises and dried cuts spread across his face and arms, making it appear as though William had run through thorns and brambles. He lay on top of the blanket, revealing bruises the size of footballs on his legs. His bandages allowed his face to peek through.

"He was admitted overnight," their mother said. "Only reason they called me was I was in his phone, which surprisingly wasn't smashed to bits."

"Who did this?" Tom asked William, who shut his eyes. With no answer, Tom finally looked at his mother. "Agnus, who did this?" He wasn't surprised that she still caked on her makeup and was adorned with chintzy and gaudy jewelry.

"He didn't cut himself," she said, their eyes meeting for the first time. "I hate it when you call me that, Tom."

If she was making a dig at him for cutting himself so many years ago, he wondered how she knew about it. Perhaps she had known more about him than she let on. "I've got nothing else to call you that you will like," Tom said, unconcerned with insensitivity. "Who did this?"

"Street hoods," Agnus said. Her thick mascara had now run down the sides of her face. "His friend that was with him is dead."

William's eyes watered up. "What?" Tom asked. "Who?"

"Carlos," William managed, wiping a tear off his cheek with his free hand, the only limb not in a cast.

"The poor boy's family," Agnus weeped. "I saw them when I came in this morning. Horrible!"

"They catch the guys who did this?" Tom asked either of them.

"What are you going to do?" Agnus asked Tom. "Stand up for your brother now that he's in a hospital bed? Beat up somebody?"

"I've been here to take care of him when you weren't around."

"You've been doing a really good job," Agnus said, her sarcasm undeniable.

"Nice of you to show up!"

"Guys," William breathed, "don't fight."

The nurse came in with her clipboard. Her tone was as sterile as her bleached uniform. "The doctor will be here in a minute to go over his vitals. Give us a few minutes, please. The waiting room is right outside." She waited stoically for the guests to leave.

Agnus smeared her mascara more while wiping her tears.

"Wait, Tom," William said with effort.

Tom drew close to William, kneeling down to him at his bedside. "Yes, Will. Whatever you need."

Annoyed with the brothers' bond, Agnus walked out in a huff. The nurse, more frustrated, tapped her pen on her clipboard.

William didn't blink. "Tom. I need you to do something for me."

"Name it," Tom said, conscious of his impatience.

"I need you to go to Carlos's funeral for me."

Tom hated funerals. Weddings too. The services were long, and everyone was overly emotional. And if someone sang, oh God, if someone sang, it was always bad. "Will, I don't think—"

"One thing," William said, concentrating on breathing. It hurt. "I can't be there."

Resigned, Tom said, "Sure. Whatever you need." With how disastrous the last few days had turned out and seeing his brother here now, he figured he might as well pile it on. "You know when it is?"

"Sir," the nurse said, waiting for him to leave the room.

"Stupid question. I'll figure it out, don't worry," Tom said.

"Okay, one more thing."

"Sir!"

"Ma'am!" Tom yelled back at the nurse, who pursed her lips so tightly it looked like her top lip somehow disappeared within the lower one. "One minute, please!" He turned back to William. "What, Will?" he asked, as tender as his rising temper would allow.

"I'm sorry if I've embarrassed you," William said, his eyes welling up. "I've always made things harder on you."

"No, you haven't. Never been prouder. You get better, okay? I have to deal with your mother now." He felt guilty for being exhausted by the thought of it. "Love you, man."

William shut his eyes and breathed heavily. Mild sedation was starting. The nurse glared at Tom sternly, and he finally left. William wept.

"My son almost died," Agnus said. The hall of the hospital was bustling with activity.

Tom walked beside her toward the waiting room, feeling like he was headed to purgatory. Forced to wait in this room with Agnus, it was like his life was needlessly wasting away.

"Glad to hear you've got a son," he said, wondering at what point William had become a son again: when he was beaten up, placed in an ambulance, or when she got the news he was in the hospital. William hadn't been a son when he needed shelter, money, or parenting when she and their father abandoned them to follow a religious crusade with some cult. That's when Tom was there.

Agnus shook her head. "Don't argue with me. I'm not in the mood for your crap."

Nothing had changed. She always thought she could just drop in and order him around. "What'd the doctor say so far?" he asked.

They approached the waiting room filled with various patients, their visitors, and crying babies. In the corner of the room, a young, pale woman was resting her head on what Tom guessed to be her boyfriend. A Hispanic woman held her crying baby and managed her rambunctious two-year-old who couldn't sit still in his seat. A bored older couple was watching the news scroll on the muted television. The only two available seats were across from each other.

"He's alive, no thanks to you," Agnus said, with more volume than necessary.

The Hispanic woman with the crying baby studied Agnus suspiciously.

"No brain damage, it seems," Tom said, unable to escape Agnus's hateful gaze. "Lucky."

"What kind of degenerates do you let him hang around with?"

"I don't smother him, Agnus. As he takes pleasure in reminding me regularly, I'm not his dad."

"Maybe you should be a better role model yourself."

"He's never been homeless," Tom said.

"He might as well have been. He wouldn't be here."

"How's James?" Tom asked, changing the subject.

"You know how he is. Six feet under."

"That bad, huh?" Tom asked, humoring himself. He had heard a rumor that their father had passed but hadn't cared enough to investigate it, barely having known him anyway. Though only fifteen years old when his parents left, he and Gilbert knew their father was somewhat of a philanderer, and he was rarely home. Later conforming to some new cult to take part of God's new plan for them, both parents abandoned them. The children, clearly disposable, weren't part of that plan.

"Oh, don't pretend you care how your parents are doing," Agnus said, laying out the guilt thick. "If I was dead too, you wouldn't care."

Agnus sat across from Tom, her cold presence jarring the Hispanic woman holding the young child, who looked away.

"We don't need to go into who cares less about the other," Tom said.

"Your father had no backbone, you don't have one, and your brother was almost killed. I gave him life. You tell me who cares less."

The Hispanic woman repositioned herself in her chair away from both of them, holding her doe-eyed baby in one arm and pulling her two-year-old's arm with the other until he got back in his chair. Tom was dismayed that even now, Agnus could turn anonymous strangers against him.

"I've got tons of backbone."

"Just like your father."

"Agnus."

"Don't call me that!"

"What do you want me to call you?"

"Don't talk to me."

He felt despair seeing her resemblance to his own profile. "What do you want me to say? If you want make it my fault, go ahead. I've been taking care of him while you traveled around to go find God or whatever with that cult of yours."

The old couple perked up to the conversation. This was more interesting than the news scroll on the television, detailing the latest global cataclysms.

"How dare you. You let him hang out with those characters! Get away from me."

"I'm sitting over here."

"Get away from me!" she screamed.

Everyone in the waiting room froze in their seats. The baby stopped crying, and the two-year-old's restlessness abated. A nurse down the hall at the service desk raised her head from her computer.

"You're nothing to me!" Agnus yelled, not caring where she was. She stood up and berated him, and the baby wailed again. "You've ruined this family! None of us want anything to do with you again! Get away, you understand me?" He got up to leave, and Agnus yelled after him as he escaped down the hall. "Your father said you were nothing!" Her screams echoed across the whole hospital wing. "Go sleep with your sluts, and stay out of my life!"

"I haven't been in your life!" he yelled back. Her irrationality hadn't changed.

"And leave your brother alone!"

Heads raised as he rushed out past the nurses' station. Fighting was pointless, and he found the strength not to argue with her anymore.

"He doesn't need you!" she screamed after him. "Yeah, leave! God will judge you!"

Tom burst out the double doors with his head down, humiliated. Inside, a nurse quickly ran to comfort Agnus, wrapping her arm around her shoulder as they made it back to the waiting area.

* * *

The computer screen stared back at Stephanie, who was in shock. Her heart beat so fast that she felt her little bony frame shaking from the nervous energy at its epicenter.

> You don't know me, and I don't want you to, but I know of a serious compromise in your organization. A spy is taking private client information and providing it to a competitor of yours. I share this information with you for no other agenda than clearing my own conscience. I have no steps to complete or sponsor to please. This is merely information I would want to know. Not to sound dramatic, but you've got a mole in your shop. Her name is Jamie Owens.
>
> Please don't try to respond to this e-mail. This temporary account has been disabled, and you'll receive no reply. Good luck.

She sat back and let her chair swivel, trying to breathe. Thoughts of Jamie fiddling around in her cute and clumsy way filled her head. She considered how Jamie avoided Martha and Janice, two of the smartest women she'd ever known. How Jamal and Cynthia had fired Westfield Shaw soon after Jamie had entertained them. And how her trip to Phoenix to acquire that little car dealer with wild dreams of expansion failed to materialize into a new account, though she had doubted it from the beginning anyway.

Westfield Shaw Advertising was her dream business. That little ungrateful *Clumsysaurus rex* was trying to destroy all of her years of hard work. She called Martha, who picked up the phone quickly and effectively concealed the anticipation of Stephanie's call in her voice.

"Hi, Stephanie."

"What was the name of that little redneck dealership that Jamie was trying to get for us?"

"Um—" Martha faked trying to remember, discounting its significance. She was bad at this. "Oh, Davey's . . . Dealios," she stuttered, hoping not to create suspicion. "In Phoenix."

"Ah, yes, Davey's Dealios. Thanks."

Stephanie hung up and read the anonymous e-mail again. She had really liked Jamie's spunk, but this was going to get nasty.

* * *

With the drapes drawn, Teri hadn't known she'd slept the whole morning. Normally, the invading sunlight in her bedroom was her alarm clock. She woke up to pounding on the door of her hotel room. After her groggy greeting to the maid, she got herself together, feeling lonesome and isolated. Having missed checkout, she took her time. Her plane didn't leave for several hours. Luigi still hadn't called her. She called him and got voice mail.

"Honeybunch, it's me. Just want to make sure you found a good place last night. I don't want to sleep away from you again. Was much harder than I thought it'd be. I don't know what flight you're on for the way back. You're going back? I mean, of course you're going back. But you're coming back today, right? Anyway . . . I guess I'll see you at home."

The following eerie silence in the room made her feel like she'd fallen into a giant abyss, with Luigi nowhere nearby to make her feel better about it. To rescue her. Luigi had stalked her, sure, but he hadn't stopped her from meeting Tom or even confronted her. Instead, he'd helped a real-live damsel in distress. He was more of a man than she gave him credit for.

She turned on the television to a channel talking about sensual couples' massages at the hotel spa. Forlorn and restless, she eventually clicked it off. She couldn't watch other happy couples engage in sexy activities. It annoyed her. She moved to the windows, opened the drapes to a small wedding in the hotel's courtyard, and gasped. The couple looked almost exactly like her and Luigi, except they smiled at each other. Their warmth made the sun seem brighter and her hotel room more dingy. She picked up her phone again to call him but decided against it, not wanting to appear as needy as she was. Her imagination about an old love past was mashing up her life recently, and it was her own stupid fault. Finding Tom on Facebook had been a mistake. Social media—technology, really—had infected her life and got in the way of her love for her lug of a husband. He needed cleaning up, that's all. She knew what he was when she married him, and she desired to have that fire-breathing passion they used to have. She had to create it, though, not just accept it. The monotony of monogamy and frustrations with Luigi's many habits had no chance against fantasy.

It was too much. She hadn't had the desire or the trust to share her feelings about Tom, and now she missed her *man*. It was time she found the strength to live the way she knew she wanted and did something about it. Unsure of how, she threw her phone down on the bed and buried herself in the pillow.

* * *

Agnus's anger had spewed loudly through the echoing halls, and that was her typical behavior. He should have expected it. Tom walked to his car, cursing himself for letting her get under his skin while his brother laid in bed looking like a bulldozer had ripped him apart, now held together by bandages and plaster. He decided that calling Jamie would be awkward. She'd probably be upset at him for reaching out to her only when he needed her. It'd be selfish to lean on her again after putting her through his identity crisis or whatever the hell he was going through.

A hand touched his shoulder as he opened his car door. Tom shuddered and turned to the petite figure behind him. "Don't come up behind people like that!"

"Because I look like a bag lady?" Homer asked. She wanted to slap God around for giving her a human form that these people didn't take seriously, for whatever reason.

"No," Tom said, "because it's annoying. Are you stalking me? You keep popping up out of nowhere like a jack-in-the-box. What's with you?"

"I can see things aren't going well."

He sighed. "Are you a gypsy?"

"Listen to me, Tom," Homer pleaded. "You've got to do things better."

"What are you talking about?" This woman was smothering him. He stood with the car door open and his emotions all over the place. And he didn't even know where he was going. "I'm sorry about what happened to William," she said, containing her sorrow. "And his friend. So, so sad."

Tom was speechless. Perhaps she *was* stalking him.

"Your brother will be okay. But your manuscript. You have to do something with it or—"

"You're interfering, Homer," God said suddenly, only Homer hearing Him.

"Will You shut up, sir?" Homer shook her index finger up at Him. "I'm making a point!" She turned back to Tom, who watched her crazy antics directed at someone, somewhere, with amazement.

"Look, lady," Tom said, reaching into his pocket. "I've got a few dollars."

She sniffed. "I'm no vagabond. Hell!"

God boomed. "You know better than that, Homer."

"Um," Tom paused, perplexed. Homer cupped her ears and held her head to her knees.

"No *um!*" she yelled, ignoring God. "I have no use for your paper currency. It's worthless, and its true value is nothing in the end. You have to listen to me!"

Tom got in his car and shut the door. He had to get away from everything and everyone.

"Wait!" she hollered through the window. "I need you to do what you know—"

"Homer!" God thundered. "You cannot change free will!"

Tom drove off into traffic, his exhaust pipe backfiring. A middle-aged couple walked past Homer, examining her strangely. She growled, and they scuttled away.

"My friend."

"I'm not talking to You," Homer said, glancing at her timepiece. The readout was fading. She only had three days left, and options were depleting. "I don't have time for it. We're through!"

"We can't be doing that," God said.

"We, huh?" She adjusted herself in the rags He had provided. "There's never been a *we*. I feel like such a jobbernowl. Go to hell."

Tom realized his brother was his only true friend right now. Work had been so consuming that, outside of his relationship with Jamie, he had no other friends. His work colleagues were just that. Even Nadia he had never spoken to outside of work, where she needed constant attention and wouldn't tolerate being ignored. His work, he decided, had been too high maintenance.

The door to his apartment felt like it was a door into a lonely dimension as he approached it, shutting himself off to the misunderstandings and ill-doings of the outside world—filled with the likes of Brent, Andre, and Agnus. Homer, he didn't understand. The crazy woman didn't even want any money. *What else had she wanted from him?*

As he lay on top of his bed, his head spun, and he realized how spent he was. A headache accompanied his equilibrium being off. He crawled onto his bed quietly, and within seconds, he was out.

He awoke to nothingness. Having slept in the same position for seven straight hours, his neck ached. His head throbbed, and he felt slow. Punch drunk. It took several seconds to read the numbers of the digital clock, his eyes slowly gaining focus. He had several text messages on his phone, but didn't have the energy to read them—even if Jamie had sent one.

He called the hospital instead. The nurse was curt in her monotone and didn't let him wake his brother, clinically saying that William couldn't take any calls. William's condition was stable but serious. She read off William's chart with the intonation of someone reading a grocery list. He found relief in that he'd likely be released in several days.

What if their mother convinced William that the beating was Tom's fault for not raising him correctly, somehow alleviating herself from any and all responsibility for a willful and negligent lack of child rearing? What if she convinced William that Tom was unnecessary in William's life while she invited herself back into it, taking his little brother away from him? He considered the prospect of having faith that it would all be okay, which he quickly discarded as pointless. He didn't have faith in anything.

* * *

William ate the last of his meal, a generic concoction of mashed potatoes, steamed broccoli, and what he thought to be processed turkey breast, complete with gristle and disgustingness. The applesauce cup had been his first voluntary caloric intake without an IV in almost a full day. It made him queasy.

"I can't eat anymore." He felt faint.

"Oh, William," Agnus said in a kind tone that was foreign to him. She was somewhat patient at his bedside. "Eat your supper. You can't wilt to death."

"Why am I so tired?" He couldn't remember her being so motherly.

"After we get you out of here," Agnus said calmly, "we're going to spend some good time together." She poured his homogenized milk into a small plastic cup. He took a drink, threw it up, and watched her clean it up.

"Mom, when are you going to make amends with Tom?"

She tried not to show her displeasure with hearing Tom's name. "One of you at a time," she said with a fake smile. "We need to get you better first."

"He feels alone a lot, Mom," William said, feeling weird saying *Mom* after so many years. "He's been great. Took care of me when I had no one and nothing. Please don't be so angry. Time heals all, doesn't it?"

"Enough about him," she said. She sat back in the upholstered visitor's chair, aggravated. "I'm sick of you two pretending that I don't exist. I gave both of you life, for Christ's sake."

"He's my brother, Mom."

She hated both of her sons, she decided. "Don't you remember that he chose that Chinese girl over us? Let your brother go. You don't need him anymore. I'm here with you now."

"He didn't choose her, Mom! He just wouldn't let you prevent him from seeing her. You know how he's always been when someone told him he couldn't do something. He was fifteen, right? In any case, you and Dad bailed on us. If it wasn't for Gilbert—"

"Excuse me," Agnus said, preparing to leave. She couldn't listen to this.

"I don't know what I'd do without him," William said, realizing how true that was.

The disagreeable meat product suddenly felt like it was moving through his intestines, and the milk churned in his stomach. He didn't notice the blood dripping slowly from his nose onto his upper lip but closed his eyes and moaned. He didn't want to lose control of his bowels if diarrhea was going to make this whole experience worse. Hopefully he'd just vomit again. Then the blood streamed.

"Oh my God," Agnus said, searching quickly for a tissue. There were none in her purse, so she ran into the bathroom in the room and pulled a fresh roll of wrapped toilet paper off of the commode. "This dirty hospital food!"

She rushed back to William to discover that his hands had fallen to his sides and that the heart monitor was emitting a long beep. His head lay on his pillow like he had been knocked unconscious.

"William!"

Two nurses quickly ran into the room, shuffling her out of the way.

"Excuse me, ma'am," one nurse said.

"What's happening?" She was frantic.

"You have to leave, miss," the other nurse said.

A female doctor Agnus had not seen before quickly emerged, pried open one of William's eyes, and inspected it with a penlight.

"Get her out of here, please," the doctor said to any nurse who would handle it.

"My son!"

"He's going into shock," the doctor said. "Defibrillator, please," she said, and a nurse escorted Agnus out. "Vitals."

* * *

Tom barely remembered what the nurse had said. He had hung up quickly, possibly by accident. His baby brother was in a coma, with internal injuries worse than the doctors had originally thought.

He couldn't cry. His body wouldn't let him. Despite the effort of initiating pain, he wanted to feel *something*. It was a dark road, one he did not want to go down again. Resisting it, he pushed it to the back of his mind.

Brushing his teeth, he couldn't help but think of his older brother, Gilbert, buried deep in the quiet, dark, cold earth, and he pictured William's lifeless body, cold and limp. Tom gagged, choking on the dryness of his throat, despite the saliva swishing around his mouth while he brushed.

It was 7:00 a.m. The light hairs on his arms glistened, absorbing the early morning light. His goose bumps rose as another Santa Ana wind brushed through the room. Abnormally, he was cold. The sharp pain from the surgical precision he had used to avoid cutting any arteries on his arms was unforgettable. He tried to blank out the elation he had felt cutting himself two decades ago. It was *feeling alive*, as he remembered it now.

That hunting knife was somewhere nearby. He could have peace.

Oh no.

In the junk drawer in the kitchen, he shuffled through pens, random envelopes, and pizza coupons before finding the hunting knife tucked against the back of the drawer itself, where it had knowingly hid from him and the world for years. Its sheath was soiled, light-brown leather like that of a worn catcher's mitt. The sheath's watermarks suggested that it must have absorbed some sort of liquid over time. Tom pulled the knife out of its worn protector. The blade was rusted and dull, looking like it was bored of being itself. The aged knife had an association and awareness to his emotions, and an everyday utensil wouldn't do.

Sitting on his bed, he inspected the blade carefully. He knew he'd like it. This was a problem, because he didn't *want* to like it—or need it—but his desire to feel that stinging tingle through his guts again overwhelmed his desire to avoid it. He had avoided doing this to himself for so long only to fall back into this self-infliction that ultimately was an expression of self-loathing. It had to be. He was morose all over again.

Back then, the sensation had become addictive. The only thing that had stopped him was going to the beach with Teri one day. Wounds, no matter how slight, would disagree greatly with saltwater. A young blossoming love with her had helped him to heal from his giving in to desire for pain, and for years, he fought against its calling.

Somehow, the knife had hidden in the back of his various junk drawers like a family secret that didn't want to die or reveal itself. Until now.

He sat cross-legged on the floor, his back against his bed frame, bracing for the pain about to surge through him. Lonesomeness and all that had been taken from him made his isolation intolerable. Chills welled through his legs. He prepared to feel something else again.

Slowly cutting his arm, his eyes watered as blood seeped from the incision. The sharp stinging made his feet shake uncontrollably. He watched the blood ooze from the three-inch cut and let it slowly drain from his veins. Cold blood droplets rolled down his arm and dribbled onto his legs, the red dots staring back at him, haunting him with their privy taunts, as if they had known that he'd fall again. It felt euphoric, embarrassing, and sick. This wasn't right, he knew, but no one was watching.

Sighing deeply, he prepared himself. *One more time.* Cutting on top of his arm, he reasoned, he wouldn't cut any arteries. He wasn't trying to kill himself. *Just stop the self-pity.*

The second cut was easier than the first, as expected. *How dare you make everything about yourself! William's in a coma, for God's sake!* Tom slit his skin faster, a five-inch cut this time. His blood seeped more quickly too, the rusty, sharp-edged blade ripping his skin like it was prepared for laceration. He wanted to scream but suppressed it. Inadequacy had taken over. Weak, the knife fell out of his hand, and he fell over onto the floor, blood rolling and dripping down his arm, onto his clothes and the carpet as he wept. Two hours later, he awoke, disoriented. Something, someone, had visited him during his sleep. He thought. *How come I feel different?* He squinted at the sunlight and rolled over. He pried his left arm off the carpet—his blood having coagulated and dried there—much like when ripping away Velcro. He inspected the dried clumps of hair on his arms and bloodstains on the carpet. Such a mess, all of it. He discounted any visitors in his apartment. *You feel different because you cut the hell out of yourself, that's why.*

Barely being able to remember life without having to look out for his brother, he started to imagine it without him. He didn't know what he was going to do without a job, and he couldn't he afford the rent on his own. *Quit making it about you.*

His eyes wandered to the torn manuscript pieces that lay around the wastebasket. Souring over the thousand hours he had invested in it, he considered its worthlessness to every literary agent he had approached. He breathed heavily and tried to forget how he'd cut himself, instead focusing his mind on the first page, how it had looked prior to being destroyed. He decided he hated the title too. The knife lay on the floor, the blade facing away like it was turning its back to him. Or worse, scoffing at his sad display of self-infliction.

Then, Tom got angry. *Enough.* He was done with weakness and wallowing in his own pathetic desolation. The self-induced pain had come from more than the knife. He had brought on his own torment with stubbornness and discontent. The fear of leaving his past wasn't yet behind him, unless he made the decision that it was where it belonged. He didn't need to reach to his past to overcome the physical obstacles to satisfying relationships with Jamie and his brother. It was strength he needed, the strength that he didn't know he needed to overcome the anxiety of failing in his writing and his fear of showing love to those he needed around him.

He stared at the knife, a cruel reminder of all he didn't want to be. In mere moments, he deposited the knife into the kitchen trash can. It was time to fix what he could of his life—and himself.

Booting up his computer, he went through it to get to the last chapter. Comments, opinions, and judgments that had been made about the material had been positive, except for the ending. He considered William's shrewd remark about how a changed ending could change his life and how important finishing it once was. That pestering homeless woman. What both agents had said, from Maroquin's bitter response and threats to Keith Levy's revelation that he was being blackballed for plagiarism—which no one would believe he didn't commit.

Taking a big breath, he highlighted the whole last chapter and deleted it. He started writing, immediately feeling closer to William, or God, or something. Whatever it was, something bigger than he was provided him the fuel to type away whatever uninhibited thoughts came to him.

* * *

Jamie had maintained a calm silence when Wanda told her what happened. *William's a good kid. Great spirit, good heart.* He was a younger, more fun version of Tom, she had sometimes thought, especially those times when Tom was lost in himself and William was out with his friends, a number of them quite flamboyant. She would have told everyone that he was gay if anyone would've asked her.

They both tried calling Tom, but he didn't pick up. Wanda's message told him to call her back when he was up to it. Jamie's had been more extensive and was successfully left without her choking up.

"Hi, Tom. I just heard. Oh my God, I know you're suffering right now. William, I can't believe it. This is so awful . . . I can only imagine what you're feeling right now, after Gilbert . . . makes me think of how quickly everything can change, how we can so easily lose what's important to us. If you need to talk or need anything, please, please call me. Or I can come over. I'm not sure it's best for you to be alone right now . . . though I bet you want to be. You're not alone, babe, okay? I don't know . . . I don't know what else to say. Call me when you can."

It wasn't until after Wanda left that she cried where she always did: the shower. The place she could let the floodgates of hurt or frustration run dry. It was like she was cleansing her insides while shampoo suds rolled down her back. She shut her eyes, and the hot streams splashed her face and warmed her skin, relieving the accompanying goose bumps that sprouted up immediately and without warning. Every time she bawled, she was grateful that it happened in the shower where she had absolute privacy. Even her mother wouldn't barge in *there*.

She sobbed so hard she couldn't stand it anymore. Crying for William, crying for Tom. For herself. Sitting on the floor of the tub, the long streams of water were tepid by the time they fell upon her head and knees. Her eyes stung. She wasn't sure if it was from shampoo in her eyes or if she cried too hard. The soap and love and impatience and hate and pain swirled, disappearing with eagerness down the drain.

* * *

He didn't feel like talking to anyone. Even Jamie had abandoned him, having quickly bounced back into the dating world. His phone stayed off. He felt guilty for not going to see William, but he didn't want to face Agnus again. There was one thing to pour his attention into, besides sleep in two-hour increments—his manuscript.

In two days, cheap ceramic dishes and flatware piled up in Tom's kitchen sink. Stark sunlight and strong Santa Ana breezes infiltrated the small space with new freedom. If Tom had thought about it, he would've realized that he was preventing the apartment walls from closing in on him.

He wrote, slept, wrote, slept. Wrote, deleted, saved, discarded. He plowed through his work. Words flowed without interruption, and the only timeline he bothered himself with was the funeral of his brother's friend.

Jamie approached Tom's front door early on her way to work. After two days of no returned calls, something was wrong. She knocked. "Tom? Are you home?"

She knocked again and waited, deciding to peer through one of the front windows, giving her a full view of the kitchen. His bedroom window in the back would have been best, but a locked gate didn't allow her back there. Her vantage point allowed her to see the back of his head as he sat at computer.

"Tom!" she shouted through the glass of the closed window. "Let me in, Tom!" It wasn't clear if he was actually writing or what, but he didn't turn around to the knocking or her muted shouting.

He continued to type on his keyboard, listening to Vangelis's electronic music on his iPod, unaware of her pounding on the window. She couldn't tell that he had earbuds blaring into his eardrums, blocking her out.

"Leave him alone."

She turned around to see Homer standing before her. "Excuse me? Who are you?"

"Please let him be. It's best for everybody."

After finishing up his last chapter, Tom took a deep breath. His new ending was tremendously different in tone, and his main character didn't die this time. He couldn't picture anyone complaining about its message being negative or *anti-God* like the previous, discarded chapter. In any case, he liked it better. The inspiration to write it made the newest version more powerful, in his opinion. After halfway printing out a full copy, he remembered he had a funeral to attend. Tom imagined William hobbling after him on crutches, berating him for dismissing the one favor he had asked before falling into a coma. Assuming that he ever woke from it.

Tom quickly browsed online and found the service to be well over an hour from his apartment, in the city. The morning traffic along the 405 over the hill would still be a bear. *Great.* He rushed to change, his anxiety turning into dread. He would be late, and seeing Agnus again—she'd surely be there—was enough to make death more distressful. An epiphany he could've done without. After putting on his best jeans with a white dress shirt and tie, he quickly loaded his printer with paper, the manuscript pile growing. He left the printer to finish its job, dashing out the front door and forgetting to lock it.

Mere moments after Tom departed, Homer emerged through the front door of the apartment and picked up the fresh manuscript copy off the printer. She had the precious pages under her control, finally. The key to saving humanity was in her hands. Now what?

Her watch read: *Twenty-one Hours Left.* After a beat, she had an idea she couldn't believe she hadn't thought of before.

* * *

It was the only suit he owned, and Eight-Ball had had it for at least six or seven years. Cheap and baggy, it hung as loosely on him as it did on its hanger and came out of the closet only for reasons he found boring and intolerable: weddings and baptisms, all of which took place in the same church, Our Sister of Guadalupe. He'd never been to a funeral, until today. With both of his parents and grandparents still alive, he feared this day that he knew would come. Burying someone in his family. He just never thought it would be his baby brother. *Manito.*

He hadn't slept at all the last couple of nights. Nightmares of his brother getting beaten to a pulp by faceless hoods made him wake up soaked in sweat. He knew that going to the funeral was supposed to be facing sorrow and addressing the loss, helping with the mourning. Regardless, he hated that he had to go and be seen grieving publicly, which was also dreadful. In no way could he not be there for his mother, though. And his parents wouldn't let him skip it anyway. He was consumed with anxiety and adrenaline. His brother was dead, and someone was going to pay. *An eye for an eye.*

He answered the door to his apartment while attaching a clip-on tie, his shirt a little too tight around the collar. Homer stood before him.

"Oh, you're kiddin' me, woman."

"Nice suit." She peeked around him. Eight-Ball lived in a compact apartment, no effort to dress it up. The carpet was beige, the walls were a bare white, and the furniture was ratty. Her cardboard hut had as much effort in comfort. Homer hadn't considered in what kind of place she'd expected him to live.

Eight-Ball knew his suit wasn't worthy of compliments. He didn't trust her. "What do you want? And how did you find me?"

"I can find anyone, once I know who they are. More on that in a moment. I've got something for you." She held out the manuscript to him.

He saw the cover page. "No way. I ain't havin' nothin' to do with either of those white boys. Do you know what we're doing with my brother's body in less than an hour?"

"I'm so sorry for your loss. I'd come back later, but there's little time." If she was insensitive, she didn't know what else to do. "I don't expect you to understand, but this is about your brother and what he would've wanted. To get this to your dad. He's an agent, right?"

"What's this you're sayin' about my little bro? What do you know about what he would've wanted about anything?" He was seething through the gap in his teeth. "That piece of shit sent you here for me to help him get a book made? My brother's dead! You people are so jacked up, man."

"I'm going to let that *you people* go, sir," Homer said, "understanding you're going through a tough time right now. Please, you don't have to read it; just get it to your father. I have no idea who he is, or I'd get it to him myself. This book is more important than you can imagine. Have you ever wanted to do something bigger than yourself? Your brother wanted your dad to see this. I can't make you give it to him. You need to want to. Just take it."

"I don't wanna, homegirl. Swear to God, I'll beat the shit out of you and those white boys if any of you ever come here again."

"Blasphemy!"

"Now I gotta bury my brother." Eight-Ball slammed the door.

She hollered through the door. "Can you tell me who your father is so that I can at least approach *him*?"

No answer. She stood there at the door, feeling foolish. Her timepiece was ticking. It clicked to read: *Twenty Hours Left.* What methods could she possibly employ to accomplish her task, which increasingly appeared to be impossible? The people she was trying to save were the exact people discounting anything she said.

"Okay, Eight-Ball, I know you're upset . . . and you need time. I'm leaving this right here. I don't proclaim to understand death very well, but more death is imminent."

The front door swung open. Eight-Ball was furious. "You threatenin' me?"

"No, no. You've got it all wrong. I was just—"

"In or out of this suit, I'll jack you up, bag lady."

"Be the bigger person and reconsider?"

Eight-Ball slammed the door again. She sighed, laid the manuscript at the foot of Eight-Ball's doorstep, and waited. Nothing. She left.

Soon after, Eight-Ball opened the door and brought the pile of paper inside. He breezed through a couple of pages, scoffed at it, and discarded it in the trash can. So angry he felt his insides shaking, he contemplated how to get even with William, and maybe even Tom, for Carlos's death. He grabbed his car keys.

* * *

The service had already started that morning. Black limousines were pulled over to the side of the loose-graveled path along the lush green lawn that spread for miles on the cemetery grounds. The single-lane road curved and twisted to form scrambled geometric patterns across the twenty-eight-acre property. Large, obstructive trees were on the perimeter of the grounds only, standing strong and firm in the ground like beanstalks, their roots quietly absorbing the nutrients of the earth. Their proud, erect silence was disturbed only by gentle winds as they laid claims to the ground as their own. Far from the shade of the monstrous trees was a congregation of mourners, comforting themselves in the company of others who empathized with their pain. The commonality of death garnered the gathering of a small assembly of dissimilar lives.

By the time Tom got to the cemetery, he had to park at the end of a long line of cars, about sixty, he guessed. From where he parked, he could barely see the two hundred or so people who stood at the grave site. Tom figured Carlos must have been quite a popular guy.

Shivering with cold, he got out of the car, his long sleeves covering his lacerated arms. Heavy clouds hung overhead. A shiver up his spine suddenly made him nervous. His mouth felt numb. Wanting to get his presence at this funeral over with, he grabbed the flowers out of the backseat, cellophane surrounding the small bouquet of grocery-store-bagged flowers. He peeled the price tag off the thin plastic and walked toward the crowd.

Homer popped her head out from behind a tree and observed Tom approaching the funeral. His slow walk toward the service softened her frustration with him. Human beings had it hard, pretending that death could be manipulated to transpire conveniently and sometime *later*. Much later. As hard as God was on her, He was definitely crueler to these poor human souls. As individuals, humanity always died. A mortality rate of 100 percent.

The preacher was sermonizing loudly to the crowd surrounding the closed casket. An easel nearby displayed a dated picture of Carlos. Like most gen Ys, his high school portrait session was the last time he'd had professional photographs taken. Flowers were plentiful on and around the casket. Agnus stood solemnly. Her tears fell, comforted by a female friend wearing just as much caked makeup. Eight-Ball stood with his grieving parents, his head down, with Carla and Skinny nearby. Eight-Ball wouldn't look up.

Other faces in the crowd included a number of friends who often gathered at Lee's Bar, including Lee himself. Wanda stood motionless and tried to keep it together, standing with Jamie, who had looked for Tom earlier but now held her head down. She figured Tom had Teri to turn to.

"Carlos Espinoza shared the breadth of life with all who encountered him," the preacher said. "His life was taken prematurely from him, and while we may be crushed by the burden of sin, he now rests in peace. There is a fountain filled with blood, drawn from Emmanuel's veins. And sinners, plunged beneath that flood, lose all their guilty stains."

Sniffling and soft, suppressed weeping filled the crisp morning air. Immediately, as if she could feel him there, Agnus saw Tom approaching the ceremony.

The preacher paused, and everyone watched the late arrival place the flower bouquet at the foot of the casket. Tom knelt down in the silence. Jamie saw him and wanted to call out, but the awkwardness of the moment wouldn't let her. She cried for him.

Tom became self-conscious of everyone watching him. *Why won't the preacher keep preaching?*

Homer popped out from behind another tree and watched Tom's uncomfortable disturbance. She wanted to jump in the middle and cause a ruckus of her own—just to make it easier on him. She noticed Eight-Ball's chin buried in his chest as he had absorbed all of the preacher's words and now his silence. Eight-Ball's stoic grieving had consumed him, and he was oblivious that the funeral service had stopped.

Tom got up from his kneeling at the casket, breathing heavily himself. He tried not to look up at the crowd that watched his every move.

"Who's that?" someone asked softly.

Homer closed her eyes and took a deep breath. She held for a second and then blew. The strength of her blow was a fifty-mile-an-hour wind that suddenly swept through the funeral crowd. Gusts of sandy debris swirled through the unsuspecting crowd as people got knocked off their feet. Two women lost their hats, and members of the congregation shouted in surprise, holding on to one another and wiping strands of hair out of their faces. An older couple fell on their rumps, and the preacher's Bible blew twenty feet away. Someone chased it as it rolled like a dead tumbleweed over the grass.

Tom stood still with his hand placed on Carlos's casket, not reacting to the torrential wind. It didn't affect him, and he didn't notice it at all. He was in his first and last moments of his brother's friend's presence, however much of it was still there. For all he didn't understand about love working out well, he understood loss.

Meanwhile, Eight-Ball squinted into the wind and saw Tom standing there, stiffly and stubbornly, while a minitornado rushed through the cemetery.

Just as quickly as the wind had arrived, it subsided. Homer watched Eight-Ball hopefully. "There you go," she said to herself. She hoped his hate would subside while he grieved. "Help him."

Eight-Ball watched Tom walk away solemnly while the rest of the crowd readjusted after the surprise hurricane that had just hit them dissipated. By the time Jamie searched for him, Tom was gone. Homer looked up to the sky, hoping for approval or acknowledgment that never came.

* * *

"You wanted to see me, Andre?"

"Have a seat."

She sat before him, knowing what was coming, feeling more comfortable in the awkward chair than everyone else before her. Already, this place felt more like hers.

"I'll need you to oversee Tom's columns, something you've wanted for a long time. Now's your chance."

Nadia smiled. It had taken a bit longer than she'd hoped. This business was ruthless, and even her boy crush wasn't going to stop her from rising up the ranks. She didn't need to sleep with Brent, either, to get recognition at Western Mag Corp.

"I know Tom's your friend," Andre said, crossing his arms and lounging back at his desk. "You sure you're fine with this?"

She suppressed her guilt. "Yes."

She and Tom were friends, even partners in a way, having had each other's backs in the workplace. It wasn't her fault that Brent and Andre both had it in for him. A competitive town had kept her from being able to write the splashy columns she dreamed of for long enough.

"You finally got what you wanted."

She smiled, not saying anything.

CHAPTER 6

The nurse gave him as much time as he wanted, but Tom couldn't take the sight of William there in the bed anymore, unresponsive to anything the doctors tried. Bandaged and bruised, William looked at once anguished and peaceful. While holding his younger brother's hand and watching him, Tom remembered their fights and their laughs, their understandings and their distance. After an hour, he left.

He drove up over the hill from the Valley, headed to Jamie's. With his brother's tragic beating and his life's misdirection, Jamie was life's grounding. His windows were down, and he drove the long, winding road of Laurel Canyon. The turmoil in his life needed to end.

The old man across the street from Jamie's house was sitting on his porch, enjoying having no company, when Tom pulled up to her driveway, surrounded by cars. Tom's run up Jamie's sidewalk seemed like a fraction of a second to the old man, Tom was at the door so fast.

"Hi," Tom said, surprised that a guy he didn't know opened the door. "Is Jamie here?"

"Who's Jamie?" the guy at the door asked someone in the house.

"This is her house, man," someone said.

Jamie appeared at the door, surprised and relieved to see Tom. "Hi." She was self-conscious of the distance between them and went up to hug him. Dark circles around his eyes made him look like he'd been up for days. "Are you okay?"

"Is that the guy?" someone asked in the background. A group of people gathered around the front door to see what was going on. Tom noticed the commotion inside but tried to ignore it. Jamie was the center of his attention.

"I've got a house, might as well use it," Jamie said, shrugging. "The postfuneral meal thingy. Heck, I've got room."

Tom nodded. Maybe this wasn't the best idea after all, but he couldn't go back now.

"You've been coping, Tom," she said, playfully hitting his shoulder. "But it's still not okay to ignore me. I called and called. You ignored me at your house the other day. It was weird today at the funeral, seeing you. I can't imagine what you're going through—"

"Jamie—"

"And William? God, my heart's breaking for him right now. I know he's the only family you've got. With everything that happened with Gilbert—"

"Jamie."

"And then I get all insecure over an ex of yours, which I feel horrible about. As a woman. It's not like *we're* in high school, right? And then I go out on a date, which was *awful* by the way."

"Jamie!"

She stopped, resigned to the fact that she could indeed go on like her mother.

"What's going on?" someone asked. More curious bystanders appeared at the front door.

"There's a couple fighting," someone said.

"Oh my God, I've got to see this," someone else said inside the house.

"Shouldn't we give them a little privacy?" Wanda asked from the living room.

"I'm not missing this," her friend said, joining the crowd. Wanda reluctantly joined her.

Pain etched across Tom's face, but the words flowed from him easier than they ever had. "I've had a bad week. A very bad week. And I've been a dildo." One of the guys in the crowd raised his eyebrows. Tom stammered, "Your ring. Where's your ring?"

"Tom. It's supposed to represent something, isn't it?"

"I've been unfair," Tom said. "I've needed to put myself out there for a long time. You said so yourself, and you were right. I need to take some risks, but I can't risk *us* anymore."

Jamie noticed the crowd behind her, quietly engaged in the moment. She couldn't imagine a bigger attentive audience. "Tom, I—"

"I'm not finished," Tom said. She buttoned up. "I'm not finished putting myself out there. I've barely started. Do you know how invigorating it's been," he asked, his careful stare not leaving her eyes, "for me to face myself? And learn that I'm finally living? Taking the right risk for the right reasons. I can't be writing a book to spite my mother or . . . prove something to people at work—that I'm not just a columnist but a *novelist*. Trying to prove to my brother that I was a worthy role model instead of having a legitimate passion. I was going through the motions before, trying to succeed, but it wasn't . . . authentic."

She had a hopeful, faint smile.

"I've put so much focus on my book and have pushed you away as I faced rejections. As I did that, I allowed someone else in. Stupid! I've realized I want to really face it all, with you beside me."

She resisted the tears. "How will I know you won't be searching out an ex-girlfriend or something again, Tom? You know I can't live like that."

"I need my best friend, Jamie." She couldn't stop welling up. "Just you and me from now on," he said.

"Where did this all come from?"

"I don't know." He really didn't. "You take the pain away. And I want to live."

"I want to live too," she said, hugging him. They kissed, and the crowd was unanimous in its oohing and aahing. Jamie's mother closed her eyes, holding it all in.

Then, a nervous energy arrived in the crowd, which slowly parted for the sinister aura making its way through it.

Tom noticed her immediately. "What's she doing here?"

Jamie turned to see Agnus approaching them. "Be nice, Tom. I know you resent her, and you have your—"

"Thomas," Agnus called.

"Please," Jamie said, grabbing Tom, "don't fight with her. It's been a hard enough day for everyone."

He couldn't breathe. The pain he had inflicted on himself a few hours ago was not yet a memory. His left arm itched from the slices he had made on himself, and the throbbing made him wonder if he had cut too deep. Seeing the woman who had caused him so much torment replaced the euphoria of seeing Jamie. Agnus's eyes pierced through him, the rich mascara unable to hide their vacant despair, haunting him as they always had.

"Tom," Jamie said. His face was flushed. "Don't let her make you into someone you don't want to be."

He looked down at Jamie, as if her words had woken him from a trance.

"Thomas."

He straightened up, composing himself.

"He's still shaken up from the funeral," Jamie offered. "I know you're worried about William, babe. The doctor—"

"You're the reason he's in that hospital bed," Agnus charged. "You've—"

"I know," Tom said.

Agnus stopped.

"I've made many mistakes," Tom said, "and I've got no one to blame for them. I used to blame you, Mother. But I don't anymore." The crowd was still, and Agnus was speechless. "I can't fault a cruel world for my own imperfections within my control. I've realized I've sometimes brought my own pain, including to those around me." Jamie didn't blink, hanging on every word. "I've got work to do to finish off this damn book I've been writing, but I'm not going to let it, or any woman, get in the way with my relationship with my fiancée anymore."

Jamie smiled at him.

"Or my family. And Mother, if you want your sons back, you can have both of them. Life is short, painful, and hard. Unless you make it otherwise. We've only got so much time on earth to do it."

Jamie hugged him tightly, and Agnus walked up and joined them. The crowd cheered with scattered applause, and Wanda wiped a tear from her eye.

Across the street, the old woman came onto the porch to find her husband weeping. The old man had been watching the display from his rocking chair and now was hunched over. He grabbed on to her apron while she stood over him, patting his head. "Oh, George. My boy."

* * *

Later that afternoon at WSA, Jamie tapped away at her desk keyboard. She searched through advertising trades for account leads, frustrated that Stephanie had called her back to the office, needing to talk to her face-to-face about something. Jamie knew leaving her mother to do the cleaning at the house would surely have consequences. She wanted to be with Tom right now, not here searching for new leads, waiting for Stephanie to get back here. It was bad enough that Stephanie knew that she was hosting a party at her house and had asked her to come in. Then Stephanie had kept her waiting for an hour.

"Jamie, Jamie, Jamie," Stephanie said with disappointment. She had marched in wearing an uncharacteristic black suit and plopped down in the chair in front of her desk.

"Hi, Stephanie." She hoped WSA wasn't closing.

"So I just got off the phone with Davey *Dealio* himself," she sighed in her Texan drawl. Jamie looked at her wide eyed. "He told me you never met with him."

She didn't see this coming. "This," Jamie laughed nervously, "is a funny story."

"He came out to meet with you," Stephanie said, "but you were gone." Her inquisitive gaze fell hard upon Jamie.

"A really funny story," Jamie repeated, trying to keep some levity. If she only would have had the guts to see the appointment through. "You see, I got their address off their website, but the place was a pit."

Stephanie stood tough. "The *old* address off the site. The pictures were new. They hadn't gotten to the new contact info. Didn't you notice that the storefront looked different from what you saw on the website? Not paying much attention to details?"

Stupid, stupid, stupid! "I don't know what to say."

"I'm meeting with Davey next week. He took my call, wasn't sure what happened to you. He's flying out here to meet with me."

"That's great!" Jamie beamed.

"Unfortunately, none of this is any good, as I've found out we have a mole in this agency who's trying to steal away our business."

"Oh no."

"Don't pretend you know nothing about it, missy!" Stephanie pointed her long fingers at Jamie. "I know all about your covert exploits an' all."

"What?"

"I pay attention to what happens to my shop. In challenging times like these, especially, I can't have the likes of you put my name in the dirt."

"But, Steph," she pleaded, standing at her desk. "I've only fought for you! For WSA!" Her heart was beating so fast, and her whole body was shaking.

"My name's *Stephanie*. Don't be trying to fool me. I'm no donkey."

"Where'd you get this information? It's erroneous."

"I know all!" she yelled. Martha and Janice poked their heads out of their offices, exchanging knowing glances of approval.

Jamie waited for the words.

"You're fired, Jamie. I can't have traitors working for me."

Martha smiled, and Janice shook her head.

"You know," Jamie said, "I can think of a couple of other people in this office who could be involved in trying to sabotage you."

"Like who?"

Jamie continued, surprised that Stephanie let her. "Um, well, have . . . have you looked at Martha? Huh? Martha. And, and . . . Janice! They're a tag team, the both of them!"

Martha gasped, putting her hand to her bosom in shock.

"How dare you," Stephanie said. "WSA would be screwed without them."

"I'm just saying! Check the facts." She counted on her fingers. "One, they're printing weird things like client histories and stuff. Two, they're always in the know in the market—"

Stephanie wasn't impressed. "That all you got?"

"No! They're . . . they're *mean*."

"You've got five minutes to grab your stuff, or I swear to the Lord, I'll have you arrested for trespassing."

Jamie, for the first time in her professional career, felt like a failure. Losing JC Traders and screwing up with Davey's Dealios wouldn't be tolerable to anyone. She should've known that if her relationship took a positive turn, her career karma had to swing the pendulum the other way.

* * *

"I'm on my way now." He needed to get his last check, or next thing, his power would be cut off.

"Hottie patottie, oh em gee," Nadia snapped on the other side of the phone. "How can you ignore my calls? You make me not want to worry at all about you. I'm praying for your brother. And Brent's a psycho around here with you gone—like he's on a crack high, which I, of course, know nothing about."

She still made him smile. He drove leisurely for a change, still warm from Jamie's embrace earlier. No deadlines to meet, no bosses to appease. He illegally held his phone to his ear, an infraction in the state of California. A trivial violation when the murdering punks who almost killed his brother were still free.

"He's a tool."

"Yes, he is. And that last guy I dated is one too. Do you know that he broke up with me via text message? Who would've thought anyone would do that to me? You can't use that kind of brevity in an e-mail, but you sure as hell can do it with a text message!" Tom let himself laugh. "And he's still checking my MySpace every day," she continued. "There's a way to check up on stalkers doing that, you know. I'm writing a whole twelve hundred words on it for next month."

"Great," Tom said, glad she wasn't that upset with him, then hearing what she had said. "Though I'm not so sure about MySpace's relevance now." Then something felt like a hammer on his head. "Oh, so you're writing feature articles now?"

"Um, yeah," Nadia said. "I got your old position." She winced just saying it.

"I can't believe it."

"Someone had to take your job, Tom. It's not like they gave me a raise. Cheap bastards."

It didn't matter. Her love life wasn't all she was focused on. "I'm coming by."

"Great." She felt guilty.

"I wouldn't come by if I didn't need to," Tom said. "I'm supposed to sign some stuff."

"Sure." A silence hung there on the phone.

"See you in a bit."

"Love you." She hung up, not believing what she just said. It had just come out. If it went over his head, she wouldn't be surprised. Her dog was more intuitive than men were.

* * *

No way is this a good idea. Jamie knew popping in to NRS unannounced wouldn't be a good move if she wanted to work at Westfield Shaw's competitor, if they were even hiring. Then she reconsidered, figuring that if they were truly gaining her old employer's accounts, they very well could have use for her. Sitting in their parking lot—which was considerably larger than Westfield Shaw's—she tried to get the nerve to do a walk-in, a memorable entrance into the job scene during these interesting economic times when they were probably inundated with résumés. Stephanie was ruining her life, and she didn't know what else to do.

Parked in her car and trying to gather her guts, she called Cynthia's cell, which uncharacteristically sent her to voice mail after two rings. If no one was going to tell her what went wrong on the account, how could she ever fix it?

Then Jamie's heart stopped. Martha and Cynthia were approaching the entrance of NRS together. She couldn't believe what she saw. *Unless Martha was fired too, and she has the same idea I do.* She rolled down her window and listened to them carefully, undetected, a mere fifteen feet away.

"And here at NRS," Martha said in a tone that reminded Jamie of what Martha's beauty pageant speeches must have sounded like, "you won't have to worry about the creative limitations you've had in the past."

"I never had those," Cynthia corrected, stopping before the entrance. "As I told you, with Jamie Owens off my account, I had no reason to stay with that shop. Once I got that call from WSA, I decided to take my business somewhere else. An agency that ignores my needs doesn't keep my business."

Jamie was shocked.

"I can assure you, Cynthia," Martha said, smiling and strutting smoothly with patronizing glamour toward NRS's door, "that won't ever happen here at NRS."

Jamie could tell Cynthia wasn't buying it, and Martha's cell rang.

"Need to grab that?" Cynthia asked her, perturbed.

Jamie grinned, knowing how ornery Cynthia could be when something didn't go her way. Her friendly demeanor could switch quickly. It had taken Jamie a while to figure that out herself.

"Just one sec," Martha said, picking up her phone. Unbeknownst to Cynthia—or Jamie—Stephanie was on the other line. "Hi."

"You have her there with you?" Stephanie asked, looking at one of her spreadsheets on her work computer. "I'll take your silence as a *yes*."

Just a few feet from NRS's front door, Martha held up her index finger to Cynthia, as if to say, *Just a second*, and concentrated on the voice on the other side of the receiver. Martha couldn't believe Stephanie's timing sometimes.

"Okay, this is it," Stephanie said into the phone, her eyes wide with anticipation of the largest dollar returns of her career. "Everything we talked about with the profit and split with NRS, we're almost there. Now with Jamie gone, Cynthia may convince NRS to hire her. I just thought of this. Jamie's no dumb cookie, so make sure you're on top of the other NRS benefits—like their great creative department there. Tell Cynthia how they won't have creative limitations there or something. Try to distract her."

Jamie observed what she could. *What the hell is going on?*

"Um, sure, Mom," Martha said into the phone, keeping herself between Cynthia and the phone to obstruct Stephanie's rising volume from Cynthia, who was growing impatient.

"Jamie was almost on to the other things we were charging them for," Stephanie continued. "Invoicing, printing costs. No doubt she would have ratted us out. I still can't believe she never discovered any of it."

"Do we really have to discuss this now, Mom?" Martha pleaded for forgiveness with her expression, and Cynthia stared at her without blinking.

"But if she and Cynthia reconnect," Stephanie said quickly into the phone, as if it was a revelation, "these things might come up now. Doggone it, we can't afford for her get this account there. Discredit Jamie so she doesn't get hired there too, got it?"

"Okay, Mom. All righty then. Bye."

Quiet and still in her car, Jamie grabbed her phone and took a picture of Martha and Cynthia in front of the NRS building. If Stephanie didn't believe her before that Martha or Janice were moles at Westfield Shaw, she'd believe her now.

* * *

Pulling into Western Mag Corp, Tom saw that recognizable cars filled the lot. This wasn't the place Tom wanted to be. Running into the rogue's gallery of fools—Andre, Brent, or any other of the soon-to-be-corporate-minded employees—would require verbal restraint and physical stamina.

Brent was at his desk formulating his eventual takeover of Western Mag Corp, and he noticed that several of the more gossipy interns had moved to the large windows.

"Is he going to try to get his job back?" "I hope he's not going postal." "His car's filthy." "He's not carrying a gun, is he?" "He wouldn't know how to hold a gun."

Brent got up and strode toward the crowd at the windows in his awkward and bumpy stride. He saw Tom down below, approaching the depressing building's front door. Unrelenting rage boiled. He'd warned him not to come back here. If Tom compromised his plans and facilitated the IPO in any way *or* further hurt his chances with Nadia, he'd have to kill him. He swung back to his desk and punched up a number on his cell. He wiped off his phone's grimy faceplate while he waited. "Did you take care of Napoleon yet?"

Coming up with a less obvious code name for his target would have been prudent, considering the close proximity of nosy interns and random, insignificant cubicle dwellers. He couldn't refer to Andre as *the silly little man* because, as far as Brent was concerned, everyone probably already called him that. Thinking now, *King Kong* would have been good due to Andre's self-destructive, stubborn behavior. *Wildebeest* would work, due to Andre's ungroomed hygiene underneath his neck, where gray chest hair poked out and greeted the world ceremoniously. If he had only spent more time doing background checks on the hit man he had hired, he wouldn't be so concerned about Andre getting spooked. The answer on the other side of the phone didn't make him happy.

"What?" Brent shook his head furiously like he was trying to get rid of a bee perched on his nose. "So this is why I haven't heard from you yet!" He met the inquiring gaze of someone in the office he didn't know and brought his voice down. Everyone in his business. "Are you playing games with me?" He noticed other anonymous interns he had never bothered to know the names of, or—a testament to their insignificance—determine if they were indeed interns. The complaining voice on the other side of the phone reeked with incompetence. Brent's meticulous plans had been made with a critical timeline, and he couldn't let Tom do anything to disrupt his ownership of Western Mag Corp. The chief editor had to be taken out *now.*

Brent hid in his cube and whispered coarsely into the phone, hanging his head down to his knees. "This was supposed to be handled this morning! I thought it was done and that he was rotting in his car somewhere. I should've known better, you imbecile! Okay, so now you're in place? Finally. What do you mean you're waiting for him to leave for lunch?"

The shooter uttered excuses on the other side of the line.

"This isn't up for debate, you twit!" Brent ranted, barely keeping his volume down. "Did I ever say this was a democracy? Now take care of it. If he gets any intel, gets it to the board, and gets this IPO through, I'm screwed. Now move your ass!" He punched the phone to hang it up. He'd definitely hire better in the future. Looking around, he noticed the interns had left the windows. Tom had made it into the building.

Otis the security guard greeted Tom in the foyer with surprise, putting an almost completely devoured apple core in his pocket. He reached out to shake Tom's hand. "Great to see you, Tom!" His gleeful voice echoed off the cement floor and empty walls. He wiped his other hand—still covered with apple debris—on his pants.

"Great to see you, Otis," Tom said, embracing the welcome source of positivity. "Keeping out all the riffraff?"

"You know it!"

Tom noticed Otis's belt. Somehow the small container of mace was supposed to deter all criminal activity. He figured Otis's wide girth coming at you was likely more formidable than the mace.

"Though you're riffraff now, according to Andre," Otis said. "Are you here to get your last check?"

"Yep." It was now that he realized this could be his last time at Western Mag Corp. He couldn't think of a reason why he would ever come back here again. "You need to escort me up?"

Otis shook his cantaloupe of a head. "Nah. Go do what you need to do. I trust you."

"You sure?" Tom asked, and Otis nodded. "Thanks, Otis. Means a lot."

"Sure thing," he beamed, looking forward to finishing his apple core.

Wading up the stairs, Tom considered his compensation for his unused vacation and sick days. You've got to love the state of California. *The rights-of-the-employee* state, though not evidenced so far.

Tom reached the platform at the top of the stairs. The door opened, and Andre appeared, leaving for lunch. Tom stopped. An unexpected run-in with the boss.

"Hey," Andre said, coolly offering Tom a fist bump.

Tom obliged him in hopes to diffuse the awkwardness. The midday fall sun burned through the large bay windows that filled the hallway like in a greenhouse. The air was stifling and stale. "Getting my last check."

Normally, his terminated employees picked their last check up the moment it was available. Tom had never been a slacker, but he mustn't have needed the money that badly. Andre quickly surmised Tom had other priorities. "I'm glad to see that you're calmer, bro. We've known each other a long time."

An uncomfortable silence hung in the stillness. "I've accepted some things," Tom said finally. "I'll find something else more suited for me. I didn't want to die here."

"Yo. You've still got the world at your feet," Andre said.

Suddenly, a bullet shot through the huge window two feet from them. It pierced Tom's chest, and he collapsed, Andre holding him up. Another shot rang through the glass, missing both of them by inches as the round planted itself in the wall behind them. Andre howled in horror and fell with Tom on top of him, trying to hide from wherever the gunshots were coming from.

Across the way on the top of an adjacent building, the gunman cursed in frustration. Brent's hired assassin shifted his rifle and took aim.

Scrambling on the ground, Andre reached up to the doorknob of the hallway door. He could barely pull the surprisingly heavy door open when lying on the floor with Tom's weight across his torso. He strained to pull the door open from the handle and started to shuffle and pull Tom with him, when a third shot tore through the glass, piercing Andre's hand. Andre shrieked and jerked his hand back, shocked by the stabbing pain in his hand and now his own blood. His shoulder and Tom's weight on top of him held the door open. Andre wailed in pain, and Tom lay silently on him, gasping for air as blood flowed down his side, soaking his shirt in crimson red.

Otis poked his head in at the bottom of the stairwell. "What's going on up there?" The surprise of the racket had knocked him out of his seat.

The shooter took another shot, whispering under his breath, "Goddamn you."

Another shot rang through the stairwell, and Otis fell to the ground and rolled, orbiting and revolving two full cycles until he hit the side of a wall, his moves more befitting a response to fire rather than a gunshot. He lay there against the wall and cupped his ears, waiting for the next one.

Andre ignored Otis's bumbling and finally pulled Tom's legs beyond the door, allowing it to slam shut. The gunman pulled his rifle away in frustration and retreated, knowing that Brent would have his ass.

Employees all over Western Mag Corp reacted to what they'd heard. Two interns hid under their desks. Brent waited patiently at his desk for his plan to be completed. The culinary writer huddled at her desk and called her mother. The sports writer hid in the lunchroom, locked the door, put his back to it, and prayed. One of Andre's assistants ran out the back door of the building screaming.

Nadia ran down the hallway to Andre and Tom and gasped. Blood was oozing out of Tom's mouth, his head resting on Andre's stomach. "Oh my God." Nadia ran to them and knelt down. "What can I do?" she asked, hoping she'd be able to do whatever it was.

"There's a sniper out there," Andre moaned. He held his bloody hand to his chest, not sure how to stop the blood. He always wished he had been a Boy Scout. He motioned to Tom. "He's got it worse."

Tom's heavy lids struggled to stay open. He could barely breathe and choked on his own blood. Some seeped from the corners of his mouth. Staring helplessly up at Nadia, he thought of Jamie looking down at him. His lungs fought to breathe in or out, whichever could happen first. Asphyxiation slowed his blood loss but increased his struggle to breathe, his mouth slowly popping open and closed like a suffocating fish.

"Tom, please!" Nadia brushed her hair out of her face in frustration and tried to pull him up, getting his blood all over her. She searched for a way to stop him from bleeding and noticed the cuts on his arms. "Oh, Tom, I don't know what to do! Please don't die on me. I need you."

Tom choked, and blood spurted all over Nadia, but she didn't care.

One of the assistants looked over all of them. "Oh my God. He's dying."

Nadia pulled Tom closer to her. She tried to hold his head up to her bosom, hoping his choking would stop. It wouldn't.

The tightness of his chest was painful, but he felt the pain slipping away. His lungs were either draining or flooding with blood, he didn't know or care, and his vision was blurring. Whatever was happening, Tom knew he had—in some way—found something within himself bigger than he could have imagined. He was breaking away from his past as his presence was becoming tolerable. The void in his life over his self-worth had been replaced by his faith in himself and the authentic love around him. His spirit had broken through to his mother, even. He'd been daring enough to find strength he hadn't known he had a week ago, living to a capacity he'd never known.

"Hey, we're both shot here," Andre whined. He was in such shock that his hand didn't hurt anymore. Someone brought him a T-shirt and helped him wrap his wound.

"There's no one out there," a brave someone said, looking outside the stairwell door.

Brent appeared over them in the hallway, surprised to see both Andre and Tom on the ground. While a nuisance, the wrong man was taking his last breaths. To him, Andre looked like he was going to be fine, once better bandaged. Did he need to finish the job himself? He should have hired better help. "What a lame-assed assassin! The worst aim ever!" he yelled.

"Wha . . . what'd you say?" Nadia asked him. "You did this?"

Andre was dumbstruck.

"Of course not," Brent scowled. He quickly departed.

Tom's eyes were vacant.

"Tom, please," Nadia said, welling up.

He choked one last time before his eyes closed. Nadia wept, refusing to let him go.

"Someone call the cops!" someone yelled.

"I already called an ambulance!"

From outside Western Mag Corp, Homer watched five cop cars, two ambulances, and a fire truck show up. A crowd was forming outside, blocking her view of who was coming out on a stretcher. A few people were crying, huddled in a small group. One writer ran to her mother, who had just arrived to the scene. Andre sat on the bumper of an ambulance, his hand wrapped in gauze, and a paramedic told him to take a seat inside the vehicle for their ride to the hospital. Homer approached the second ambulance and saw a white sheet placed over Tom. She stood motionless as he was put into the vehicle, and the doors closed.

* * *

Zipping into Westfield Shaw's parking lot, Jamie rushed into the building with her phone. She finally had something on Martha and, surely, Janice was in on it too. She rushed up the stairs, skipping every other one with precise coordination. Somehow she hadn't stumbled the littlest bit, in her normal clumsy fashion. Adrenaline was sharpening her up. "I've got something for you to see," Jamie said, marching into her former boss's office.

Stephanie took off her reading glasses. Anyone busting into her office unannounced, especially a terminated employee, was unacceptable. It disturbed the balance and symmetry she had strived for, with the pleasingly color-coordinated furniture and her Texan version of feng shui. "I don't have to be scared of you and call the cops, do I?"

"No." Jamie was still panting. "Remember when you said that I was a traitor? Well, I'm not, and I've got proof!"

Stephanie stared at her in awe, and Jamie waited impatiently for her phone to pull up the picture, wanting to scream at it.

"Look! Here, you see," Jamie said, pointing. "That's Martha with Cynthia in front of NRS. She's your mole!"

Stephanie ignored the picture. "Jamie—"

"Look right there!" Jamie insisted. "She's the one trying to destroy your agency! Not me!"

"Jamie."

"You didn't believe me before, but you've got to believe me now, right? I knew it, I knew it. I've always trusted my intuition before when something was wrong."

"I can't believe she's trying to hurt us," Janice said, appearing in the doorway.

Stephanie stood up and approached Jamie. "Your intentions are ill conceived, Jamie. But I admire your tenacity."

"She's a true detective," Janice added coolly.

Confused, Jamie wondered how she could've gotten this wrong. "I don't understand."

"It's all quite simple. Martha and Janice—"

"Or *Janice and Martha*," Janice corrected, moving forward a couple of steps into the office. Suddenly, Jamie felt trapped in the boutique office.

"Shut up, Janice," Stephanie dismissed, turning to Jamie. "Those two women are my biggest advocates for this agency. They helped broker a deal to keep Cynthia and Jamal on board by working a new partnership with NRS. We were about to lose them, Jamie, because of you, I'm told."

"You're *told*?" Jamie asked. This was unbelievable. "By who?"

"By *whom*," Janice corrected.

"Shut up!" Jamie and Stephanie yelled in unison.

"There isn't room at Westfield Shaw for account managers," Stephanie said, "that say they're going to do something and then don't do it, under any circumstances. We can't be compromised."

Martha joined Janice at the door opening, wearing her blood red lipstick. Jamie felt claustrophobic.

"What are you doing here?" Stephanie asked, eyeing Martha up and down. "You're supposed to be with Cynthia at NRS right now."

"Cynthia left," Martha said.

"What do you mean she *left*?"

"She didn't even make it in the door," Martha said, avoiding Jamie's disbelieving glare. "She said the way she did business was misunderstood, and we had it all wrong."

"What'd you do?" Janice yelled, pushing Martha in the shoulder.

Martha shoved her back twice as hard, knocking her against the wall. "Don't push me!"

"You always tell me what to do, and then you go and screw this all up!"

Now Stephanie raised her own voice. "Ladies!"

Martha and Janice ignored her and slapped one another, going at each other like hyenas fighting over a carcass.

The intercom beeped. "Cynthia is downstairs for you, Stephanie."

Stephanie caught her breath, and everyone froze.

Just moments before, the glass door of Westfield Shaw had opened, and Cynthia strode through it, angry, hurt, and betrayed. Elegant as she was, no one pushed her around or abused confidentiality privileges. She wasn't a commodity and wouldn't be treated as such. Coffee and tea were commodities. Grains, vegetables, precious metals. This puny ad shop was lucky she didn't arrive with a baseball bat in hand—and even luckier that she kept her husband at bay, who probably would have driven his Escalade through the door.

Still, Cynthia couldn't believe Jamie was pulled off her account. Being the client, she should've been consulted for approval and input. Her business was moving to another ad shop. She didn't know to whom yet, but she was definitely out of WSA, where the leadership was going to get a piece of her mind.

"Don't let her leave," Stephanie said, closing her office door behind her, leaving Martha and Janice to stew in the room with Jamie. The two statuesque stepsisters' hostile glares penetrated her like daggers.

"What, are you going to beat me up now?"

Janice ignored Jamie. Instead, she attacked Martha, who had proven to be a worthless ally and completely undependable in foiling the system. "I can't believe you allowed her to follow you. You're awful at this."

"What do you mean I'm awful?" Martha snorted back. "Without me, you'd still be doing makeup for Miss California. Go to hell."

Janice stood there with her hands on her hips, tapping her foot. The nerve. "She took a picture with you in front of NRS with Cynthia! You're full of fake promises and, like, are the worst aspiring criminal ever! You go to hell!"

Martha was steamed. "You're not coming on our cruise now. I'm canceling it."

"You can't do that. I booked it!"

"Well, I'm canceling it!"

In an instant, the two bumbling cohorts slapped and pushed each other again, not noticing Jamie slip away.

Cynthia waited impatiently in the small lobby downstairs, alerted to Stephanie's approach by her brisk clicks and clacks down WSA's stairs, moving as fast as her skinny little legs in black Jimmy Choos would allow.

"Cynthia," Stephanie said, smiling widely. She didn't know why Cynthia was here, but something was wrong. She never swung by.

Cynthia turned to her. She had been reading a framed puff newspaper article on the wall that announced Westfield Shaw's arrival as a new budding boutique advertising agency in Los Angeles years ago. She was more cynical of the piece now than she was when she had first read it. The cramped, boxy lobby had felt charming before. Not anymore.

Stephanie moved in to hug Cynthia but was rejected by Cynthia's chilly businesslike manner. "Oh, okay," Stephanie said nervously, unsure how to react to Cynthia's unfriendliness. "How are things? Did you need anything from Westfield Shaw? How's business these days?"

Her questions sounded as poor to her own ears as they did to Cynthia's, who believed when she saw Stephanie that there was no state in the union she hated more than Texas.

"So what's this with the spies you've got here, Stephanie?"

Stephanie held her palms open in front of her and shook her head, confused. "Um—"

"Oh, I'm no fool," Cynthia warned. "Don't be thinking that you can fool Jamal and me. There's *nothing* we hate more than spying white people. Lying white people, actually. Who are just as bad as spying white people!"

Stephanie's fake smile vanished. "We've done no spying, Cynthia. This is prepost—"

"Don't you worry, I'll be sure to make sure this gets out to the whole community. The *whole business* community, the Better Business Bureau, even city hall. Don't be surprised if I go to Fox News with this."

"Cynthia," Stephanie said with a softened tone, "there's a misunderstanding here. I can assure you that in no way did WSA mistreat you. And Fox News? Really?"

"They're fair and balanced, don't you worry," Cynthia dismissed.

Suddenly, Martha and Janice appeared in the lobby, which now felt so crowded that Stephanie wondered why she had thought that such a tiny lobby was in any way functional.

"Jamie left," Martha said.

"Just left!" Janice added, exasperated. "She must've gone out the back door. Why didn't we think of that?"

"You!" Cynthia pointed at Martha. "Working for both shops! Who do you think you are, a double agent or something? Wow. Jamie was right."

"Jamie?" Janice said.

"That bitch," Martha muttered.

Stephanie searched for words that would ease the situation, but stuttering was all she could muster.

"Never in all my years of business," Cynthia said, speaking authoritatively like a judge in court, "have I seen such a pathetic display of professionalism. You pulled the one person off my account I trusted. She's informed me of all that's going on here."

"Whoa, whoa, wait," Stephanie said, trying to calm her down. "You've got some inaccurate information here, Cynthia."

"Your two little—well, neither of them are little—but these two intrusive, unprofessional, let me say *women*—so I don't go all profane—gave confidential information I gave you, and only you, to my competitors? How dare you give my billing and account details to another ad agency so they could exploit me! I never gave you that authority!"

"They didn't do that," Stephanie pleaded. Her throat was so dry that her speech struggled to be coherent. "There was no sharing of information. I cut a deal with NRS to share an account or two, due to economic forces, that's all. To help keep WSA afloat is all. All the financials stay here, right, Martha?"

"We did what we had to do. Janice, let's go," Martha said, quickly ascending back up the stairwell.

Stephanie longingly watched Martha disappear. For the first time in her career, she didn't want to be left alone with a client who she knew, if pressed, would kick her ass.

Janice stood with her arms folded. "You're on your own with this."

Caught off guard, Stephanie turned to Janice. "What did you two do?"

Cynthia crossed her arms. "Please tell."

Feeling the heat of the inquisition, Janice briefly considered her fruitless partnership with Martha. She couldn't keep quiet anymore. "You know how hard it is to compete out there."

Cynthia's eyebrows arched, observing the showdown. It was as she suspected.

"You shared her financials?" Stephanie asked, theatrical in front of Cynthia. She couldn't believe she'd been duped. "What are you trying to do, use her information to get competitors to take her business away from us *and* NRS? Ruining us in the process?"

"You say it like it's a question," Cynthia said.

"It wasn't my idea," Janice said nonchalantly. "Martha wasn't happy enough with your promises, Stephanie, of making us partners for bringing in business to NRS. We were supposed to become our own bosses, owning our own accounts. Accounts like JC Traders would follow us when they found out that NRS and Westfield Shaw were both scam shops."

Cynthia shook her head. "Ironic."

"I'm a victim here too, you know," Janice said.

"Get out," Stephanie said, pointing at the door.

Janice stood there.

"You lame-assed amateurs!" Cynthia yelled, jolting Janice to thrust herself out the door, a swift gust sweeping through the small lobby until the door shut behind her.

"I'm sorry, Cynthia," Stephanie said, gesturing toward the only two chairs that would fit in the lobby. "Have a seat with me here. Or would you like to come to my office upstairs? We can work this all out like partners."

"I'm not sitting," Cynthia said, standing rigid. "I've got business to do, and it's not here. I'll tell you now, Stephanie. I'm not going to be quiet about this."

* * *

Homer moped. The way she saw it, God's commitment to free will was what was killing humanity. He could pretend her assignment to save humanity from Him had honor in it, when evidently, He allowed the world to kill itself. She had to do something about Earth's impending doom. *Something.* She herself didn't think much of human beings or their often-misguided plights on Earth, but observing human tragedy had affected her. Deception and betrayal had worn Tom down, as did his poor judgment and full engagement of his own free will. But he'd overcome it. She'd seen it.

But Tom's anonymous killer had sent her over the edge, with the sight of Tom's limp mortal form being transported to the vehicular monstrosity with the whirling red lights. The thugs who had assaulted her were still living on Earth too, as was Tom's graceless and jealous coworker, Brent, and the elusive criminals who brutalized William and killed his friend. So God had allowed free will to murder the chance of humanity's survival? With Tom having exited his mortal existence, her services down here were no longer necessary. What else could she do? God called after her, but she refused to answer, instead withdrawing to her flimsy cardboard shanty and writing feverishly in her tablet, knowing she had limited time to finish it before He pulled her away. She wore a heavy set of headphones—a gem of a find—she had acquired from one of the nearby trash cans to cover her ears from His booms. Should they come.

Last Day, Western Clouds, Early Evening.

There are mere hours left before humankind will be wiped off the Earth. It's with great sorrow that I share this with you now, without misguided theory or hypothesis. This is fact. My forthcoming banishment into solitude pales in comparison to the degree of imminent and unnecessary catastrophe that the Great One requires. Free will, even when misguided or ignorant, is more important to protect than billions of lives? How atrocious of a task He required of me. Rather than provide me the tools to efficiently implement His request, He reduced me to an impotent observer—as usual—with less input than the male partner of a black widow here on Earth. After copulation.

Regardless, dear reader, I blame myself for humanity's impending death.

It is only these noise-canceling headphones of some sort that I'm fortunate to have scavenged from human refuse that are providing any recourse from His constant attempts to reach me, diffusing His overbearing and intrusive booms. (Apparently, human beings have become quite successful at developing tools that assist in omitting His voice.)

How so much evil can fill this world is a question no one, however enlightened, can answer with any certainty or even mild accuracy. Earth's crying children continue to call out in different ways, even if among themselves, with little faith in the Almighty One. Human death is certain, yes, but it is preceded by the evils of murderers, dictating oppressors, slave drivers, rapists, drug traffickers, drug developers, racists, vindictive ex-spouses, child molesters, environmental destructionists, thieves, liars, money launderers, conspiracy theorists, tax collectors, tax cheats, and Democrats and Republicans, many themselves who are tax cheats or possess one or more of the aforementioned unfortunate characteristics.

Dear reader, this is admittedly a bleak outlook in a world that is filled with jealousy, fear, anger, pain, genocide, betrayal, abandonment, child endangerment, animal cruelty, hatred, physical and mental abnormalities, deception, obscenity, selfishness, pride, political corruption, God bashing, God fabrication, adultery, intolerance, hypocrisy, racism, sloth, violence, destructive self-interests, assault, emotional abuse, scandal, natural disasters, authority abuse, religious oppression, fake religion, religious self-righteousness, and war.

All of this, I admit, gives me mounting stress. What is left? Hope, faith, love, and compassion are supposed to counter all of this? It's little wonder that God's creation, humankind, has trouble finding its way, or—more accurately—His way. But goodness, if it exists, shouldn't be destroyed in its entirety due to my ineptitude.

The young men I followed, Thomas and William, offered hope. Possibly the last hope. It's with great sadness that I address my failure to assist the Almighty One's request of this nebulous book being published without diluting His all-important free will, while allowing death to transpire in my unsuccessful wake. This, while William's precarious livelihood awaits an intervention of its own, divine or brought about by flawed and ineffectual human mechanization. With the loss of Tom, I hope I haven't inadvertently assisted in expediting the eventual end of times. My own state of healthy self-assessment—as well as existence—I admit, is now forever compromised. But at least free will is not! (You should be reading this as facetiously as intended.)

It is with this that I leave you now, dear reader, leaving this writing tablet, should its availability be allowed by the powers above, as (hopefully) irrefutable proof of His desire to see humanity destroy itself.

Signed,

Homer, Your Defeated Servant of the Heavens

She lay in the cardboard shanty for what she knew would be her last night down on Earth. Drowning out His constant booms for her attention with the headphones—a surprising insulator from what would have been excruciating eardrum busters—she pondered what would become of Tom's manuscript now. She tried to find a comfortable position. The dusty and filthy blankets draped over her, and the hard concrete pressed against her back. The glory of gravity. A flea landed on her cheek while her head rested on the dingy pillow, but she ignored it as much as the muffled booms. She closed her eyes but couldn't sleep, the earphones pressing hard against her head, giving her a migraine again. Her thoughts pounded in her head like a vice, pressing her temples together, but it was better than hearing *Him*. She imagined Tom's work, what God had thought it could do—if it, indeed, could do anything. How the work was *so important*. How ridiculous her task was, and how she had been unable to get the manuscript in the right person's hands. Or *someone's* hands. Time was quickly disappearing, as were her chances for a tolerable existence. Chills rushed through her, there in the dark. She realized her concern for humanity had trumped her fear of everlasting solitude for herself. The plight of humans was infectious somehow. She had rooted for them, on an individual basis anyway, setting Thomas and William apart from assemblies of soldiers and packs of troublemakers.

She got up and discarded the last few empty pages of her journal in the trash can from which she had acquired the earphones. Her business here wasn't done.

Cupping the earphones to her head, Homer approached Tom's apartment and—because she had previously locked the front door herself— she snooped around it, looking for a way in that wouldn't cause a lot of racket. No doubt, she sometimes made things harder on herself.

The calm October night allowed little light to guide the last leg of her journey, barely illuminating the locked wooden gate at the back of the building. She jumped it.

Landing on the other side of the gate, she fell upon several trash cans in a glorious cacophony of metal slamming against metal and then landed clumsily on the concrete. It was pitch-black in the alley, and Homer tried to find her balance after falling onto another trash can. Its lid rolled in circles—the metal discordant clamor disturbing the otherwise-silent night—and it spun around in smaller, tighter circles until it finally rested. She scrambled for her flashlight, but it had fallen out of her pocket somewhere, and she lost her headphones. Another trash can fell down on its side, and a white cat screeched, tearing over her head. The flashlight fell back in her lap. What did she have to do to escape the disgusting environment of smelly rubbish and human refuse? And what was it, exactly, about these scavenging felines that attracted humans to ever acquire them as domesticated pets?

A light turned on in a neighboring apartment, providing Homer welcome relief to plan her escape from the piles of human filth. Shards of light poked at the darkness around her, and she heard more commotion. She lay still, camouflaging herself within the trash cans and piles of large trash bags. An old, cranky man poked his head out the window to inspect the source of the ear-splitting commotion. Homer shut her eyes as if it made her more invisible.

The last thing Homer needed was to get arrested in this Godforsaken place. She had heard how human beings imprisoned each other. It was a soul-wasting pre-purgatory of sorts, where a small quantity of people then found God. She was sure He'd leave her there for a while to contemplate how much she'd failed Him again. Yes, He'd leave her there to rot while the other angels got a huge kick out of it.

The crookedly old man studied the garbage disaster, when suddenly the white cat jumped into his arms through the window. "Angel Kitty," he scolded. "Making such a mess." He shut the window behind him, and Homer opened her eyes.

She crept down the deserted alley lit by the kitchen's ambient light. She found Tom's apartment and peeked in through the open bedroom window. The kitchen light in the alley clicked back off, leaving Homer in almost total darkness, unable to see three feet in front of her.

"Egad."

She took her flashlight out and scanned it across the room, the light bouncing as only a burglar would handle it. Surprised by the lack of much characteristic individualism in the bedroom, she wondered how good Tom could have been as a writer.

The grandfather clock's ticktock gave way to its top-of-the-hour chime, startling Homer enough to fall down on her rump back onto the cement, dropping her flashlight inside the window. "Oooommphh!" The headphones fell apart onto the ground.

After sitting still in the dark waiting for any authoritative reprimand from the old man or anyone else—that never came—she got up and jumped through the window. She saw that her flashlight had rolled to a trash can—that Homer was grateful to be a small plastic one—and Tom's ripped-up manuscript lay next to it. Staring at it in disbelief, she picked up one of the shreds of paper and inspected it, the ticktocks of the clock pounding in her head. The unnerving grandfather clock in the corner felt like the Grim Reaper without the scythe as it stood there, watching her every move.

Unaware that the manuscript was an old copy, without Tom's refined final chapter, she considered her options. She hadn't been successful in getting the last copy to one agent, but what was stopping her from sending copies of it to *all agents*?

"I know, I know, I'm running low on time!" she whispered angrily, monitoring her watch that was draining in power as it faintly read *Three Hours Left*. "And no, I'm still not talking to You!"

Cowering with her ears covered, His booms never came.

She scrambled to collect the bits of paper and put them all in a pile and sat in front of them with her legs crossed and the flashlight at her side, closing her eyes. She inhaled. The clock spoke to her in the deafening, ominous language it knew. Ticktock. Ticktock. Ticktock. Homer didn't move. Ticktock. Ticktock.

The manuscript pieces started to quiver and shake like the earth was rumbling below them, yet the ground didn't move at all. The white paper bits lifted from the floor a couple of feet and collected in an elaborate round swirl, forming an elegantly spiraling eddy, puff-white like a cumulus cloud. The pieces started to light up like fireflies, twirling around her as she sat in the calm eye of the hurricane. A small hum accompanied their mystical presence, the small beads of energy collectively lighting up the room like a living, revolving Christmas tree. Homer's eyes opened wide, and she watched the aesthetic spectacle which was quite debonair, if she said so herself.

She took a deep sigh, and a rush of wind carried the magical vortex of manuscript pieces out the window, billowing into the crisp night air, the pieces following each other blindly and instinctively as birds did when migrating. Homer rushed to the window to watch the fall winds carry them into the night where they suddenly winnowed and dispersed into hundreds of directions, fluttering away until the disappeared.

The bedroom was silent now except for the clock's intrusiveness. Looking at her timepiece, Homer could barely read the lettering now.

With minds of their own, the paper pieces followed and—in some cases—created their own currents, whiffling through the atmosphere in hundreds of directions. Some of the small balls of energy carried dozens of miles and others thousands. They glided over plains and sailed over water bodies and danced over mountain ranges until they reached the doorsteps of their destinations. Each piece settled with its stoic presence undetected, magically growing into a complete copy of the original, discarded manuscript, many picked up immediately by the strangers who came upon them.

One was picked up by an inquisitive man who had happened to have a late night and came upon it at his doorstep. He picked it up and scanned the first page—and then cursed the ever-invasive Internet for rewarding the aspiring writer's impressive hunt for his home address.

On the East Coast, a woman picked her copy off her doorstep and flipped through it quickly while she hailed a cab. In Germany, a piece sailed undetected through an open window until it miraculously became its full version on a kitchen table by freshly unwrapped bratwurst, ready for its reader. In France, an agent received his pile of mail from an assistant, the manuscript appearing at the top of the pile as the assistant spilled the agent's coffee and then was berated by the haughty agent.

Homer closed her eyes in relief. Something had to work.

Then a crash of thunder ripped through the sky. Relentless and torrential winds swept the pages away from the hands that held them, reverberating all over the world. Reams of paper were pulled by flurrying gusts, the pages disappearing into the air away from their owners, many of whom fell down and were dragged by the wind themselves. The pages floated away carelessly from some owners who unsuccessfully chased them down the street. Strong gales sucked the pages off of kitchen tables and out windows, souring their readers. The woman hailing the cab watched her manuscript fly away after briefly laying it on top of the car as she got herself together. "Oh, shoot!"

After all of the new manuscript copies disappeared from their old owners, the fragments appeared in another flurry back in Tom's old bedroom at Homer's feet. She watched in horror as her last opportunity to save mankind from itself was sucked away by God's overbearing order. His will couldn't be ignored. Humanity couldn't be handed the keys to survival, trumping any plan Homer had devised. All that she knew felt frail and cold, and she watched the last small pieces of ripped paper fall to her feet and the beads of light died out. She had failed. Again.

And it was silent.

CHAPTER 7

Jamie poked at her food. Despite her protests, her mother had ignored her requests to not come over. She would have rather slept in.

"Veggies in your eggs almost ready," her mother said at the stove, pulling them out of a steamer. "These are organic too. None of those evil pesticides." Proudly wearing the apron she'd had since sometime in the 1970s, she took her cooking seriously. It was her way of making sure her daughter knew how appreciative she should be to have the type of mother who would cook for her with such unconditional love. Just to be clear.

"You didn't have to do all this," Jamie said, taking a small and judicious bite out of wheat germ pancakes.

"Very healthy, child. You'll always have your mother here to care for you. As long as I'm around, anyway."

"Mom, don't talk like that."

"I'm just saying," her mother said. She dumped five times more eggs than Jamie could ever eat on her plate, but Jamie was too tired to argue with her. "I'm not going be around forever. I've still got to do a whole slew of things before I go. I decided to sing in this charity function next month. I'm trying to figure out if I should sing Cher or something by Barbra Streisand. The theme is movie soundtracks."

"What's the charity?" Exhausted from having been up most of the night after all that had gone down at Westfield Shaw, she'd thought that Tom would be there for her, but yet again, her BlackBerry was quiet with no returned call. If they were ever going to work, he had to be a better partner.

292

Her mother dropped the pan back on the stove and took off her apron. "It's a somethin'-or-other for the environment. I'll do anything for charity."

"Mom," Jamie said dryly, "you'll do anything for attention."

Her mother tried to think of something clever to say and, instead, sat and prepared to eat when there was a knock at the door.

"I'm kidding, Mom," Jamie said, patting her affectionately on the back before going to the door. On the other side of it, she was surprised to find her former boss at her house, dressed in the colorful suit of the day—green like money, which Jamie found ironic in every sense considering the clients she'd lost.

"Hi, Jamie," Stephanie said, cold without her jacket. She had been ill prepared to be out this chilly morning.

"Hi."

"Can we talk?"

Not believing she was using such a ridiculously convenient excuse, Jamie said, "Um, my mother's here for breakfast right now—"

"Later," Stephanie said, her arms crossed as she fought off the crisp air. "My office tomorrow morning? I want to offer you your job back."

"What?"

"Tomorrow," Stephanie said. "You were set up by traitors that used to work for me. I fired them today . . . and I want you back."

"I don't know," Jamie said, fighting the urge to ask Stephanie in. She clearly was cold out there, but Jamie didn't want her mother to have at her. With the quizzing and thorough examination, Stephanie would be here for an hour.

"With a substantial raise. We're going to get a whole bunch of our accounts back together."

Jamie couldn't believe what she was hearing.

"As you know, Cynthia came to see me yesterday," Stephanie said, shivering. "You would have known what happened, but of course, you left. But I don't blame you." She wasn't used to pleading to anyone for anything. "She's back with us and, if all goes well, could double her annual budget in a year or two, back to normal levels, but only with you as part of the deal."

Staring at this woman—who shifted her feet one right after the other like it would keep her blood from freezing—Jamie thought of all she had told Tom about going after what he wanted. Going after what his life had in store for him, if he had the guts to take on the risks involved.

"I'll pass." Jamie surprised herself.

Stephanie was dumbfounded. "You can't pass, Jamie! Martha and Janice are gone, and you've got ownership of my largest account. It's what you've always wanted!"

It stung for Jamie to hear Stephanie refer to JC Traders as *her* largest account. Cynthia had called her the night before and explained all that had gone on at WSA and how Martha and Janice had double-crossed Stephanie, who had tried to double-cross Cynthia. Jamie couldn't believe the plot had almost succeeded. "Not all I've wanted, Stephanie."

Stephanie hadn't seen this coming. This woman was going to be her undoing, after all. "This is an opportunity you won't get again."

"I know. I'll figure it out," Jamie said, satisfied. Her dream of self-fulfillment was, somehow, near.

"It's not easy, you know. Going out on your own."

"I know."

Just what she needed. Another competitor. "Okay!" Stephanie huffed, shaking her head before running back to her car.

Closing the door, Jamie shut her eyes and leaned against it, shocked at herself, but excited. She was doing it.

* * *

Finally, Luigi's cab pulled up to the house on Shadow Hill Lane. A couple of days out of the city had been good for him. Resentment had succumbed to the emotional exhaustion of frustrating his wife. He no longer wanted to possess his insecurities and had gotten enough apologetic text messages from his wife to coax him home. After walking up the long and winding driveway, Luigi slammed the front door and walked in the house. Teri was there as he'd expected, freshly showered after her workout and primped to the nines, pumps and all. He loved her in pumps, which she hadn't worn for a while. They were no good for the gym and coffee with girlfriends, the only things she had done much of lately besides her quick trip to LA. Her five-foot-ten height now raised to six-foot-one.

"Hi, honey," Teri said as she ran up to him, hugging him with a foreign enthusiasm that startled him.

"You need money for a new Coach bag or somethin', buttercup?" he asked, cross-eyed. A woman extraordinarily friendly and out of character was dangerous.

She put her arms around his neck and looked down at him, two inches shorter than she was. His protruding stomach made it hard for her to have the kind of close facial contact they'd had just a few years ago, before his love of pasta and high-carb frozen meals received more love and attention than she did.

"My Luigi . . . my sweet, sweet Luigi." Teri caressed his short hair around his ears and gleamed down to him. Luigi burped, blowing the discharged air above her, which she showed her gratitude for by smiling widely at him. "My darling, you thought I'd be upset at you for following me, didn't you? Stalking me as you did?"

"Um—"

"Baby," she stopped him, putting her finger to his lips. She nonchalantly wiped a stray bread crumb from the corner of his mouth. "Do you know how much it meant to me that you cared so much about me to follow me like that? Trying to catch me losing my way."

This could be a trap. He wasn't sure what to say. "Which question you want me to answer first?"

She laughed. He couldn't remember the last time she was so enthralled with him. Maybe when he had proposed. No, she was more loving now.

"You are my man," she said. "What you did back in LA to that rapist guy . . . you are my man, Luigi Steffanci. I'm sorry for putting you through so much all the time."

"Of course, you're my woman."

She continued to pet him. "Yes, I am. Just don't ever follow me again."

"Listen," he said, wrapping his arms around her waist, "I've been doing some thinking."

"Yes . . ."

"I know you needed to go see that Tom guy and stuff."

"That's over now," she snapped quickly, then remembering to be tender with him. "No one will come between us again."

"Well, I kinda got an idea how that can happen."

She didn't know what that meant. It was impossible that he was having an affair, wasn't it? He wasn't *that* rich.

"Well," he continued, "I know that I've let myself go a little bit."

"You have," she agreed.

"It's totally messed up too," he said, and he blew out a quick gust of gas from his rump. He felt his buttocks reverberate as the repugnant air escaped. "I'm sorry," he gushed.

Teri rolled her eyes affectionately at him. "My man," she said, shaking her head.

"I'll get a stomachache!" he blurted. "But I just picked these up." Luigi pulled a small prescription bottle from his pocket. "These, my doctor says, will help with that. I just took one. After a few days, it should all dissipate, sweetness. Pharmaceutical companies to the rescue with symptomatic remedy pills I have to take for the rest of my life, ya gotta love it!"

"Luigi, you didn't have to do that. But good. Take another one."

"Sweet God, I did," he said, and he kissed her.

"I thought you didn't believe in God," she smiled.

Luigi paused. "Whatever I believe in, whatever is, is. But I know I want to work for us, Teri."

She looked into him, speaking with a kind conviction, having thought this out. "I need to appreciate you more—like my mother said. You're the man that's taken care of me. I'm the kind of woman that needs that. If you didn't want that kind of woman, you should've gotten a different one."

"Yes, I should have," he said. "But I started to tell you something. About someone else between us." A crease emerged between her eyes as she frowned. "I know you've always wanted a child, and my ridiculously low sperm count has prevented that. A sperm count that ain't my fault, by the way, and it's also not a sign of poor genetics, I might add."

"Okay," she said slowly, not sure where he was going.

"And since my sperm is dead—"

"It's not dead," she interrupted, trying to be nice.

"Might as well be," he breathed, "but let's adopt. Let's have a family, Teri. I want our love to grow, and I can work at it. On our terms, not anyone else's."

"You mean it?" He had always refused to be a proponent of adopting, which she didn't understand. Her parents too, for they wanted a grandchild from their bloodline.

"I say we do it, but you don't need my permission," Luigi said. "It's your parents you need to convince."

"They'll have to deal," Teri said. She kissed him, and they fully embraced. "It's our decision. And we'll give love to someone who needs it. I love you." For the first time in her marriage, she felt free from the lost love of her life and didn't wish it was Tom that was holding her.

"I love the heels."

* * *

She wanted no more part of Him and what He had in store for her next. God called upon Homer, who was folding up her cardboard home and about to head somewhere other than here.

"Homer, you have to talk to Me."

She kicked the box. "No need."

He paused, acknowledging her pain. "I know this is not what you had hoped for."

She pounced on the box to make it flat and eyeballed up at Him. "You know all, don't You? I bet You know that I don't want to be part of this anymore. What You do here." She picked up the box and slid it near the trash cans with their backs leaned up against the cinderblock wall. Nice and tidy, the way He liked everything. She cradled her tablet in her arms. Her last testament. She wiped any leftover debris off and bunched up the old, flea-ridden, foul blankets that now had obscene holes in them. Holy blankets. Nice.

"Tom and William both—"

"What?" she boldly interrupted. "You're bringing them up to me?"

The couple with the dachshund walked by a few yards away, increasing their pace to a brisk walk when they saw her hollering to the empty heavens.

"Homer," He said, "now Tom's here with Me."

She stopped and took pause. This was little consolation. "Well, I hope so. After all this." She tossed the disgusting blankets by the trash cans, hoping to never see, smell, or encounter anything like them ever again.

"You think I'm unfair, don't you, Homer?"

"I'm furious with You." Her tone was out of line, but she wasn't pointing up at Him. He should appreciate her restraint, actually.

"You will soon understand."

"Torrential winds, sir? I thought I had it there at the end."

"I know you did. Very nice trick, Homer. It might have even worked, if free will did not matter and that copy of the manuscript had been the right one."

She hated Him. He was the one with the tricks then, leaving wrong manuscripts around for her. "I guess—as far as the Christians are concerned anyway—Jesus wasn't the savior if You're still sacrificing people. You're throwing religion after religion into a tailspin here, You know, if they find out. No wonder no one down here knows what's going on with You or what to believe. You've got to always keep them guessing, don't You?"

God sighed. Homer was definitely the feistiest of all the angels. Despite the challenges of working with her sometimes, she had been perfect this time.

"Homer, I did not *sacrifice* Tom, so this has nothing to do with one religion over another. I will *take care* of him. Do not be concerned with earthly religion either, Homer. While important, the language I speak transcends this understanding, in a language all can understand if desired. Your follow-through was impeccable, my faithful servant."

"Oh, puh-leez, sir!" she cried. "I couldn't even get the manuscript to the bald thug fellow. There's no agent, no publisher, no book."

"Not yet, Homer. But there will be. And it's because of you."

She didn't believe Him. "Lies!"

God took a different tact. "Homer, because of you, humankind will see the new version of this book that I need to be seen. Because of you, billions, not millions, of lives will be saved and will not have to perish before their time. Wars will end, others will never begin. Starvation will cease, and diseases will be fought on a global scale unlike ever before, and children will play. Because of you, humankind will be extended for ages.

You, faithful servant, are a hero among heroes and need to quit sulking around."

"I'm not sulking." She wasn't sure what was going on, but she still hated Him.

"I wasn't sure you had it in you, Homer. But you have rewarded My own faith in you."

"You know all. Don't patronize me with Your blatherskite!" Spit trickled down her chin.

"Eventually, I do know all," He smoothly responded, "and none of what I speak is nonsense. Calm down, Homer." All of His creations being unique, she had ascended to the top of His list. "The League of Angels does not even deserve you, young one. But to the heavens, you belong with Me."

She searched for what to say. Abusively violent human beings that He created had ended Tom's life of mortality. Was He not responsible by association? "I'm—"

"Dutiful one," He interrupted. "You've questioned, you've trusted as you desired trust. You searched for what you couldn't find, understood what you didn't know, and risked Me being angry with you to think of someone else above yourself. You put the risk of failure and the weakness of fear of changing yourself aside and found strength within yourself that you didn't know you had. It was faith that you needed. Now, you belong with Me and the court of the greatest angels."

The living space He had provided her was still disgusting. The cardboard shanty stood folded up in between two of the old trash cans that, upon closer inspection, were drawing flies. She kicked the pebbled gravel with her shoddily sandaled feet, certain that the conditions of this assignment couldn't have been worse.

"Sir. Did you have to take him?"

"Oh, Homer."

In a flash, she was pulled up to the heavens, her eyes wide with the excitement of a soaring thrill ride of communion. Deafening wind howled through her whole being as she glided upward, propelled by the organic force that streamed all around her. She saw herself rise from Earth below, where an abandoned construction project was being bulldozed. The advertising billboard near it was getting farther and farther away, but she could still read it: New Nature Preserve Coming This Spring. Two foxes hunting the land together looked up, sensing a commotion in the air they didn't understand.

Soon, Homer felt neither hot nor cold, high nor low. Her tattered, homeless garb disintegrated and disappeared as she morphed into a celestial being, more spirit than physical presence. Her tablet disappeared.

"Wha—"

"You won't need that. Also, Homer, your human form was meant to blend in but not provide you the privilege of the power of influence without substance. You couldn't use the stereotypically pleasing physical aesthetics of this culture that provided you no need to stretch your talents. The very best comes out of the people on Earth when they can become more than themselves. And you succeeded."

"You mean instead of putting me down here as a rich white dude?" She may have been a spirit again, but God still somehow made her physically ill.

"My most boring creation ever, I admit."

She got dizzy as she continued her meteoric rise into the heavens. "Now, I will show you how this young man saved more than your wholeness could ever comprehend, Homer, all unbeknownst to him. I treasure all of My children, but it is Tom, who lived without envy despite all that transpired in his years, that I need to especially provide for."

"I better not be hornswoggled again!" At least she couldn't have hives anymore. "If You're lying to me . . ."

God ignored her. "He's oblivious to our doing, so you can see it's not My ego, Homer. For this young man shall continue to live, and we shall go see him now."

"What about William? The killers? So much pain, sir. What exactly I did right, I still don't know." Completely removed from her mortal existence, she now resided in a more comfortable, invisible entity, relieved that she was out of the cruel, drab, earthly clothing. But she ached for the younger one. Leaving chaos on Earth after He was done with an objective was His way. After Jesus had died, wars had erupted with millions of people dying in His name.

"Quiet now. Look." He showed her a vision of the world below, opening a number of small chasms of space for her to see through. Smoky windows reflecting the future. "There is still pain . . ."

Wanda was at Jamie's door, sharing the news of Tom's death, Jamie falling in her arms, her engagement-ring hand falling limp to the ground. Through another window He had provided her, Homer saw Agnus bawling at William's bedside.

God showed her the rest of the windows. "But Homer, there is also justice and redemption for others."

Jamie was running her own ad agency, and she and Cynthia went over more growth plans into other states. Davey Dealio arrived, and Jamie introduced him to Cynthia.

In a boardroom, a vote was being taken, and Western Mag Corp's IPO was declined. Andre grimaced.

Andre and Nadia watched on as Brent and the hit man were put into a police car, their heads delicately protected as they were pushed into the backseats. The formerly unseen partners of the firm escorted Andre out of the building, holding his cardboard box of personal belongings, the box's middle giving way and splattering all of its contents onto the ground. "*Oy vey*," Andre muttered.

Wanda and Blaine were getting married.

Don was washing dishes in jail, dishes upon dishes thrown at him faster than he could clean them, making him fall over with exhaustion.

William awakened from his prolonged clinical sleep. Wanda and Agnus greeted him, ballooning with smiles as they rushed to his bedside. He gazed into nothing but into something, trying to remember where he was.

Martha and Janice were diligent worker bees in a prison cafeteria, serving food to the hatemongers who had beaten up William and killed Carlos. The women dreaded their new employment as they threw slop on the plates of ungrateful inmates and then at each other.

"Food fight!" someone yelled.

"But, Homer," God said, "it is through these last two windows that you'll see what makes Me most proud."

Homer moved on to see Keith Levy with Eight-Ball and his family in Eight-Ball's house. Levy noticed the manuscript in Eight-Ball's trash. Out of curiosity, he picked it up.

"That's trash, Dad," Eight-Ball said. He swiped it away from his father.

"I'll be the authority on that," Levy said, snapping it back from him. "You have to get over yourself, son."

"This has nothing to do with me," Eight-Ball protested. "You know who this has to do with."

"You're not the judge and executioner, young man." Levy approached his son. "You've got to move on like the rest of us. It's okay."

Eight-Ball stared at him fiercely like it was his father he hated.

Homer was befuddled.

"Just watch," God said.

Levy stood mere inches from his menacing son. "Don't let yourself become weakened by hate, Eduardo. Your mother and I may have split, and I blame myself for that. But you've got blessings. And we need each other."

Eight-Ball's hatred visibly started to wither away, despite his efforts to hold it.

"We need each other," Levy repeated. "I need you. You lost your brother, but I can't explain what it's been like losing Carlos. My stepson, yes, but truly a son to me. My youngest son. Can you find it within yourself to let the hate go? Otherwise, it's like we ourselves are dead."

Eight-Ball put the manuscript on the counter and embraced his father, letting his hate go. It was as if Eight-Ball and Levy were erasing their years of distance and despair.

"Interesting," Homer said.

"And finally," God said, "this last window into the future."

He showed her Levy and Maroquin fighting over the manuscript, negotiating with each other in her office over who had rights to it. GQ and his young wife observed the goings-on.

"You don't have a contract," Maroquin said. "My partners here have, despite my protests, agreed to represent Tom Summers. Through his estate."

"You had your chance," Levy protested. "I don't even know why I agreed to discuss this with you."

Maroquin felt the trophy wife's stare. "Because you owe me, Levy. You know I run this town. Though, I don't believe in its viable publication myself as it is. I've read it, they haven't."

"What's it going to take?" GQ asked. "The subject matter itself is invigorating. I'm going by instincts here right now. Give us a chance to read it? Possibly bid you for it?"

Levy stared at the GQ couple in their designer clothes—the New Yorkers who thought they ran the world. "Oh, you'll read it," he said, with an air that came off to Maroquin as grandstanding. "But bid on it? This isn't eBay, you two. This is publishing. When you can afford it, you should go Hollywood. They'd love your style! Oh, and Maroquin. There's a revision you haven't read. With a new final chapter."

Maroquin was horrified. "What?"

"Yes," Levy said. "And it's amazing." He prepared to leave. "By the way, I didn't take kindly to your false accusations of plagiarism. This book is an original piece of work. His brother—who now is the rightful owner of the manuscript—gave me his computer, with files of all the old drafts. Incidentally, he's insisted on working with me. After all . . . we're like family now. I don't understand how a poorly run shop like yours is open. Good day!"

Maroquin's heart sank, and GQ was enraged. His wife couldn't contain her wild smile.

"It is now in the right hands," God said. "You, my faithful servant, found a strength you didn't know you had and delivered beyond your capacity and faith. This time, you didn't use your powers to harm, embarrass, or compromise humanity's free will. You found your true power beyond the crutch of pride. Now come. We must attend to other matters soon."

The powerful force of Homer's ascent made her unable to gasp as she continued to rise into the heavens much faster than she had fallen. She was sucked up into the crisp coolness with a surge of heat that shot through her essence, hot-wired and projected somewhere into the universe. It was at once familiar and unknown, where she felt heavy but agile, where light was abundant but scarce. Joy overwhelmed her, and she imagined how she would address the other disbelieving and jealous angels. She tried to speak, but instead, her voice sang in peacefulness, and she was drawn beyond the clouds with a silent whisper.

ACKNOWLEDGEMENTS

The Silent Partner would not exist if it weren't for the many people who had inspired, coached, and endured me through its progress.

First, my editor, Wendy M. Grant. You championed the story's development and helped me bring it to new heights. You dealt with my relentlessness and restless vision that sometimes weaved off course, and I'm extremely grateful for your detail, and friendship.

Peter Ettinger, my brother. You effortlessly assisted me with an overhaul of earlier drafts so that the story became a much more improved version of itself. (I basically started over, throwing out all earlier drafts. *In their entirety.*) Peter, I damn thee. (But seriously, I love you, man!)

Angela Ettinger, thank you for your faith in me and excitement about the project. When times got dark, you were always there cheering me on, waiting for the next kernel I would send you.

Brian Kennedy, thank you for supporting my vision from the very beginning and reliving *TSP* rewrite after rewrite. Your advice and our brotherhood was important in keeping my spirit on track. I'm eternally grateful.

Jami Lee Sanders, Mitch Fleck, Jason Patz, Tina Washburn Patz, Amie Becker, Chris Angelo, Michelle Jones, David Follman, Tracy Woodworth, Paul Guinn, Chris Angelo, and Magali Garcia: thank you for your notes on the chapters that I provided you. I heard every one of them. Your assistance, as well as your encouragement, helped me think through things I otherwise wouldn't have, and improved the final product.

My sisters: Dorelie, Verena, and Deanna: Thank you for never doubting. Verena, thank you for your advice and assistance once I was done with the book. Your knowledge of PR and social media assisted beyond anything I can ever repay you.

Randy Zussman and Debora Maciol: Thank you for supporting me and understanding my neurosis with rewrites and the perpetual isolated late nights with my laptop in coffee shops. Your love is priceless, and always will be.

Eric Atilano: Your faith in me with *TSP*'s book trailer——from the first time we talked about it over java——will be something I'll always remember (sans Alzheimer's). The layers of our friendship through the whole process has been extremely rewarding, and everything you led so that we could complete that trailer with our limited resources is nothing short of amazing.

Michael C. Poole: Your own visions continue to inspire me. Thank you for your faith and assistance. You're a true artist that I respect.

Christina Cervantes: I miss working with you, and I appreciate your dedication and assistance to this project. I couldn't have done the trailer without you.

Amy Lane: Through you, I met Christina. Thank you for believing in me.

Jeff Amante: Thank you for your patience in developing the book cover design. We went through multiple ideas and, thanks to you, we came up with the right one. You, my friend, are awesome.

Paul Wade: As a fellow writer, your guidance was invaluable. Thanks for your great ideas that improved the book's layout. We're a great team.

Lynn Palmer: My friend, I'm grateful for your support of me, always, as well as introducing me to Wendy. Our talks, your support. I'm beyond grateful.

Jerry Jao: Thank you for your friendship and vision. With everything.

Mike Marucci and Honor by August: Mike, thank you for believing and illustrating my vision to the band. Michael Pearsall, Evan Field, Brian Shanley, and Chris Rafetto: thank you for your support. Your music is brilliant and I'm honored that you allowed your work to be included in the book trailer. Chris: thank you for lengthening your fantastic instrumental!

To my friends that, whether you knew it or not at the time, your words inspired me to keep going: Eric Atilano, Frankie Vinci, Mitch Fleck, Mitch Kelly, Shannon Grotbeck, Donna King Lewis, Martin Victor, Vickie Starling, Paul R. Guinn, Paul Guinn, Rachel Lueras, Mark Sturcken, Tina Bowles, Sarah Dobbins, Noreen Ippolito, Sandi Banister, Michael Hull, Jami Lee Sanders, Debbie Wagner, Sean Johnson, Steve Lees, Robin Lees, Stacy Lees Hughes, Tracy Barber, Jerry Jao, Clare Madsen, Dave Ezratty, Katy Bennett, Francesca Albanese, Derek Sante, Brad Samuel, Diana Hoffman, Dave Saunders, Gloria Valenti, Russell Wolf, Alison Beck, Jill MacMillan, John Katsilometes, Russell Robertson, Paul Wade, JohnJay Van Es, Rich Berra, Kyle Unfug, Rachelle Taylor, Jimmy Steele, Cindy Spicer, Jenny Savage, Rebecca Naomi, Kelly Neff, Michael Rannazzisi, Liz Peterson, Brandy Newman, Vanessa Lops, Tina Mosely, Gee Young Lee, Doug Hyde, Ian Howfield, Lisa Poe Howfield, Dave Goldberg, Francesca Albanese, Cathy Cuizon, Barry Smith, Pascal Ferrari, Jeremy Everly, Maria Dunton, Cathy Deary, Mary Deary, Sean Cassidy, LeAnn Brodecky, Brad Booker, Bernadine Addis-Fredriksen, Allyson Carboni, Chip Franklin, Tracy Harven, Joe Haze, Michelle Kalanja, Michaela Meade, Gina Raroque, Sofia Cain, Troy Reierson, Todd Speelman, Adam Rinella, Amy Owens Roach, Ellen Phillips Scruggs, John Steffanci, Michael Green, Robert Alvarado, Isa Ann, and Greg Toderov.

Those who helped me promote the book trailer, thank you! Honor By August, Eric Atilano, Verena King, Dorelie Guinn, Deanna King, Randy Zussman, Mitch Fleck, Jerry Jao, Frankie Vinci, Sandi Banister, Geena the Latina, Jesse Lozano, Casey Bartholomew, Tyler Anderson, Russell Wolf, Robert Alvarado, Francesca Albanese, Jennifer Douillard, Michelle Jones, and Alicia Jarvela.

When we showcased the trailer, the following of you came and supported to the point that the showcase was virtually *free*. Thank you all for your support! Verena King, Jerry Jao, Eric Atilano, Michael C. Poole, Christina Cervantes, Rico Telles, Lolly Boroff, Dave Saunders, Gary Filips, Linda Sakane, Barb Brosius, Greg Todorov, Roni Kugelmass, Kyle Greco, Amy Lane, Sonya Fry, Cathy Cuizon, Isa Ann, Krista Yost, Michelle Trudeau, Sarah Dobbins, Jill MacMillan, Elizabeth Bryce, Mary Deary, Cathy Deary, Mike Ippolito, Noreen Ippolito, Bryan Stevens, Alicia Mendez, Diana Hoffman, Russell Robertson, Kylie Gard, Amie Becker, Carrie Marriott, Che Jones, Monica Jones, Fernando Guerrero, Chris Bradshaw, Mario Portillo, Heather Portillo, Frankie Vinci, Rachel Gold, Clint August, David Kitting, Delana Bennett, Dominique Gilbert, Dorothy Tran, Chris Fuentes, Geena Aguilar, Jeremy Everly, Ashley Shapiro, Paul Wade, Kristine Wade, Sheena Milligan, Alicia Jarvela, Amy Dowell, Kristy Dowell, Laura Dowell, Nina Hicks, Peter Nguyen, Daniel Travers, W Demitrus Willis, Harry O, Richard Price, Jim Bergen, Joyce Bergen, Mal Hall, Doug Timmerman, Joel Kelly, Kyle Bruen, Sofia Cain, Kariann Van, Christine Vargo, Sandy Feldman, Chris Canann, John Nelson, Jeff Amante, Michael Green, James Gagnon, Carlota Noceda, Trevor Hamer, Mary Hamer, Joe Troutman, Melissa Brewer, Katy Bennett, Sean Johnson, Debbie Wagner, and Alyssa Deetman.

At the time of this printing, the following Facebook fans of the book helped promote *TSP's* existence. Thank you for believing. Eric Atilano, Michael C. Poole, Rachel Lueras, Amy Lane, Christina Cervantes, Dave Schroeder, Eva Carter, Barry Poles, Michelle Kalanja, Angela Walsh, Debbie Popiel Winner, Amy Beth Frankel-Steinberg, Blair Giesen, Brad Samuel, Dave Saunders, Debra Woolery, Andrea Barthel, DeAnne Sheehan, Danielle Roth, Vincent DeCarlo, Becky Peabody Estepp, Deanna Matthes, Dan

Allen, Jason Patz, Jimmy Philips, Gabriela Moreno, Dawn Boquet, David Follman, Michelle Jones, Amie Becker, Jason Rogers, Ashley Shapiro, Harlan Flagg, Jack Foster Mancilla, Gary Welsh, John Adamo, Clarke Smith, Doug Hyde, Frankie V., Lorrie Stocks Scheller, Dore Rodine, Erica Kramer, Eric Dahl, David Madsen, Erin Hansen Baughman, Lauren Schroeder, Mitch Fleck, Dirk Hanson, Dorelie King Guinn, Verena King, Peter Tweezy Nguyen, Maria Dunton, Jane Ezratty, Randy Zussman, Erin Malsom Guidera, Noreen Ippolito, Steve Virissimo, Cathy Deary, Brett Schlank, Athena Matiskas, Dave Caster, Jamal Parker, Debora Maciol, Alan Mollet, Robin Crook, Angela Ettinger, Ann Lackomar, Sarah Dobbins, Tina Washburn Patz, Anthony Graziano, Sarah Beebe, Ashley Pearson, Ross Garcia, Tatiana Saunders, Felix Barela, Hula Ramos, Rose Hughes, Sandi Banister, Mary Deary, Ashley Perschall, Scot Sturtevant, Louis Perschall, Debbie Stein, Francesca Albanese, Ricardo Telles, Dave Goldberg, Donna King Lewis, Brittany Donnelly, Vickie Starling, Maureen Ferreira, Sarah Jones, Erika Nazem, Sofia Cain, Richard Berra, Todd Speelman, Mike Derry, Sean Johnson, Elisabeth Hession Klos, Deanna King, Gregg Cantor, Mike McNamara, Isaura Dafonseca, Jerry Jao, John Katsilometes, Amy Dowell, Chalea Pierce, Tracy Barber, Paul Wade, James Gagnon, Russell Robertson, Dominique Gilbert, Daniel Travers, Katy Evans, Cathy Cuizon, LeAnn Brodecky, Casey Bartholomew, Rebecca Naomi, Jenny Savage, Marsha Harszy Sinnock, Kelly Neff, Miguel Verde, Mark Sturcken, Tracy Harven, Joe Love, Laurie Welsh, Victoria Andrade Rock, Lisa Poe Howfield, Ian Howfield, Jennifer Gartz, Michael Hull, Derek Sante, Mindy Allen, Ellen Phillips Scruggs, Mitch Kelly, Shannon Grotbeck, Lori Summers, Lee Smith, Jill MacMillan, Steven Nagelberg, Kristin Baker, Gee Young Lee, Samya France, Rebecca Sommers Esparza, Kari Kuh, Brandon Baxley, Taylor E. Schuss, Tina Mosley, Shivanee N. Ramlochan, Whitney Lynn Shepherd, Rik McNeil Bollman, Amy Stone, Troy Reierson, Mike Marucci, Lynn Palmer, Karolyn Knight, Aaron Crowley, Kirk Greenquist, Missy Fredriksen, Heather Cramsie, Taylor Van Arsdale, Chris Angelo, Shanon Plumlee, Allyson Carboni, Rene Garcia, Eric Eisenberg, Bill Lubitz, Tom Chase, Greg Swiszcz, Wendy DeMay, Carter Mason, Junior Solis, Michaela Meade, Trista Thorp, Stephanie Cooper Heiner, Rey Buenrostro, Joe Haze, Kelly Bridges, Cassandra Jacob, Blanca Vasquez, Christopher Rafetto, Kelly Stewart-Baizar, Robert

Alvarado, Rachelle Taylor, Adam Rinella, Rachel Gold, Jeremy Everly, Paul R. Guinn, Sean Leckie, Amy Lee, Brandy Price Newman, Stephanie Simon, George Pappas, Mario Portillo, Stacey Miller Eisenberg, Joel Kelly, Paulette Harris, Nando Guerrero, Rob Rodz, Mia Larae, Alicia Moore, Loraine Palmer, Coty Atwood, Elena Elizabeth, Troy Heard, Rodsyl Vega Aldebol, Wendy M. Grant, Andy Waage, J.C. Simon, Stephanie Fowler, Karolyn Johnston, Laura Mounier Gaughan, Kristian Madsen, Leslie Goldman, Todd Romano, Lety Beers, Trevor Andrew Hamer, Gina Raroque, Efe Erdogdu, Honey Boudreaux, Randil Ramsess, Russell Wolf, Andre Biebel, Adam Wolf, Kelly Donahue, Idris Cakir, Karina Zajaros, Elia Esparza, Connie Thomas, Jason Gnerre, Zoe Elmore, David Dorudiani, Achraf Refifi, Jeff Amante, Kent Kimberlain, Christy Spearing, Megan Kelly, Katy Bennett, Michael Pokocky, Bryan Stevens, Dax M. Tucker, Shauna Moran-Brown, Cindy Spicer, Stephanie Konstantinis, Rosy Posy, Andrea Stewart, Aaron Anavim Mario, Kelli Kunkel, Sway San Diego, Dan Heilbrun, Joe Troutman, Sinergia Ministerios Juveniles, Kelly Del Monte, Tyler Anderson, Cammie Buerry, Leslie Brown, Ramon Salido, Kristine Agricola Wade, Mike Puckett, Rob Guthrie, Pamela Witte, Marot Kinberg, Julie Anne Lindsey, RachelintheOC Thompson, Ron Voigts, Greg Johnston, Cindy Rose Swanson, Ruppert Lindemann, Tarek Hassan Refaat, Lisette Brodey, Rosa Shah, Anthony Newman, John Scherber, Robbi Sommers Bryant, V Kumar Som, Renee Pawlish, Stef Mcd, Michael Rannazzisi, Renfrow Fred, John Martin, Stephen Jennison-Smith, Paul Rice, Tim C. Taylor, Virginia Lee, Jorge Salgado-Reyes, Carol Gordon Ekster, Teresa Kennedy, Rebecca Nolan, Amy Lichtenhan, Joel Blaine Kirkpatrick, Jamie Sue Wilsoncroft, Larry Enright, Tim Greaton, Lavinia Thompson, Caren Widner Hanten, Judy A. McNutt, TJ Rama, Matthew Pizzolato, John McCuaig, Amanda Young, Kim Mullican, Simon Williams, Barry Crowther, Melissa Webb, Reggie Ridgway, Kim Zaugg Krey, Jeff Littorno, Rexcrisanto Delson, Brian Hutchinson, Gayle Feyrer, Cindy Pahl, Mel Comley, Patti Roberts, Tracey Alley, Heather Paye, Jonathan Gould, Christine M. Butler, Susan J.P. Owens, Helen Yee, Aryn Badorine Rannazzisi, Stephanie Alexander Rehmann, SJ Wist, Michael R. Mathias, Anna Tan, Carolyn Arnold, Ara Grigorian, Sean E. Thomas, Philip Parry, Terry Simpson, Karen A. Einsel, Pat Gragg, Maria Savva, Kyle Bruen, Alicia Mendez, Joseph Oreb, Calista Taylor, Cathe Esparza Young, Tim

Queeney, Terry Kliz AkaLuzia, Rebecca S. Scarberry, Walter Eckland, Micheal Rivers, Cathryn Wellner, Alison DeLuca, Jay Squires, Dave Ezratty, L.J. Kentowski, Kenneth Hoss, Pam Asberry, Brian Meeks, Becky Tsaros Dickson, Dawn Kirby, Russell Blake, L. Carroll Lor Mandela, J.C. Martin, Dina Santorelli, Ranee Dillon, Jamee Rae Pineda, Kim Cormack, Al Boudreau, Jill Metcalf, Genna Sarnak, Sharon Buchbinder, Julia Joanne Black, Craig Stone, Sarah Patton, Joseph Rinaldo, Maureen Hovermale, DeAnna Knippling, Emlyn Rees, Paul Callaghan, Chaela Sumner, Peter Carroll, Tiffany Aller, Dee Bibb, Erica Negi, Callie Norse, Kimberly Gore Wehner, Tyffani Clark, Dave Zeltserman, Cari L. Pedstelak, Joey Av, Peter Hindley, Dane John Cobain, A.I. Davroe, Travis McDougald, Lucille Vitale Dunn, Kate Kelly, Ben Woodard, Peter Adler, Brian Wilson, Jeannie Walker, James Anest, Bert Carson, Doug Timmerman, Leandri Geldenhuys, Jesse Lozano, Jess Almodovar, Faith Helen Mortimer, Stacy Lees Hughes, Lian Dolan, Melissa Hurley, Jami Lee Sanders, Alex Will, Leslie Tucker Morris, Obaapa Akua Boatemaa, Stacey Shaw, Meghan Sandoval, Florida Schaal, Mark OBrion, Jo Landis Shields, Julie Jackson, Mulalo Jennifer, Megan Gibson, Ashley Wiederhold, Nientunnuk Finweno, Gigi Rena, Neeraj Tripathi, Rachel Heeter, Laura Knox, Angel May Chan, Alain Nguyen, Niraj Patel, Sadhna Mitra, Anne M. Carpenter, Jeannie Bolinger, Rita Lanning, Mohammad Sartawi, Andrew Connell, Marni Setless, Alwin George, Mikey V, Kristen Negro, Jess Richards, Rolf Gehrung, Erin Brophy, and Lori Ello.

My friends, you make me feel deceptively popular.